I am Cuba

Fidel Castro and the Cuban Revolution

I am Cuba

Fidel Castro and the Cuban Revolution

Matthew Langdon Cost

Encircle Publications, LLC
Farmington, Maine U.S.A.

I AM CUBA © 2020 Matthew Langdon Cost

Paperback ISBN 13: 978-1-64599-028-4
E-book ISBN 13: 978-1-64599-029-1
Kindle ISBN 13: 978-1-64599-030-7

Editor: Cynthia Brackett-Vincent
Book design: Eddie Vincent
Cover design by Deirdre Wait, High Pines Creative, Inc.
Cover photographs: © Getty Images

Published by: Encircle Publications, LLC
PO Box 187
Farmington, ME 04938

Visit: http://encirclepub.com

Sign up for Encircle Publications newsletter and specials
http://eepurl.com/cs8taP

Printed in U.S.A.

ACKNOWLEDGEMENTS

If you are reading this, I thank you, for without readers, writers would be obsolete.

Getting to this final written piece of *I Am Cuba: Fidel Castro and the Cuban Revolution* has truly taken a village to achieve.

The idea of writing this historical novel germinated back in my senior year at Trinity College in Hartford, Connecticut, in the classroom of Dale Graden. His passion for Latin America inspired me to take the miraculous story of Fidel Castro and the Cuban Revolution and run with it. I finished the first draft a year after graduating college.

I was not much of a writer and had never been to Cuba, which turned out to be two major stumbling blocks. I set the manuscript aside, and for 30 years I honed my craft, made use of numerous helping hands, and visited Cuba, following the revolutionary war trail across the island nation.

I am grateful to my mother, Penelope McAlevey, and father, Charles Cost, who have always been my first readers and critics.

Much appreciation to the various friends and relatives who have also read my work and given helpful advice.

I'd like to offer a big hand to my wife, Deborah Harper Cost, and children, Brittany, Pearson, Miranda, and Ryan, who have always had my back.

I'd like to tip my hat to my editor, Michael Sanders, who has worked with me on several novels now, and always makes my writing the best that it can be.

Thank you to Encircle Publishing, and the amazing duo of

Cynthia Bracket-Vincent and Eddie Vincent for giving me this opportunity to be published. Also, kudos to Deirdre Wait for the fantastic cover design.

Most of all, I'd like to thank Fidel Castro for creating such a compelling story for me to put down on paper.

Cuba 1952-1959

Havana

Santa Clara

Sierra Maestra

Santiago

PART ONE

The Revolution Stalls

Willard L. Beaulac
American Ambassador to Cuba
Habana, Cuba

July 25, 1953

John Foster Dulles
Secretary of State
United States of America

Dear Mr. Secretary,

This should be my final letter regarding the state of affairs in Cuba. I will be returning to Washington D.C. for reassignment to make way for President Eisenhower's new appointee, Arthur Gardner. I must confess to some trepidation turning over this seething cauldron of a country to a man unfamiliar with Cuba, but I will do my best to bring him up to speed.

Cuba has been in a state of turmoil since the Platt Amendment. The coup d'état of Fulgencio Batista on March 10th of last year is just a continuation of the corruption that lurks in every crevice of Cuba. To offset the loss from low sugar prices, Batista has invested in tourism and invited organized crime from the United States to open casinos, hotels, and cabarets. It is entirely possible that every single government official is accepting some sort of bribe so that this mafia can operate in plain sight.

While there is no overt rebellion to Batista since Rafael García Bárcena and his *Movimiento Nacional Revolucionario* (MNR) were arrested, there is a growing rumble of dissonance in the dark alleys of Habana. The leader of this opposition would be former President Carlos Prío and his Auténtico

Party, who hosted an opposition group conference in Montreal with the purpose of overthrowing Batista. There have been rumors of a new rebel leader, a man named Fidel Castro, but it doesn't appear he was even invited to join in this Montreal Pact.

We have extended diplomatic relations to the government of Batista, even though he came to power through force, his regime has welcomed organized crime, has proven corrupt, and violently represses the many opposition groups.

Sincerely,
Willard L. Beaulac

1

July 25th, 1953, Eastern Cuba

Vicente Bolívar pulled the 1952 Buick to the side of the road as he crested the hill overlooking Santiago. He was weary from the 500-mile-plus drive from Havana, but the sight of the sprawling city below illuminated by the midafternoon sun at his back revitalized him. It was as if he were home, even though he'd never been here in his life. He opened the door and unpeeled himself from the seat, breathing in deeply the air that was his heritage, his birthright, and his freedom. At just nineteen years of age, Vicente was embarking upon the adventure of a lifetime, a thought that didn't slightly hesitate as it raced through his brain and disappeared over the mountains and into the sea.

His grandmother had told him endless tales of his ancestors—men and women who'd roamed this eastern end of the crocodile shaped nation of Cuba. At the same time, this wizened woman had imparted little information about his own parents, who'd died before his memories began. She had grudgingly revealed to him that the men of Batista had assassinated his father after the Sergeants' Revolt of 1933, his crime being loyalty to the deposed president, Machado. Of his mother, she spoke not a word, and it was his uncle who finally told him she'd disappeared, but it was rumored that several sailors from the United States had killed her. Her crime had been that she refused to have sex with them. A cousin told him a similar account, but in his version, it was two wealthy gamblers visiting from New York City who saw his mother dancing, and assumed that everything had a price, but were dismally disappointed to discover their money couldn't grant them what they desired. As always, just the thought of his unknown parents caused a tear to well up in the left eye of Vicente, and he absently rubbed it away with his fist.

The day was stifling hot, the humidity rolling up from the ground where it was battered about by the strength of the sunrays, but Vicente didn't notice. His grandmother told him that his blood was made up of the soil from so deep within the history of Cuba that it could not be affected by anything so trivial as air temperature. He squinted his eyes to better see through the haze, as he gazed in wonder to the left of Santiago, where the town of Baracoa must lay hidden behind the mountains. Over 400 years earlier, his ancestor, Guamá, had arrived on this easternmost tip of Cuba. He'd accompanied the great *Cacique*, Chief Hatüey, and 300 warriors in long canoes, who traveled from Hispaniola to bring warning of the impending arrival of the Spaniards. A shiver went through Vicente as he thought of the valiant battle these ancient Taino natives had put up for years, before being all but exterminated by superior weapons, numbers, and disease.

In Bayamo, Vicente had dropped five men at a safe house. They would be part of the distraction to detract from reinforcements coming from the garrison located there. He'd continued on alone, and for the past four hours the car had been silent, or as quiet as his thoughts allowed for in the close confines of the Buick. The road had bumped along the edge of the Sierra Maestra, a mountain range that his grandmother's grandmother had fled to after the failed Aponte slave uprising. The jagged land spiked its way into the sky, hiding valleys housing sharecroppers, tenant farmers, and bandits. Somewhere in those peaks she'd discovered an oasis of black liberation in the area of El Frijol, a community known as a *Palenque*. In these rugged hills, this group of former slaves escaped detection for generations, and it was here that both his grandparents were born.

When José Martí and Antonio Maceo had landed an invasion force near Baracoa in 1895, his grandfather had joined their quest for independence from Spanish colonialism. He'd watched both men succumb to injuries sustained on the battlefield, but the spirit of the revolution continued. Riding at the side of the legendary general, Calixto García, his grandfather had been witness to the growing swell that rose like the tide and swept the Spanish interlopers into a cowering mass within the walls of Santiago. The *mambises*, Cuban peasants who began the war with machetes and now carried rifles, began to have their senses tickled with the sweet taste of freedom like sucking upon the peeled sugar cane in the fields. Vicente could feel this history pulsating in his veins, his feet plunging into the earth as if rooted, while his soul soared through the mountains and his face was splashed with the sea crashing upon the rocks. He was home. He again rubbed his left eye with his fist.

In 1898, with victory and Cuban sovereignty all but realized, the United States had swooped in and stolen their triumph, and forced Cuba to henceforth be subjugated to their will. For the past fifty-some years, this peonage had resulted in the advancement of the monetary interests of powerful American companies. Now, in 1953, the infrastructure and wealth of Cuba was foreign-owned. His grandmother had painted the history of Cuba with broad strokes that resonated within his being, but it was Fidel who had filled in the canvas by enlightening him to the tragic politics that had cursed the majority of Cubans to a life of poverty, poor health, and illiteracy.

The green palm fronds glimmered in an almost translucent white in the glare of the setting sun. Down below, a peasant led his burro stacked high with sticks. A chicken wandered the side of the road looking for food, and Vicente could see a ship, either coming or going, in the port. This serenity would all be shattered tomorrow. He climbed back into the car and continued down into Santiago. His first stop was the Rex Hotel to pick up three men, and then the train depot for the arrival of Raúl Castro. Fidel's younger brother had just turned twenty-two, but his baby-face made him appear much younger than Vicente. On the outskirts of town they idled in the shade of a small cluster of palm trees until several more cars arrived, and then the caravan proceeded eight miles to the village of Siboney. A light on a tree signaled the thin road to the farmhouse where the rebels were gathering. Vicente was one of the few who knew why.

"In two hours we'll attack the Moncada Military Barracks in Santiago. This is not a training exercise." The young lawyer spoke quietly in the early morning darkness of the isolated farmhouse in Siboney. Vicente glimpsed the shocked faces in the flickering candlelight, for most thought they were being rewarded with a trip to *Carnaval*, while others believed it was just more play-acting at being revolutionaries. It was hard to believe that soon they would be fighting—and almost certainly killing—Cuban soldiers. Emotionally, many were unready to take the leap from rhetoric to action. "In a few hours we'll be *victorioso o derrotado*," he continued, "but regardless of the outcome of this battle, this movement will triumph. If we succeed tomorrow, Martí's aspirations will be fulfilled sooner, but either way, they will be realized."

The rebels bowed their heads as they commemorated Martí, the father of Cuban independence, the man who had instilled in them this will to be free at all costs, and the one they prayed to instead of God. The lawyer, Fidel Castro, wore a brown uniform; as did those who surrounded him, the only difference being the sergeant's stripes on his shoulder and that his tunic was too small for his large athletic frame. He was noticeably taller and broader than the average Cuban male, surpassing six feet in height and with evident musculature.

Fidel continued to speak at length, but for Vicente Bolívar, all noise had condensed into a steady hum seemingly generated from the very earth itself. He'd known, after all, that his training over the past year was for exactly this moment, the violent overthrow of Batista's regime. Yet, that'd all been more like a game. This was real, as his dry throat and sweat-soaked shirt reminded him. He could smell the fear in the room as over a hundred people processed the importance of life and death.

"Our plan is dangerous, and anyone who leaves with me in the morning will have to do so willingly." Fidel's brown eyes gazed at each of them in turn, their expressions hidden in the darkness as was his, vague glints in the candlelight behind his glasses. His tightly curled black hair was cut short, and Vicente noted that he'd recently shaved his mustache. His newly bare face made him look even younger than his twenty-seven years, his smooth cheeks giving him the appearance of a boy and not a man. "Remember, we're not assassins. Only kill as a last resort." Fidel held out hope that the barracks could be taken without violence, but he knew that it was highly unlikely.

"We couldn't kill anybody if we wanted to." A high-pitched voice pierced the room.

Three of the men beside the speaker, also university students, nodded their heads in agreement. "We've hunting rifles and shotguns, and they've .30-caliber Springfield rifles," one of them said.

"They won't get the chance to use those rifles because we'll surprise them in their sleep." Fidel replied. "And then we'll be the ones armed with modern weapons."

"There are barely a hundred of us and there are over 400 of them," another student chimed in. "This is madness."

"I'll make no man risk his life for freedom who chooses the safety of chains," Fidel retorted, his deep voice rising. "But I can't allow you to tip off the authorities and ruin our surprise. Pedro," he gestured at the suddenly apprehensive complainers. "Lock these men in a room until we're safely gone."

Vicente shifted his feet nervously and checked his watch. *What chance do we really have?* He wondered.

"The rest of you...pay no attention to them. Many of the soldiers will be gone for *Carnaval*, and those that are left will be sound asleep, drunk as sailors. Once we take Moncada, we'll raid the arsenal and melt back into the mountains, arming the peasants for our revolution."

There were sixteen automobiles, many of them hidden inside the now-empty chicken coops, as Haydée Santamaría and Melba Hernández, the only women among the revolutionaries, had strangled and roasted the birds the previous evening to feed the 120 men. The weapons had been stashed in the well until just a few hours earlier, the rifles now stacked against one wall with about thirty assorted handguns on a table, firearms that Vicente and two others now began to distribute along with the meager ammunition that went with each. The face of Juan Almeida spoke for all of them as he received an ancient .22 that might or might not work, and in any event, was certainly no match for the high-powered machine guns carried by the soldiers. Juan swallowed his objections with difficulty and shuffled on leaden legs back to his spot in the room.

Vicente stumbled through the dirt like an automaton, his feet following orders that his brain couldn't quite comprehend. They were *really* going to do it. It was more than talk and argument, more than bluster, more than anger and fancy words—it all was about to become as real as blood and bullets. Once they were all armed with some ancient relic of a weapon, Vicente read off the car assignments, and the rebels filtered out into the lightening sky of eastern Cuba where revolution was just another day in its history. Vicente had been slotted to drive the Buick he'd arrived in, but at the last moment Fidel decided he should drive and banished him to the backseat.

Fidel was vigorously tapping his left knee-high boot, anxious to get started. The V-8 rumbled to life, and the other automobiles followed suit, stirring like ancient monsters awakening from a deep slumber in the quiet countryside. It was not yet 5:00 a.m., still almost an hour before sunrise. Lester Rodriguez had fallen asleep in a chair on the front porch and was almost left behind, but Melba noticed him, waking him just as the caravan began their journey.

Vicente turned to the man on his left. "Vicente Bolívar." He saw no reason for secrecy at this point.

The bearded man behind the driver's seat wrestled a hand free to give a short shake. "Gustavo Arcos."

"It seems as if we've a full mornin'." Vicente noticed a missing patch of hair on the chin of the man in the midst of the thick-black beard.

"This is a fucking shit show," Arcos whispered, his eyes on the back of Fidel's head.

Vicente ruminated over his answer, for his knee-jerk reaction was to agree, but his loyalty demanded more. "We do what we must do," he finally replied.

"Must we die?"

"A few months ago I drove Fidel on a fundraisin' trip in Pinar del Rio." Vicente nodded toward the driver. "He told me about this man named Sock-ra-teeze," he stumbled over the name, "who lived thousands of years ago on some island called Greece, much like Cuba in size, but far across the ocean. He was found guilty of treason for speakin' out against the government and sentenced to die, unless he apologized for his words and actions."

"What did the man do?"

"He mocked the gods and corrupted the youth with different ideas."

"What happened to the *hijo de puta?*" Arcos asked, wiping his brow, for even at this time in the morning the car was like an inferno. "Did he apologize?"

"No. He swallowed the poison as he'd been ordered and died."

"Ay, *cabrón*," the man cursed Socrates for being a dumbass. "And that's supposed to make me feel *mejor*? You sure know how to pick up a man's spirits."

Vicente rolled his tongue over his teeth, pursing his lips. He had pondered this story for weeks before speaking further with Fidel about it. "We all die," he told Arcos with the tone of a student and not a teacher. "But we've the choice to be square with ourselves before we die, or we can sell out and live a little longer. I choose to live akin to what I know to be right."

"Shit," Arcos mumbled. "Not much to be done now, though, is there?"

If Vicente thought anybody cared, he would've written a quick note to be delivered upon his impending demise. The death of his grandmother five years ago had severed the last bond of love and affection he had in this world.

The only person who might care was a young Italian beauty from the United States he'd recently befriended; they'd shared coffee a few times and exchanged life stories. There was something about Sophia he couldn't quite put a finger on, but her laugh lived within him, even though he was quite certain she hadn't a thought for him.

The men and women he was with now, they were his only family. There was no chance that he'd back out; there was no choice but to proceed. He held the sawed off .44 Winchester rifle loosely, the butt having been cut from the weapon to make it easier to handle. As the car raced through the morning darkness, he steeled himself against the urge to flee, vowing to do his part, to face the enemy, and to make Fidel proud.

"What's Boris doing?" Fidel asked from the front seat. The car in front of them had pulled to the side after having gone no more than a few miles down the road. It was a flat tire, probably from overloading the vehicle and then driving over the deeply potholed roads. The rebels found space for four of the men, but they had to leave four others behind, further reducing their numbers.

Vicente sighed, shaking his head. He understood that great risk led to great results, or so Fidel had drilled into their heads, but the day's strategy already reeked of disaster. There was no time to dwell upon these ominous signs as they left the forest behind, and the buildings of the city beginning to appear as dark shadows. Santiago was a jumble of two- and three-story buildings crowded upon narrow streets, the structures looming on either side blocking what little light the impending sunrise might bring. The caravan of cars slowed, carefully easing past these ghostly edifices lining the quiet streets of the city.

Fidel cursed again from the front seat, wondering aloud where his brother was going. The plan called for Raúl Castro and Lester Rodríguez to lead an attack on the Palace of Justice, an important vantage point from which to provide cover fire for the main attack. Unfortunately, they'd just turned the wrong way to reach that destination. There was nothing to be done, and the bulk of cars continued on to Gate 3, where the main assault would occur.

Abel Santamaría and twenty-three rebels, the third group, would occupy the Saturnino Lora Civilian Hospital. This vantage provided a direct view into the interior of the fortress and would allow them to support the attackers once they were within the walls of Moncada. The only drawback of the hospital's location was that from its upper floors one could see the parade ground of the fort, but not the gate or street where the attack would originate.

The Buick in which Vicente rode paused to let the car behind them pass, and he realized they'd arrived. Rising imposingly just across the wide avenue was the yellow buildings topped by craggy battlements of the Moncada Barracks. The very ruggedness of the bastion sent a shiver down Vicente's spine. They were a few minutes behind their 5:15 a.m. timetable that had been selected to coincide with the patrol being on the far side of the compound, and thus, Fidel impatiently waved the car behind them to pass.

The Mercury roared past them to the narrow entrance where the three sentries slouched sleepily, the last thought on their minds being that this was an insurrection. "Make way for the General!" Renato Guitart yelled out the window at them as the automobile screeched to a stop at the gate. The guards instantly saluted, giving the rebels the opportunity to spill from the car and take them captive. Four of the rebels ran up the outside steps of the barracks to commandeer the radio, while the others hastily dropped the simple chain across the gate so that the carloads of rebels could access the compound.

As Fidel began to nose the Buick toward the gate, the two-man patrol that they'd planned to avoid appeared on the street outside the fortress wall. Without hesitating, he veered towards them away from the entrance. "We must take them prisoner before they rouse the entire barracks," he whispered in a hoarse voice as he drove at them, hoping they'd pass as partygoers returning from the Carnival. He opened his door, which was shielded by the car from the patrol's line of vision, ready to jump out with his pistol and capture them. Vicente tightened his grip on the rifle; willing his nerves to be still and hoping that he wouldn't embarrass himself, even as the tightness in his stomach threatened to paralyze him and cold sweat blurred his sight.

One hundred feet. Ninety. Eighty. And then the two soldiers suddenly turned and leveled their Thompson sub-machine guns. One yelled something they couldn't hear as Fidel gunned the motor and sent the car hurtling at them, its tires striking the curb and rocking the passengers forward and back and stalling the engine. The two

Maceo Regiment soldiers opened fire, spraying bullets into the automobile, but return fire erupted from the car behind them, and the two soldiers pantomimed puppets on a string before crumpling to the ground.

"Everybody out!" Fidel yelled, but he was talking to an empty car as the rebels had already flung themselves to the ground, using the automobile as a barrier between them and the fortress.

Soldiers began raining down fire from numerous windows, at first sporadically and then in concert until the air was filled with the deafening cacophony of gunshots and the sound of bullets tearing into the metal of the Buick shielding the rebels. Behind the staccato gunfire belched the deep wails of the alarm, as if all the long dead oppressors of Cuban freedom were clawing their way out of the ground to wreak vengeance on those who wanted liberty for the island nation. Vicente realized he'd yet to fire a single round and hastily rose from his huddled position to snap a shot at nothing in particular, firing blindly into the wall of the fortress.

"Fidel, take cover," Pedro called, the urgency of his tone cutting through the din surrounding them. Vicente turned to look and saw Fidel in the middle of the street, waving with his free arm while shooting his pistol with the other, urging the others to follow him towards the gate down a gauntlet of death. Two men grabbed him and pulled him to the ground behind the Buick.

At the gate, it was only the occupants of the first car who had penetrated the fortress. In their haste, they'd left the vehicle blocking the entrance so that no other cars were able to gain access to the stronghold. Vicente watched helplessly as Renato fell, shredded by a .30 caliber machine gun that had begun peppering the rebels with large rounds that tore limbs from bodies and chunks from buildings. Ramiro Valdés suddenly appeared in the opening of Gate 3, firing back over his shoulder, and Vicente came to one knee to give covering fire, actually shooting at a target for the first time.

"Start, *hijo de puta.*" It was Fidel, now back in the driver's seat trying to get the son-of-a-bitch Buick to turn over, but the engine was either flooded or shredded by bullets.

Pedro leaned in the window, yelling in his ear in an effort to be

heard over the clamorous commotion surrounding them. "We have to get the hell out of here."

"Running away is for cowards," Fidel replied.

Pedro grabbed Fidel by the collar of his too-small military uniform, jerking him to the window. "This is a fucking mess. Die if you must, but don't take all these boys with you."

The panic in Fidel's eyes softened slightly. He became aware of heavy machine gun fire accompanied by hundreds of rifles shooting and realized that his plans had been butchered. "What do we do?" He cast a pleading look at the experienced soldier clutching him by the shirt.

"Take whoever is left and escape to the mountains like we planned. I'll cover you."

"No, I'll stay while you go," Fidel retorted. "I'm to blame for this disaster."

"The Movement is over if you die," Pedro replied simply, but inside he was screaming for this man-boy to stop the theatrics and get the hell out of there.

"It was a ghastly mistake to drive at the patrol. I should've followed the plan and driven through the gate and all of this would've gone differently," Fidel said, barely controlling his voice. He slid out of the driver's seat, hugging the ground, suddenly terrified.

Pedro looked at Vicente as he tilted his head at Fidel. "Get him out of here, Bolívar." Vicente grabbed Fidel by the arm as Pedro and the others abruptly began a covering fire. A bullet ripped a hole in Arcos' back and exited his stomach in a shower of red as they broke into a darting zigzag course for the car back across the street. Vicente could feel the hair on the back of his neck bristle as he braced for the lead that must surely find their exposed bodies, but somehow they reached the safety of the cross-street.

"Those pigs have us pinned down," a rebel soldier complained bitterly as they reached his position. "We're drowning here."

"It's time to hit the road," Vicente said when it became apparent Fidel was still tongue-tied. "We'll meet back at the farmhouse as planned. Do you have room in your car?"

"No. We're bursting at the seams."

"You go then." Fidel indicated with a wave of his hand, regaining some of his composure. "Vicente, you stay with me, we'll catch a ride with somebody else." As the automobile disappeared down the murky street, there was a brief pause in the firing, and the two men peered around the corner. "What's happening?" Fidel asked, his dark eyes staring fixedly at Vicente without moving or blinking.

Vicente realized that Fidel had removed his glasses for the assault. It seemed to be a bad time to not see so well, but he knew that Fidel's vanity often interfered with common sense. "I'll go tell them we're splittin'. You wait here." Shocked at his own insolence, Vicente ran towards the barrack's gate before Fidel could countermand his statement. He knew that it was a suicide mission to run back into the teeth of the enemy, but he understood that if a life were to be sacrificed, it should be his and not that of their leader.

Bullets splattered against the road all around him as the hulking machine gun from the elevated position within the compound tried to pick him off at six hundred feet. He could hear the hefty chunks of lead cleaving the street around his feet, rending gashes into Trinidad Avenue. As Vicente approached the barracks, the buildings shielded him from the machine gun's wrath, buying him a temporary reprieve.

There was a firefight raging at the gate as soldiers were counterattacking against the few rebels who'd actually gained access to the fort. Lying dead on the ground were four rebels, their bodies splayed awkwardly. One man had half of his skull missing, a gooey red bowl that left Vicente wondering who it was, whether he'd known him. "We've got to tear ass," he yelled at the remaining men, a mass of half-dressed soldiers shooting at them from the barracks' windows. The front car was parked at the entrance, providing cover from the soldiers in the compound, its hood and grill checkered with bullet holes, its windshield smashed and tires flat. "We're the only ones left."

They hurriedly clambered into the second car as bullets clattered around them. The driver threw the vehicle into reverse and sent the automobile careening backwards across the wide avenue, trying to gain the safety of the buildings on the other side. As they spun onto Garzon Avenue, there were several men running in a crouch, among them the unmistakable figure of Fidel. Even bent over he was a full head taller than the others. Vicente yelled and pointed, the car slid to a stop, and the rebels jumped in. They fled the city, crossing back over the San Juan Bridge, returning to the farmhouse in Siboney to lick their wounds. As they pulled into one of the chicken coops and got out, Vicente saw the sun peeking over the horizon.

* * *

Haydée Santamaría had spent the previous day ironing 120 uniforms for the rebels to wear in the attack on Moncada, and then, along with Melba Hernández, the only other woman, she'd made a chicken dinner for all the men. After she and Melba had finished with all the "women's work," Fidel had the audacity to tell them they were to stay behind at the farmhouse for the assault. It'd taken a full hour of wrangling to get him to relent, but finally he gave in to their demands, and they'd been assigned to her brother, Abel Santamaría, who was to take command of the civilian hospital.

Occupying the hospital had been as simple as pulling the three cars up to the front doors and approaching the front desk as if checking in for an appointment. A security guard had been asleep by the door, and once Boris liberated his gun, the rebels continued up to the second floor to support the attack on Moncada. Three men were left below to make sure none of the staff sounded the alarm, all while allowing the doctors and nurses to go about the business of caring for the patients. The remaining eighteen rebels had lined the second-floor windows facing the compound.

As the recon intelligence had noted, from their vantage point they had a clear view of the courtyard inside the military barracks, but couldn't see the gate nor help in the attack they knew was coming. Fidel's logic was that, as the rebel attackers gained access through Gate 3, the soldiers' defense would make them sitting ducks for the *fidelistas* hunkered down in the Civilian Hospital.

"*Vaya*, what's taking so long?" Abel Santamaría wondered aloud as he nervously paced back and forth. His ears protruded at sharp angles from his head, pushed there by black horn-rimmed glasses, giving him more of a comical air than that of a desperate rebel.

Appearances notwithstanding, he was second-in-command overall of "The Movement."

The silence was broken by the strained sound of a car motor suddenly revving, and then gunshots pierced the morning solitude, sporadic and then more frequent, but still they could see nothing from their position. The shooting steadily intensified, and then they heard the noise of a large-caliber machine gun opening up, its boom-boom-booms coming in rapid succession. The acrid smell of gunpowder seeped into their nostrils, but there was no sign of rebel intrusion into the courtyard. *So much for the plan*, Abel thought, scratching his head anxiously.

"What do we do, boss?" Boris asked, his normal smile gone as his eyes slid from left to right searching for something, anything, to shoot at.

Abel didn't answer for a long moment, but then shrugged his shoulders and shook his head in exasperation. "We wait." They sat tight for several minutes, the gunfire accelerating as more soldiers became involved.

Sudden shots down below led to a rebel clattering up the stairs with the news that several policemen had come to check on the hospital and the rebels had been forced to open fire, killing one of the officers. The other two had returned fire and escaped to spread the alarm. Abel ordered the men to spread out to defend their position, no longer merely facing Moncada, but in all directions. It was soon obvious that the Batista forces were slowly circling the hospital, cutting off any means of escape. The steady barrage of weapons and deep wails of the Moncada alarm were augmented by screaming babies in the maternity ward, disrupted by the noise but mostly angry that they hadn't yet been fed this morning.

"If we're going to hit the road, it's now or never." Boris was at Abel's elbow, having just come back from a thorough check of the hospital to take stock of the enemy. "Soon we'll be trapped like snakes in a barrel." His face was flushed and his eyes dilated, but he managed to keep his voice even.

"If we vacate our position, then we might condemn the mission to failure." Abel removed his glasses and rubbed his eyes nervously.

"I don't know what's going on with Fidel at the gate, but we have to stay—there's a chance we can still help them—either with their attack or their retreat."

Boris nodded his head as if they'd just agreed to spend a quiet morning drinking coffee. "We should save our bullets, then."

"Pass the word." Abel turned back to the window, raising and lowering his rifle several times at soldiers inching their way forward before he realized that Boris hadn't left. "What?" he asked, turning back to his friend and second-in-command.

"Your sister and Melba?" A bullet shattered the light behind them, causing both men to flinch.

"Tell them to go so that people will know what happened here."

Boris smiled bitterly. "She already told me to do things to myself that I don't think are possible." Haydée was not only Abel's sister, but was also Boris' fiancée.

Abel chuckled sympathetically, "*Envíalos a los dos*. I'll speak to them."

A few moments later, Haydée stared defiantly at Abel, her large teeth bared, daring him to dismiss her. A lock of dark hair with glints of lighter color twisted its way down between her thick eyebrows onto her broad face. "*Pendejo*, don't bother sending us away."

It was not the first time she'd called him an asshole, but it'd be the last. "We're almost out of ammunition and will certainly be killed or *capturados*," Abel said as calmly as possible, a twitch in his right cheek betraying his anxiety. At the same time, he was slightly afraid of his sister's stubbornness that he knew so well. "Somebody has to survive to tell the story."

"And we're not children." Haydée nodded her chin to include Melba at her side. "We're not just women, either. We're *revolucionarios*. If you stay, we stay."

"I shudder to think what Batista's soldiers will do to you if we're taken alive."

"They won't touch us," Melba spoke up, her thin face angry. "The people of Santiago would tear the soldiers apart. They might dare to rape women in the countryside," she gestured roughly out the window to where the surrounding hills were just becoming visible in the gathering light, "but they'd never dare here in the city. We're safer than you, Abel. Now, let's go about our business."

Abel raised his hands in defeat. "Go back to your posts then."

The rebels waited to hear news from the attack on the gate, but none came. The sun had fully emerged in the east by the time Boris reported that they were totally out of ammunition, having fired as sparsely as possible—yet, they still had to push back the incursions that the soldiers attempted. "One of the men suggested that we disguise ourselves as patients. Most of the people here are on our side."

"Hide like *cobardes*? I don't think so," Abel replied haughtily at such a cowardly suggestion.

"What then? Do we punch while they shoot?" Boris mimed the posture of a boxer with his trademark smile plastered stiffly on his face.

"We face them proudly and defiantly. We've no reason to be ashamed."

Boris tapped his empty rifle absently on the ground. "There's no shame in living." He walked to the window, staying well to the side, looking out to the Sierra Cristal in the distance, wondering if the rest of the rebels were already seeking safety in the rugged terrain of those mountains. "We don't know what happened to Fidel. If he's been killed, then you're in charge."

"They'll never fall for it. We're all suddenly just gone? It'll never work." Abel vainly tried to check the rising pitch of his voice.

Boris nodded, his tall, thin frame even ganglier as he towered over the seated Abel. "I've had that thought as well. We can't disguise all of us, but a few? Haydée and Melba could pass as nurses. You and one or two others could become patients of the hospital."

Abel shook his head vehemently. "I'll not hide like a common criminal. But you're right, we can slip a few between the cracks."

"No."

Abel raised his eyebrows. "No?"

"You have to escape." The two men locked eyes. "For The Movement."

They went down the stairs and borrowed supplies so that Boris could bandage Abel's eye, disguising his face. "You look like a mummy," he cracked, standing back to admire his handiwork.

Abel changed into a hospital gown and slipped into a cot between two other men who'd recently had cataract surgeries, while Haydée and Melba donned nurse's uniforms in the maternity ward. Two other rebels were swathed in wraps as if they'd just come from the operating room and placed in beds far apart and between patients that appeared sympathetic to the cause.

The remaining *fidelistas* gathered in the downstairs lobby with their arms raised in surrender, but the soldiers streaming in were not in the mood to quietly take prisoners. "On your knees!" the man who appeared in charge yelled, striking a rebel in the knee, the crack of the bone loud in the confined space.

"There are more of them hiding as nurses and patients." The words were blurted from a man in a hospital gown as he rushed up to the soldiers. "I'm Carabia. I was here last night and woke up to these vultures overrunning the place." Unluckily for the rebels, Carabia Carey was the civilian press chief for the Moncada Barracks. He'd kept his mouth shut and bided his time before betraying each and every one of them. "Come with me. There are two women disguised as nurses, and their leader is bandaged up like an eye patient."

His gown flapping behind him, Carabia led the soldiers to the maternity ward. "Those two over there," he said pointing. The soldiers grabbed Haydée and Melba roughly, dragging them along to find Abel, who started to rise from the bed, only to be knocked flat. As he tried to raise himself again, the soldiers beat him back down with their gunstocks, tipping the cot over and spilling Abel to the floor like a sack of potatoes.

The two women were thrown into one of the administration rooms and the door locked behind them. A man lay on the floor, partially under a desk, his face and body so beaten he was beyond recognition. They wrestled him into a chair; his body draped forward over the writing space, where he scribbled on a piece of paper; *I was taken prisoner—your son.*

Melba looked into his eyes and realized it was Raúl Gómez García, the young poet who'd drafted the Moncada Manifesto to be distributed upon their victory. "I'll make sure your *madre* gets this," she promised, knowing that this was only possible if she lived.

After twenty minutes, a group of soldiers came into the room, one of them kicking García back to the floor. When Haydée screamed for them to stop, the man raised his rifle and shot the poet dead, looking over at her with derision. She went at the man in a fury, but never saw the blow that connected with the back of her head and sent her tumbling to the floor. After a bit, she licked her lips and tasted blood, her brain clearing enough to realize the soldiers hovered above them in a circle, talking and smoking cigarettes.

"That tall one didn't give up even a little," a soldier remarked to another.

"The bastard got what he had coming to him," a thick, brutish bull of a man replied.

"It might've been different if you hadn't bashed him in the back of the head," a third soldier remarked, who looked slightly queasy at the sudden violence unfolding around him. "He was tough with his fists."

The first soldier nodded his head in agreement. "And he still never gave us nuthin'."

"I'm not so sure that's true," the brutish soldier retorted. "His black and white *zapatos* fit me perfectly." He looked down at his feet, pleased with his acquisition. "Plus, he gave me his life. That's something."

Haydée looked at the man's feet and recognized her fiancée's shoes. The day before, Boris had tried on ten pairs of new boots, and, when none would fit him, he'd pulled on his dress shoes instead. He'd laughed, saying, "I'm ready for the dance tomorrow." And now he was dead. Her eyes glazed over with coldness, her brain suppressing the pain, locking it away into a tiny corner. She'd cry later, but not now, not in front of them. Her jaw muscles worked furiously as she stared at the thick bastard who'd killed her man, marking down the details of his crooked face, noting how his nose was flattened and the scar by his right ear, saving the image for another time, another place. Flicking their cigarette butts to the floor, the soldiers exited through the door.

The two women were scheming how they might escape when the door again burst open and a sergeant entered. He was obviously a man to be feared, judging by the deference of the five soldiers with him, all of whom stood almost at attention, their hands clasped behind their backs and eyes staring at the floor in contrast to the undisciplined assassins they'd thus far had contact with. "Which one of you is the *hermana* of Abel Santamaría?" the sergeant brusquely demanded.

The two women stared impassively at him, no hint of recognition crossing their faces. "Who?"

The sergeant laughed harshly. "No matter. I know it's one of you." He paced the room, one hand behind his back as if hiding something.

Haydée spat at his feet, her anger threatening to explode. "I don't know what you're talking about."

"How could you've known?" The sergeant stopped in front of her, his black eyes burning into her, an intense violence in him lingering from the not-so-distant past.

"Known what?" Haydée felt trapped by his gaze, his words, and some secret that was rushing toward her, a secret she didn't want to know.

The sergeant brought his right hand around and held it out to her, slowly spreading his fingers. Haydée tried to stop herself from looking, didn't want to know, didn't want to touch, but unable to prevent herself, she reached her own hand out to catch what was dropped. "How could you've known your *hermano* was about to lose his eye?"

Haydée stared into her brother's sightless eye. With her free hand she punched the sergeant as hard as she could in the chin. He retaliated with a sweeping hook that exploded into the side of her head, though no blow would've been strong enough to obscure the sensation of her brother's eyeball popping in her hand as she involuntarily squeezed it. Two soldiers picked her up off the floor and set her roughly into a chair, her knees too wobbly to support herself, her neck unable to prop up her head as it lolled side to side. From her mouth dribbled spittle, and blood flowed freely from her nose.

"Where's the rendezvous point?" the sergeant demanded. "If you tell me where Fidel Castro is, I'll stop at an eye for an eye. Do you understand? I don't want to have to kill him slowly or kill him at all, I just want that *maricon* Castro."

Haydée's mind spun back into orbit. *Fidel was alive.* She righted her head over her shoulders, licking her lips before replying in a cracked voice, "If Abel wouldn't tell you anything even after you took his eye, what makes you think I will?"

2

September 5th, 1951, Havana

"**D**o me a solid. Come with me, and at least hear him talk. He's a real gone cat," Félix said. "He says that The Man can't take our pads without shelling out some dough." "What *good* will it do?" Vicente Bolívar retorted, irritated. He was tired from driving all night, having made a delivery of rum and cigars to Camaguey, eight hours with an over-loaded truck on bad roads, only to pack it full of beef for the return trip to Havana. He'd slept for four hours in his tiny shack before Félix, his roommate, had woken him to cajole him out onto the Havana streets to hear some rich lawyer spout out nonsense. "President Prío is a *cabrón*—just as dirty as they come. He's not gonna give us a single peso. If we protest too loudly, he'll just send his *gángsters* in to rough us up."

"Just come with me. Hear the man speak. He's a real hipster, I tell you. He'll clue you in."

Vicente groaned, "*Mierda*! Let me get dressed and we'll go hear what this Fidel Castro has to say."

The room was not much to look at, a space of twenty-feet by twenty-feet with two meagerly stuffed mattresses on a dirt floor. Their hut was built of palm fronds from the walls to the roof, and weathered a dark-gray by the sun and rain, one of thousands of such abodes crowded haphazardly into this poverty-stricken neighborhood. But, Vicente had a regular job and was off the streets for the first time in years, so he considered 1951 to be a banner year indeed. His meager pay from driving the truck was enough to allow him to share this room in La Pelusa, possibly the worst slum in Havana, but it was better than the alleyways where he'd been sleeping since leaving his grandmother's *choza* upon her death. That crowded shack with its chickens scratching in the yard and the mango tree at the foot of the garden had been the only home he'd ever really known.

It'd been more difficult than he'd have thought to find a job in Havana, most positions requiring a *contragolpe*, the boss man with his hand out taking a portion of his scant pay. With little experience and minimal education, he'd been fortunate to find an older driver who'd taken pity on this sixteen-year-old boy alone in the city. At first, he'd been a passenger, loading and unloading the truck for the driver who suffered from rheumatism in his back, but over time the man had taught him how to drive the truck, starting him off on the central highway when there was little traffic, and once he was proficient, had paid for him to get a driver's license.

"Fidel says that it's time for the Cuban people to rattle the cage, for the workers to get with it instead of the fascist oppressors," Félix spoke excitedly, stumbling over the unfamiliar words, as they worked their way through the maze of winding dirt alleyways that was La Pelusa. It wouldn't take much to level this neighborhood stretching across the outskirts of downtown Havana, where in marked contrast, the tall buildings were of stone topped by tile shingles. It was an eyesore for any wealthy Cuban or rich tourist who mistakenly turned off the main boulevards into this slum, but the dwellings were home to thousands of poor who would otherwise be homeless without the slanted roofs, crooked walls, and sagging doorways. Though the buildings may have been dilapidated, it wasn't for the lack of spirit or *alégria*—the joie-de-vivre—of their inhabitants, for the people in the yards and on the sidewalks emanated an energy and vitality that challenged anybody or anything to diminish their existence. "Fidel," Félix was saying, "speaks in such a nifty way that you can almost believe that what he says is possible and that we'll one day be free of the bogus chains of exploitation."

"What are these 'chains of exploitation'?"

"It's how the *rico* keep us *pobre*," Felíx replied simply.

"But what does he want?"

"Are you writing a book? He wants to light up the tilt sign, is what this cat wants. He refuses money, because we don't have any. They say he'll visit the market and take a mango, or a banana, or some other bite to eat from those that hang their hat in La Pelusa, and they refuse to charge him, and this he does accept. The *guajiros* have come to trust him," he said, and then paused to collect his thoughts. "And if a peasant trusts him, if the cane cutters trust him, don't you think maybe he's worth listening to? Can you dig what I'm saying?"

Vicente paused to look at an old woman smoking a cigar, her face a virtual roadmap of La Pelusa, each wrinkle etched by some hardship she'd experienced in her many years of life. She reminded him of his grandmother, a tough old woman who'd known right from wrong. He felt the familiar tear well up in his eye and hastily rubbed it away. "I've heard of this Fidel Castro," he said carefully. "People say he's the son of a rich sugar tycoon. That he's grown up *con la cuchara de plata en la boca*." When Vicente had been a valet for the hotel in Matanzas he'd seen many of these wealthy people growing up with the silver spoon always in their mouth, never understanding the hardships all around them.

"That may be so. But here in La Pelusa, we don't sweat a cat by his past, but only by what he is now."

"*La gallina de arriba se caga en la gallina de abajo.*" The rich get richer and the poor get poorer was just a fact of life. Vicente thought of the casinos, the bars, the fancy hotels, the cabarets, and the houses of prostitution that filled downtown Havana. La Pelusa hardly had a corner *bodega* selling dry goods and beer, much less a casino or even a brothel. Nobody here could afford a single peso for entertainment or women, but many they passed even at this time of day had a bottle of rum with them, to numb their brains to the lot they'd been cast. "Money brings out the *diablo* in man."

"I'd gladly trade my soul for some bread." Félix laughed. "But I dig

seem
oxymoronic

you. That's the hip thing about Fidel. If he truly grew up with plenty of biscuits, what's he doing with us?"

"Unless there's somethin' in it for him, you mean," Vicente replied, frowning as he considered what Castro's scam might be. In Cuba, there was always a con. "So he makes noise just long enough to be bribed to drop the case? He's probably just another *bisnero*, out to hustle money pretendin' to be an honest businessman."

The fact was that blocks and blocks of the neighborhood shanties were to be torn down so that a Civic Square could be built, a symbol of prosperity to efface the reality of poverty that flourished in so much of Havana. This proposed whitewashing of the neighborhood was similar to the clothes that Vicente wore in an attempt to cover up his dire finances. The white shirt and dark jacket hung loosely on his thin frame. He'd found them cheap in a second hand store, the sleeves frayed and a stain or two on the shirt. As long as he kept the dark jacket on, however, he could pass for a sophisticated man of means, at least in comparison to the men and women they passed. His hair was rich and abundant, minute traces of dark brown highlighting the black waves combed carefully to one side, his forehead high and narrow. His nose was petite, almost effeminate on his face, while his dark golden skin spoke of black, white, and native ancestors. If it weren't for the intensity of the fierce eyes that made one think of a pirate, he might almost have been pretty.

Crowds had gathered on the corner where there was a long-neglected garden overgrown with weeds. The heart of their neighborhood was about a mile and a half west of the University of Havana and about the same distance south of the Malecón, the wide roadway, sidewalk, and seawall along the Strait of Florida. They'd no sooner arrived than a murmur of anticipation traveled through the throng signaling that the man of the hour was approaching.

Vicente followed the gaze of hundreds of men and women to see the approaching storm that was Fidel Castro, walking quickly as he talked animatedly to his companion while they wended their way around slower-moving pedestrians. He waved his hands and arms energetically as he spoke, his teeth flashing white against his youthful olive complexion, his face clean-shaven, almost adolescent in its exuberant features. Castro dwarfed those around him, and Vicente realized the man was almost a full foot taller than his own five-foot-five-inch frame, with a striped blue suit jacket failing to conceal an athletic physique.

Without breaking stride, Fidel picked up a wooden box discarded on the side of the road, and making his way to the center of the gathering, set the box on the ground and climbed atop of it in one fluid motion. He raised his hands and spread his arms, almost like a preacher, and the crowd gradually quieted. After a pause, he began to speak.

"Fellow citizens of Havana, you who live in the *barrio* of La Pelusa, I want to assure you that you're no less deserving of your rights than the people of Miramar. Although your dwellings may not be as exalted as the wealthy capitalists who live in the mansions of our city, they are still your homes. You're the farmers while they're the manure that grows their wealth. If your humble *choza* pales in comparison to the Presidential Palace of Carlos Prío Socarrás, our mighty, learned, and honest leader,"—at this, the crowd burst out in derisive laughter—"it's a question of his morality and not of your decency. If you must struggle to feed your family, it's a problem of our corrupt government, not of your desire to provide."

Fidel went on to attack the system that forced them to live in poverty and then to sacrifice their very homes for the benefit of the excessively rich men who oppressed them without just compensation. "If *El Presidente* is determined to build a Civic Square on the sacred ground where your families live, he must pay you a fair sum so that you may start over elsewhere. When the inspectors come around, you must tell them of the improvements you've made. You must tell them of the mouths that are dependent upon you and of the people whom the roof keeps dry and warm at night."

Vicente felt as if Fidel were looking directly at him, those dark eyes boring into his spirit, the words opening up his conscience, letting him know that there was no shame in being poor, that he could take pride in the honest, if modest wage, he earned. It was his right—and a noble one—to struggle against a system that devalued his worth, and he deserved more. "Dignity begins with one small step and grows until you've run a marathon. I'll defend you in court. I ask for only one thing in return. You must stand together. You must show your solidarity when the *matones* come around trying to scare you off. You must stand up to the police who are paid to force you out. You must realize your self worth and defend it."

Vicente had spent the day with his mind buzzing from what he'd heard. That night he was unable to sleep even though he was exhausted, his intellect racing with the new thoughts swirling around in his brain. The next morning, Vicente paid a man to fill in for him driving that day, and instead went to the door of a second floor office in Old Havana at 57 Tejadillo Street. This was the banking district and also where many of the lawyers in the city had their places of business, though most of the buildings weren't as run down as this one.

This was the oldest neighborhood of Havana, and the businesses, two- and three-story edifices, had ornate balconies rising above the sidewalk and crowding the narrow street on either side. The narrow sidewalk in front of Castro's law office was littered with debris that'd apparently fallen off the building above. Vicente looked up apprehensively and then hurried through the doorway before some falling missile could strike him. Up the stairs he found a small reception room, noting the new desk and several shelves lined with books. The plaster walls were cracked in places and shedding their paint in irregular patches, while the ceiling appeared as if it might've weathered a fire at some point. The furniture, gleaming brightly and smelling of fresh polish, seemed the only concession to lawyerly propriety. There was no one in the room, but Vicente could hear a clattering noise coming from the lone door, slightly ajar, that appeared to lead to an inner recessed office.

"Hello?" he called, easing his way towards the door. There was no answer, so he knocked lightly, and the door swung open under his knuckles. Fidel Castro was rapping away madly at a typewriter, his fingers banging the keys as if he were angry with them, and at the same time he muttered disjointed, indistinct words that Vicente couldn't quite hear. "Hello," he said again.

Without looking up, Fidel replied, "Come in, then. I take it you're not here to kill me or you would've done so by now." He continued his work, and then, presumably having come to a suitable stopping point, pulled his hands back to the edge of the desk and looked up. Perspiration dotted his brow. "Sit." He nodded to a chair. "What can I do for you?"

"I live in La Pelusa," Vicente spoke slowly and hesitantly, not sure why he'd come. "I heard you talkin' yesterday about fightin' for us. My name is Vicente Bolívar."

"Good to meet you. May I call you Vicente?" Fidel didn't follow the normal conventions of Cuban formality, preferring to use first names, for himself as well as others. Upon a nod of assent, Fidel continued, "What is it that you do for work?"

"I drive a truck, Señor Castro." Vicente studied the face of the man across from him, trying to see some signs of greed lurking behind his features. "Why are you fightin' for us? You know you'll never get paid?"

"Call me Fidel," Castro said offhandedly as he took a breath. "The government of Carlos Prío is corrupt through and through. It's nothing but an agglomeration of *gángsters* looking to line their pockets with the money of the poor. I aim to let them know that the voice of the poor can be as loud as that of the rich. If they must have your homes, they must pay for them. It's that simple."

"I heard you grew up the son of a cane owner."

"You heard correctly. My *padre*, Ángel Castro, came to this country penniless and through hard work and crookedness built an empire in Oriente Province," Fidel admitted to the charge as his mind wandered to his actual childhood, spent mostly away from home at school, first at the La Salle School, and then with the Jesuits at Dolores School, both in Santiago.

Vicente decided to let the 'crookedness' go for a moment. "How's it that you fight for us, yet want *nada*?"

Fidel stood up slamming his chair back into the wall and stalked across the room, his boots banging the floor angrily. He'd always hated injustice, starting with the authoritarian rule of his father, his Jesuit teachers, professors at the University, politicians, and so many wealthy people who thought their position of power equated somehow with them being *mejor que otros.* "Is my father better than another man who has no money? Does my father need so much or should he share it with those less fortunate? Does the United States have the right to use our country as their playground, milk cow, and garbage can just because they're more powerful and wealthier?" Fidel warmed to his favorite topic, that of the unequal distribution of money and the convenience of strength. He paced in the tiny office, making Vicente draw his chair further back to the wall with each circuit, the tall man's words hurtling through the tight confines of the space and his arms chopping the air with a vengeance.

"My father grew up a poor peasant but was able to raise himself up through hard work and careful investment, as well as by selling his soul to the devil that is United Fruit. He doesn't quite understand that the next step is to share with his fellow man." He abruptly came to a stop directly in front of Vicente, his gaze scrutinizing the young man in front of him, veering away from the uncomfortable topic of his own father, a man he loved, feared, and despised. "But what of your father?"

"My, uh, father?" Vicente stammered. "What about him?"

"Exactly. Tell me about him."

"He was a soldier loyal to Gerardo Machado," Vicente said defiantly, knowing only what his grandmother had told him, but well aware that the prevailing opinion of former President Machado, deposed in 1933, was unfavorable, and that most were happy he'd been overthrown.

Fidel walked back to his chair and sat down slowly. "Back in 1924 Machado campaigned with the slogan 'water, roads, and schools.'" He tapped his fingers on the edge of the desk. "These are ambitious goals that I can agree with. He built a road from Havana to Santiago, connecting our island nation like never before." Unexpectedly he slammed his hand down hard on the table. "And then the power went to his head, and he rammed through changes to the Constitution to stay in power." This power play had resulted in growing unrest in Cuba, finally forcing Machado to step down under pressure from the United States. When the interim government had proven equally unpopular, an army uprising led by Fulgencio Batista had taken power in a coup that came to be known as the Sergeants' Revolt. Fidel took a deep breath. "There are worse traits than loyalty. What happened to your father?"

"Batista killed him when I was six months old." Vicente had heard that his father had been intelligent and loyal, but stubborn to a fault. If he'd repudiated Machado after his fall, his life may have been spared, but the hardheaded young soldier had refused to join the growing opposition. He'd backed Machado when he had tried to wrest power back from Batista, and when it was reported that the former president had taken flight to the Bahamas, it was too late for Antonio Bolívar. "His body was found shot full of lead in an old buildin'," Vicente said simply. "It was clear who done it."

Fidel stared inquisitively, although kindly, at Vicente. "Your father was devoted to a man who believed that men of color shouldn't be able to advance above a certain level in the army?"

"My *abuela* told me that my father had always been that way, *terco como una mula*. Once his mind was set, whether it be on which way to travel or the best way to shine a buckle, there was no changin' it."

"So what can I do for you?"

Vicente reached into a place he wasn't used to going, realizing that he wanted to help this man, to listen to him and to learn. He felt strange, almost elated. "I'd like to be of use to you," he said simply.

"Why?"

"Yesterday when I heard you talkin'…" Vicente groped for the right words. "It's like I been out fishin' for a week with nothin', and then I see the ripples in the water, and know my luck's 'bout to turn 'round."

"You're a driver?" Without pausing for an answer, Fidel continued on, "I've desideratum of a chauffeur on occasion. It just so happens that tomorrow is one of those times. Meet me here in the morning. Now I must go, for I'm late for an appointment and must first drop off this article at *Alerta*." Vicente found himself on the sidewalk pondering the meaning of the word Fidel had used, deciding it must just mean need.

The next day Vicente was outside the office building as the sun first peeked its head above the horizon. Fidel hadn't mentioned an exact time he was to be here, only that it should be in the morning. Lacking a watch, he'd set his mental clock to awaken him when the church bells rang at six a.m. Vicente had brought a newspaper with him and he opened it up and attempted to read it.

"Daddy-O, you fracture me. You need to read like a horse needs a cigar!" Felíx would say, laughing at him as he sounded his way through the headlines of discarded newspapers, but Vicente refused to concede his ignorance. Learning to read, he'd concluded, was a doorway to greater things. There was an article discussing the next spring's election. If he understood the words correctly, Fulgencio Batista, the very man who'd ordered the execution of his father, was running a distant third in the polls and stood little chance of winning the presidency.

Two hours later, when Vicente had been about to sneak off for a *cafecito*, Fidel pulled up in a Pontiac Sedan with a man in the passenger seat. They both got out. "This is my brother-in-law, Rafael." He nodded at the man with him, and then looked back at Vicente. "This is my new driver, Vicente." Fidel stepped to the rear of the car and yanked the door open. "We've some business to discuss and some papers to peruse. Do you know where Batista's Kuquine Estate is?" Vicente nodded. "Good. That's our destination."

Vicente climbed into the driver's seat, confused. He was inspired by Fidel's vision and personal magnetism, and he was only too happy to unquestioningly climb aboard the man's runaway train, but to pay a visit to Fulgencio Batista? Batista had controlled politics in Cuba from the Sergeants Revolution of 1933 until he easily won the presidency in 1940 in a landslide, his popularity in Cuba at its zenith. Under the terms of the Constitution of that same year he'd stepped down in 1944 at the completion of his term, retiring to the United States where he split his time between New York City and Daytona Beach, living in luxury, obviously having purloined a fortune in kickbacks and outright theft during his time ruling Cuba. He'd run for the Senate in 1948 in absentia and thus began to ease his way back into the politics of Cuba—as if he'd ever really left. The man was now, once again, running for president.

As they motored slowly down the long winding drive of Batista's *finca*, various animals were scurrying around the immense front yard.

A doe with a fawn pranced past the car, not the slightest bit nervous of the vehicle and its occupants, while hutui—large rat-like animals with white and brown fur—cranes, and dogs crowded around the car when they stopped.

Batista came striding out of the extensive house, emerging from under an awning that ran around the entire structure, two men who must've been bodyguards a few steps behind him. He wore a white linen lounge jacket over a button-up white shirt. Tiny gold stars matching the glint of the gold watch on his wrist dotted his dark tie, and his mulatto skin, flashing smile, and overall ruggedly handsome features gave him the appearance of a movie star rather than a politician.

Rafael Díaz-Balart, the brother of Fidel's wife, Myrta, and a close friend of Batista, was the first out of the car. The two men hugged and kissed each other on the cheeks while Fidel and Vicente silently got out. Vicente made as if to scratch his arm and instead pinched the soft skin of his forearm. Two days ago he'd been delivering meat and cigars, and today he was standing ten feet from the man who had his father killed.

A crane with long stilted legs and a red head topping his white feathers poked his beak inquisitively into Fidel's pocket. "Panchito, leave the man alone." Batista shoved the crane away, only to have a small pack of dogs surround the startled Fidel. A tiny Pekingese jumped and yapped excitedly, joined by a Dachshund only slightly larger with sad eyes, and finally a hulking Newfoundland that stood aloof and to the side, seemingly not caring about their arrival. "Mr. Castro, I've heard much of you over the past few years." The two men shook hands, ignoring Vicente and the two bodyguards.

"Senator Batista." Fidel nodded, his own athletic frame more than matching that of the other man. "Thank you for inviting me."

"The pleasure is mine." Batista motioned towards the house. "Come into my study, please." They entered into a room with walls covered by shelves filled with books. "I read about how you defended yourself after the fiasco in Cienfuegos."

"They'd every right to be demonstrating," Fidel replied angrily, his eyes sliding over the titles of the books on the shelves, from *The Prince* by Machiavelli to *Discourse on the Method* by Descartes.

"Of course they did," Batista said gently. "I only meant that your arrest and abuse at the hands of the police was a fiasco."

"President Prío has brought shame upon Cuba with the vast corruption that he allows to flourish in every facet of his government."

"That's why I'm running for President." Batista offered a cigar to Fidel, who accepted the token of peace, taking his time over the ritual of first holding it to his nose and inhaling, nodding almost unconsciously at its dark aromas, then snipping the end before lighting it as if a man with all the time in the world.

"How can you expect fair play from that nefarious and unscrupulous aristocrat? Perhaps you should have a coup now, why wait for the elections?" This last Fidel dropped in almost mockingly, looking through the smoke at his host.

Batista froze momentarily, his suave demeanor shocked by the brazen suggestion. "You're suggesting that I overthrow the current government?"

Fidel smiled back at him, "I believe that I'd be able to support you in a *golpe de Estado*. Otherwise, my hands are tied by my Orthodox Party and our candidate, Roberto Agramonte."

Batista walked over to a bust of Abraham Lincoln and an elegantly framed copy of the Emancipation Proclamation. He appeared to be reading the words that had freed the slaves in the United States almost one hundred years earlier. Batista himself was a poor black *campesino* from Banes in eastern Cuba. If he'd been born fifteen years earlier, he might himself have been a captive laborer. "I believe that we must fight for our freedom, but the time and place must be right. Dissatisfaction with our government must follow a process, and only if that process fails should," he paused slightly, "*otras acciones sean consideradas.*"

After an hour of civil conversation that included nothing on what "other actions" might be considered, Fidel politely thanked Batista for his hospitality, and made to leave. He paused by one of the bookshelves on his way out, admiring the titles, before saying, "But you are missing one profoundly significant book."

"And what would that be?"

"A work by Curzio Malaparte," Fidel said casually as he looked through a telescope that had once belonged to Napoleon Bonaparte. "*The Technique of the Coup d'État.*"

Batista chuckled as he guided Fidel to the door. "You're a stubborn man, Fidel Castro. I can see that the stories of you hold merit. You'd certainly make a better friend than enemy." It would be the last time the two men would meet face-to-face.

Rafael had decided to stay behind, and thus, for the return trip, Fidel rode in front with Vicente. He spoke about the Prío administration's malfeasance, until Vicente finally interrupted him, "Would you really support a coup by that man?"

Fidel laughed harshly. "I'd never back that *singao*. That son-of-a-bitch is in bed with the American mob and is selling our country out to the imperialists. But if one is trying to uncover whether or not another is planning a putsch, the delusion of complicity is justified to gain the other's trust, don't you think?" Without waiting for an answer, Fidel continued, "But I'd bet everything I own, which is not much, that he has plans to that end. Polls show that he'll lose the upcoming elections—and badly, and that *perro* doesn't know how to accept defeat. Mark my words, that old dog has something up his sleeve."

"What can be done about it?"

"There's nothing to be done. We must go on about our business as normal. Prepare for the elections. What will be will be."

Vicente digested that thought. "I'd like to help."

"Do you have a pistol? Or more to the point, do you know how to use one? I'll occasionally need a driver, but I've many enemies, and a weapon would be helpful to dissuade them." Fidel looked pensively out the window at the outskirts of Havana. "We've people who know how to handle guns."

"I can get one." Vicente didn't have the first clue about guns, but really, how hard could it be? "But I only ever shot off a shotgun before so, err, mebbe...."

Fidel turned to face him, his unbroken stare seemingly prying into the deepest recesses of Vicente's being. "No need to worry, we'll find you an able teacher." He'd just met Vicente the day before, and already he'd begun trusting him with his secrets and safety. He recognized a corresponding stubbornness in those flat eyes, a steadfast resolve to move forward, to break down obstacles rather than circumvent them, as well as loyalty leavened with kindness. "I'm also in need of help investigating the corruption of President Prío."

"What for?"

"I plan to expose his fraudulent behavior, but I must first make sure my allegations can be proven, or it could wreck my own political aspirations. Remember Eddie Chíbas?" Once Castro's mentor, Chíbas had called out the Education Minister publicly only to have the incriminating documents mysteriously disappear. "When those papers were withheld, Chíbas' honor left him only one route." Fidel's voice lowered in memory of this tragic time.

Vicente remembered the day in August when Senator Chíbas had ended his Sunday night broadcast with a call for Cuba to awaken in the name of economic independence, political liberty, and social justice. The broadcast had then cut to commercial, and it wasn't until the next day that he and most of Cuba learned that Chíbas had shot himself. He'd meant to do so live on air, but had gone over his allotted time, and a technician had switched over to a commercial for Café Pilon.

"Where do I start?" Vicente asked hesitantly. "It's only," he paused, "I'm not so good with papers. Or numbers."

Castro reached over and clapped him on the shoulder. "That, too, we can help you with. Just start by talking to people. Go to the casinos and cabarets and ask questions. But don't drink or gamble. Don't play games with the devil for you'll surely lose. When you find some impropriety, let me know. I need proof or it's no good. Do you understand?"

As Vicente began walking home from the parked car, he thought of the mass of information he'd been swarmed with on this day. It was overwhelming, but at the same time, he sensed the winds of change his grandmother spoke of during her stories, and he smiled broadly. Where this Fidel Castro would lead him, he did not know, but he already knew he'd follow him into the inferno if asked.

* * *

Over the next few months, Vicente's daily life went from the boring to the bizarre. One day, he was talking to "the girls" about who came and went from the upstairs VIP rooms of their brothel, and the next he was tailing men who'd met with Prío. He had to give up his job driving the truck, but Fidel managed to pass him a few pesos here and there to get by. He moved out of La Pelusa and into the apartment of Fidel's sister, Lidia, who fed him and darned his socks. Fidel made sure that he carried a newspaper wherever he went, and offered help at first with words, and then with ideas.

One day, Vicente had slammed the newspaper down in frustration, cursing that it was too difficult and he'd never understand most of what was being said. Fidel had looked at him, his fierce eyes gentled, and softly implored Vicente to keep trying. "If you're unable to learn," Fidel had said, "then what I wish for Cuba is an impossibility." Vicente had quietly picked up the *Havana Times* and continued the struggle. He never again complained about the difficulty.

Vicente now carried a pistol, which he still didn't know how to work. Almost daily, he drove Fidel somewhere, either accompanying him as a bodyguard or staying in the car to read up on the news. This day, he'd followed a man who'd lunched with Carlos Prío, back to the Hotel Nacional. The sweeping arches and chandeliers of the hotel continued to fill him with astonishment, even though for the past few months he'd been frequenting establishments such as this as he pried into Prío's private and not-so-public life searching for some proof of exploitation or nepotism.

The lobby was long and narrow, with the check-in desk to the right as you entered the hotel, the elegant dark wood counter and marble floors meant to intimidate those who didn't belong. The porters and doormen were all black, a deep burnished obsidian that almost allowed Vicente to pass as white, but he knew not to push that envelope. Thus, he refrained from passing through the wide glass doors leading to the back veranda where wicker furniture was scattered in groups providing a comfortable setting for cocktails, cigars, or even a meal. Beyond the veranda stretched an expansive lawn overlooking the Malecón and the Strait of Florida, site of frequent society weddings, dances, and other functions.

There seemed to be a wedding taking place even now as Vicente slid casually into a buffalo leather armchair, slightly protected from view by the planted palm tree that provided ambience to the sophisticated lobby. And that's when the girl approached him. "Excuse me, but I believe that's my purse underneath your chair?" Her voice was soft but not apologetic, quiet but not meek. Her features were Italian, yet her accent was unmistakably *norteamericana*.

Vicente reached underneath and found the missing small red clutch in shockingly bright vinyl. He stood and thrust it towards her as if it might bite, his mind recognizing how ridiculous his behavior was but somehow unable to prevent it. He'd never spoken with anyone as sophisticated and beautiful as this.

"Thank you, Señor," she replied with a coquettish smile. Her black brows framed long lashes that fluttered at intervals above brown eyes that Vicente found himself immediately lost in. "*Lo siento, hablas inglés?*" she apologized, realizing that he might not speak English. In the brief time she'd been in Cuba, she'd yet to have a conversation with an honest-to-goodness Cuban. "My Spanish could use some work."

Vicente shook his head to break the trance. "I speak English." He smiled proudly. Vicente had worked for three years in Matanzas as a yard boy for a wealthy American family and had picked up the basics, and this had allowed him to get a job in a hotel as a valet for several more years. "I'm glad that the bag wasn't lost."

"I'm Sophia," she said boldly, her short hair a combination of thick lush curls and small kiss-me ringlets, sculpted around her generous cheekbones.

He pointed at his chest. "Vicente Bolívar. Good to meet you." He attempted a small bow but came dangerously close to head-butting her and stepped hurriedly back.

"Whoever you are…I have always depended on the kindness of strangers."

"What?"

Realizing that he'd probably not seen the film, *A Streetcar Named*

Desire, Sophia decided to move on rather than trying to explain the quote. "Are you staying here at the Nacional?"

"No, I was, uh, meetin' a friend."

"Too bad." Sophia pouted.

"Why's that?"

"I thought we might get a cup of coffee together," she replied.

"The con, con, *conserje*, he just delivered me a message," Vicente said. "To say that he's not to come today. I'm sitting here two minutes wonderin' what I'm to do now." He grinned like a three-year-old having finished a particularly messy finger painting.

"Fabulous," she said, her red lips savoring the word. "I'd be happy to pay as reward for finding my purse." She took his arm, brushing slightly against him, and steered him out the front door. They walked out the long drive of the hotel, around to the left, and down the hill to the Malecón. Sophia delivered them to a small café facing the seawall across the street, settling them both at an outdoor table with two chairs. "*Café con leche*," she told the waiter, who nodded, and turned to Vicente.

"*Cafecito*," he said, still taken aback by the abrupt turn of events. They sat in silence, watching the spray from the waves crash over the seawall onto the walkway until the waiter brought the small cup of bitter coffee for Vicente and the larger cup of espresso with hot milk for Sophia.

"You're not Cuban," Vicente stated the obvious. "Um, I mean to say, you're in Cuba why?"

"The gorgeous weather and splendid dancing bring me to Cuba. That, and my uncle, who works in the casino business." Inwardly, she was still quite angry with her uncle for having forced her to leave Larry. She was certain she didn't love the man, but when he kissed her neck and touched her breasts she was able to banish the thoughts of her dead parents and the car crash that had killed them so abruptly. "But even though your English is good—I'd call it 'hotel English'—I'd guess that you are Cuban."

"I'm as Cuban as they come, Señorita Sophia," Vicente replied, very proud of his ancestry, a pride instilled by his grandmother through stories she passed on to him as he grew up. "My ancestor fought with Hatüey back in the early 16th century."

"Hatüey?" Sophia wrinkled her nose; an expression that Vicente would come to realize was her look of deep thought. "Who is that?"

3

July 26th, 1953, Siboney, just outside of Santiago, Cuba

The Pontiac slid into the chicken coop at the Siboney farmhouse, and the eight men crammed into it piled out. The newly risen sun was bathing everything with a red glow. *Red sky in the morning, sailor's warning,* flashed through Vicente's mind amidst the chaos of what had just occurred. It was hard to believe that they'd left this place a few hours earlier filled with heroic dreams of becoming the saviors of Cuban democracy. A man whose name Vicente didn't know was whimpering in pain, biting down on a belt so as not to scream. A bullet had smashed his kneecap, and from thigh to ankle was a mess of blood, gristle, and bits of bone.

Fidel yelled that they should've gone on to Bayamo to join with the group that had ambushed the fort located there. Nobody would meet his eyes, all of them thinking about either escape or surrender. "They killed Raúl." Fidel stormed through the house. "I made a mess of everything." Mad with shame and grief, he held his pistol to his head, and just then a gunshot rang through the chaotic noise. For a moment, Vicente thought he'd actually killed himself, but then realized the shot had come from outside.

"*Hijo de la gran puta.* You shot me," Nito Ortega shrieked at the son-of-a-bitch who'd accidently discharged his weapon, the bullet striking him in the ankle.

"We've gotta' give up!" a young mechanic from Artemisa said loudly, his voice pitched high with hysteria.

The bickering went on for almost an hour. The men vacillated between the frenzy to do something, anything, and calmer calls to regroup and retreat to the mountains. Some of the men had spent time in jail and swore they wouldn't go back, no matter the cost.

"Today didn't go as planned," Fidel finally said in a firm, calm voice. The noise in the room immediately diminished, even the injured quieting their moans. "Bad luck plagued us from the start, especially that patrol appearing out of nowhere, but these things happen. The important part is not that we were defeated, but how shall we react to this debacle? Shall we roll over and play dead? Shall we turn ourselves in and promise allegiance to the government? Or, shall we continue with our plan?" He was silent for a moment. "I'll go on fighting the revolution from the Gran Piedra Mountains and welcome any that wish to come with me. We leave in one hour."

"*Yo iré con usted Fidel.*" Vicente found himself on his feet agreeing to accompany his mentor, moved by the words of passion, angered by the weakness he'd been feeling, and yet a bit surprised to be acting so boldly.

Their immediate goal was to move northeast towards Ocaña Heights, and this they did with haste, hoping to break free of any attempts to encircle them. They'd just passed a farm when they came upon a small cabin in the woods, home to an elderly black woman who called herself Chicha. She'd no food but instead offered the services of her grandson to guide them into the mountains. Sensing their trepidation she produced a letter signed by Antonio Maceo in 1895 that declared her a patriot messenger. "I fight for in-dee-pen-dence with the men of Martí and nothin's changed in the past sixty years," Chicha remonstrated. "I might not be as pretty no more, but you can trust me, and you need a guide if you don't wanna git lost."

After hours of tramping silently onward, they stopped at a honeyberry tree, the men greedily picking and devouring its peso-sized, cherry-like fruit. Continuing down the rugged trail, Vicente's mind wandered, his thoughts turning to the young woman, Sophia, whom he'd met at the hotel in Havana. Over the course of the last year and a half they'd become quite close, meeting often for coffee, occasionally for a meal or to hear music. He wondered if he was falling in love though they had not exchanged so much as a single kiss. The only contact between them was when she took his arm as they walked, or the slightest brush of her hair and back against his hand when he pulled a chair out for her. She was a twenty-three-old Italian girl born in New York City, a brash talking *mujer joven* with a smile that lit up her entire face and dark eyes whose pull was inescapable.

As Vicente walked into the mountains with the weight of the Cuban Army in pursuit, he found himself smiling at the way she chewed her pinky when in thought, played with her hair when nervous, or whistled slightly when she spontaneously laughed. Sophia had lived most recently in Miami with her uncle, Samuel Franco, who had taken her in when her parents had perished in a car accident eight years earlier. Her uncle, a pit boss, had come to Cuba to work at the prestigious Montmartre Club at the corner of 23rd and P in Havana's Vedado district, just a few blocks from the Hotel Nacional where they currently resided.

Vicente was certain that Sophia had at no time ever kept company with a poor, semi-literate, dark-skinned man such as himself. Although, Vicente reflected, he'd done well for himself in the past year. He now wore a suit and tie everywhere, in stark contrast to his soiled delivery outfit. But more importantly, Fidel had insisted that he fill every spare moment with reading, lecturing that it was education that separated the classes in Cuba, and that with equal opportunity, this social stratification would disappear.

In Miami, Sophia had spent one year at the Catholic Barry College, run by Mother M. Gerald Barry, but had grated against the strict religious doctrine that suffocated her English and history classes. As a result, their discussions had come to include the Church, both of them having doubts as to the existence of a superior and loving being. It was here that she began to make the transition from the

European Spanish that she had spent four years of private school learning to Cuban Spanish.

As he trudged on, Vicente looked at his comrades plodding ahead and behind, chuckling silently as he imagined what they might think of her. She was the embodiment of what The Movement was against—niece of a wealthy casino operator from the United States catering to rich foreign tourists while much of Cuba suffered in poverty. This was why Vicente avoided being seen with her in public; both of them, in fact, avoided their own kind, she preferring places not frequented by *Yanquís*. It was almost as if they were having a clandestine affair, if a very chaste one. As it was, their intimacy was taboo, and neither one of them was ready for anything more than just such a platonic affair, although Vicente spent many sleepless nights imagining just such a tryst.

Up ahead, Fidel's mind was far from romance. Although his stomach rumbled, he'd been hungry before and paid it no mind. No, it was the fear that seemed to shadow the sun that he couldn't quite shake free of, the terror that the army would find them at any moment, the dread that he'd ruined not only his opportunity to strike a blow at Batista, but very well might have destroyed his life, and others, including that of his brother, Raúl.

Not far from here, in the town of Birán—much of which was owned by his father—Fidel had spent his early life, times he fondly remembered. How naïve he'd been, not yet aware that the inhabitants of the village were little more than slaves of his father, working long, brutal hours for a pittance, mistreated and abused. In his innocence, they'd been good days filled with playing games, swimming, hunting with slingshots, and fishing. Then, when he was older, to improve his education as well as to escape persecution of the local populace who knew he was a *bastardo*, his father had sent Fidel off to be educated at the Marist Brothers' La Salle school, followed by the Dolores School, both in Santiago, and later the Bélen Jesuit Preparatory School in Havana.

Although he'd attended the best institutions in the country, those schools had taught him a bitter lesson indeed. His classmates, often more impressed with heritage than money, looked down on him from their aristocratic perches, insulting him, "*Eres un campesino y un bastardo*," belittling his unwed mother and rural home, and it was on this battleground that he first learned to fight. It was true that at home chickens roosted around the house and that the family often ate standing up—a habit that Ángel carried with him from Spain—and that he was a *bastardo*. But neither the chickens nor the lack of legitimacy made him feel inferior.

He was more interested in athletics than academics and was a champion at baseball, Ping-Pong, basketball, and especially track. Dictators like Mussolini and Hitler fascinated him, and he spent much of his free time studying them in detail as he tried to understand what made them so charismatic and powerful. As a child he was known as "*El Loco* Fidel" for crazy stunts like making a bet that he could ride his bicycle into a brick wall without being injured—a stupidity he had three days in the hospital to reflect on.

Dawn brought the buzzing of airplanes searching the area along with the light of a new day. An Afro-Cuban peasant with legs withered by polio directed them to the house of a man who owned a radio. It was here at the home of Feliciano Heredia that they heard the dictator Batista address the nation, recounting the recent assault of the Moncada Barracks. He claimed that thirty-three rebels had been killed in the fighting, and among the names listed was Emilio Hernández, a young man who had turned back from the mountains because his shoes were hurting his feet.

"Emilio wasn't killed in the fightin'."

"As far as I can tell, there weren't any more than eight of us who fell in the fighting," Fidel responded. "They must be killing the prisoners."

"There will be no surrender!"

"No," Fidel replied. It was clear that capitulation was no longer an option. All that remained was flight. "We should redirect for the Sierra Maestra. It's much larger, and once there we can better establish the resistance movement."

"Batista lied," Vicente said in disbelief. He couldn't quite get over the radio broadcast they'd just heard. "We didn't torture soldiers or patients in the hospital. Abel would never have hacked up innocent civilians with a knife."

"And this wasn't a result of the Montreal Pact," Fidel added. "But with this speech Batista has married us to a lie and it won't be easy to separate us from that lie in the minds of the people." He resented being identified with other parties that opposed Batista. Just two months earlier, former president Carlos Prío had convened an opposition conference in Montreal whose attendees had solemnly vowed in writing to defy Batista's tyranny and overthrow him. Fidel hadn't even been invited, and it was this rejection that had cemented his decision to attack the Moncada Barracks sooner rather than later, a brash action that had been intended to prove that he was a man to be reckoned with.

* * *

"In nomine Patris, et Filii, et Spiritus Sancti. In the name of the Father, and of the Son, and of the Holy Spirit. Amen," Archbishop Pérez Serantes recited while crossing himself. He then got straight to the point with the members of the Joint Committee of Civic Institutions of Santiago known as *los Fuerzas Vivas.* "We must end these senseless killings. There must be a balm in Gilead."

Present for the meeting was Magistrate Subirats representing the administrative local judicial power: José Medina Puig, president of the Rotary Club and Venerable Master of the Libertad Masonic Lodge; Mariano Roca Gutiérrez, president of the Lions Club; Rector Felipe Salcines Morlote of the University of Oriente; the powerful businessman Teófilo Babun Selman; Enrique Canto Bory of Catholic Action in Oriente Province; and editor Carlos Dellundé of the Oriente newspaper.

The Archbishop looked at each man in turn before continuing in his precise and articulate pattern of speech. "Those dying are not some faceless criminals from disreputable families. It's our very own young men, *de familias honorables*, disillusioned by the illegitimacy of the current regime, shot on back roads, interrogated and killed in torture chambers. As the Apostle Paul enlightens us in Romans 14:19, 'Let us therefore follow after the things which make for peace, and things wherewith one may edify another'."

"I'm *emocionado*, quite thrilled actually, to hear that the Catholic Church is standing firm in opposition to this sickening misuse of power," José Medina Puig said. As president of the Rotary Club and Master of the Masonic Lodge, he was the only one whose authority might equal Serantes'.

"This we can agree on," Archbishop Serantes replied with a smile beginning to emerge at the corners of his mouth as he gently teased his friend. "But I'm certain that if the Pope were to see me conversing with a Freemason that he'd consider it a venial sin." The two men had a standing game of Canasta once a month, played with two other civic leaders behind closed doors to avoid the scandal. These two local *líderes* saw only positives from working together, even if the institutions they represented had diametrically opposed viewpoints on faith.

"They attacked the barracks!" Teófilo Babun Selman cut in. "They cut open patients in the hospital with knives. They are worse than criminals." Teófilo profited from the military presence in Santiago, supplying them with uniforms, weapons, and food supplies using his fleet of ships in the harbor and trucks on land. "In times of crisis extraordinary measures must be taken."

"I've been assured that the stories of carving men up are false. On the contrary," replied the archbishop, "most in the hospital speak very highly of the rebels. They say that they were very polite young men, and women—as I understand it there were two such members of the fairer sex involved. Perhaps the army isn't telling the whole truth. A righteous man hateth lying: but a wicked man is loathsome, and cometh to shame."

Serantes' ties to the Castro family were long, deep, and complicated, a history going back twenty years when he'd arranged for Fidel's father, Ángel, to obtain an annulment of his original marriage, and to wed his former maid and mother of three of his children, who'd then been baptized, and so legitimized, even if only in the eyes of the church.

"I won't argue with you," Serantes continued, "that the actions of the young Castro boys and the others were wrong, but this barbaric slaughter of prisoners is wrong as well. As the First Thessalonians teaches us in chapter five, verse fifteen, 'Make sure that nobody pays back wrong for wrong, but always strive to do what is good for each other and for everyone else'. We can't change the past, but we may still be able to affect the future. I believe the rebels that have escaped into the country will surrender once they know they won't be executed. Let the courts determine their fates."

Teófilo bowed his head in agreement. "You are right as always, Your Excellency."

"Let's say that we're able to convince the army to arrest, rather than butcher, the rebels that remain at large," Mariano Roca Gutiérrez of the Lion's Club tentatively interjected into the ensuing silence. "Would these boys get a fair trial?" All heads swiveled to Magistrate Subirats, the most influential member of the judiciary in the city.

"The law states that thirty years is the maximum sentence for insurrection against a legitimate government," Magistrate Subirats responded gravely. "The army wouldn't dare pressure us further than that. In other words, we can save their lives if properly arraigned, but I'd hesitate to suggest finding these boys anything but guilty would be acceptable. Chaviano is a sadistic murderer and wouldn't think twice before making a magistrate disappear."

Rector Felipe Salcines of the University of Oriente cleared his throat. "Public opinion resides with these young men. I don't think the army would want the bad publicity that'd go along with executing passionate youths, and certainly not the assassination of magistrates."

"Batista has his censors in every newspaper and radio station in the entire country carefully culling every word before it's shared with the populace." Carlos Dellundé of the Oriente newspaper shrugged his shoulders. "I doubt that any impropriety by the army would see the light of day."

"The Grand Master of the Masonic Lodge in Santiago, Luis Savigne, has been in contact with the Grand Master in Havana, who managed to obtain a personal audience with Batista." Medina had saved his hole card for just this moment, flexing the strength of the Masons at a table of the most important people in Santiago. "*Sus súplicas de piedad fueron escuchadas*, or it would seem the pleas for mercy were noted, because he personally heard Batista cursing

Colonel Chaviano over the telephone and demanding an end to the violence."

"*Maravilloso!*" Enrique Canto Bory of the Catholic Action in Oriente Province exclaimed. "Although, Chaviano would be more amenable to leniency with the prisoners if he were approached by Archbishop Serantes with this plea for indulgence," he added, preserving the importance of the Church in these proceedings.

"I will remind the colonel of the words of Matthew, 'for if you forgive other people when they sin against you, your heavenly Father will also forgive you'," Archbishop Serantes replied softly, his eyes searching the response of those at the table.

"We'll await the verdict." Magistrate Subirats settled into his chair. "Make sure he understands that we're all united on this matter." In this way, he cemented the strength of the courts by giving voice to the path to be followed.

In just over an hour the archbishop was back from his meeting with the commander of the Moncada Barracks. "Colonel Chaviano was very courteous and sends his regards to all of you." He swept his arm in a semi-circle that encompassed the group of the most preeminent men in Santiago. "He claims that the only rebels to have been killed are those who fought back."

Magistrate Subirats snorted, a surprising sound coming from one as venerable as him. "I've heard multiple reports of dead prisoners taken into the woods by truck, arranged with rifles as if they'd fallen in combat for photographs, and then brought back to be buried. *Que Dios tenga piedad de sus almas.*" He bowed his head in a silent prayer for mercy on their souls.

Archbishop Serantes nodded his head. "I am only telling you what was said to me. The Colonel agreed to respect those who submit for trial, and they will be treated with decency if they turn themselves in."

"Another lie," Magistrate Subirats said flatly. "He will continue to kill those that surrender and claim that they fought back."

"The only way to force the Colonel to keep his word is to publicize his guarantee of civility, otherwise it will have no effect," Dellundé interjected vehemently. "You must send a pastoral letter to the media outlets so that all can see that Chaviano has promised leniency. Even the censors wouldn't dare to delete orders from Batista and backed by Colonel Chaviano's word."

"Agreed." Magistrate Subirats struck his fist down on the desk. "This must be done immediately."

"Unfortunately my secretary is not here today, and I have no idea how to work that machine." Archbishop Serantes nodded to the typewriter on the desk at the far end of the room, trying to subdue the tension.

"You must dictate to me then." Medina moved to the chair in front of the typewriter. "Wasted time means more wasted lives. And where does your secretary keep the carbon for copies?"

When the document was finished, they each took a carbon for further copying and distribution to the various news outlets, the radio stations, and the cable office so it could be sent on to Havana. "There is one more thing," Archbishop Serantes spoke out just as they were about to leave upon their tasks. "Major Andrés Pérez-Chaumont was also part of the meeting with Chaviano, and he told us that his soldiers demand *venganza* for the cowardly attack. Major Chaumont hinted that the slightest incident could set them to killing every last rebel they encounter. It sounded almost like a threat."

"You must go search for them to protect them, Your Excellency," Canto said very plainly, spreading his hands, palms up, beseechingly. He was a businessman, as well as the founder and president of the Catholic Action in Oriente Province. "The people have taken to calling Major Chaumont '*Ojos Bonitos.*' Apparently he's developed a fondness for carving out the eyes of his prisoners. I'd venture a guess that this sort of man doesn't make idle threats."

The following day the article "Enough Blood" was printed and broadcast the length and breadth of the country. This public assurance professed by the army and supported by the civic leaders of Santiago led thirty-two rebels to turn themselves in to the mercy of the courts, but Fidel was not among them. A few days later, as mass was ending, Canto arrived at the church with urgent information that the last holdouts were ready to turn themselves in. Within minutes, the archbishop joined him in a Jeep along with a reporter from the Havana newspaper, *Diario de la Marina.*

"We must hurry," Canto implored. "It's Fidel and seven others. They're waiting in a ravine by the road just before the El Cilindro Farm, but on my way to get you I passed a patrol going in that direction."

A half hour later, as their Jeeps rounded a sharp curve just seven miles from Santiago, a man appeared on the side of the road and waved them down, anxiously peering left and right, apprehension rolling off him with the sweat. "There are eight men in my cabin," he gasped out, "waitin' to turn themselves in, but the army is here huntin' for 'em. I told 'em to come out just before the entrance to the farm." The farmer climbed into the Jeep, ducking his head as they drove. He didn't want to be seen and associated with those protecting the rebels from the brutal retaliation of the soldiers. "Hurry! If they're found in my *bohío*? I'm *jodido*." The man crossed himself. "Sorry Your Excellency."

"One of them is Fidel?" Archbishop Serantes fixed the peasant with his severest stare. "Fidel Castro?"

"That's what he said," the man replied, and then added, "just 'round this corner." Canto slowed the Jeep for the curve and then pulled up next to a barbed wire fence. There was nobody there.

Archbishop Serantes got out of the Jeep and began walking the road, scrutinizing the trees and foliage when suddenly a burst of machine-gun fire split the air. The farmer slipped through the fence and disappeared into the woods, and the newspaper reporter from Havana dove underneath the Jeep. Five dirty and ragged men emerged further up the road in a small clearing, all looking back over their shoulders to where the shooting had come from.

As they reached the fence a soldier suddenly burst from the woods several hundred yards behind them. "Halt!" he shouted, firing his gun into the air to emphasize his order.

Another soldier appeared, rifle at the ready, yelling down the road, "*Dejaros asesinos!* Stop or die!"

Archbishop Serantes ran across the ditch towards them waving his arms and startling a murder of crows that went fluttering into the sky. "Don't shoot. Stop! These men are under my protection."

"And who the hell are you?" the first soldier demanded.

"Archbishop Serantes."

"I don't give a *mierda*. These assassins are my prisoners."

"Colonel Chaviano has promised the safety of these men." Archbishop Serantes moved himself between the soldiers and the rebels, who'd now raised their arms in surrender and were crowding behind the man of God. "Be merciful, just as Your Father is merciful."

In the woods nearby, Fidel sat at the table inside a small shack made of palm fronds in his underwear and shirt, tense with fear at the sound of gunfire. He'd exchanged his torn pants for a borrowed pair that was too tight and hadn't yet managed to struggle into them. Vicente had badly twisted his ankle and turned himself in with ten others when the public assurance of safety had reached their ears in the countryside a few days earlier, and then five more men had just left the shack for the same purpose. That left Fidel and two others still hoping to journey to the Sierra Maestra and continue the insurrection from there.

"Will we bring all the guns or just what we need?" Oscar Alcalde asked, nodding his head at the pile of rifles discarded by those who'd just left.

"They will only slow us down," Fidel replied wearily, his plans having disintegrated into nothing. "We'll have to move quickly and silently. The *maldita* soldiers are everywhere."

He paused, reflecting on the damn soldiers, when more gunshots rang out, coming from the direction of the road. Before he could stand, the door burst inward, striking Oscar in the back and toppling him from his chair. "Come out you *bastardos*! Show yourselves or we'll cut you down," a man yelled from outside the door. To emphasize his point, a machine gun rattled, and both Fidel and Felipe joined Oscar on the ground. "Surrender, you motherless dogs. Come out now or so help me God we'll shoot this hut so full of holes there won't be anythin' left ta' burn."

Fidel stared at his hand, which was trembling uncontrollably, and a fresh film of sweat had sprung up on his skin, reeking of fear. "We must yield or become martyrs," he said. He picked up the nickel-plated pistol from the table and threw it out the door. "We're coming out. Don't shoot!" He stooped slightly to ease out the door, his hands raised above his head. Oscar followed him cautiously, while Felipe wisely hid himself in the shadows.

A sixteen-man patrol, weapons leveled and at the ready, stood in a semi-circle facing the cabin. A short, wiry, black soldier jostled his way up to Fidel. "You are Castro." His face was twisted and his lips could barely mouth the words. "*Dicen que es un gigante de un hombre*, and while you are no giant, you're certainly tall enough."

"My name is Francisco González Calderin," Fidel said, his voice high with stress. "The one you speak of was with us several days ago but has long since left."

The soldier levered a bullet into the breech of his Springfield rifle. "My *hermano* is dyin' in Santiago because of your attack. Don't lie to me. I'll have my vengeance." He brought the weapon to bear on Fidel and started to squeeze the trigger, but an officer knocked his arm down.

"Private Seguí, we'll not kill anybody here today." The private looked at the tall, black lieutenant who'd spoken. He made another half-hearted attempt to bring his rifle to bear, and the officer again pushed the barrel downward.

"But Lieutenant Sarría, these pigs murdered our friends and family," Seguí insisted vehemently. "That one at least must die. Whether or not he's Castro, I don't like the look of him. He's an *asesino*."

"You are the assassins," Fidel countered. "It's the soldiers who are killing unarmed prisoners."

"I'll kill one more right now!"

"You do not kill ideas," Lieutenant Sarría stated, such a strange remark that both men looked at him, breaking the tension. "So follow orders or I'll have you punished."

Felipe was dragged from the cabin, and the soldiers lashed the rebels' wrists tightly in front of them. Tied in such a fashion, sitting in his underwear, hands quivering, Fidel felt an abject humiliation. "How'd you know where to find us?" he demanded of the lieutenant.

"Where are the others?" the lieutenant retorted, suggesting that not only had he been tipped off as to their whereabouts, he also knew there were supposed to be more of them.

Fidel bowed his head. "If you haven't yet shot them, they're on their way to turn themselves in to Archbishop Serantes."

"Find this one's pants," Lieutenant Sarría ordered. "And put them on him. We must get back to the truck."

On the way, Fidel asked to speak alone with the lieutenant, who obliged and lagged behind, leading his captive by the rope that bound him. "I'm the one you seek," Fidel admitted, trusting his life to the benevolence of this middle-aged, low-level officer.

"Of course you are."

"You must tell no one or I will be shot," Fidel urged. "You must keep me safe."

Lieutenant Sarría stared passively at him, pausing in the trail. "You do not kill ideas," he murmured again, before giving a tug on the rope and continuing on, moving faster to catch up.

At the farmhouse, Felipe and Oscar were put in the back of the army truck with the soldiers while Fidel was ordered to sit in front between the driver and Lieutenant Sarría. They'd gone less than half a mile before happening upon the archbishop's Jeep. The man of God now stood between five quivering rebels and two soldiers who were sporadically shooting their weapons into the air while hurling curses at the prisoners nonstop.

"Put them in the back of the truck," Lieutenant Sarría ordered.

"These men are under my protection," Archbishop Serantes insisted.

"They'll be safe enough with me," Sarría said. "But you may follow to make certain nothing happens to them."

They'd just reached the city limits of Santiago and were approaching the Árbol de Paz, the tree of peace memorial to the Spanish-American Armistice, when another Jeep pulled across the road blocking their way. Colonel Chaviano got out of the passenger seat and approached the truck. "Is that ragged man really Castro?" he asked, peering in the passenger window.

Sarría let a few seconds tick by before giving a subtle nod to the affirmative.

"Good work, Lieutenant. I see a promotion in your future. Follow me to Moncada."

"These men are my prisoners and I'm bringing them to the city jail," Sarría answered.

"Lieutenant." Colonel Chaviano rolled the word out in several slow syllables. "I'm ordering you to follow me to the Moncada Barracks."

"I'm sorry, sir. But these are my prisoners, and I don't think they'll be safe there." Sarría sat defiantly in the cab of the truck in the increasing heat of the summer morning. Just a week ago the man next to him had led an insurrection, killing numerous soldiers, and raising the ire of those that survived. He knew that by thwarting the colonel he was almost certainly throwing his career away, but he also understood that one must do as one's conscience dictates.

"I'll have you arrested and thrown in the back of the truck if you don't obey me immediately," Chaviano said, his thin lips trembling.

"What is the hold up?" Archbishop Serantes had disembarked from his Jeep and now approached the two men. "Colonel Chaviano, it is good to see you."

"I'm afraid that to bring these men to Moncada would be a death sentence, Your Excellency," Sarría spoke stiffly without even looking at the man of God. "I'd like to bring them to the *vivac* where they'll be safer, but Colonel Chaviano disagrees."

"They must of course be afforded every chance to be brought to trial for their actions. We'll continue to the city jail, then, and let the police be responsible for them instead of the soldiers." Archbishop Serantes fixed the man with a level stare. "God is our refuge and strength, an ever-present help in trouble."

Colonel Chaviano stood in the sun, simmering with rage. He'd given the archbishop his assurance of the rebel's safety, not really believing he'd have to keep this promise—and certainly not to let someone else take credit for this prize captive, Fidel Castro. At the same time, Chaviano understood that to go against the archbishop in Santiago would make it very difficult for him to continue to live any kind of pleasant existence in Oriente Province. "Of course." He finally managed to squeeze the two words out between pressed lips.

* * *

"Honorable Judges, never has a lawyer had to practice his profession under such difficult conditions; never has such a number of overwhelming irregularities been committed against an accused man. In this case, counsel and defendant are one. As attorney, he hasn't even been able to examine the indictment. As accused, for the past seventy-six days he's been locked away in solitary confinement, held totally and absolutely incommunicado, in violation of every human and legal right."

Fidel was dressed in his favorite blue-striped suit and freshly-pressed red necktie for the trial, sophisticated attire that was now covered by the borrowed robe he wore as his own defense counsel. He paced back and forth in front of the judges crowded into the small nurses' room. It was the very same hospital that Abel Santamaría and other members of the *Movimiento 26th de Julio*, the moniker now ascribed to the *Fidelistas* due to the date of their insurrection, had taken control of a few months earlier during the failed Moncada Barracks attack. The authorities had decided that Fidel would be tried separately from the other Moncada rebels to contain, if not silence, his vitriolic accusations against the government. He'd been held separately in isolation while the trial of the other rebels progressed. Just three days earlier, twenty-nine rebels had been found guilty and transferred to the prison on the Isle of Pines.

"As this trial has continued, the roles have reversed: the accusers now accused, and of horrendous, venial crimes of torture, murder, even rape." Fidel paused, and made eye contact with each of the three magistrates who were on his left, next to the prosecution. The proceedings unfolded in a single, cramped room typically used as a classroom for the nurses. The doors had been thrown open to allow a faint breeze to waft in, a small respite from the stifling heat. Two military police stood guard to each side of the doors and six reporters filled chairs just in front of the magistrates.

"It was not the revolutionaries who were judged there; judged once and forever was a man named Batista—*monstruum horrendum!*—And it matters little that these valiant and worthy young men have been condemned, if tomorrow the people will condemn the dictator and his henchmen!" Fidel warmed to the task, pointing at the three magistrates with whom his fate rested, angry, not with them, but at the egregious offenses of the government, men honoring the legacy of democracy punished randomly.

Fidel pointed out the door to the left in the direction of the fortress. "Moncada Barracks was turned into a workshop of torture and death. Some shameful individuals turned their uniforms into butcher's aprons. The walls are splattered with blood. The bullets imbedded in the walls are encrusted with singed bits of skin, brains and human hair, the grisly reminders of rifle shots fired full in the face. The grass around the barracks is dark and sticky with human blood. And what were their orders? General Martín Díaz Tamayo arrived from Havana and brought specific instructions from a meeting he had attended with Batista, along with the head of the Army, the head of the Military Intelligence, and others. He said: 'It is humiliating and dishonorable for the Army to have lost three times as many men in combat as the insurgents did. Ten prisoners must be killed for each dead soldier.' This was the order!"

Fidel paused, then allowed that the magistrates had no choice but to find him guilty, as Batista would not permit any other outcome, before summing up his defense with a roar. "I know that imprisonment will be harder for me than it has ever been for anyone, filled with cowardly threats and hideous cruelty. But I do not fear prison, as I do not fear the fury of the miserable tyrant who took the lives of seventy of my comrades. Condemn me. It does not matter. History will absolve me."

PART TWO

The Revolution Continues with a Splutter

Arthur Gardner
American Ambassador to Cuba
Habana, Cuba

November 7, 1953

John Foster Dulles
Secretary of State
United States of America

Dear Mr. Secretary,

I have now presented my new credentials as Ambassador to Cuba to President Batista and have formally begun my duties. The ceremony was heartwarming. President Batista has sworn to cooperate with the United States in exterminating the insidious communist threat that menaces our well-being. Not only is he actively distancing himself from the Communist Party within Cuba, he has promised his support in our endeavors to expel this rot from Guatemala.

Cuba has really started to boom. This is an obvious reaction to the steady governing hand of President Batista, and the close alliance with the United States. The people here really appreciate this relationship, due largely, I believe, because the US helped liberate them in 1898. For the first time in their history, Cubans have a sense of security. I think that it would behoove our interests to continue the Sugar Act, giving them preferential treatment in keeping this solid relationship positive.

The final trials of those misguided youth who attacked the Moncada Barracks ended on October 16th with a guilty verdict for Fidel Castro. He was sentenced to fifteen years for his role in the insurrection, a very just and fair verdict, and one that speaks to the generous nature of President Batista. I have endorsed the order to supply the Cuban army with the mortars, hand grenades, rocket launchers, and anti-tank guns to help fight the spread of Communism.

President Batista has called for democratic elections on November 1, 1954. Although he does not have the popular support to win at this time, I recommend we do what we can to get this strong ally duly elected.

Sincerely,
Arthur Gardner

Cuba

Havana

Santa Clara

Trocha

Camaguey

Yara

Sierra Maestra

Bayamo

Santiago

4

May 15th, 1955,
Isle of Pines, Cuba

It was high noon on May 15th of 1955 and cheers were ringing out at the entrance to the Presidio Modelo penitentiary on the Isle of Pines, just seventy miles south of Havana and thirty-five miles to the mainland. "Hip, hip, hooray!" "Long Live Cuba!" "Castro! Castro! Castro!"

Thirty-six different groups in Cuba, as well as the United States government, had brought pressure to bear on Batista to free the political prisoners. With one stroke of his pen, thinking that his position was so secure as to be beyond threat, Batista had set Fidel and his followers free.

Vicente walked down the steps of the prison where he'd spent the last eighteen months a changed man. He'd come to know the deeper meaning of the *Movimiento 26th de Julio* and had a far greater appreciation for the concepts that Fidel espoused. His literacy had increased dramatically as well, giving him an opportunity to read, reflect, and write on a much higher plane.

On this day, Vicente wore the formal white guayabera shirt that'd arrived in the mail from Sophia. Pinned to it was a brief note: "As you will most likely be photographed quite a bit, you might as well look dashing." The four pockets on the front were carefully buttoned, and its sharp-vertical pleats made him look taller.

To the cheering throngs and gathered journalists, Fidel raised a fist in triumph, a salute to the world, and the rest of them waved their hands. Vicente doffed his Panama hat, also a gift from Sophia, and held it aloft victoriously as the exuberance washed over the small band of former political prisoners.

"Juan, you'd think that we were movie stars or baseball players returning from winning the *Yanqui* World Series," Vicente said in a hushed voice, awed by the elation in the air. He fingered the tip of his mustache, carefully groomed like Fidel's—actually he'd been thinking of *el bigote* of Benny Moré, the crooner who Sophia thought so handsome she might melt.

Juan Almeida shook his head, no less stupefied than Vicente. "To breathe the air as a free man is enough to make me choke, but to be a hero? This is more than enough for me. I need no more. If I die tomorrow, I die happy. This moment in time erases the failure of Moncada, the hiding in the mountains, the trial, and the imprisonment. We've a purpose, *amigo*."

"Some go to Santiago in July for *Carnaval*," Vicente said. "But it appears we went to spark a revolution of the people."

Later that night, led by Fidel, the recently released prisoners boarded the steamer *El Pinero* for the trip back to the mainland. Fidel gathered the men together in the steamer's spacious central cabin and began to speak, slowly and softly, but then with more and more power and passion, as if he were a preacher. "The people of Cuba must realize that we fight for our freedom even at the price of our existence. Our freedom shall not be feast or rest, but battle and duty for a nation without despotism or misery. There is a new faith, a new awakening in the national conscience. To try to drown it will provoke an unprecedented catastrophe. Despots vanish, people remain."

Fidel paced the room, flinging his arms energetically as he invoked the spirits of previous rebels who'd martyred themselves for the cause. "First there was Hatüey, that valiant Taino chief who refused to surrender to the Spanish in the 1500s and burned for his belief in *libertad*, and then Black José Aponte who sought to free Cuban slaves in 1812 and was hung and decapitated for his ideals. And that brave guerilla officer, Antonio Maceo, who just seventy-seven years ago refused to accept the Treaty of Zanjón, because it neither realized freedom of the slaves nor achieved independence for Cuba, principles that were beyond negotiation. And of course, there is our beloved José Marti, who never compromised the basic principal of self-rule, and perished charging when the order was to retreat. Like those heroes before us, we, the *Movimiento 26th de Julio*, will never accept anything less than that Batista must be removed from office and the people of Cuba should rise to power."

Castro paused, his brow furrowed. "You are my most trusted brothers and sisters." Here he nodded to Melba and Haydée. "You who've been with me from the start, who fired those very first shots at my side, who spent time in prison with me, I tell you the true revolution begins now. So, a small pause to celebrate overcoming this first obstacle, and then *trabajar*, to work, *mi camarados*!"

As the sun crept over the horizon, they steamed into the port city of Batabanó. Even this early in the morning there was a crowd of hundreds cheering as sailors tied up, but Vicente had eyes only for Sophia Franco. She stood to the side, slightly aloof from the crowd; her loosely curled black-hair partly covered by a wide-brimmed floppy hat with peach-colored ribbons fluffed around the crown. Her sheer black dress fit her body perfectly, reaching just below the knees, thin shoulder straps light against the dark of her cocoa-butter skin. As her eyes scanned the debarking men, she waved a small Cuban flag, the single star in a triangle with the blue and white stripes. The hurrahs and clapping, the hooting and hollering, all went silent until he could almost hear her whisper his name as she smiled at him, her dress rustling as she shifted her hips, and the flag slapping the air with a rhythmic cadence like the blood coursing through his veins. He walked to her and managed a small bow, sweeping his Panama hat from his head.

"Hello, Vicente."

"Hello, Sophia." He shifted his feet nervously. "You look nice."

"It's good to see you."

"What're you doing here?" Vicente stared somewhere over her right shoulder. "I mean—I'm glad you came, but why?"

"Do you need a ride?"

Vicente hesitated, deliberating upon his answer. "There's a train going to Havana, but the smoke and soot of those contraptions always makes me feel sick."

"I've a car."

"Let's go, then." He stole a glance over his shoulder as he allowed her to guide him towards the automobile. Fidel and the rest of the released prisoners were parading towards the train depot surrounded by admirers, oblivious to the two of them sidling away together.

"I've a confession," Sophia blurted as Vicente steered the vehicle onto the road to Havana. "While you were in prison I took a job as a dancer," she said all in a rush.

"What kind of dancer?" he asked, perplexed, never having known this about her.

"The kind that doesn't wear very much for clothes," she replied in a faint but defiant voice.

They rode in a thick silence for a bit before Vicente was able to banish the image of a mostly nude Sophia performing for leering men enough to ask the question burning in his mind. "Why?"

"Power," she replied. "Independence."

"I don't understand."

"We're not so different in what we want, you and me. It took me a long time to understand why you'd raise up a rifle and become a killer of men."

"You dancing naked for men is the same as me fighting for freedom against a corrupt government?" he asked incredulously.

"Society ignores you because you're nothing more than a poor mulatto." Sophia picked her words carefully. "You want to be judged not by the color of your skin or your bank account, but who you are as a man."

Vicente was set to argue, but instead, nodded his head. "This is true. But I still don't get…"

"You think women have it easier?"

"What do you mean? Women have everything."

"Everything?" Sophia glared at him. "I depend on my uncle for an allowance until he's able to marry me off, and then I will serve the whims of my new husband. I'm not supposed to work, vote, or do anything but look pretty and be pleasing. You call that everything?"

"And taking your clothes off for money helps how?"

"It gives me power over men and independence from men at the same time."

"You mean to say you're exploited by men." Vicente veered around a slow-moving automobile in front of them.

"Exploited?" Sophia asked heatedly. "I ask you, who is more exploited, the sugar cane worker or the dancer? He works for half the year for a dollar a day doing fourteen hours of back-breaking work while I make five times that dancing on a stage."

Vicente spent the next ten minutes digesting this thought, before grudgingly grunting, "Perhaps you have a point." They spent the rest of the drive into Havana, slightly more than an hour, chatting about anything but politics, dancing, or the nature of their relationship.

As they approached the edge of the city, Sophia asked, "Where will you be staying?"

"I don't know."

Sophia pursed her lips, a gentle blush inching up her cheeks. "I've a friend. A dancer. She's gone to Matanzas for the week to visit her family and left me the key to her apartment."

"And your uncle?"

"I told him that I'm watching a friend's apartment while she's away." Sophia brushed away a curl that'd escaped from behind her ear. "Although I'm a bit nervous about it, as it's a slightly rougher neighborhood than I'm used to."

Vicente nodded as if deep in contemplation before flashing a bright white smile. "Perhaps I could help out. After all, I am a hardened revolutionary."

As he bathed away prison and travel, Sophia cooked him some beans and rice with a bit of ham, which he devoured upon emerging from the tub refreshed, even if exhausted. Then, she led him to the bed where he now found himself. It was a solid four-poster with cotton shrouding that Sophia pulled around to block out the light, but not so much as to prevent the breeze from the fan. It smelled nice, a feminine smell, one that'd been conspicuously absent from his life, even though the scent wasn't Sophia's, who hadn't joined him, but had merely tucked him in. Perhaps her fingers had brushed his cheek as he fell into a dark, dreamless sleep and found himself waking in the mid-afternoon disoriented and aroused, a situation that necessitated time to relax, before he ventured onto the balcony to find Sophia reading *The Old Man and the Sea*.

"It's about an old man in Cuba who has gone eighty-four days without catching a fish. Can you imagine? Going out every day and failing? But this day is better, and at noontime he hooks a fish that he's sure is a marlin."

"I know this man. When I was a boy I used to go out on a fishing boat that belonged to my uncle. My job was mostly swabbing the deck, baiting hooks, and cleaning the fish. One day we put into port in Cojimar so that my uncle could deliver a gift of *cigarros* to his *amigo*." Vicente was standing at the railing overlooking Zulueta Street, absently watching people hurrying about their business, while others gathered in knots talking.

"How old were you?"

"Ten."

Sophia thought about the cocoon she'd lived within when she was ten, but remained silent so that he might continue.

"His *amigos* name was Gregorio, a name that sticks with me because my uncle yelled it so gleefully when he saw him. He was a small, thin man, maybe fifty years old? As we were leaving, a fat," here Vicente paused, shook his head, and corrected himself, "a robust American came down to the boat with a fishing rod, his hair slicked back on his head, with a bushy mustache hiding his upper lip. Gregorio introduced my uncle to him as Mr. Hemingway, and my uncle couldn't stop shaking his hand."

"You must've been quite impressed yourself," Sophia said.

Vicente chuckled, a low rumble of embarrassment. "I'd no idea who he was until about six months ago when Fidel gave me a book called *For Whom the Bell Tolls*. He told me that the author was a Cuban at heart and one of the greatest writers of our time. When I saw the name Ernest Hemingway, that day in Cojimar came rushing back to me."

"You worked on a fishing boat when you were ten?" Sophia was constantly surprised at their different upbringings. When she was that age, she was attending private school, learning to ride horses, and going to birthday parties.

Vicente turned and sat down in the iron chair next to Sophia, a small narrow table between them. "I began when I was eight, I believe, working when my grandmother wasn't teaching me to read, write, and do some numbers."

"And you said your grandmother raised you? Was it just the two of you?"

"No. I lived in a house with uncles, aunts, and many cousins."

"It sounds like an Italian family." Sophia laughed. "I was an only child but have more cousins than I can count. It was almost a relief when my parents moved to Miami for my father's work. It was nice to have peace and quiet at home instead of constant chaos."

"Being crammed in with thirty-some others at the Presidio Modelo for the last eighteen months reminded me a lot of my childhood."

"You must miss them all horribly. Did any of them visit you?"

"One moment, Sophia. Is there coffee here? I'd be happy to make it." Vicente stood and entered the apartment, rubbing his left eye with his fist. Sophia followed him into the single room, with a kitchen in one corner, the bed in another, and a table tucked against the back wall, between two doors, one leading to the stairs down and out, and the other leading to an open terrace with a few pieces of wicker furniture.

"Here's some Maxwell House instant coffee." Sophia pulled the can from a cupboard. "I'll make it if you tell me why you avoided my question."

"Don't bother. Water is fine. Maybe even stronger than that *mierda*." Vicente mentally cursed for his expletive. "Sorry for my language."

Sophia laughed and put it back. "Tell me about your family," she persisted.

"None of them visited me," Vicente replied. "I was hated from the day I walked into their house with the teetering steps of a toddler.

I believe it had to do with my mother and father getting married, but I was never told. The only person who was nice to me was my grandmother. When she died, I kissed her cheek goodbye, and walked out the door with nothing but the rags on my back." He didn't add that the reason his family had disliked his mother so much was because she'd met his father dancing in a club much like Sophia had been doing.

"And you haven't talked to your family since?" Sophia pictured three-year-old Vicente entering a home where he was loathed, gradually coming to that realization over the years, and never understanding why.

Vicente absently opened and shut several cupboards with his back to Sophia, delaying his answer, which was muffled when it finally came. "No."

"I haven't talked to any of my family since my parents' funeral." Sophia's mind went back to the blur of powerful emotions that was the car crash, the funeral, and the custody fight that embittered the family, as they blamed her uncle for the move to Miami. Yet her parents' will had been clear, and she'd become the ward of Samuel Franco, the black sheep of the family. "My uncle treats me fine, but he never seems to look at me." They moved to the veranda and sat in wicker chairs facing each other.

"I don't believe anybody ever looked at me before the day I met Fidel. He has a way of listening to my actual words without judgment. I never had that in my life. And then you," Vicente said softly. "The first day we spoke I was petrified of what would come out of my mouth. I could tell that you were interested in me, who I was, what my thoughts were, and that was something special and terrifying all at the same time."

"You know you don't have to act with me Vicente. You don't have to say anything and you don't have to do anything. Not a thing. Oh, maybe just whistle. You know how to whistle, don't you, Vicente? You just have to put your lips together and…blow."

"You might listen to me, but I don't know what the…I don't know what you're saying half the time."

Sophia laughed in delight, a tiny whistle escaping through her parted lips. "Sorry. I just remembered that line from Lauren Bacall in a movie based on an Ernest Hemingway novel. It seemed to fit the conversation. You do know how to whistle, don't you?"

Vicente gave a low, piercing whistle before continuing, "But I do like that I don't have to act with you."

Sophia nodded. "I go around each day as the niece of Samuel Franco, and men hold doors for me and compliment my appearance. But if any conversation gets past the day's weather or what I'm wearing, their eyes glaze over. I thought that by dancing, people would actually see me, the real me, but I was wrong. I wasn't a person, but the reminder of a lost love, or an object to be used for pleasure and discarded like a once-read book. That's why I quit it after only three months."

Vicente breathed a sigh of relief. "I can't believe anybody would ever place anything but a pedestal underneath your feet."

"They surely appreciated my looks," Sophia admitted. "But what I wanted recognized was…me, and that was not on display."

"At least people notice your body." Vicente mentally kicked himself. "I mean, they appreciate your beauty," he stammered. "To be a mulatto in Cuba, uneducated, poor, with bits of Indian thrown in? I was like a stray mutt, not paid much attention to—until I became annoying."

"I thought that black people were treated terribly in New York," Sophia said with care. "And then I moved to Miami, and it was so much worse. My uncle would use the most ugly words when he spoke about black people, and if one were to speak to me? I'd met a very nice man who worked in the casino as a dealer. He'd the nerve to ask me to get a cup of coffee, having no idea who I was. When my uncle found out, he had him beaten and fired. I went to the man's home to offer solace and he wouldn't let me in the door. He asked why I wanted him dead. It was only then that I realized how naïve I'd been, that my behavior might cost a man his life just because the color of our skin was different." Sophia failed to mention that she'd kissed the man, full on the mouth, and their tongues had touched.

"And so that is why we can't be seen together by anybody we know. Word of us together would piss your uncle off." Vicente shook his head as if to erase his words, "I mean put your uncle on a warpath."

"I don't understand why he separates himself from others in this way." Sophia looked wide-eyed at Vicente, hoping for an answer to a question she'd struggled with for the past few years.

"Karl Marx stated that social reforms are never carried out by the weakness of the strong, but rather, by the strength of the weak," Vicente recited. "I suppose it just means he's scared."

It was dusk as they emerged onto Zulueta Street in search of food. The fruit vendors were packing up for the day, but there were plenty of old women rolling cigars at card tables, offering the finished products for sale at a steadily lower price as the daylight dwindled. Just down a ways the Zombie Club's neon sign blinked on and off, its marquee blaring that Silvano "Choricera" Shueg would be playing timbales later that night.

"Do you mambo?" Sophia inquired, her eyebrow raised hopefully, and yet skeptically at the same time. She'd worn a straw hat pulled down low on her head, a partial disguise, but still felt very conspicuous after her conversation with Vicente.

"Of course I mambo." Vicente laughed at her. "I'm Cuban, after all. But first we must eat. Should we go to Sloppy Joe's?" More of a bar than a restaurant, it still had excellent sandwiches. "It's just around the corner."

"How do you know about Sloppy Joe's?" she asked. "Anybody from New York new in town, that's where they always want to go."

"Back when I was driving, I used to make deliveries to José, the owner, and he'd always give me a sandwich when I showed up. So, maybe a tourist place—but with great grub!" In just a few steps, they were there, and Sophia entered, with Vicente following.

Although it was packed, as always, they managed to find two seats at the sixty-foot gleaming mahogany bar, crowding onto the stools wedged between boisterous Americans, some enjoying the seven-year-old house rum, others sipping one of the eighty other cocktails offered with ingredients imported from all over the world. "Why is it called Sloppy Joe's? Is the man unkempt?"

Vicente smiled, thinking of making deliveries five years back. "Not personally, he's not, but he tends to leave his business rather, shall we say, a complete mess." He shrugged his shoulders. "So people called it Sloppy Joe's, and José embraced the name and made a sign proudly proclaiming it."

Vicente was celebrating liberation from prison, so when the barkeep came over he ordered the signature drink, the Sloppy Joe, for Sophia and himself—cognac, pineapple juice, port wine, curacao, and grenadine shaken well and poured over crushed ice.

The drinks were delivered to them in two tall Collins glasses with straws. Sophia took a small sip, approving the taste with a murmur and a smile. "You're spot on with this drink, Mr. Bolívar. So, do tell me, shall you be ordering dinner for me as well?" There was a bit of a bite to the question, suggesting that she wasn't happy that he'd ordered the drinks without consulting her.

"There are really only two choices, as far as I'm concerned," Vicente responded without hesitation. "Either a ham and cheese on rye or *ropa vieja* on a bun."

"*Ropa vieja*? What does 'old clothes' have to do with a sandwich?"

Vicente chuckled. "Its a loose meat sandwich with peppers and onions. Although it looks like *mierda*, oh, I'm sorry, I mean to say very similar to a pile of colorful rags, but it tastes great."

"I think that I'll have the ham and cheese on rye, and you'll get the old clothes, and then I'll sample yours."

They ate, drank cautiously, and spoke of trivial matters. A little before nine they paid and went back to the Zombie Club to hear Choricera play the timbales. As the curtain rose, a large black man wearing a short-sleeve button down white shirt with a red handkerchief around his neck appeared onstage, and, with a howl of rage, begin beating the drums. Then he began to run around the stage, tapping beer bottles filled to different levels, each creating a different sound. This was not all—he thumped pans, boxes, the wall, and even the stage floor.

All the while, he sang in a full-throated husky voice and juggled different props between, during, and after songs such as "Fruits from Caney," "Gravedigger," and "Don't Cry for Her." Vicente began to explain what these songs meant to Cubans, but it was impossible to hear, and Sophia pulled him to his feet to dance with the rest of the crowd, spinning and trying to keep pace with the furious beat set by the man known as the "wheeler and dealer." They started with the mamba, moved to the rhumba, and finished with a conga line along with the rest of the patrons.

Several hours later they emerged from this alfresco venue, leaving the crazy scene in the garden behind them to return to Havana. The Zombie Club, like so many places in Cuba, was mostly outdoors in an enclosed area surrounded by buildings on three sides.

"That was fabulous." Sophia bounced down the sidewalk, the music still pulsing through her body. "I can't believe I haven't heard of him."

"He doesn't get outside of Marianao very much." Vicente had seen the man play twice before. "Should we go to Floridita for a nightcap?"

They slid into a table, the bar a little quiet at midnight, most of the serious partiers having moved on to cabaret shows or brothels. There was a raucous group in the far corner of the bar from them, and one of the men caused Vicente to lean across and squeeze Sophia's arm. He nodded towards the clamorous cluster, "I believe that is Ernest Hemingway. He doesn't look much like the man I saw some ten years ago, but I recognize him from the back of the book you're reading."

Sophia stole a peek, and sure enough saw a grayer version of the author of *The Old Man and the Sea*. "I think you're right. You'd never guess he's a famous author. He seems to be your normal drunken American." Hemingway was telling a loud story about a woman he'd met in Key West.

"Fidel tells me that his gift is that he's just a real person who writes about what he knows. In the book I read, there's a man named Robert Jordan who leaps off the page like he's sitting next to you. As a matter of fact, this character reminded me of my grandmother's stories about my ancestor, Calixto Bolivar, who fought during the Ten Years' War for Cuban Independence."

"The Ten Years' War was from '68 to '78?" Sophia turned her eyes back from Hemingway to the man she was with.

Vicente raised his eyebrows in surprise. "Exactly. How'd you know that?"

"I've been reading up on my Cuban history. I figure if I'm going to date a revolutionary, I should know more about what makes him tick."

She gave him a coy smile, but the waiter interrupted the moment by bringing them two daiquiris in enormous glasses.

Dating? Vicente had been thrown into turmoil by this solitary word. It was after all, what he hoped for more than anything else, but his shyness prevented him from asking for clarification. "My great-grandfather, Calixto, rode with the *mambises* of Antonio Maceo."

"*Mambises?*" Sophia asked, chewing on her pinkie.

"The mixed race rebels who fought for Cuban Independence," Vicente replied, not without a little pride. He went on to give a glowing account of his ancestor who'd ridden next to Maceo in their failed quest for Cuban independence from Spanish Colonialism.

"When did Cuba finally become an independent country?" she asked when he was finished with the sad tale of defeat and death.

"Let me tell you on the way home," he replied, finishing his drink. As they emerged from the swinging door onto Zulueta Street, Sophia mistakenly bumped into three sailors jostling to enter.

"What d'we have here, Billy?" the closest American seaman slurred.

"It looks like some wop broad picked up a darkie for some bedroom sport," the man who must've been Billy replied.

"She ain't bad lookin' for a guinea," chimed in the third man, his white uniform and hat offset by his red cheeks. "Maybe she wants a real man instead of a houseboy?"

He'd barely gotten the last bit out before Sophia hand slapped him hard across the face. The man staggered and was setting to return the blow when Vicente slugged him in the ear, knocking him to the ground. With one motion Vicente shoved the other two men through the swinging door and grabbed Sophia's hand.

They ran down Obispo Street, so busy during the day, but now desolate, with the sailors giving chase. It'd been easy enough to duck around several corners on the narrow cobblestoned streets of Old Havana, and once out of sight, Vicente pulled Sophia into a dark courtyard. Hidden in the shadows, they watched the seamen thunder by, Sophia giggling as Vicente pressed a hand to her mouth.

They were standing clutching each other, when the emotion of conflict, flight, and safety turned to desire. Sophia suddenly stopped her laughter and pressed into his body, his arms enveloping her as they tried to inhabit one being. She turned her face up, lips poised and shimmering with the faint light of the moon, and Vicente leaned in, his mouth devouring hers.

All time seemed to stop, and then Sophia pulled back, her hands on his chest, her breathing ragged. "We can't."

Vicente knew that neither one of them was prepared for the fallout their relationship would create, but it wasn't until they were almost back to the apartment before his senses were able to recognize this. *Our time will come*, he promised himself, *of that I am sure.*

5

December 2nd, 1956, the Caribbean Sea off the coast of Cuba

Vicente stood at the bow of the sixty-foot wooden yacht named the *Granma* searching for a hint of land. It was the early morning hours of December 2nd, 1956, and he and eighty-one other men had been at sea for the past seven days in an attempt to invade Cuba from Mexico. The journey hadn't gone as planned; the boat built to take twenty-five people at the most was vastly overladen, causing it to travel significantly more slowly than originally thought. As a result, they'd missed the uprising that the Santiago underground had concocted to coincide with their homecoming, and now the Batista forces knew their arrival was imminent.

There'd been no food or water for the past two days. When the sea had become rough, almost all the men vomited, and as Universo Sánchez commented, *mierda sus pantalones*, they were unable to prevent themselves from shitting in their pants. They'd rinsed their soiled clothes in the salt water and put them back on, only changing into their olive green uniforms several hours before their approach to the cove that was their intended landing. Getting off this overcrowded and leaking pleasure yacht would be a relief to all of them, even if they beached it in the middle of the entire Batista army.

Vicente's ruminations drifted back to the last time he'd been in Cuba, some fourteen months ago, and of course, Sophia. Their relationship had flourished, even though it was entirely platonic. Neither of them had had anybody in their lives they could share their deepest thoughts, their personal fears and dreams with—until now. This emotional merging of their souls was tempered by an estrangement they couldn't bypass; perhaps what kept them from becoming lovers. She was, after all, the embodiment of Cuba's problems, the white niece of an American gangster working in the casino owned solely by foreign interests. How could he fully commit to her and still be faithful to Cuba? And how could she love him knowing that her family and friends would never accept him? Or, worse yet, that he might be killed by the police?

This fear had come close to being realized a few months after being released from prison. Vicente was returning from a clandestine meeting when abruptly a burlap sack had been dropped over his head and he was knocked unconscious by a vicious wallop. Vicente came to in the trunk of an Oldsmobile. He managed to pop the trunk open with a tire iron and tumbled out of his rolling casket onto the Malecón, the broad avenue that ran along the sea in Havana. He staggered across traffic and into one of the narrow and cobbled streets and disappeared before his assailants even realized he'd escaped.

Two days later, realizing that his life was in jeopardy, and that his presence would compromise the group's activity, Vicente booked a berth on a steamer bringing sugar to Mexico and followed Fidel into exile. Unable to face Sophia, he left her a note explaining his great affection for her but that nevertheless, their friendship could not exist in the current climate. Circumstances forced his flight, and absence for the time being, but he would be back. The ship brought him to Altamira, and he took a bus from there to Mexico City where Fidel and a band of twenty other exiles resided.

Fidel had acquired the services of Alberto Bayo to begin training the exiles in guerrilla warfare. Bayo had fought for eleven years with the Spanish Army against the Moors in the North African Rif in the 1920s. He'd then gone on to further study, and teach, this strategic style of attack-and-disappear combat before again becoming involved in the Spanish Civil War. When the loyalists lost, he'd gone into exile in Mexico, seemingly waiting for the *Movimiento 26th de Julio* to come calling. Fidel had persuaded this now graying sixty-three-year-old man to give up his furniture factory and instead train a force that as yet had no weapons.

One day as Vicente rested from the heat, he'd asked Bayo if there was a chance that a small group of men could defeat an entire army. Bayo had told Vicente that the guerrilla is invincible when he can rely on the support of the peasants in place. When Vicente discussed this with Fidel, he learned that Celia Sánchez was busy developing just such a network of sympathetic locals in Oriente Province, and that they'd invade somewhere along that southeastern coast before the following year was over.

Now here he was at sea on a leaky, overcrowded yacht slowly approaching the Cuban shore on this lightless December night. Looking over the railing of the *Granma* as it puttered through even darker water, he hoped that this Celia Sánchez had indeed developed a structure that would render them invincible, and wondered what waited for them out there in the darkness.

* * *

Hundreds of miles away and several days earlier, deep in the heart of Oriente Province, Celia Sánchez had indeed thoroughly prepared for the arrival of the *fidelistas*. This society-girl-turned-revolutionary was probably the unlikeliest of agent provocateurs, but she had developed a carefully cultivated network that she activated on the next to last day of November by simply visiting the house of Crescencio Pérez, the latest of many sojourns to this powerful, if salacious-minded, older man. His home was in Ojo de Agua de Jerez, nestled in the rugged mountains of the Sierra Maestra, and close to the planned landing spot of the *Movimiento 26th de Julio*. Crescencio had agreed to help her support the invasion of this Fidel Castro, mainly because he liked being around her, but also because he detested Batista's country soldiers, the *Guardias Rurales*, who were always harassing him.

Of late, Crescencio had become too powerful for them to bother him much, as his reach covered almost 1,500 square miles in the Sierra Maestra. The deep ravines, high ridges, impenetrable jungles, numerous caves, chilly nights, hungry mosquitos, and torrential rains creating slithering mud made it a hard place to live, but also, a hard place to find. The population of this region was comprised of the outcasts and outlaws, marijuana farmers, miners, and poachers eking out an existence just outside the boundaries of civilization.

Crescencio had become the patriarch to all of them, acting as lawyer, judge, protector, lawman, friend, and even father to this coarse group of men and women who called home the almost uninhabitable mountains of eastern Cuba. He had nine wives and several other women vying for his attention. He was sixty-one years old, of medium size with grizzled gray whiskers, and a crooked mouth that gave him a distinctive look. His charisma and those intense flashing eyes turned this deformity into handsomeness that women enjoyed and men feared.

"It's happening, old man. Fidel Castro is due to arrive tomorrow." Celia strode into the room, teasing the outlaw. She wore her favorite dress, a zebra striped affair, and high heels that were conspicuously out of place in these foothills of the mountains.

Crescencio smiled, his tilted grin crinkling his face into an impish charm. "I know that he's on his way. But not tomorrow."

Celia cocked her head, casting a derisive glance down her angular and pronounced nose at the man before sitting at the table. "And you know this how? Did he, perhaps, call you?"

"Changó told me."

Celia froze momentarily, surprised by this revelation, but quickly gathered herself. Of course the old peasant was a follower of Santería. Many of the people tucked away into Cuba's most rural areas believed in this religion that merged Catholicism with ancient Yoruba religious practices. "He told you directly?" She raised one of her pencil-lined eyebrows in an arc of genuine incredulity.

"We had a ritual last night, and when my *santero* went into a trance, Changó came to visit in the body of his son. He told me that a great man was coming on a boat to make many changes, and that though it would be a rough landing, the hero would survive." Crescencio looked narrowly at the doctor's daughter to see her reaction, knowing that many did not believe in the ancient African gods who peopled Santería's pantheon. At the same time, almost nobody in Pilón would discount the possibility of their existence. Sensing no mockery or astonishment, he continued, "he also said that this conqueror would be late but in time for the festival honoring Changó." This ritual celebration was always on the fourth of December, in just a few short days.

Celia had to admit that she'd consulted *santeros* and *santeras* before to guide her in difficult decisions, but she took this advice with a grain of salt, much as she did Christianity. She also knew better than to openly doubt that Changó, the god of fire, lightning, thunder, and war, had taken over the body of the son of the *santero* and then discussed Fidel's arrival with Crescencio. "Did he tell you anything else?"

"Not this time."

"He's spoken about the invasion before?"

Crescencio shook his head. "The *santero* has looked at the coconut pieces and cowrie shells and then read my *pataki*, making clear from this story that my destiny lies with this Fidel of yours."

"And what does Changó or Fidel want with some old thief?" Celia flirted lightly with the peasant lord, knowing that this would encourage him to continue.

Crescencio laughed, a short hard chuckle. "I'm not too old to teach you a trick or two in the bedroom young lady." He paused, and when his offer was ignored, continued, "nor a thief for some time now, but perhaps I'll accept *bandido*? For your information, I'm the third oldest son of Changó in this entire region. As you certainly know, he himself fucked—excuse my language—around in his younger years before he learned the fine art of diplomacy, royal grace, and charm. He teaches us there is still a chance to redeem ourselves, even after a lifetime of mistakes. Maybe even an old bandit can be reborn, especially if he aids this Fidel of yours, him and his friends. Who am I to argue with my *Ori?*"

"You certainly can't change your destiny," Celia agreed. "Well, it would seem then that I've got the right man for the job. If you could spread the word that the invasion is tomorrow…or soon thereafter, I would be in your debt." She lightly licked her lips; smoothing the Stormy Pink lipstick from Revlon she'd so carefully applied earlier, not missing the fact that the old bandit was mesmerized.

Crescencio broke his gaze from her tongue and lips and went into his bedroom to prepare. It was some time before he re-emerged wearing his best clothes—a white guayabera, white pants, and a black lariat around his neck that matched his shiny shoes. With a flourish, he added the finishing touch, topping his head with an exquisite felt hat.

"And what do you think you're doing?" Celia asked exasperatedly. "You're going to go all through the mountains inviting your crew to welcome a wanted fugitive and help him overthrow the government, and you dress up in your finest clothes?"

"I've thought this through." Crescencio grinned. "If I'm stopped by the *Guardias Rurales*, I'll simply tell them I'm going around to invite my family to the wedding of my nephew. If there were indeed to be a wedding, this is how I'd be dressed."

Celia laughed and shook her head. The old man was brilliant.

* * *

That same night of November 29th, just over a hundred miles to the east, Frank País was going over the final checklist for the planned Santiago uprising. He'd be twenty-two in one week, but though young, there was nothing brash about him. Everything he did was incredibly thorough and well planned. There was no doubt that this would be no different, for men's lives were on the line. "Again, from the top. Léster, you lead off."

"I'll put the mortar in my trunk when I leave here. Then I'll go to the Los Ángeles flower shop and gather the 30.06 tripod machine gun. At 6:00 a.m. I'll pick up Caleb, Josué, Orlando, and Camilo from

the safe house and proceed to Vista Alegre. At 7:00 a.m. on the dot
we'll begin shelling the Moncada Barracks and keep the soldiers
pinned down so that they can't come to support the *policía*."

País had just the faintest inkling of peach fuzz dotting his
upper lip. It was his first try at growing a mustache in an attempt
to look older. His thin face and large ears made him appear to be
no more than seventeen, the age at which he'd begun to organize
his resistance movement in Santiago. Upon the release of Fidel
Castro from prison in the spring of 1955, País had merged his
well-developed opposition group with that of the *Movimiento 26th
de Julio*. It was with trepidation that he was letting his youngest
brother, Josué, fire the powerful machine gun that would defend the
mortar as it lobbed explosives at the Moncada Barracks, but there
was no denying his right to be a part of this revolution.

"Jorge?"

Jorge Sotús had the square chin, high forehead, and combed back
hairstyle of a movie star. "Our group will stay in Sorribes tonight.
Quiala and Alonso will take the bus in the morning to the maritime
estación de policía. They'll approach the guards at the main entrance
and shoot them. I've assigned four others to create a diversion by
throwing Molotov cocktails. At this point we'll drive through the
gate with two cars of men and go around back where we'll gain
access to the building. Once we're in control we'll wait for further
orders."

Frank País looked over at his good friend Pepito Tey, who was
responsible for the most important piece of the overall strategy.
Years earlier, they'd met at the Teacher's College, at first both vying
for the same political office of president of the students' association.
But now their talents merged, País in charge of the planning and
Pepito leading the action as second-in-command.

"I'm going to kill me some *hijos de putas*, is what I'm going to
do," Pepito said. He had a swarthier complexion—and more of a
mustache than his *amigo*, but Rosario, País's mother, always joked
they had identical ears. He was a fifth-grade teacher at the De La
Salle School, while País had just recently resigned from his job at
the El Salvador Baptist School. When asked the reason for leaving,

País had merely said, "Cuba needs me."

"How do you propose to kill you some...*policía*, exactly?" País asked patiently.

"Those *bastardos* are either going to run away or die, and then this fucking city will be ours." Pepito stalked up and down the room, his emotions too hot for him to sit still.

"Humor me and tell me how you're going to take the *estación de policía*." The soft-spoken País smiled slightly at his friend.

"Why didn't you just ask in the first place? Otto and his men will enter the Visual Arts School and set up a machine gun on the roof to give supporting fire. Francisco will drive into Jesús Rabí Street and control that side of the building. I'll lead two cars to the main entrance and get into the building, killing any *hijos de putas* that don't surrender."

País nodded at his friend and turned to one of the several women present. "And are the first aid kits all in place, Vilma?"

Vilma Espín was the daughter of the Bacardi family lawyer. She'd grown up wealthy, and was one of the first women chemical engineering students in Santiago, even going on for further education at MIT in Massachusetts. Upon returning home she'd met Frank País, and the entire direction of her life had changed. "We've two nurses each taking the chests to the six locations just before 7:00 a.m. We also have five alternates in case anybody is sick or changes their mind."

"That should do it then." País rubbed his hands together, perhaps the only one in the room who was not sweating from anxiety. "The members of the command center will spend the night in Punta Gordo with me. The first mortar shot at 7:00 a.m. will signal the beginning of the insurrection. Good night and God bless."

None of the young men and women slept well that night, and Frank País was no exception, finally going and sleeping in the car while the rest of the leaders tossed and turned indoors. He was up before 5:00 a.m., pouring a cup of hot coffee, and then standing outside watching the waves of the ocean crash onto the shore in their uninterrupted rhythm, not bothered by the machinations of man. It was the best cup of coffee he'd ever had, he reflected, and the most peaceful.

Less than an hour later he strode into a private residence near Céspedes Park, expropriating the location for his base of operations, and sending the Rousseau family and their servants away. They were nervous at having their home be the center of the uprising, but fully supported the action, and thus, left without a word. Soon after arriving, there was a commotion outside, and País followed the others to the balcony where two cars drove by honking their horns. Pepito Tey and other men leaned out the rolled down windows, shouting, *"Larga vida Fidel!" "Larga vida a la revolución!" "Abajo con Batista!"*

País smiled faintly at the cheers for Fidel and the revolution along with the condemnation of Batista, knowing that it was impossible to cool his friends' hot Spanish blood. He was the last one to return inside, watching the empty street long after his best friend had passed by on his mission to capture the *estación de policía* and take control of the city.

Just before six, Lester went to the safe house and picked up the others, crowding the five men into the car as the sky began to grow light from the rising sun. As they nosed their way down the ten blocks to the school where they would deploy the mortar, two official Jeeps suddenly blocked their way. The *policías* ordered them out of the car at gunpoint. To fight back would've been futile, to run, suicidal, and he'd no choice but to try and talk his way out of the predicament, but when the officers found a map with the title *Operation Mortar* in Lester's pocket, the jig was up. They were all thrown down, spread-eagled, flat on their stomachs, with their hands cuffed behind them and their faces in the dirt. The sergeant in charge popped the trunk open, and discovered the mortar and machine gun, and Léster and the others were brought to the jail.

Jorge Sotús sat in the passenger seat of the 1955 Chrysler Windsor as his friend Roberto Roca drove them the twenty-odd blocks down Paseo de Martí. They'd left a bit early, anxious to begin this terrifying ordeal before they could change their minds, and were now driving slowly so as to time their arrival with the mortar fire. Quiala and Alonso had left earlier, taking the bus, each with a pistol stuck down in his waistband, covered by their suit jackets. Four others had also taken the bus, a bag of Molotov cocktails in one man's arms, their job to cause a distraction on the side of the building, while the two carloads of men attacked the primary entrance to the maritime station.

Quiala and Alonso got off the bus at the clock tower, about a hundred feet from the two guards at the main gate of the headquarters. They'd agreed that whether they heard the mortar or not, they'd take out the two *policías* when the clock struck seven. There was a little activity at the train station next-door, but not too many people were up and about yet at that early hour. The two men looked at each other, and with a slight nod, began walking, hearts pounding. *What if the cars were late?* Three pelicans swooped down past them in perfect formation, heading back to the bay for some fishing. In the distance a train whistle blew, announcing an arrival or departure. The two men matched each other's strides, first looking at the clock and then zeroing in on the two sentinels, and then looking away so as to not be so obvious.

The first chime suddenly pierced the still morning air, and Quiala pushed his sports jacket back and drew the revolver like a cowboy from some western movie, pulling the trigger and repeatedly hurtling bullets into his intended target, semi-aware that Alonso was doing the same next to him. The two guards crumpled to the ground in a shower of blood. They pushed open the gate as the two cars appeared right on cue and shot through the opening, one pulling around to the primary entrance in the back and the other to a side door.

Jorge jumped out of the Chrysler before it'd fully stopped, rounding the car with the one Thompson machine gun the group possessed. A sudden stinging on his cheek was followed by a distinct crack, and he realized a bullet had just brushed him. He looked up to see a sailor again aiming his rifle at him when the man suddenly slumped over as Danny Fong put a slug from his .44 Winchester through his left eye.

The officers inside had managed to lock the door, and, as Jorge sprayed rounds through the windows into the interior, Roca and two others broke it down with a crash. Jorge followed them into the maritime *policías* day room, as Roca suddenly cursed loudly in pain, having taken a hit in his right foot. Jorge fired three shots into the desk clerk's chest while the other man threw down his gun and fell flat on his face, screaming, "*Rendición! Rendición!*"

One of the rebels bent to take the surrendering sailor's weapon, the rest of them moved to the stairs, scurrying upwards with shouts and gunfire. It was enough of a cacophony that only one man resisted them at the top, and he fell with a bullet in his shoulder, the rest throwing down their weapons and begging for mercy. In less than five minutes the maritime building had been taken and was now in the possession of the *Movimiento 26th de Julio.*

Pepito was infuriated as he listened to the report from his source at the *estación de policía.* It was 2 a.m. on the morning of November 30th, and he was just learning that the police had apprehended a key player of his team. According to the source, who worked as an operator at the headquarters and happened to be a friend of his mother, a *Movimiento 26th de Julio* member from a small town outside Santiago had been picked up on suspicion of insurrection, and had spilled the details of the raid slated to start in five short hours. Pepito reminded himself that it didn't matter, for this raid was merely a diversion for Fidel's landing, so they had to proceed, even if failure was assured.

Otto and eight men took two cars and left first, as it was their job to provide covering fire for the main assault. They were cruising down San Carlos Street, about to make a right on Padre Pico, when the windshield of the lead automobile exploded, bits of glass scratching faces and coating their olive green uniforms. The driver slammed on the brakes in apparent confusion. Otto realized that they were taking gunfire and ordered everybody out of the stopped car, a statement that didn't need to be repeated as men spilled out of the car in wild panic. He motioned for them to follow him as he cut down Padre Pico toward the Visual Arts School at a dead run.

The shots were coming from the second floor of a house just across the block. *We've been ambushed!* Otto thought. Nobody was hit, not yet anyway, and by now they'd gained the protective cover of the school. They broke down the door, and rushed through the building to the central patio. Two men slid a table against the wall and then climbed up to the roof, passing the Madsen machine gun up to be assembled. Within minutes they were returning fire both at the ambushers and also sweeping the back of the *estación de policía* with bullets. Otto found himself wondering if the firefight had drowned out the sound of the mortar that was supposed to signal the start of the fighting.

Pepito's assault team had diverged from their route to pass by the command center at the Rousseau House. Even before they reached their friends' position, the twenty-some-odd men in three cars were hanging out the windows hollering their support of The Movement, of Fidel, and their disdain for Batista in extremely colorful language. As they passed under the command group gathered on the balcony, Pepito pumped his fist towards his best friend, País, his eyes smoldering with a promise of success or martyrdom.

The *estación de policía* was less than a half-mile from this command center in Céspedes Park, and as they came down Santa Lucia Street and approached it, gunfire erupted from around the corner, and Pepito assumed that Otto had begun his clash with the police. A machine gun sounded from the front of the *estación de policía*, causing Pepito to rethink his original strategy of driving the car up the meandering drive to that entrance, forcing them to circle the building to get to the front. That might have been effective if this assault had remained a surprise, but now it'd be suicide.

He quickly decided to stop at the bottom of the Padre Pico steps and attack up those famous stairs. The *policía* wouldn't expect the attack to come from here, especially if the informant had shared the plans with them. This would put them just over a hundred yards from their objective, but he hoped that the deviation from the plan would bewilder the *policía* enough for them to be successful. Tony Alomá led the group of twenty men up the fifty-two steps, each as wide as a street. The men ran as a pack up and up, hoping they could reach the top before they were spotted. It was not to be.

When they were about halfway, several *policía*, along with two soldiers, appeared at the top where the steps narrowed, firing down into the charging revolutionaries. Right in front of him, Pepito saw Alomá's head explode in a shower of blood, brains, and ooze. Just the night before, Alomá had rejoiced in the birth of his first child, a child who would never know his father. The other men paused and stared at their fallen friend in bafflement. Pepito realized the perilous position they were in and pushed forward up the stairs yelling and cursing for the others to follow him.

Otto heard the gunfire spewing from the front of the *estación de policía* and knew that the strike force was in trouble. He realized that firing into the back windows of the headquarters wasn't distracting the eighty men inside from concentrating a deadly fire upon the assault team. Something more needed to be done if his friends out front were to have any chance at all. He handed off control of the Madsen with terse orders to cover him, and then climbed down from the roof carrying a bag with several Molotov cocktails and two Brazilian grenades.

At the back wall he took a deep breath and broke into a zigzag run towards the back of the building housing the police. Gunfire spit at him as several sentries fired from the second floor, but a burst of machine gun fire silenced one of them, and the other decided it'd be more prudent to stay out of sight. Otto threw one of the grenades into a smashed window but nothing happened, so he lit and tossed a homemade bomb into the building. This was more effective, as he heard the roar of a fire inside the room. He repeated this at two more windows with equal success, and made a dash for the safety of the Visual Arts School just around the corner. He'd just about reached the protecting wall when a single shot rang out. Otto felt like he'd been punched in the back of the neck, and his throat was spread all over the wall in front of him, the red stain the last thing he saw before death.

Pepito reached the top of the steps and realized the *policía* and soldiers had retreated to the safety of the station, from which thick black smoke now billowed. He ran down the street to the main door throwing a grenade at the base, ducking back and shielding his face for the explosion that never came. *I knew these little pineapples weren't worth a damn,* he thought. The chatter of a machine gun made him dive for cover. When it paused, he came to his feet in a crouching run, trying to get to the safety of the concrete wall. He'd taken just two steps when several bullets struck him. He fell on his face, rolling over to look at the brightening sky as he died.

Back at the command center, the telephone was constantly ringing with different groups calling in to report their progress. They heard the thunderous volley from the *estación de policía* that went on and on, and farther in the distance the maritime station attack. The first bad news had come before it all started, País learning that Lester had been picked up and the mortar lost, forcing him to order sharpshooters to Moncada to try to pin the soldiers down in the barracks. Several street leaders communicated that the insurgents in the olive green uniforms now controlled the streets, but more bad news soon came; the prison had not been taken. The best news, however, came when Jorge rang to tell him that the *Movimiento 26ᵗʰ de Julio* was in command of the maritime station. Just before 9:00 a.m. the first two survivors of the failed attack on *policía* headquarters arrived.

Vilma, the typical broad smile missing from her face, brought the men to País as he was finishing a phone conversation. "Well?"

Luis fumbled with the hat clutched in his hands, his face sooty from the fire and the shooting. There was a bandage wrapped around his forearm, a red smear bleeding through. "We failed."

País nodded. "Tell me about it."

"I was on the roof of the Visual Arts School with Otto providin' covering fire for the assault team. Otto went to set the buildin' on fire and was shot and killed. About thirty minutes later Ramón pulled up out front and yelled for us to come with him, that the strike had failed, and we ran for it. We dropped three men off under the command of Agustin to control the streets and came straight here to report."

"And what of Pepito? Where is he?"

Ramón was a thick-squat man, about as wide as he was tall, and at thirty-seven years of age, one of the elder statesmen of the revolution. "He didn't make it."

País looked away out the window over the balcony and into Céspedes Park, the square center of the city of Santiago. His vacant stare lit upon the bust of the father of their country, Carlos Céspedes, and he thought about the words inscribed there, words he couldn't see now but knew by heart. "His head is crowned by two bay leaves that symbolize the force and the justice."

"Didn't make it? Meaning what? They captured him?"

"He's dead. I saw his body with my own eyes. And then I ran. They also killed Alomá and several others."

A hush fell over the room as all had been eavesdropping on Ramón's words. A small tear trickled down Vilma's cheek, and the phone rang once and then fell silent as if in respect for the dead. A fifth-grade class would be without a teacher come Monday morning, a revolution would stumble on without a great leader, and Frank País would mourn his closest friend, but for now, the business of insurrection had to be continued. "Do you have the Madsen?"

Luis nodded.

"Report to Moncada, where we have a few men attempting to keep the soldiers pinned down. Although their mission isn't a total success, they've succeeded in distracting the military from Fidel's arrival. With any luck, he'll arrive soon with his men to help us capture the city."

Unfortunately, an hour later, Celia Sánchez, who was watching for Fidel's arrival, managed to call in to say there'd been no sign of him or his invasion force. About the same time, a truckload of soldiers arrived at the maritime *estación de policía* ready to dislodge the rebels under Jorge, who called to say that they were going to have to vacate their occupation. "That's it then." País put down the phone receiver in the cradle. "We're closing down operations here so that we might carry on the fight tomorrow and the next day and the next." He shook his head wearily. "You all know the drill. Everybody change back into civilian clothes. Leave in pairs and return to your lives. It's probably best if you can find another place to stay for a bit, as I'm sure the backlash from the *policía* and soldiers will be brutal and extensive. We don't know how much they know."

* * *

Fidel Castro rubbed his bristly cheeks. He hadn't shaven since setting sail, according to the dictum set by their military instructor of the past year, Alberto Bayo: the guerilla soldier must be able to live without the comforts of civilized life. It'd been quite a journey since

Fidel had been released from the Isle of Pines Prison. He'd hoped to carry on the insurrection from Cuba, but the police had harassed him at every step, and even made attempts upon his life. As a result, he'd been forced to go into exile.

Soon after arriving in Mexico City, he'd met the man who'd become his most trusted advisor. Ernesto "Che" Guevara was an Argentinian fresh from Guatemala, where he'd been fighting for President Árbenz to bring land reform to that country. Everyone called him Che because of his Argentinian dialect, that habit of dropping in that little word at the start or end of a sentence in order to add emphasis. Che had first befriended Raúl, the two bonding over their shared interest in Marxism.

When Fidel had followed his brother into exile in Mexico, Raúl knew that he had to introduce these two men. By the end of their first meeting, when they'd talked long into the steamy July night, Che had joined the *Movimiento 26th de Julio*. His wide intellect created from a voracious appetite in books matched Fidel's, and many conversations between the two men had further laid down the path that would be taken, first to remove Batista, and then the true objective, that of land distribution and economic, medical, and social reform free from North American interference or influence.

That fall Fidel had taken his message to the United States in a seven-week tour of speeches, meetings, and most importantly, raising money. In front of 800 Cubans at the Palm Garden Hall, on the corner of 52nd Street and 8th Avenue in New York City, he first made the promise that he would invade Cuba by the end of 1956. This claim he'd repeated again and again for the past year, and thus, when others had argued that the training was not complete, that the *Granma* was not a large enough vessel, when Frank País said the Santiago underground was not strong enough; he'd overridden their concerns because he'd made an inviolate promise to the people of Cuba.

And here they were, on the second day of December almost a year later, peering into the darkness, trying to spy their homeland once again. He was so close he could smell the sugar cane, the palm fronds, the tobacco, and the good earth that was Cuba. In New York City, Tampa, Miami and other cities he'd spoken heatedly about the evils of Batista and the concept of a free Cuba, and at the conclusion of his speeches cowboy hats had been filled with the donations of all those sympathetic to the Cuban plight. Now he'd put those dollars to good use.

A bit more than a month ago, Fidel had returned to his borrowed rooms in the home of Orquídea Pino, a sympathetic Cuban-born lady who'd married a wealthy Mexican businessman, to find Frank País playing the piano. He listened through the remainder of the lovely piece before striding across the wide room to shake the man's hand. He'd first met País a few months earlier and had been greatly impressed by his attention to detail, organization, and commitment to the cause. "I trust your flight was smooth?"

"Very much so," País replied, rising to return the greeting. His frame was diminutive in comparison to Fidel's, but his eyes projected a mental strength matched by few.

"I'm glad you were able to come. We've much to talk about."

"There was little choice, as my communication is one that must be delivered in person." The two men moved to the inner veranda where Fidel lit a cigar, offering País one as well, which he declined. "There's no reason to beat around the bush, so I'll just come out with it. We must put off your planned invasion as we're ill-prepared for an insurrection in Santiago."

Fidel stared fixedly at the end of his cigar, perhaps only the tightening around his eyes belying his emotion. "In what way are you ill-prepared?"

"There are three main reasons. I don't like how our underground is currently organized, and believe it could use a good reshaping. Two, the preparations for a general strike have been haphazard at best, and finally, the action commandos are untrained and poorly armed and will be no match for the *policía* and soldiers."

A silence descended as Fidel digested these comments. "I've made a promise to the Cuban people that I'd return by the end of 1956, and that I intend to do," he finally said in a voice that brooked no argument.

País spent five days in Mexico City pleading for a delay, but the sheer force of Fidel wouldn't allow for compromise. He'd promised the people of Cuba, and his word would be kept. But he became increasingly more impressed with the acute mind of País, and made him National Action Chief, handling all of the urban resistance in Cuba.

Eighty-two men had crowded onto the yacht in the early morning hours of November 26th, Fidel the last to board, and they puttered down the Rio Pantepec River and into the Gulf of Mexico. He'd sent the cable to Frank País that they were on their way to Playa las Coloradas below Bélic and south of Niquero in the Oriente Province, and would be arriving on November 30th. This had been a terrible misjudgment, as he'd not planned for the high winds of El Norte once they hit the open water, nor the slowness of the overburdened yacht.

Singing the Cuban National Anthem and the 26th of July Anthem, they started their journey into the Gulf, but by the end of the second song men were retching over the sides of the boat, vomiting on themselves and each other. Fidel quickly realized that they'd not be making the seven-plus knots he'd estimated once they hit the high seas. The vessel sprang a leak, and the next day and a half was spent bailing until they discovered that a drainage plug hadn't been inserted correctly. On November 30th Fidel listened to the scratchy radio, along with the others, as the newscaster reported the squashed uprising in Santiago. If he could only fly, he thought, he would've been there to support those that had died in his stead. But now, finally, they were approaching the shore, the final phase of what had been a 1,200-mile odyssey.

6

December 2nd, 1956, Oriente Province

With their eyes on the Cabo Cruz lighthouse the *Granma* motored into the Niquero channel. It was the morning of December 2ⁿᵈ, and they were two days late in arriving. The first hint of light was barely peeking from the eastern horizon at 4:20 a.m. when the yacht ground to a shuddering, screeching halt, still miles from their destination. "What is it?" Fidel demanded.

"We're stuck fast on a sandbar," one of the three sailors replied. "But the coast is only about a hundred yards in."

"Can we break free?"

"Not until the tide changes."

"When the sun comes up we'll be sitting ducks," Che spoke quietly but urgently.

"Grab your weapons and as many bullets as you can. Hold the guns high, and into the water you go. We must get to shore before the daylight truly breaks," Fidel ordered. There was a mad clambering over the side, and splashes as they hit the knee-high water. Even within a few feet of the ship, however, men sunk into the muck up to their chest. "Move toward the shore. Keep your weapons high. To get your gun wet is to die."

The eighty-two revolutionaries scrabbled their way through the small surf, washing up on the shore miles from their original destination. Celia had planned to meet them with transportation, but that was two days ago and fifteen miles away. The "mainland" where they'd come ashore was actually a mangrove swamp, the water often deeper in places than the ocean they'd just encountered, the gnarled and twisting scrub trees hooking their ankles and tripping the men as they fought through a jungle of tangled vines and jagged pronged leaves.

"Stay together. We must stay together," Fidel directed through gasping breaths. It took them two hours to bushwhack the mile necessary to clear the swamp. They could hear, but not see, the airplanes flying overhead. They assumed that the air force had spotted the *Granma* stuck on the sandbar and was now methodically searching for the rebels. The sound of cluster bombs could be heard detonating, as the bombers hoped to get lucky and blindly strike the invaders by dropping these special bombs that released numerous smaller bombs before hitting the ground.

The rebels came to the house of a charcoal burner, and Fidel strode right up to the door and announced, "Have no fear. I'm Fidel Castro and I'm here to liberate Cuba." In the coming days, Fidel would learn humility and the importance of discretion, but in this case, his arrogance worked, and the man gave them food and water.

Vicente was the last to leave the man's small shack. "*Gracias, amigo*," he said, grasping the man's hand.

The gnarled man blackened with soot nodded to where Fidel was disappearing into the woods. "I've heard of him. It's said he'll finally bring freedom to the *campesinos* of the Sierra Maestra."

* * *

Celia sat at Crescencio Pérez's dining table, her distressed expression communicating someone in a deep dilemma. There was a large map of the southwest region of Oriente Province spread out before her. This was her third day here, having set up her command post at the crossroads of Fidel's three possible arrival points. The soldiers would now be suspicious of any strangers in the area after the recent Santiago uprising. As well, her network of people had been conspicuously absent from their jobs for the past two days. It was time to call it off. She'd lingered one more night hoping that the invasion force would miraculously appear. As of yet, she'd heard not a whisper, somehow making the waiting worse. She shook her head in frustration. Certainly they'd have gotten word out if they had been forced to land elsewhere, or been discovered by the Cuban navy or air force. Maybe the old bandit had been right about Changó telling him the *Granma* would be delayed.

Celia was not quite your typical hard-faced revolutionary. She wore a narrow brown dress that would have been more appropriate for a dinner party. Even today she'd taken time to apply a dark pencil to shape her eyebrows and red lipstick to her lips, bringing color to her homely face. Her thick black hair was pulled back into a ponytail exposing her marble skin. At thirty-six years of age, Celia had had a host of boyfriends and suitors, yet there'd been no serious interests in her life since her first love had died tragically when she was but seventeen years of age.

She'd listened to the radio reports of the atrocities committed in Santiago after the failed uprising two days ago, meant to coincide with the arrival of Fidel, and was glad that Frank País had seemingly survived, thinking back to the day she had guided him and Miret along the coast to pick a landing spot for this very invasion. Celia's mind wandered to her meeting with País at his parent's house at 266 General Bandera Street. They'd recognized in each other similar organizational abilities and a deep passion for the cause. Their reputations had preceded them, but it immediately became obvious as they discussed tactics and strategy that neither one was prepared to leave anything to chance. As soft music played on the record player in that middle-class living room to drown out their plotting from prying ears, País had entrusted her with the transportation of the guerrillas into the mountains. Not only did she go on to develop a network of peasants to hide the rebels, truck drivers to transport them, and women to sew their uniforms, but she also had local doctors instruct the peasants in first aid procedures while she also collected medical supplies.

Thus, it was Celia Sánchez who was in charge of the many lives being risked in support of this phantom landing. *This is it. I have to pull the plug.* The words she tried to push away echoed in her head. She could no longer endanger the clandestine network she'd so carefully cultivated. Celia summoned Beto Pesant and César Suárez, her two most trusted advisors, and told them to gather their things. Then, she drove the Jeep to her old hometown of Media Luna and dropped César off with orders to assess the damage created by the delayed landing. They'd rendezvous with him in Manzanillo. After the uprising in Santiago, there was no doubt that the *Guardias Rurales* would be arresting people, and any man absent from work the past few days with no good excuse would be suspect.

Celia continued on to Campechuela with Beto, driving down the main street past the company store, a tailor shop, and several *bodegas* with men drinking beer and rum out front of these small markets, before parking in front of the feed store. Here, they parted ways, each off to sound out their various contacts on to what degree the failed insurrection had compromised the operation and individual members of the local resistance. They agreed to circle back, meeting at the small bridge on the side of town towards Manzanillo later in the afternoon.

Celia went to a bar on the corner named La Rosa, intent on checking in with Enrique, one of her operatives there. He was the bartender of the establishment and the typical rebel at twenty years old; wearing a white t-shirt with a pack of cigarettes rolled into his sleeve, his hair carefully coiffed back and a smirk upon his face. She'd no sooner approached the small glass bar than six men, four in the uniform of the *Guardias Rurales,* entered with guns drawn.

"Celia Sánchez, you're wanted for subversion against the government." One of the officers stepped up, pressing a pistol to her forehead. "You," the portly man in charge said to the bartender, "keep your eyes on the floor and serve us a drink."

"What you gonna' do to her?" Enrique asked as he came out from behind the tiny bar puffing nonchalantly on a cigarette, but his shaking hand belied his calmness. A soldier knocked him to his knees with the butt of his gun where Enrique rethought his question with bowed head, a thin red strand of blood dripping from his nose to the floor. "We know that you're involved in the uprising in Santiago." The man in charge came up behind the chair that Celia had been thrust into. He ran his hand down her cheek and over her chest, cupping her right breast affectionately, almost tenderly. "We've had eyes on you for some time. If you do what we say, you might just live through the day."

"What do you want of me? I just spent the night with a friend in Media Luna and stopped here on my way back to pick up supplies." Celia wasn't able to keep her voice from quavering.

"For now, all I want is for you to stay here with a few of my men. I've some business to attend to and then I'll be back." The leader snapped his fingers and three men followed him out the door.

Celia sat by herself, but two men remained at the adjacent table. She peeked sideways at them, realizing that she knew one, a grim-faced man named Hatüey, aptly nicknamed "Machete King" for his use of the broad side of the blade to beat his victims senseless, ending more than one mill strike with this violent approach. Celia searched her brain for where else she knew the man from, other than the stories told about him. The other was vaguely familiar as a member of *Los Tigres de Masferrer*, an elite paramilitary unit formed expressly to protect Batista.

They're going to kill me. No, they're going to rape me, torture me, and then kill me. Her thoughts reflected the knowledge of the dangerous game she'd been playing, and their suspicion alone was enough to entail the most horrible of death sentences. *But wait, why am I just sitting here in the bar, by myself, with no threats other than to not leave?* With a rush, the realization came that they were waiting to see who might be coming to rendezvous, who her acquaintances were, whom else she might implicate. She had to escape or die trying.

She looked at Hatüey and smiled, shaking a cigarette out of the pack. "Do you mind if I get some matches?"

Hatüey turned so that the scar on the side of his face glimmered at her in the glare of the sun. "Go ahead," he grunted, his voice rough, but with a tinge of apology within. Now she remembered—he was a patient of her father.

Celia went to the small glass bar that had cigars and cigarettes below, while behind it was a shelf with some bottles of liquor. "May I get some matches, please?" she said aloud to Enrique, and then mouthed the words, "be careful." She'd no way of knowing that later that day he'd be dragged outside and shot forty-two times and his shredded corpse left in the street. She returned to her seat and smoked casually, attempting to give the appearance of indifference, as if she truly believed that she might live through any interrogation that followed. She crushed the butt on the table, making a face and running her tongue over her lips as if the cigarette had left a bad taste in her mouth. "Do you mind if I get some Chiclets?"

"As you wish."

Celia stood, gathering her courage, and walked to where the gum was stored in a small glass case that stood on legs by the door. She reached into the case and then turned, launching herself through the door and into the street. As it was Sunday, it was market day in Campechuela, and the narrow lanes were crowded with people and stalls piled high with merchandise and fruits and vegetables. Both men came out firing their pistols at her as the stunned pedestrians froze and then scrambled for cover, adding to the commotion.

Celia ran as fast as she could, impeded by the narrowly-cut brown dress she wore, wishing for the olive-green uniforms they'd prepared for Fidel's arrival. Luckily, she was wearing flats and not heels, but the tight material didn't allow her to extend her legs fully as she ran. She scurried from building to building until she finally came to the Dos Amigos Sugar Mill at the edge of town and crawled into a thorny grove of thick trees. She spent the rest of the day motionless, staring up into the sky watching air force planes whizzing overhead, and realized that Fidel must've arrived.

* * *

After the disastrous landing and once clear of the mangrove swamp, Fidel led the invasion force in a desperate attempt to reach the protection of the rugged Sierra Maestra before the soldiers could track them down. After three days of almost nonstop marching, their feet blistered and their bodies undone by exhaustion and lack of food, the rebels were forced to bed down in a thicket of underbrush below the protection of a small hill just as the sun was rising on the horizon, most of them falling asleep immediately.

Vicente woke from a deep slumber to the sound of raised voices. He kept his eyes closed, not in an attempt to feign sleep, but rather, because he wasn't yet ready to wake up and begin the marching again. Fidel and Raúl were bickering, as brothers will, but in this case life and death were involved. "We should break into smaller groups and rendezvous in the mountains where it's safer," Raul said, to which Fidel replied, "We must stay together and present a front of unity and force." Che was attempting to moderate, but having little success as the two Castros butted heads, the confusion and exhaustion adding to the squabble.

Vicente grinned as he imagined the frustration of the Argentinian, Che, as he strived to mediate between the two headstrong Cubans. He'd found himself chatting with the man on the journey aboard the *Granma*, amongst other things learning that Che had taken time off from medical school for a 5,000-mile motorcycle trip across South America where the exploitation of workers in the copper mines of Chile and the extreme poverty of the rural peasants in Peru made him begin to examine his established beliefs.

"We'll stay together and that's final." Fidel thundered into Vicente's reverie, causing his eyes to shoot open. The sun was starting its descent, indicating it was midafternoon. "Wake the men up and hand out the rations," Fidel continued in a growl, "and then we'll move out to the east."

Raúl had just distributed the rations of sausage, a cracker, and condensed milk, when all hell broke loose. Gunfire exploded from every possible angle. Vicente dropped the food in frustration, almost willing to take a bullet for just one bite. His rifle was at his feet and he swung it up, firing blindly at first, and then recognizing figures of the *Guardias Rurales* moving in on them. Fidel was yelling furiously. "Fight back. Kill those *bastardos*. Do not run away." But there was no chance. The camp was in chaos, and it was every man for himself, many leaving their weapons behind as an unnecessary burden.

Vicente saw his *amigo* Nicó gesturing for him to follow and the two ducked behind a rock, taking turns shooting at the enemy from behind this scant protection. He saw Che take a bullet in the shoulder and slammed to the ground with a cry of pain. Over by the cane field Faustino and Universo were pulling Fidel under cover of the shielding stalks. As Vicente watched, he realized with horror how the *Guardias Rurales* had found them; there was a trail leading right to the camp, the trampled plants of eighty sets of feet and discarded cane peelings and bagasse that the men had sucked the sugar out of from the previous evening. "Nicó," he said. "We have to make a break for it."

"Head for the cane. I'll cover you." Nicó pointed with his rifle. "When you get there, cover me and I'll join you."

Vicente broke into a stumbling run, ready to take a bullet at any moment, wondering idly what it'd feel like, whether it would hurt or numb him, be quick and painless or long and drawn out. He passed by a fellow rebel standing out in the open with his hands over his ears yelling for everybody to quiet down, clearly having lost his senses. In a panic Vicente dove into the outcropping of the field, rolled over, and turned to see Nicó with his hands raised, his rifle at his feet. Three men crowded in upon him, jabbing at him with the tips of their machine guns. An officer walked up to Nicó, put a pistol to his head and pulled the trigger, and his *amigo* dropped to the ground, his life gone just like that.

Vicente beat his hand on the ground in pain and frustration. When he raised his head, it was to see similar variations of brutality playing out as those rebels who dropped their guns and surrendered were being beaten, tortured, and killed. The buzzing of airplanes came roaring in low over the cane field, firing at anything that moved, picking off the remaining rebels. There was nothing he could do but try to escape. He crawled back into the sugar cane in the direction he'd seen Fidel and the others going.

* * *

Che Guevara was standing with Jesús eating half of a sausage and two tiny crackers on the afternoon of December 5th when the ambush came. He was leaning against a tree, making small talk with this Cuban about their children, the first chance to talk idly since the journey aboard the *Granma*. Che had just turned his head towards his comrade to better hear him when there was a sudden popping noise, and then it was like the heavens opened up and a thunderous roar filled the air with deafening capacity. It took him just a split second to realize that it was gunfire and they were under attack. He picked up his rifle, a bulky relic dispensed to the man who'd been brought as the guerillas' doctor, although perhaps the best shot of all of them. He craned his neck to locate the enemy, but before he could fire, a man ran by dropping a box of ammunition at his feet and continued on in complete panic, arms waving over his head. Che realized he should be first looking for cover instead of standing like a target on a knoll, and bent down to grab his medical bag, only to realize that he couldn't carry it and the box of ammunition. With little time to deliberate, he made the snap decision that the bullets were more crucial to the lives of the guerillas than the bandages.

With his rifle in his right arm held pointing up and the ammunition box under his left, Che broke across the clearing towards the cane field. He found himself running next to Emilio when the ground came up to meet him with a rush. Rolling over he saw Emilio on his knees, vomiting blood, a burst of bullets having shredded his midsection, and realized that he himself had been wounded as a piercing pain ripped through his chest and neck. *I'm fucked,* he thought in despair. *There's nothing to do but wait for death. If I'm to die, let me do so honorably.*

A man was screaming that they should surrender, and Che heard Camilo Cienfuegos yell in reply that nobody was going to surrender, adding for emphasis, *you prick!* Juan Almeida bent over him and grabbed Che's collar and began dragging him to the sugar cane, urging him to help himself, that it wasn't his day to die, that they must move, because to lay still was to invite capture and torture. Reaching the sugar stalks, he regained his feet and followed Juan and several others through the field and to the safety of the woods, just in time as airplanes came whizzing low over the ground strafing the sugar cane with bursts of machine gun fire.

Fidel crawled through the cane with Universo Sánchez and Faustino Pérez right behind him, his only thoughts focused exclusively on escape. His hands were being torn up and knees scraped, but he kept going for a good half-mile before stopping. *The planes will be able to see the sugar cane stalks waving and know that we're here*, he thought with sudden panic. He could almost feel the heavy-caliber bullets from the single-engine spotter aircraft ripping into his body, tearing his flesh, such that every iota of his being urged him to move, to flee, to escape this coffin of death. Instead, he forced himself to take a deep breath.

With only the smallest tremor in his voice, he turned to the two men behind him and realized that Vicente had also joined their ranks. "We need to stop here and wait for dark." They spent the remainder of the afternoon and early evening nestled into the field, barely breathing, the smell of smoke from burning sugar cane acrid in their nostrils, the sounds of planes flying low-overhead, the shouts of soldiers, and the occasional burst of gunfire as other guerrillas were discovered. When the protective cloak of darkness came they continued to move towards the east.

As the sun came up, the four of them continued to stagger forward, exhaustedly putting one foot in front of another. Fidel heard the drone of the plane before he recognized its importance. "We've been spotted!" Faustino broke into his reverie. Slightly ahead of them was a stand of three marabou trees in the middle of the wide expanse of the fields and they made for that, hoping for the better coverage of this thorny bush-tree, but they were not to make it, as the plane swooped in upon them. They dove under-cover of the cane stalks as the machine gun kicked up dirt around them.

Somehow, none of them were hit. "We need to move before he comes around again," Fidel said, his voice high despite his best efforts. "They think we're going for the marabou so we must head the other way." They moved in spurts for the next hour, but by then several planes were strafing the area and they were forced to dig themselves into the soil and cover themselves with straw. They could hear infantry searching the ground, promising horrible deaths if they didn't surrender, but yet they lay still. Fidel found himself nodding off, but he feared capture and torture worse than death, so he made himself stay awake. When he realized sleep was inevitable, he placed the butt of his rifle between his legs and the muzzle under his chin. With his finger resting on the hair-trigger, he finally nodded off to sleep.

When Fidel woke it was dark, but he could sense the enemy out there, the soldiers ringing the field, knowing the guerrillas were there somewhere. *This is how it happens,* he thought. *This is how all of my dreams come to an end, lying in a sugar cane field like a common criminal and a coward, sniveling and praying to God for forgiveness, no better or different than any other.* He was scared, and he knew he'd be unable to fight back when discovered and equally incapable of killing himself, impuissant for the task at hand. *I'm only thirty years old!* His inner soul deplored. *I've so many unrealized dreams, not just for myself, but also for my country. I cannot die and become but a footnote to history.*

Fidel heard the slight rustling from the other men and knew they were also awake and that he couldn't act the coward in front of these brave souls who had tied their fate to his, had followed him on this ill-conceived invasion, and now lay in the sugar cane pissing and shitting themselves from necessity and fear. He steeled his nerves and cleared his throat before speaking, "We are winning. Victory will be ours." His voice was firm in the hollow silence. "The rule of the guerrilla is to escape to fight another day, and we've done that. Soon, we'll continue our way to the safety of the Sierra Maestra, where we'll reunite with the others. Once in the mountains, with the support of the *campesinos*, we'll gather our strength and then sweep out of the mountains at the head of an invincible army."

Once Fidel began to speak, he was unable to stop, his words pouring forth for the next four days and nights. Barely taking time to sleep, occasionally pausing because soldiers could be heard searching nearby, he otherwise spouted a steady stream of the dreams he had for himself and Cuba. "We'll exile all those who accepted corruption and execute those who profited from more heinous crimes once we're in control." At first the words were for the ears of the three with him and a lament for what he feared would never be, a cry for his shattered hopes, but gradually they became his reality.

"There'll be no races, but only Cubans. Everybody in need of medical aid will receive it. Education will not be only for the wealthy, but will be available for every single Cuban. No longer will the rich prey upon the poor. The *Yanquís* will no longer control our economy." He went into detail of the utopia he'd created within himself, somehow forgetting he was hiding in the mud and straw of a sugar cane field with no food or water. His voice grew raspy as his throat became raw, but still he talked, giving himself one last chance to be the person he always knew he was destined to be, living in the paradise he'd created.

On the fifth day since the ambush at Alegría de Pío, during a momentary lull in the Fidel monologue, Vicente pulled himself from the soil and his own filth to his knees and cautiously lifted his head above the sugar cane stalks. "I think the soldiers are gone," he said.

Two days later they approached an isolated *bohío*, the house of two brothers who were sympathetic to their cause, giving them their first food and water in a week. They were then brought to the home of Guillermo García, a local mule driver, and he guided them to safety, crossing the heavily guarded highway through a drainage culvert that ran underneath. It was Celia Sánchez who'd brought this short squat, peasant into the network of the *Movimiento 26th de Julio*, and it was he who found and guided the shattered guerillas to safety after the ambush at Alegría de Pío. On the morning of December 16th, Guillermo delivered Fidel, Universo, Faustino, and Vicente to *Cinco Palmas*, a ranch house on the Vicana River that belonged to Mongo Pérez, Crescencio's brother. Five-palm trees rose thirty-feet above the house that was built in a small glen, the mountainous inclines and canopied forest shielding the building from the air.

The rebels bedded down in the sugar cane field adjacent to the house, gently refusing the offer of sleeping in the barn as unsafe. Two days later, Guillermo returned with Raúl and four other rebels. A joyous reunion occurred between the two brothers, especially when Raúl informed Fidel they'd brought five rifles with them. Fidel shouted out in the middle of the cane field, "Five…and with the two I have, this makes seven! Now, yes, we have won the war." Vicente, perhaps not yet fully recovered from the previous weeks' disasters, kept his mouth shut, for there was no arguing with Fidel.

There were rumors of more guerrillas in the area, and thus, Fidel moved the small remaining force further from the ranch house to a small stream to wait. After three days, Guillermo delivered Che Guevara, Juan Almeida, and two others to their hiding spot. Fidel met them with hugs, ecstatic to see his army rejuvenating itself. "Tell me of your journey," he demanded of Che once the joyous greetings had died down.

"*Che*, I took a bullet in the shoulder when we were ambushed back at Alegría de Pío and thought I was done for, but Juan convinced me otherwise, dragging me to safety." Che slapped his *campeñero* on the shoulder affectionately, knowing that the close-mouthed Cuban wouldn't share that Che had been blubbering and fully panicked at the time. "We joined up with three others and walked the coastline, knowing it would take us east to our destination. Along the way we stumbled into Camilo with two others, missed detection by soldiers on several occasions, and finally found a small hut where the peasant family fed us, our first real meal in nine days. Like the phoenix, we are reborn from the ashes to fight another day."

"Where are your rifles?" Fidel's face had narrowed during the recap of Che's adventures.

Che dropped his eyes to the ground. "*Che*, we decided to split into two groups and leave our weapons behind so as to not draw attention if spotted," he replied tentatively. "Camilo and two others should be here soon." He shuffled his feet, and continued to fill the silence, "I apologize for leaving the rifles behind, but any mistake that has been made has been paid thrice over by the ordeal of reaching this rendezvous point."

Fidel was rocking from foot to foot, his face growing redder by the moment. "You have *not* paid for the error you committed, because the price you pay for abandoning your weapons in such circumstances is your life. Your only hope of survival, in the event of a head-on encounter with the army, was your guns. To abandon them was criminal, and *estúpido*."

* * *

Sophia set the newspaper down next to her on the table. She was sitting at a table under the palm grass thatched cover of a cabana next to the kidney-shaped pool of the Hotel Nacional. Across the way she could see Meyer Lansky playing his afternoon game of gin rummy with his cronies, and she wondered in what ways he was plotting to purloin pesos from the Cuban population. She hadn't heard from Vicente in more than a month now, and then the rumors had begun to circulate of an invasion from Mexico. This gossip had been replaced with the real news of the uprising in Santiago that'd been brutally repressed by the *policía* and soldiers. Soon after the media had reported that Fidel Castro had landed in Oriente Province and been wiped out, but Sophia knew better than to believe the government-controlled Cuban newspapers. Today, however, it was in *The New York Times*, and she could no longer ignore the reality of it.

The New York Times

Cuba Wipes Out Invaders
Leader is Among 40 Dead

Havana, Dec. 5—Cuban planes and ground troops wiped out a force of forty exiled revolutionaries who landed on the coast of Oriente Province tonight.

Government leaders said Fidel Castro, leader of a revolt against President Fulgencio Batista, was among those killed. He had been exiled to Mexico after an abortive attempt to overthrow the Cuban Government in 1953.

The Government spokesmen said the revolutionaries landed from a Mexican yacht on the southern coast between the port of Niquero and Manzanillo.

Vicente is dead, Sophia thought. "Vicente *está muerto,*" she said it aloud, softly, in Spanish, as a single tear appeared under her large, round sunglasses and rolled down her right cheek. There was emptiness to the thought. How was one supposed to feel when somebody dies? She'd never quite understood the proper etiquette of death, even after her parents had been torn from her. Everybody had been so kind, apologizing as if it'd been their fault, claiming to know how horrible she felt—but in reality, it was just a numbness that had gripped her like the flu and wouldn't let go.

She'd only know him a few years and much of that time was spent in prison and exile. She knew him on paper. But at the same time, she knew him better than she'd ever known anybody. The way he held the door for her when they went out, held her arm in a crowded street, and listened carefully to every word she spoke. There was a diffidence to him that was endearing, but at the same time a passion smoldered in his eyes, a dangerous simmer under the surface.

For the thousandth time she asked herself the single consuming question, both in English and Spanish, to be fair. "Do I love him? *Lo amo?*" She cried when she thought of him growing up an orphan in a family that hated him, catering to rich Americans, living on the streets, hustling just to live. Sophia had marveled at the transformation in his intellect during the days leading up to Moncada, and then the time spent on the Isle of Pines, not just the improvement in his speech and writing, but his capacity for introspection. "*Lo amo?*" Not that it mattered, for he was most certainly dead.

PART THREE

*The Revolution Travels
a Rocky Road*

Arthur Gardner
American Ambassador to Cuba
Habana, Cuba

December 28, 1956

John Foster Dulles
Secretary of State
United States of America

Dear Mr. Secretary,

The *Servicio de Inteligencia Militar* (SIM) has been unable to spend adequate time on investigating the communist threat in the country due to the civil unrest posed by many groups in Cuba against the Batista regime. Thus, the *Buró Para Represión de las Actividades Comunistas* (BRAC) has been created under the tutelage of CIA Director Allen Dulles.

During my weekly canasta game with President Batista last week I was able to broach the troubling subject of the police invasion of the Haitian Embassy at the end of October. He apologized, but stated that tempers had flared due to the assassination the prior day of Colonel Blanco Rio at the Montmartre Nightclub. They were certain that those involved had taken refuge in the Embassy, but we will never know for sure, as they executed all ten suspects on the spot.

President Batista also assured me that the uprising in Santiago and the rebel landing led by Fidel Castro has been effectively stamped out. The military had engaged the rebels within days of their disembarkation and wiped them out. Fidel Castro was among the dead, thus, we should hear no more of him.

The major opposition to President Batista seems to come from lower-middle class University students. The *Directorio Revolucionario* (DR), under the leadership of José Echeverría, shut down the University on November 30th as a protest. The wealthier young men could care less about politics, and have been termed the *niños bitongos*, or spoiled brats, by the more radical students.

Sincerely,
Arthur Gardner

Eastern Cuba: The Oriente Province

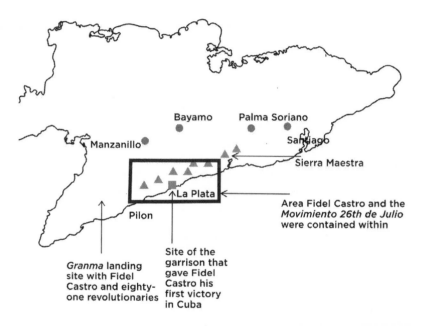

Bayamo

Palma Soriano

Manzanillo

Santiago

Sierra Maestra

La Plata

Pilon

Area Fidel Castro and the
Movimiento 26th de Julio
were contained within

Granma landing
site with Fidel
Castro and eighty-
one revolutionaries

Site of the
garrison that
gave Fidel
Castro his
first victory
in Cuba

7

January 7th, 1957, Sierra Maestra, southeastern Cuba

"The pork is good, my friend?" Eutimio squatted down next to Vicente, a broad smile creasing his narrow face. "Do you need some more honey and brandy?"

Vicente shook his head no, wanting the sweet sharp liquid, but already afraid that it was clouding his judgment sitting on a stomach that'd so often been empty of late. "Maybe later. You're kind to offer."

Fidel approached, the embers from the fire casting his face in shadow, darker patches where his beard had begun to grow. "Eutimio, you're a wonderful man. The kind of person this revolution is based upon. Without you…" Fidel shrugged his shoulders, "We'd all be dead or in prison being tortured by Batista's thugs."

Eutimio beamed and replied, "It's nothin', *señor*. We hear *muchas cosas buenas* about you from Guillermo and Crescencio. They say you want to improve our lives, make the land ours. I hear that you and your men pay for the food you eat and treat our women well. That ain't true of the *Guardias Rurales* who steal our food and rape our daughters."

"Tell me about the military garrison at La Plata," Fidel directed, his mind planning the first offensive of the *Movimiento 26ᵗʰ de Julio* since their return to Cuba over a month earlier. They'd had time to rest and recuperate, carry out some training exercises, and regain their strength while bolstering their numbers. Recruits had been sent up from Manzanillo with more rifles, explosives, and ammunition. To the eighteen survivors of the *Granma* landing, Fidel had added fifteen more men.

"I know little of the place, Señor Castro, but I do know where it is. Perhaps I find you a woman who has cooked or cleaned there?"

Eight days later, on January 15ᵗʰ, the guerrillas emerged from the tiny path through the jungle that'd been hewn for them by the peasant, Melquiades Elías, a friend of their guide, Eutimio. They'd just passed over a ridge that ran from the Sierra Maestra to the sea, a particularly rugged climb, and the men happily slipped out of their clothes and into the Magdalena River that splashed its way out of the mountains. There was one more hill of a smaller height to ascend, and then they crossed La Plata River to within striking distance of the fort there. A coast guard cutter was anchored in the harbor and appeared to be ferrying men to and from the land, thus, Fidel decided to hold off on the attack for another day to better determine the situation.

In the morning they moved within sight of the fort, which was currently under construction, the zinc roof of the new barracks shining in the bright sun. Partially dressed men emerged from their thatched-roof quarters to work on the new buildings. As the guerrillas descended from the hills to the dirt road that wound its way along the coast, they came upon two beekeepers who informed them there were about fifteen soldiers and sailors stationed at the fort, and also that the notorious overseer for the Laviti family, Chicho Osorio, was due to show up at any moment. The family had built an immense fiefdom in the area through violent means, and maintained it through brutal repression inflicted by thugs like Osorio. The beekeepers said the man passed on this road every day at this time. The sun was descending over the horizon when a man astride a donkey with a young boy riding behind him appeared on the road.

"Halt." Universo Sánchez stepped into the road with his rifle leveled. "In the name of the *Guardias Rurales.*"

"Mosquito," blustered the rotund man astride the ass. This was presumably the code word for safe passage, a most appropriate one for the place and time as a swarm of them had increased in numbers since dusk.

Fidel strode into the road with Vicente at his side. "Dismount," he ordered with a curt tone, "and come with us." Vicente took the reins of the two beasts and they moved safely off the road and out of sight.

"Who the hell is you?" the overseer demanded, his voice slurred with drink. "And what da'ya want?"

"I'm a colonel sent with direct orders to find out why the rebels haven't been caught and killed yet," Fidel replied sharply. "But the real question is…who are you and what're you doing on this road?"

"I'm Chicho Osorio, and I run the biz-nus of the Laviti family. If you want to remain an officer you'd best treat me with more respect." Food stains ran down the front of the man's shirt, and tobacco dotted the stubble of his chin.

"My orders are to investigate the soldiers at the garrison and determine whether or not they're in collusion with the rebel dogs. You seem a man of authority in these parts." Fidel turned away slightly to hide the smile he couldn't quite contain. "Tell me what you know of them."

"The sol-das are most def-in-lee not helping the guerilla pigs, but they do little else other than sit around their barracks and eat and drink," Chicho admitted, producing a bottle of rum from the pocket of his filthy white linen jacket. He took a long swig, smacked his lips, capped the bottle, and slid it back inside his pocket. "But I…" he patted his chest importantly, "can tell you what peasants around here are likely helpin' those traitorous pigs from Mexico." He proceeded to reel off the names of men that were sympathetic to the rebel cause, and proclaimed proudly those that remained loyal to Batista.

Fidel again had to muffle a chuckle at the thought of this man calling him a pig. "I've been in the woods trailing that damn Castro," he explained the reason for his unshaven face. "And once we find him, that'll be the end of it."

"I'm with you there," Chicho rejoined loudly, causing Vicente to cast a look in the direction of the fort not that far distant. "If I come upon that shit eater...I'll cut his *cojones* off and hang 'em 'round my neck for everyone to see. Same with that bandit Crescencio Pérez, but I wouldn't hang his wrinkled nut sack around my neck." Sensing disbelief, Chicho blustered, "I've already killed one of those Castro sons of bitches. It's he who sup-sup-sup, gave me these fine boots." The fat man stuck out his foot to show the finely crafted Mexican footwear that most of the original eighty-two aboard the *Granma* had worn.

Fidel ceased interrogating the man at this point, as the drunken fool had just signed his own death warrant. "We're going to do a surprise inspection in a few hours, and you'll be coming with us. We'll pretend you're our prisoner," he ordered, excusing himself to meet with his commanders, leaving the overseer under the watchful eye of Crescencio, the Cuban that Chicho had just claimed he'd castrate if given the chance.

On their approach to the fort, Chicho shared information about where the sentries would be posted, never guessing even though his hands were now tied behind him that he was actually in the hands of Fidel Castro and the guerrillas of the *Movimiento 26th de Julio*. They came to within forty yards of the fort around 2:30 a.m., a full moon lighting up the buildings that housed the soldiers. Vicente had been given the task of executing the overseer, Chicho, and was hanging back behind the others when Fidel signaled the attack with two quick bursts of his Thompson machine gun, the *rat-a-tat-tat* splitting the early morning air.

As soon as he heard these gunshots, Vicente took a deep breath, stepped up behind Chicho with a pistol, and shot the man behind the right ear, his head shattering with a sickening dull explosion. The crass overseer teetered for a long second, and then his legs went slack and his body slammed to the ground, the noise drowned out by the gunfire. Vicente stared at the lifeless corpse for a long ten seconds, the first man he'd ever killed. He'd fired at men at the Moncada Barracks, but didn't think he'd even come close to hitting his target. At the ambush of Alegría de Pío he'd shot a man in the leg from a distance, but this was different. Standing not two feet away, he'd put his pistol to the back of a man's head and pulled the trigger, the man's brains gleaming dully in the scant light as the bullet exited. Like Sophia had said, he was a "killer of men."

The attack was a three-pronged effort. Julio Díaz led a squad on the right side of the palm-thatched barracks, Fidel commanded the center assault, and Raul and Juan Almeida struck from the left. The soldiers rallied themselves rather quickly, returning fire and holding the guerillas at bay until Luis Crespo crept up to the barracks and set the roof on fire, one sailor flying out the door to be immediately shot in the chest and falling dead before he hit the ground. The rebels began to advance in a tightening grip upon the remaining soldiers, raining bullets into the hut from three angles, until cries of surrender were heard over the thunderous gunfire.

The victory gained them eight Springfield rifles and a Thompson submachine gun along with about 1,000 rounds of ammunition, cartridge belts, knives, and some food stores. Two soldiers had been killed, five wounded, and three additional men had been taken prisoner. Che treated the wounded enemy and then the rebels left them in the care of the other soldiers after setting fire to the four buildings in the compound, initiating a pattern of mercy that they'd follow throughout the revolution. Surprising to all, there had been no casualties among the rebels, and two hours after the start of the attack, they moved out towards Palma Mocha with a newfound confidence as fighters. They'd just won their first battle, carried new weapons, and had begun to believe that victory was possible.

The guerrillas trekked steadily north and then west to return to the Caracas Peak in the shadow of Pico Turquino. Eutimio had asked permission to return home to check on his family the day before the ambush, which was nearby, but gave them explicit directions on the course they were to follow, and promised to rejoin them soon. True to his word, he reappeared four days later, coming upon them in a coffee field at La Olla and bringing gifts of candy. Eutimio reported that the army was close, and they moved up into the steep hills of Caracas Peak, the elevation and terrain too difficult for the army's tanks. Thinking the enemy had been left far behind, Fidel felt comfortable enough to requisition a deserted wood cutter's hut with an abandoned stove outside and set a fire alight, the warmth—and hot food—being a comfort after their constant roaming.

Vicente was given the task of boiling the yucca root on the stove, a food even blander than plain potatoes, but luckily they'd liberated some salt and pepper from the garrison at La Plata. This was not enough to help with the meat portion of the meal, as five hutia had been slain, and then cooked upon spits, the four-pound rodents supplying protein for their bodies but little for the taste buds. After eating, Eutimio was sent out to scavenge food from the local inhabitants for the following day, and the men took time to clean their weapons, listening to revolutionary teachings from Che as they did so. He spoke of the history of class struggle, a topic beyond the intellectual capacity of most of them, and shocked them with the call to abolish all private property. It was his comment on the equality of women that sparked the biggest reaction.

"You can't be suggesting that women are the equal of men?" Ramiro Valdés interrupted Che's discourse.

"*Che*, Marx was quite clear on the topic," Che replied. "I believe he said 'anyone who knows anything of history knows that great social changes are impossible without feminine upheaval. Social progress can be measured exactly by the social position of the fair sex, the ugly ones included.'"

Fidel laughed abruptly, a barking, but genuine, if unfamiliar sound, from their leader. "I believe that women have a position in the change we hope to achieve. Hell, if it weren't for Celia, we'd all be dead now. But why does your fellow Marx have to emphasize that the ugly ones should be included?"

Che smiled, an impish look suggesting perhaps he'd found a hint of rum to go with his meal. "Don't underestimate the power of an ugly woman. *Che*, you've met my wife. What say you of her?"

This brought quiet to the group of men relaxed for the first time in quite a while, but suddenly tension returned, for it was not seemly to speak of another man's wife, and those that'd been in Mexico and met the woman could attest to the fact that she was not that attractive.

"She seemed a fine woman," Fidel gathered the nerve to say. "The type of person you could build a revolution around."

"*Che*, my wife is one of the ugliest women I've ever met," Che stated firmly. "And it's for this reason I married her. She'll always work harder than a pretty one, she aims to please me in every way possible, and the chances of her cheating on me are slim."

As they prepared to bed down with a warm meal in their bellies, Fidel, suddenly apprehensive, ordered them all to move several hundred yards further up the spine of the mountain, a shift that was met with grumbling. Vicente fell asleep wondering about the soundness of Che's argument, for the only woman in his life was Sophia, and he thought her the most beautiful person he'd ever seen. He was quite certain that Sophia, chewing the little finger of her hand, would not be happy with how Che spoke of woman, even if his claim was that they were crucial to the revolution. But that was as far as his thoughts got in that direction, for the image of Sophia chewing her pinky made him jealous, and he wondered what it would be like to nibble on her hand, her shoulder, and her neck.

In the morning, as the camp was waking from sleep, the men rising from their huddled spots and packing away their blankets, they heard the low rumble of airplanes approaching. Fidel gave a short whistle and raised his hand for the men to pause and hurry under cover. It was not unusual to hear planes out searching for them, and the men crouched down under the scrub trees of this higher altitude to avoid detection.

Suddenly a small spotter plane glided over the peak at their backs, flying low, and continued on down the mountain towards where the stove was and where they'd almost slept the night before. Following close behind was a squadron of five P-47's Thunderbolts, squat jug-shaped planes whose stubby wings were mounted with .50 caliber machine guns. The huge guns opened up as they passed overhead, the heavy bullets tearing apart the previous night's camp. Vicente gasped in disbelief, his ears so deafened by the noise he at first didn't hear the bombers coming in, Douglas B-26s supplied by the United States like the Thunderbolts, dropping their explosives and laying waste to what little was left of the encampment.

"Che!" Fidel said, looking downhill apprehensively as if expecting soldiers at any moment. "Take Chao with you and see if you can make contact with the forward guard down below. Don't bother trying to salvage anything. The rest of you, get your things and let's move out." In less than a minute the camp was emptied, the men melting into the forest.

Two days later, Vicente was on sentry duty, when Fidel came up behind him. "We escape death again," he said, squatting next to Vicente on a small ledge overlooking a valley. "Batista keeps sending planes, tanks, and men to extinguish us, yet at the same time, he's claiming we're all dead."

Vicente pondered the words, knowing that Fidel wasn't just making conversation; there was always a purpose to what he said. "It'd be important for the people of Cuba to know *estamos vivos* and are resisting the government," he commented.

"Not just Cuba, but the world needs to know we live," Fidel agreed. "We need to stop the United States from supplying the government with weapons to be used against us, and we need to gain sympathy from the rest of the world if we're to succeed."

"Maybe a story to be published in the newspapers?" Vicente ventured, following Fidel's lead.

Fidel stood and tossed a rock into the space below. "We need to invite a journalist to come witness that the leaders are alive and well, and that the rebellion continues actively."

"Who'd be *loco* enough to come into the Sierra for an interview?"

"Not just anybody. It has to be a foreign correspondent if we want the world to hear and believe the story. Preferably, this would be somebody from *The New York Times*."

Vicente spat on the ground. "It'd also be nice if we had some tanks and airplanes, but that's not likely."

Fidel laughed and slapped Vicente on the shoulder. "You don't believe it's possible, *compañero*?"

"I think it's difficult."

"That's why I sent Faustino to Havana last month. He's assuming command of the underground there, but the first order of business is to make inquiries and find a journalist willing to come to us."

Vicente stood and faced Fidel. "How do you plan on getting a journalist here?"

Later that day, Crescencio found himself guiding Vicente down out of the mountains on his journey to Havana. Vicente had been curious for some time about Crescencio, this older man with a perpetual smile on his face, a man treated with so much respect everywhere they ventured in this region of the Sierra Maestra. After passing a small cluster of four peasant huts, the inhabitants greeting Crescencio reverently, Vicente saw his opportunity. "You're treated like a king in these mountains."

Crescencio laughed and turned his head slightly to reply, his feet instinctively knowing the way. "I've taken what I wanted and done what I will, but the *gente de las montañas*, those that inhabit this region of the mountains always come first for me, and everybody knows this. It's I who have fought abuses by the *Guardias Rurales*, provided jobs farming and tending cattle, and it's I who dispense justice fairly."

"That's what they tell me," Vicente spoke cautiously. "But what I don't understand is, when you have such power and respect, raising yourself up hand over hand, rung by rung, why endanger all that you have to join us?"

There was silence for the next half hour, the only sound Vicente's ragged breathing, as he wasn't yet used to the elevation and exertion of hiking the rugged terrain, descending from a height of over 4,000 feet. When Vicente had given up on an answer, Crescencio spoke, breaking the stillness with a thoughtful response. "I've followed the path of Changó for my entire life. I've lived, as a man should. I've been so drunk I couldn't walk. I've fucked many women. I've fought and killed. But at some point I realized that I'd become the chief of an entire tribe of people, men and women who looked to me to fix their lives. I've done my best, but they're still hungry, poor, uneducated, often sick, and abused by the *Guardias Rurales*."

They both reflected quietly for a few minutes on the hardships of the average Cuban, much less the peasants of the Sierra Maestra. "And then the doctor's daughter visited me. Celia Sánchez. She grew up without a mother, always at her father's side, a girl who matured into a woman. From the earliest age she'd a heart the size of the mountains and loved everybody, poor and rich, ignorant and intelligent, healthy and sick, it didn't matter; all that she hated was injustice. She first came to speak to me several years ago asking me to join her fight against Batista." He shrugged, pausing, and Vicente saw a flicker of regret pass across his face. "But I was too caught up within myself at that time, and I refused her out of hand. Recently, Changó came to me and told me that my life was out of balance, and that I was meant to be more than just a pleasure seeker, but rather, a leader of *mi gente*, my people. As you know, after Changó hung himself and came back to kill the enemies of his people, he learned the art of diplomacy and leadership."

Vicente had first heard the stories of Changó, both as a mortal and as a god, from his grandmother, as she rocked in her chair, he sitting at her feet. As a mortal, Changó had been the most powerful king on earth and often rode the edge of immorality. One time he'd performed a sin so overbearing (stories vary as to what the sin actually was), he'd hung himself. But when his people needed him, he'd risen from death, and returned to save them from their enemies, becoming a god in the process.

"I hope to improve the lot of my people. Celia told me that many have tried to create real change, but that it would take a special man to fix Cuba's ills. This leader would have to be a true warrior to expel the current regime, in this case, Batista. But, this *caudillo*, he has not only to kick *los ricos* in the ass, for the rich shall never willingly turn over their wealth, but must at the same time keep the *Yanquí* beast at bay. This man would have to possess the qualities of Changó. He'd have to carry the double-edged axe of the warrior and speak with the silver tongue of the politician, yet his heart would have to beat in rhythm with the people. I think that Fidel is this man."

Vicente knew that if it weren't for Crescencio, the *Movimiento 26ᵗʰ de Julio* wouldn't have existed at all. It was he who'd put the word out to hide, feed, and protect the shattered rebel forces after the Alegría de Pío disaster. It was the peasant network established by their patriarch that found, guided, and reunited the various fragments of rebel groups, and now allowed them to elude the soldiers and to move about in the mountains without starving or being captured. Lost in his thoughts, he didn't see that Crescencio had stopped, and almost ran into him. The old man raised a hand, peering around the side of a tree, before motioning Vicente forward.

A Jeep was tucked into a small grove of banana trees with two people in the front seat. One was a striking woman in a zebra-patterned dress casually smoking a cigarette. A man sat cradling an M-1 rifle in the passenger seat, his face impassive behind dark sunglasses. They both got out, and the woman approached Crescencio and gave him a hug. He kissed her on the right cheek, his arms lingering slightly too long around her slender figure, making her smile and push him away in mock anger.

She turned to Vicente then, her eyes taking him in from head to foot. "I'm Celia Sánchez."

"Vicente Bolívar."

"I'll take you to Manzanillo and from there we'll find a way to get you to Havana and hopefully back with this journalist." She turned and raised her eyebrow at Crescencio. "You'll not be going with us?"

"If you're inviting me…" Crescencio replied good-humoredly, joking, but always with the small hope of success. *It never hurts to try*, he thought.

"I would, but the guerrillas require you in the mountains." Celia smiled brightly. "Fidel needs you more than I need you." She turned and climbed back into the driver's seat, gesturing to her companion toward the back and patting the front seat for Vicente to sit. "You're not like the others." She gave him a knowing look once they were on the way down the rough trail that couldn't be discerned by the naked eye, yet was here being used as a road. "You're more like Crescencio than the university boys up there with him. Almost as if you belong here." Most of the small rebel army was indeed made up of students from Havana University.

Vicente nodded. "I lived in Havana when I was very young, but then grew up in Matanzas with my grandmother. She told me many stories of my ancestors, many of whom lived their lives here in Oriente

Province, but I know as little of this terrain as any other man from Havana."

"The land is here." Celia put her hand over her heart, steering the Jeep with one hand, a little too casually for the comfort of Vicente on the rocky path. "And here." She touched her head lightly. "You're part of this place, whether or not you've been here before, I can sense it."

"And you?" Vicente asked. Crescencio hadn't been the first to sing the praise of this intellectual woman who'd masterminded the quite complicated and effective resistance movement in Bayamo, Manzanillo, and all of the smaller towns surrounding the Sierra Maestra. "How does an educated white woman fit into Pilón? Isn't that just a backwater?"

"My father didn't think much of Havana." She looked at him briefly with a small grin. "He's a country doctor at heart, so after he graduated from medical school, he came to Oriente, first Media Luna, and then Pilón. He believes that the salt of the earth live outside the shadows of cities. He was never one to believe that things like social standing, money, or education dictate the worth of an individual."

"But what brought you to revolution?"

Celia looked appraisingly at him. Nobody had ever asked her that, and she hesitated a few moments before answering. "I was brought up to care for people. My mother died when I was six. My father raised me. He's the most extraordinary man alive. He taught me compassion and respect. His patients, the *campesinos, cortadores de caña, y los pescadores* became my mother, filing through my house to see the doctor when they got a break from farming, cane cutting, and fishing. It's hard to explain the love that I have for these people."

"It's better than hate." Vicente thought back to his childhood when he'd been angry with everybody and everything, and it was only his grandmother who'd kept him from serious trouble.

Celia nodded, whether in agreement or just in acknowledgement of his words, it was tough to tell, before continuing, "I almost entered into a normal life, falling in love with an older boy when I was fifteen. But when he died suddenly of a rare blood clot…" Celia shrugged her shoulders. "When I'd finished mourning, it was as if the scales had dropped from my eyes. I saw the poverty all around and felt it when I looked at my father's patients, so many of them desperate and beholden to moneylenders and landlords. When Batista took power and brought in the American mobsters, it became too much to bear. My transformation from peaceful protest to more forceful resistance came when a girl that I was a godmother to was kidnapped by Batista's secret police. I later discovered that she was delivered to a casino in Havana to become a sex slave." Celia fingered the cross that hung around her neck on a chain, a medallion that had belonged to the girl. "She was ten years old." She hadn't ever spoken of this to anybody, and it was a relief to unburden her mind on this stranger next to her.

After a short drive they came to a farmhouse on the outskirts of Manzanillo where Vicente changed into the civilian clothes that Celia had brought him. An Oldsmobile was waiting to take him to Havana. The driver was an extremely thin man of about thirty who smoked the entire time and badgered Vicente about things he shouldn't have, places and people and events that were none of his business. He only stopped when Vicente pretended to doze off.

In reality, Vicente was visiting Sophia in one of his favorite memories. It was the day they'd gone to the beach in early August of 1955, near the end of the time he spent in Havana after prison and before exile. They'd packed a picnic lunch of braised pork shoulder sandwiches that included ham, onion, pickles, cheese, and mustard on homemade bread, with sides of corn-on-the-cob and potato salad. Vicente had borrowed a car from a resistance fighter, insinuating that it was needed for *Movimiento 26th de Julio* business, and off they'd gone, driving the sixty-some miles to the narrow spit of land, ten miles long and no wider than a half mile at any point, that was home to Varadero Beach, just past Vicente's childhood home of Matanzas.

When Sophia had changed into her bathing suit, a white lined cotton one-piece with a zipper in the back to pull the fabric tight, Vicente had spent the next hour looking at anything but her, and then the rest of the day looking at nothing but her. As it turned out, Sophia was recognized by one of her uncle's associates, who confronted her the next day about whom she'd been with. Two days later, Vicente had awoken in the trunk of an Oldsmobile, barely escaping with his life.

He wasn't sure if he'd been kidnapped by thugs working for her uncle, or the SIM on the orders of Batista, or maybe a combination of the two. Either way, Vicente fled into exile in Mexico soon after. His last thought before he fell into a fitful sleep was how good it would be to see Sophia again.

The next morning, Vicente was dropped off at Faustino Pérez's apartment in Havana and found that Frank País was also there. Soon after Vicente arrived, Armando Hart and his brother, Enrique, pulled up in a boat-like Pontiac to take them all to a meeting in the Vedado district where they met with a dynamic young man, José Antonio Echeverría.

"Faustino will be assuming the leadership of the *Movimiento 26th de Julio* in Havana for the time being at least," País spoke quietly, a reserve somewhat at odds with the intensity in his eyes. Vicente had heard that he played the piano beautifully, and that he wrote moving poetry, but had put these pursuits on hold to become leader of the *Llano*, which was all of Cuba outside of the Sierra Maestra. "He'll speak on all matters for Fidel as well as myself."

Echeverría nodded at Faustino. "We know each other. He's a good choice to represent your party here." At twenty-five, Echeverría had been an active student leader before Batista's coup, and had headed the university student opposition afterwards. He was almost movie-idol handsome, with jet-black hair brushed carefully back to reveal a strong forehead—his sharp cheeks readily revealing a broad smile. "Armando has joined you in Santiago?"

"For now. We're having to rebuild our network after the uprising in November." País was still raw over the loss of so many good men killed in support of Fidel's disastrous invasion, the most troubling that of his close friend, Pepito.

"I'm sorry we were unable to do more. We had to go underground after Colonel Blanco was killed." He discreetly omitted that it was his organization that had pulled off this assassination. "But things have quieted down and we're planning a fresh action and would welcome your aid and support." Echeverría looked at Vicente, unsure how much he should share in front of this man he didn't know.

Faustino caught the glance and interjected. "Vicente has been with

Fidel since before Moncada, which he fought in, and went to prison along with the other veterans of that attack. He went into exile in Mexico and returned aboard the *Granma*. He's here on a mission for Fidel."

"My compliments on your loyalty. From Moncada? And one of the eighty-two?" He bowed his head in respect, before continuing with the shocking undertaking the DR was about to engage in. "We're planning to assassinate Batista, take the Presidential Palace, and spark an uprising of the people."

"What's your timetable?" País asked in a low voice.

"Within the month."

"And what do you want from us?"

Echeverría chose his words carefully. "Your backing in our uprising. Any intelligence, manpower, and weapons that you can spare."

"The *Movimiento 26th de Julio* is weak in the capital right now." País ducked his head, as if in apology. "We've focused thus far on developing our strength in the eastern part of the island."

"I understand," Echeverría replied.

"I will bring your request to our National Directorate. We meet next week."

Echeverría stood, indicating the meeting was over. "Thank you. I'll wait to hear."

The effort to find a foreign journalist made a significant leap a few days later, just after the tribunal of Faustino, País, and Vicente had confirmed the recommendation of Javier Pazos, the son of a local economist, to join the guerrillas in the mountains. Faustino then asked Javier his thoughts on founding a school to teach revolutionary philosophy, history, and tactics to be named after Ñico Lopez, who'd been killed at Alegría de Pío. This idea was preliminary, even controversial, as the most basic of details—where it would meet and who would teach the classes—still had to be worked out.

"It's difficult right now to pull people into the movement," Javier said cautiously. "Many don't know whether Fidel is dead or alive."

"I've been searching for a journalist willing to travel into the

Sierra Maestra to prove he is alive, but local journalists fear for their lives and foreign correspondents don't want their credentials revoked," Faustino replied.

"A foreign journalist?" Javier posed the question with a tinge of excitement that caused his voice to quiver. "My father is a good friend of Ruby Phillips, the correspondent for *The New York Times* here in Havana. I'm sure that he can get us an audience with her."

The next night there was a clandestine meeting at the Bacardi Company. Ruby was hesitant to be of assistance, not wanting to ruin her relationship with the President of the country, but she told them that there was a very eminent *Times* writer arriving in Havana soon for a vacation with his wife. "Herbert Matthews is the kind of guy who will jump at the chance to write this story. As he's not based here in Cuba, he'll not face the same repercussions from the government that other journalists would."

Later that night, Vicente had his first free moments since arriving in Havana five days earlier, and called Sophia, whose voice was oddly flat. They agreed to meet at La B del M, a bohemian bar in Old Havana. There was a trio playing music, two men on guitars and one with maracas, all of them blending their voices into a low melody, a suitable backdrop for conversation and dining. Sophia wore a white off-the-shoulder dress with a wide cummerbund cinched tight at her waist. On her head a white chimney pot hat with purple orchids perched jauntily, bringing color to the outfit.

"I thought you were dead," she accused Vicente in a displeased voice. They sat against the wall hung with numerous pictures of the famous people who'd patronized the place over the years. "When the papers reported that the invasion force had been wiped out, a piece of me crumbled and disappeared. For two months and four days I thought I'd lost you forever," she said, her voice rising until she suddenly reached across the table and slapped him, hard. Vicente sat back abruptly, one hand rubbing his cheek.

"I guess I deserved that," he said finally. "But when you work for the revolution, your job is…"

"Oh, don't give me that tired crap, Vicente." Her voice was weary. "You could've gotten word to me somehow."

"It's been a very difficult time." Vicente acknowledged gravely. He understood that she was irritated, but would it have been better if he were dead? "Many of us died in an ambush soon after landing in Cuba, but a core group of us survived with the help of the local peasants, and we're now building our strength in the Sierra."

"Why're you here?"

"To prove that the *Movimiento 26th de Julio* survives." Vicente saw no harm in telling Sophia this. She was hardly one caught up in his world.

"And have you had any luck?"

"Yes. There's a journalist arriving soon from New York that I hope will return with me to the Sierra Maestra."

"I still can't believe you waited so long to reach out to me. Not even a letter."

"I'm sorry, but I've been very busy. I shouldn't even be here now."

"And why's that?"

Vicente looked around the small bar. He used to come here to buy a sandwich and a beer. A group of locals huddled over their drinks listening to the music, while a few American sailors prepped themselves for a long night on the town with shots of cheap rum. Nobody, it appeared, was paying attention to the quiet couple in the shadows. "The Bureau of Investigation would be extremely happy to find me here, that's one reason. I'm sure that they'd ask questions of me that might jeopardize my whole mission—and in ways that obliged me to answer."

Sophia softened, realizing he was putting his safety in jeopardy. "The Hotel Ambos Mundos is right down the street. We can buy some rum and sit in the room and talk without fear."

"I've no money." Vicente shrugged his shoulders. "As a matter of fact, though I can afford these drinks, I was going to find an excuse to avoid a meal, even if you were hungry, which I was hoping you were not." The money that Fidel had passed to him in the mountains was now gone, and Vicente was living on the generosity of the *Llano* resistance fighters.

"I have money." Vicente looked at her with one thought burning in his mind, but that terrible thought stayed unexpressed behind immobile lips. Sophia laughed at his expression. "Don't worry, I told you I'd given up earning money from…dancing. I make money the old fashioned way, corruption. My uncle has gotten me a job working for the casino, something to do with the accounting, that I don't really do, but receive a paycheck nonetheless." She threw some money on the table and stood, grasping his hand. "Let's go. I can't imagine you've much need for pesos in the jungle."

They bought a bottle of rum and some Coca-Cola, and then Sophia checked them into a room, sneaking Vicente in a back door. There was certainly no need to flaunt that this beautiful white socialite was shacking up with a sun-hardened mulatto in a cheap suit. The hotel was a five-story brick affair and their room was on the fourth floor. They avoided the Otis screen-cage elevator and chose the stairs instead, passing by a marble basin of water with turtles sleeping in it.

"What do the people in Havana say of our guerrilla movement in the Sierra?" Vicente asked as soon as they had settled into the two straight-backed wooden chairs in the room. The second drink of the night had been enough to loosen his tongue.

"It depends on who you're talking to, I suppose. If you talk to the government, then you don't exist. I guess that's why you're here. If you speak with the owners of the hotels, clubs, and casinos…well, they won't hear of any such nonsense. As far as my uncle and his cronies are concerned, Oriente Province is a different country and a world away from Havana. The tourists don't give a hoot unless you interrupt their party. Yet there are some people who do speak of a group of survivors in the mountains defying the soldiers." She poured them both another half-cup of rum and added a splash of Coca-Cola. "Cuba Libre," she said, raising her cup in toast.

Vicente tapped her cup with his own, taking a small sip of the sweet drink. "And who are these people and what do they say? And how do you know them?"

Sophia looked mischievously at him, her fingers brushing his arm as they sat on either end of the tiny business desk. "You're not the only one in this room who is part of the resistance."

He shook his head in confusion. "Are you saying that you've become one of the dissidents?"

"More than that. I've become a courier for the DR, a student group planning a series of protests and strikes to bring the government to a standstill."

"The Revolutionary Directorate? You're working with José Echeverría?"

"You know him?" Sophia realized she'd grown slightly tipsy, and that perhaps she was sharing too much confidential information, but was he not also a revolutionary with the same aim and purpose? "He's such a charming young man. They plan to bring the government to its knees by non-violent means, and replace Batista with a duly-elected president."

Vicente snorted involuntarily. "And what's it that you do for this charming man?"

Sophia chose to ignore the barbed suggestion to the question, eager to share her own importance. "Everybody knows me from Lansky all the way down to the floor men, and as a woman, I'm practically invisible. Many government officials, high profile police, and army officers frequent the Montmartre, and I pass along the intelligence that I overhear."

"I don't suppose you shared with Echeverría that Blanco was going to be at the Montmartre Nightclub last October?" Vicente realized instantly that he'd said too much, but his worry for this woman he loved overcame his caution.

"Blanco? The secret service chief that was assassinated...." Her eyes widened as realization kicked in.

"Look, Sophia, I'm not opposed to the DR. I met Echeverría earlier today, and he certainly has liberty for Cuba at the front of his mind. And yes, he's a terribly engaging man. But don't for a second think that you're not in danger and that the agenda of the DR is anything but a violent overthrow of the government, the same as the *Movimiento 26th de Julio*. Our path is to the same destination—if perhaps by taking a slightly different route, but Fidel and Echeverría agree on one thing: the insurrection is going to be violent, bloody, and will not end in a week or a month."

The moment was ruined, and although they managed to work the conversation back to more pleasant topics, they both realized they might've overstepped the boundaries of what should be said. Once secrets are openly shared, passions tend to take a back seat. Vicente's restless sleep caused him to rise before the sun came up. He left her a note that he'd call before returning to the mountains, not realizing that this wasn't a promise he'd be able to keep.

8

February 9th, 1957, The Sierra Maestra near Caracas Peak

Fidel and Almeida were discussing plans over a cup of coffee when a new recruit from Havana approached wearing a black bowler, a sure sign he was fresh from the city where this was all the rage. With him was a farmer who carried two sacks of grain, one slung over each brawny shoulder.

"What is it?" Fidel demanded harshly, perhaps more so than he intended.

"This man, sir, this man says that the valley is filled with soldiers."

Fidel turned to the farmer who held his stare without flinching. "And who are you and what bullshit do you bring?"

"I'm Adrian Pérez, and I bring no *mierda*. I come to tell you that there are a great many soldiers massing in the valley below. I also saw the man, Eutimio, who is your *amigo* and guide."

"Can you show me?" Fidel was less concerned about the proximity of the soldiers than the presence of Eutimio with them. He'd recently begun to suspect that their peasant guide had turned traitor.

About a half hour later, after they'd covered nearly four kilometers, the farmer led him out of the scrub to a rock outcropping. From this vantage point, Fidel was able to spot the buzz of activity in the valley below clearly through the scope of his rifle. Hundreds of *casquitos*, or little helmets, as the rebels had taken to calling the government soldiers, were forming to march into the hills directly towards the guerilla encampment. He could clearly see Eutimio speaking with an officer and gesturing up the mountain.

Once back at camp, he thanked the *campesino* for his information, and then broke the rebels into two groups, one under the leadership of Almeida and the other with him. As they were leaving, Ciro reported that Eutimio was leading the soldiers up the rocky terrain towards them. "We can't be bothered with that now," Fidel said. The man was already dead to him, and another piece of Fidel's humanity stripped away. There were so few people he was able to trust in his life, and this only added to his growing cynicism. "There will be a day of reckoning with that traitor, just not today."

The two groups of about fifteen men split off in separate directions and withdrew further into the mountains to escape the approaching soldiers. Four days later they reunited as planned at the rendezvous point, *El Lomón,* a mountain peak in the western part of the Sierra Maestra. From there they hiked to *Los Chorros*, the farm owned by Epifánio Diaz, who had two sons marching with the guerrillas. They arrived as the sun was sinking over the horizon and made a hasty camp using what little light was left.

It was here that the first National Directorate meeting of the *Movimiento 26th de Julio* was to be held, an important moment and one for which Fidel had long waited. The farm was on the outskirts of the Sierra Maestra, making it accessible to members of the *Llano*, the urban guerilla organization whose leaders had traveled to meet with Fidel and his top officers. Fidel had received a message from Vicente that he was also bringing a correspondent from *The New York Times* to interview him here quite soon.

In the morning Fidel was up with the sunrise, leaving the camp in the trees to cross a field to the farm when he came upon Celia Sánchez and Frank País. The two had just arrived in the back seat of a ramshackle Ford, their driver a bold volunteer peasant who had driven the borrowed car through several checkpoints with a wedding cake carefully posed in the seat beside him, claiming he was shuttling people in for his sister's wedding. Fidel had met País several times in Mexico, but never Celia, and he was instantly smitten. She wasn't beautiful in the way his wife Mirta had been, or a ravishing feline as Naty was, no, Celia Sánchez possessed an artistry that painted itself from the inside out. He could feel her passion straightaway, and sensed quite quickly that she might be the piece missing thus far from his life.

"So, you are Celia."

"And you are Fidel." It was as if there was no more to be said. She knew this man almost as if they'd grown up together.

Raúl Castro broke the spell, approaching with a hearty greeting for País and then introductions to Celia, who'd packed a box of cigars as well as ham, candy, and other delicacies, which they shared with the rest of the guerrillas before going off to a cane field for a picnic lunch. Afterwards, Raúl took País to review the men and speak with them of tactics and strategy.

Fidel and Celia strolled through the cane field into the forest and along a stream, talking of many things other than revolution. He talked of his mother and she of her father, avoiding the cheerless subjects of her mother dead at a young age, and his father recently deceased, though it was true his father had been emotionally absent from him even when Fidel had been a young boy. Her house had been located on a sugar plantation in the small town of Pilón, while Fidel grew up in similar circumstances in the comparable town of Birán. Within each of them burned the indignation of a Cuba that was being abused by a few people at the expense of many. They spent the day together, sharing a festive chicken stewed all day in a pot by the farmer Diaz for dinner, talking, talking, and then in the early morning hours in a small lean-to—and no surprise to either of them—making love.

Vicente arrived at the farm with Herbert Matthews of *The New York Times* at sunrise on the morning of February 17th, having completed the final leg of the journey hiking in the dark. A man was sent to the guerrilla camp to inform Fidel that they'd arrived. A message soon came back claiming Fidel was at another camp and would arrive in a few hours, giving them a chance to grab what sleep they could. Vicente smiled at the news, knowing there was no "other" camp, and that this suggestion that they had multiple posts was meant to impress Matthews. This fiction of the two camps was only the first act of a well-planned show of smoke and mirrors that Fidel would present to this American journalist during his stay. At eight in the morning, Almeida came down to get them.

Fidel opened a box of brand new Habaneros as soon as introductions were made, and offered one to Matthews, cutting the end off with a knife he took from his belt. He then pulled a Zippo from his pocket and lit both their cigars, taking several luxurious puffs. The two men made small talk about the trip from Havana and their mutual friend Ernest Hemingway, before getting down to business.

They talked for hours, smoking cigars, with Fidel waxing eloquently about the guerrilla movement, indicating that while the soldiers were massed in columns of 200, his men worked in groups of ten to forty, failing to mention that there was only the one such group, and it was currently comprised of just thirty rebels. He had the men march past in formation, and then they changed shirts and marched past again, creating the image of an incredibly lively and busy camp of hundreds of fit, well-equipped men. He talked of regularly defeating the Batista troops, even though their only triumph to date had been the rout of the tiny garrison of La Plata.

Once the interview was over, a driver took Matthews away and the National Directorate of the *Movimiento 26th de Julio* convened to map their strategy going forward. Fidel and Raúl represented the Sierra; País, Armando Hart, and Haydée Santamaría spoke for Santiago; Celia operated out of Manzanillo; and Faustino Pérez as the new leader in Havana.

Fidel lay his main agenda on the table with his opening statement, "Every part of the movement is here to accommodate the Sierra. The *Llano* should spend their time recruiting new guerrillas to join us in our armed fight, as well as raising money to supply us with weapons and other necessities for our struggle."

País was the only one to put up nominal resistance to this. "In Santiago we have the full support of the people. If we have the weapons and manpower, I think we'd be able to take control of the city in two years."

"The Sierra is the face of the revolution." Fidel strode in circles around the forest glen where they were meeting. "We're the magnet for money sent by those in exile, and men will migrate to us like bits of steel. Without us, there's no revolution. We've thirty men now and are a thorn in the side of the soldiers. Give me a hundred armed men and we'll control the mountains so that General Tabernilla is afraid to send troops into the hills for fear of their destruction. Once this journalist's article comes out in *The New York Times*, the world will know who we are and what we're fighting for, and people and money will flow to the Sierra."

Nobody argued with Fidel for long, and it was agreed that the *Llano* would work to supply the Sierra with men and weapons. Faustino then broached the subject of the palace assassination attempt that Echeverría was organizing in coordination with the Havana students. "There's no date set, but the plans are in motion, and they hope to carry their action out within the month."

"Their plan is to take control of the Palace when Batista is in residence and kill him?" Fidel lit another cigar, the smoke keeping the mosquitos at bay.

"That's how I understand it." Faustino looked at País, who nodded his agreement. "They're looking for the support of our underground in the attack."

"Last October they carried out an assassination on Blanco at the Montmartre." Fidel paused and looked up at the darkening clouds. "To slay Batista will only result in his replacement, probably by General Tabernilla. It's not the man we need to defeat, but the army and the entity that it represents." He didn't reveal his true purpose in denying aid to the DR in its proposed attack on Batista, which was that he feared Echeverría's growing popularity, which rivaled his own. Victory through assassination would put him in a position to dictate the future of Cuba if it were successful, while Fidel would be left in the mountains of eastern Cuba.

"I'll tell Echeverría that we're unable to support his efforts."

Fidel turned and glared at Faustino. "You'll tell him that we don't agree with his tactics and that we choose not to participate in a hapless endeavor with no positive outcome possible."

"And the idea of opening a second front in the Escambray Mountains?" Faustino asked, having known that Fidel would never agree to his organization playing second fiddle to a perhaps spectacular assassination. No fool, he'd presented that piece of business first, and he was now getting to what he really wanted.

"What exactly is your concept?"

"I propose we open a second front in Las Villas Province that can be supplied more easily by the underground in Havana, creating a nuisance on the western side of the island, and thus, making the army further dilute its forces elsewhere."

"That would also decrease the supply of men and weapons to the Sierra Maestra, would it not?" Fidel puffed reflectively upon the cigar. "Which, I believe, we've already decided is our primary objective?"

They were interrupted at this point by Ciro Frias who was standing guard about fifty meters away along with four others. "*Comandante,*" he said approaching the group and addressing Fidel. "A man has come up from the farm to say Eutimio has arrived."

Fidel blew a smoke ring and watched it grow larger and waft away. "Have Mario go retrieve him. You and Fajardo intercept them on the way and search him for weapons and then bring him to us."

Mario was a peasant recruit who knew Eutimio well. He was unaware that Eutimio had broken their trust, and he greeted his friend effusively, and they were soon on their way back up the hill. Part way to the camp they came upon Ciro, who greeted Eutimio with a huge hug, closing his arms around the smaller man in a vise. Fajardo stepped out from behind a tree holding a Thompson machine gun, the short deadly barrel and film canister size roll of ammunition disconcerting to the traitor at such a short distance. Ciro frisked him, finding no weapons, but taped to his chest under his shirt was an official looking envelope.

"Don't open that, I beg of you," Eutimio said, his hands now bound behind his back.

"I won't," Ciro replied. "But I'm sure Fidel will." They marched him back to the meeting to deliver the prisoner and the envelope, which turned out to contain a pass allowing Eutimio safe conduct through the army patrols. Colonel Alberto Del Rio Chaviano, the commander in charge of the army's Sierra operation, had personally signed the document.

Fidel read the script aloud and interrogated the traitor, discovering he'd been offered a farm as well as the $10,000 reward if his betrayal led to the capture or death of Fidel. The first trial of the Sierra was convened, with all present, to decide upon the appropriate punishment for this Judas in their midst. "How do you plead?" Fidel for once had the opportunity to act as the prosecuting attorney.

"I know that my life is forfeit and that what I've done is *mierda* and that you have no choice but to kill me. I only ask that you take care of my children." The man who had been their friend and apostate stood simply in front of them. He didn't cry and ask for forgiveness.

As the dusk started to roll into the mountains on the crest of black thunderclouds, the leaders decided that there was no point in waiting, that a bullet to the head would be the most merciful end. Eutimio was pulled to his feet and placed with his back against a tree. *Who would pull the trigger?* Vicente thought back to the overseer he'd executed at the start of the battle of La Plata and hoped that the job would not be his once again. Killing a defenseless person at close range was bad enough, but this was different. The man had been their friend. It'd be much easier if he'd acted the coward, but instead he accepted his fate. The man was just a poor peasant who'd been lured into corruption and betrayal by the promise of his own farm and money, more money than he could even comprehend. The time dragged slowly by, until finally, Che Guevara stood and walked over to Eutimio as lightning in the hills behind them illuminated the scene. Che raised a pistol to the man's ear and pulled the trigger at the same time as a tremendous clap of thunder echoed through the mountains, bringing on its heels a torrential downpour of rain, the men leaving the executed turncoat to return to the camp with bile in their throats and sadness in their souls.

That rain lasted for the next ten days before finally breaking on the eleventh day. It was hard to march as the small waterfalls cascading down from the mountain paths forced them to change direction time and time again. The rebel band had been in a dismal mood since the execution of Eutimio, but today the first bright news in quite a while had arrived. A courier had delivered three copies of *The New York Times* article by Herbert Matthews.

The motley collection of bedraggled men gathered in a clearing so that Fidel could translate the pertinent pieces into Spanish. Most of them were barely dressed, as they were taking the first opportunity in more than a week to dry their soaked clothes and boots. They were thin to the point of being emaciated, unshaven, and exhausted from the weather and marching. Fidel still feared that the army would find them if they stayed in one place, and thus they moved every day to a new location, never having the time to build any sort of shelter. The stop and the sun invoked old habits, however, and many set to cleaning their guns as they listened.

Fidel began by sharing the date, Sunday, February 24th, that the article had been in the newspaper, before reading the headline, "Castro Is Still Alive and Still Fighting in Mountains." Camilo whistled loudly and Almeida added a whoop of encouragement. This one headline would accomplish the task of disproving the government rumor that Fidel was dead and the revolution wiped out with him.

Fidel smiled at his *comandantes* before turning back to the story. "Fidel Castro, the rebel leader of Cuba's youth, is alive and fighting hard and successfully in the rugged, almost impenetrable Sierra Maestra at the southern tip of the island. President Fulgencio Batista has the cream of his Army around the area, but the Army men are fighting a thus-far losing battle to destroy the most dangerous enemy General Batista has yet faced in a long and adventurous career as a Cuban leader and dictator." The men broke into louder cheers to hear themselves referred to as dangerous.

"Havana does not and cannot know that thousands of men and women are heart and soul with Fidel Castro and the new deal for which they think he stands." Fidel paused to let the words sink in.

"That is the problem with narcissistic and fascist dictators!" Che chimed in. "*Che*, they can never understand when they're hated." Che had finally managed to light the damp tobacco in his pipe. "If the people support us, then we've won the revolution."

Fidel nodded his agreement. "Juan, you got your name in the newspaper," he said, skimming ahead. "The captain of this troop was a stocky Negro with a black beard and mustache, a ready, brilliant smile and a willingness for publicity. Of all I met, only he wanted his name mentioned—Juan Almeida, one of the eighty-two."

"Of course he wanted his name mentioned. He thinks he's a movie star now." Ciro laughed.

Almeida flashed that wide smile, but then grew serious. "I just wanted my family to know I was still alive."

The men fell silent at a thought common to them all, and Fidel took the moment to continue. "As the story unfolded of how he had at first gathered the few remnants of the eighty-two around him; kept the Government troops at bay while youths came in from other parts of Oriente as General Batista's counter-terrorism aroused them; got arms and supplies and then began the series of raids and counter-attacks of guerrilla warfare, one got the feeling that he is now invincible. Perhaps he isn't, but that is the faith he inspires in his followers." Fidel looked around at the small group of malnourished and fatigued rebels and grinned, repeating the most important word, "Invincible."

He finished up with Matthews quoting him, "Batista has 3,000 men in the field against us. I will not tell you how many we have, for obvious reasons. He works in columns of 200; we in groups of ten to forty, and we are winning. It is a battle against time and time is on our side."

Vicente interrupted the silence, "Did you forget to mention that we have only one group?"

* * *

Sophia was naked; her arms stretched high above her head, bound at the wrists by a rope drawn tight over a rafter. Her eyes had been taped shut and a rag reeking of cleaning fluid stuffed into her mouth, her own hoarse breathing the only noise she could hear. She'd no idea how long she'd been here. Rolando Masferrer, Batista's thuggish enforcer, had been waiting in the lobby of the Nacional when she had gone for a walk three days after the Palace attack. The bellboy had delivered a message from Joe Westbrook the night of the attempted assassination, warning Sophia to keep a low profile, but she couldn't bear being alone.

After several days of being cooped up in her room, she'd pulled on a floppy hat, donned sunglasses, and was exiting the hotel when Masferrer had approached her from behind and guided her wordlessly but forcefully into an idling sedan before she was even aware of what was happening. As they'd driven down the street, Sophia was still rationalizing that she'd be able to talk her way out of this. The man refused to tell her what it was all about, only that he'd some questions for her. They pulled in behind an abandoned warehouse building down by the port. Masferrer stepped from the car, extended his hand to help her out, and then led her into the building. At one point it'd been a repository for sugar to be loaded onto ships, but now was empty and cavernous. He'd unlocked a door in a corner of the vast room and she'd stepped into a dimly lit office with a desk and several chairs.

"*Sentarse*," he said, pointing at a chair. He took his jacket off and hung it on a hook before sitting across from her at the desk. She, of course, had heard the rumors about this man who'd rebelled against Machado, fought in the Spanish Civil War, and once opposed Batista's coup. Masferrer was a survivor though, and when he'd realized that Batista was here to stay, he'd become a staunch supporter. He was a senator, newspaper publisher, and a thug enforcer for the dictator. He'd developed a secret police force, *Los Tigres*, to defend Batista. This group was notorious for its bloody interrogations, torture, and butchery.

"*Cuál fue su participación en el ataque del Palacio?*" When Sophia didn't reply, Masferrer leaned forward and brushed a curl back from her face. "Perhaps I should speak in English? What was your involvement in the Palace attack?" The questions had been civil at first. "How do you know José Antonio Echeverría?" After Sophia had feigned ignorance to question after question, Masferrer had hit her, an open-handed shot to the side of the head that knocked her from the chair, the floor rushing up to deliver a second blow. Sophia lay on the floor stunned that this nattily dressed man with the broad face and wide smile of a Texas rancher had just struck her a vicious blow. There was a musty smell to the concrete that reminded Sophia of the garage in the home her parents had bought in Miami right before they died.

The plan had been minutely detailed, and might have enjoyed success, all but for the cowardly nature of man and the unfortunate placement of an elevator on the wrong floor at the wrong time. Echeverría had arrived at the radio station CMQ at precisely 3:14 on the afternoon of March 13th, and entered the building with ten other students, while a group of five guarded the door. They subdued the employees without violence, and Héctor and Floreal took over the job of radio announcers, reading a supposedly official communication from the general staff of the government that an attack was taking place at the Palace. They went on to claim that an uprising had occurred at Camp Columbia by junior officers and soldiers, and that General Tabernilla had been placed under arrest. After a break for commercial about Norwegian cod, cigarettes, shoes, and chocolate, the announcers had returned to report that the President of the Federation of University Students would be making a statement about the rebellion at the Palace. Echeverria read from a scripted speech: "The dictator Fulgencio Batista has just met revolutionary justice. The gunfire that extinguished the bloody life of the tyrant may still be heard around the Presidential Palace. It is we, the Revolutionary Directorate, the armed hand of the Cuban Revolution who has accomplished the final blow against this shameful regime still twisting in its own agony."

Sophia had been privy to the planning of this strike at Batista and had tuned into CMQ safely in her room. This nightmare was the result. Masferrer came around the small table and picked her up from the floor while his two henchmen watched impassively. He held her by the throat with one hand and slapped her head back and forth with the other. "Give me names and I'll let you go." There was blood in her mouth, a taste of iron that she'd never known. Her eyes were so teary that everything was but a blur, or was that because her brain was retreating into mute terror? Either way, she didn't reply, whether heroically or confusedly, she wasn't sure.

Masferrer stopped buffeting her skull, holding her limp figure aloft on her toes for all of twenty seconds, waiting an answer that was not forthcoming quickly enough. With a snarl he hurled her forward over the table, ripping her dress from her body like wrapping paper from a package. In an obviously well-practiced move the two thugs by the door quickly moved in, tying her hands in a slipknot rope attached to the two corners of the table so that she was unable to turn around or fight back in any way. And then he raped her while she screamed and cried, the fear, loathing, humiliation, terror, and pain all wrapping itself into a quivering ball of rage that was the only thing that allowed her to survive until he was done.

The attack on the Palace that the radio station was announcing began one minute after the announcers claimed it was already over. Two cars and a red truck with "FAST DELIVERY" written on the side pulled up in front of the Palace. Carlos Gutierrez Menoyo led the charge on the guards at the main gate, splaying bursts of machine gun fire from his Thompson. Nine others, comprising the advance commando unit, spilled out of the cars and were closely followed by forty more men from the truck. The sentries posted outside went down under a hail of bullets, and the men gained entrance, flooding into the Palace. Unknown to the attackers, many of their supporting force had backed out, choosing life over honor. Of the hundred men whose role had been to control the streets with gunfire, only fifty showed up. Other rebels whose task was to deliver the three .30 caliber machine guns and the one .50 caliber failed to do so.

Soldiers from the third floor began sweeping the street with heavy fire, the delivery truck being peppered with bullets and stragglers to the attack falling under the heavy barrage. As the advance commando unit entered the first floor they were temporarily slowed by a sergeant firing steadily from behind a marble column. Menoyo was able to drop him with a burst from the Thompson, and the force moved to the stairs. The Palace was three stories high, with the second floor having an interior balcony overlooking the first, and this landing area was now filled with soldiers directing a fusillade into the students storming up the steps. The first group reached the top of the stairs, leaving many of their friends mortally wounded behind them. They turned to the left and down the Hall of Mirrors to where Batista's office lay. They had been meticulous in their planning and knew that he'd be present at that hour. Menoyo tossed a grenade through the open

door, waited for the ensuing explosion, and then the five of them crowded
through the gaping entrance, blasting everything in front of them. When
the smoke cleared, they realized that neither of the dead men on the floor
were Batista.

Unbeknownst to the rebels and in a cruel twist of fate, Batista had
just been on the second floor, but for some reason decided to work in his
small office on the third floor, and had recently taken the elevator back up.
The only way to access the top floor living quarters was by this lift, which
at the time of the assault was sitting on the top floor, out of reach of the
commandos. The DR commandos had no way to reach their prey, and most
of them died, shot like fish in a barrel without even the chance to surrender.

Masferrer zipped his pants, his cowboy hat still atop his head. He
walked around the front of the table and dropped several pictures of
Sophia with members of the DR, and even one of her with Vicente.
Her arms were still stretched wide and her face was pressed into the
wooden surface. Masferrer grabbed her by the hair, jerking her head
up so that she could see the photographs.

"We've been watching you. We know that you've been delivering
messages for the DR. Give us something and we we'll let you live.
Keep silent, and you will have a long stay with us." The two goons came
forward, releasing her temporarily only to tie her hands together, a
loop of rope thrown over the rafter, with Sophia forced up onto tiptoe
with arms high. It was then that they taped her eyes and gagged her
before leaving her alone, or alone as far as she could tell.

Sophia awoke to a shift in the air from the opening of a door.
She sensed the presence of others, but no word was spoken, just a
sharp pain as the blade of a knife traveled slowly between her breasts,
down to her stomach, flicking her belly button, and coming to rest on
the edge of her bare vagina, before being slowly retracted. When the
rag was pulled from her mouth, she told them everything she knew,
which was not much. When she was done, the rag had been put back
in her mouth and they had left.

Jose Antonio Echeverría motioned for the others to follow him after
reading the statement that the DR had been responsible for the assassination
of Batista and the taking of the Palace, quite unaware that neither of these
events had actually occurred. The plan was to return to the University,

high on the hill of Havana, where the defense of the insurrection would be centered in preparation for retaliation from the army and the police. The men clambered back into the three cars and split off in separate directions, gunfire echoing in the distance. The streets were clear of traffic, as the word was out that a major disturbance was underway.

Echeverria was in the front passenger seat as the car hurtled down the empty streets, plotting the next step, when the driver shouted that the police were coming at them. He looked up to realize a patrol car was coming the other way, and before he could tell everybody to remain calm, Carlos, always the impulsive hothead, leaned out the back window and sent several shots at the oncoming vehicle, which slid sideways and slammed into them, the two machines colliding with a scream of ripping metal. Echeverría was the first out of the car, firing a burst from his machine gun, but the police fired back from inside, their bullets slamming into him, knocking him to the sidewalk, where Joe Westbrook pulled him to cover in a doorway. The patrol car reversed with another tortured squeal and sped off. The others had already fled, slipping down an alleyway in the confusion. "I am gone," Echeverría said to his loyal friend. "Go."

* * *

The sharp retort of Fidel's telescoped rifle split the early morning air. A flash illuminated his position on the hill overlooking the El Uvero military garrison that was protecting the sugar refinery and lumberyard just east of Pico Turquino in the Sierra Maestra. His single shot was the signal to begin the attack, but while the sun had come up on the mountaintop, it was still pitch black lower down where Vicente and the bulk of the rebel army hid.

The fort had four guard posts surrounding a main barracks with a few other buildings for civilians. Juan Almeida was leading the squadron given the task of taking out the northern post. This would allow Raúl and his group to capture the barracks housing the bulk of the soldiers. Vicente was part of the advance guard unit under the leadership of Camilo Cienfuegos. He realized they were out of position, slightly lost in the dark, as soon as return fire from the garrison began to light up the blackness.

"We're too far left," Vicente yelled, firing the M-1 carbine, still smelling of its cosmoline packing grease, the weapon having just been received in a new arms shipment, sadly the product of recent disaster. Two months earlier, the DR had suffered a devastating blow in an attack on the Palace attempting to assassinate Batista, and now with more weapons than men, had agreed to sell them to País to raise capital.

"Nothing can be done about that now," Camilo responded in a firm voice. "Press forward!" He'd also secured an M-1 and appeared to be quite happy with the devastation this weapon delivered. The outpost guards in the small sentry hut laid down a withering fire, causing Vicente to drop to the ground to seek shelter.

Further to his left, along the coast road to Peladero, Vicente could see the group led by Jorge Sotús and Guillermo Garcia advancing on the southern sentry outbuilding. Guillermo had been one of the original peasants to join the rebels after their disastrous landing, and Sotús had been the leader of the unit that'd taken the Maritime Station in Santiago on the day the *Granma* was intended to land.

"Keep crawling," Camilo urged Vicente and the three others of his squad. "We have to press the bastards." They found themselves worming their way forward next to the men in Raúl's squadron, the momentum pausing when Eligio, who'd stood up, took several lethal bullets, his body jerking spasmodically before crumpling to the ground.

"There's no cover," a man shouted in opposition to the suicidal notion of hastening into the teeth of the enemy's defenses, for soldiers had run from the barracks and jumped into a large trench that'd been built just for that purpose on the yard's perimeter, the *casquitos*, popping up to fire at the exposed guerrillas.

Celia aimed down the M-1 carbine and pulled the trigger, sending fifteen shots in as many seconds in the direction of the barracks, the wooden stock slapping her shoulder in an oddly comforting manner. Working in the urban resistance had entailed hiding from the police by using constantly changing houses and disguises, but now she was finally able to confront the enemy. She'd not earned this new semi-automatic weapon, as they were doled out by seniority with the guerrillas in the mountains, but Fidel had handed it to her, and that was that. It may have been that at thirty-five inches long and five pounds six ounces it wasn't too much weapon for her diminutive frame. Or it may have been that they'd been lovers ever since she'd first met him.

Celia had been back in the mountains for just over a month now, ever since she'd brought a television crew to interview Fidel on April 23rd. Robert Taber and Wendell Hoffman, the television reporters, had come from the United States under the pretense of interviewing three young Americans who'd joined the guerrillas, but in reality were looking to do a piece on Castro and the *Movimiento 26th de Julio*. The newsmen spent several weeks following the rebels through the Sierra, culminating with an interview on Pico Turquino, the highest peak in the Sierra.

There, Fidel had disavowed any inclinations towards communism and again expressed the concept that the guerrillas were invincible. "Batista," he'd articulated, "says time and again that we are dead, that there is no revolution, and claims that when soldiers die here in the mountains, it is by accident. Well, there have been a great many accidents here in the Sierra Maestra as of late, that I can tell you."

This attack on the garrison protecting the sugar mill would result in many more of those "accidents," and add to the luster of Fidel's movement. Partway down the hill from the central command, Che was settled between the trees with his new Madsen machine gun. Because the range of his Madsen was limited, he and his team had had to move closer than the central squadron, and were now about 150 feet from one of the guard posts, keeping up a steady barrage of fire on the structure. A crew of four men helped in keeping the weapon firing while also protecting his position. A man nicknamed Cantiflas, because of his incessant nonsensical babble when nervous, was refilling the thirty-bullet clip.

Che was working on his timing with the trigger, giving bursts of eight to ten bullets, the casings spinning out the bottom after being fed in from the long clip on top. The past six months had been a difficult time for him as the hot and humid weather caused his asthma to act up with limited medicine to treat it. But here, now, in this heady, terrifying moment, he was truly a revolutionary, attacking the forces of the corrupt dictator, fighting for the people. This was what he was meant to be, not a doctor nor philosopher, but a warrior. In the previous months, he'd not been idle. With a proven gift for leadership and tactics, he'd quickly assumed responsibility for the initial training of most of the new recruits. He smiled when he thought of those fresh-faced recruits as Fidel welcomed them to the base camp with a small speech. "The war is only beginning now. It may last five, ten, fifteen, twenty years, or more. We had less than thirty men until your arrival, and most days we are lucky to eat one small meal. Not everybody has a weapon. We never sleep in the same place twice. The only thing that I can guarantee is that you will not be run down by a bus."

These men, many from the more urban *Llano*, had either read or heard of the article by Herbert Matthews touting the romantic, heroic, and invincible nature of the guerrilla fighters. In a way, the rebellion was all of those things, but not quite in the way they imagined. These new recruits had adapted for the most part, although there had been a few desertions. He was glad that the two youngest American boys had left the mountains with the CBS reporters, and now only the nineteen-year old, Ryan, remained.

"We have to mop this mess up." Camilo had crawled over to where Vicente was stretched out in a prone position firing into the structures. "There'll be reinforcements and aerial support coming any minute."

Vicente looked over his shoulder down the coast road where there was another fort just ten miles distant. Crescencio had been given command of a group of men to dissuade these possible reinforcements, but he wouldn't hold out for long against their superior numbers. Fidel had estimated that it'd take an hour for these soldiers to arrive on the scene, so it was imperative that they take the garrison quickly. "Let's do it then."

The two men stood and began scuttling towards the guardhouse as the squadron under Almeida did the same. Vicente briefly saw Almeida jerk with the impact of bullets and fall to the ground, and then he concentrated his fire on the trench where several small helmets poked their way cautiously up. He took aim, sending a burst of bullets and saw one of the heads explode, the projectile piercing the thin armor of the helmet. The few men left alive dropped their weapons and raised their hands in surrender.

The battle had been won, but not without cost: six of the rebels had been killed and another nine were seriously wounded, including Almeida. The capture of fresh arms and ammunition, as well as the incredible morale boost of defeating the soldiers in open combat was well worth the losses. As it turned out, the initial exchange of gunfire had sliced the telephone wires, and the soldiers had been unable to call for backup of either troops or air support, a lucky break for the guerrillas as the battle had raged for almost three hours. The rebels took what weapons and food that were there, burnt the buildings, and turned the prisoners loose to find their way down the coast to the next garrison, before melting back into the hills. The air force would soon be flying overhead, and they needed to be long gone by the time that happened.

9

July 30, 1957, Santiago

Frank País sat calmly in the kitchen of the businessman, Raúl Pujol, on a burning hot day in Santiago, with a small, detached smile on his face. He knew that he shouldn't have come, as there was no escape route, the only way in or out being through the front door. But it was hard to see any of it really mattering. A member of the Civic Resistance had just stopped by, alerting him that Colonel Cañizares and his brutal police squad were searching houses in the neighborhood, but País had assured the sympathizer that Pujol was on his way with a taxi to move him to a safe house, and that he'd wait. The past few months had been tough for País, possibly the most difficult of his young life, maybe even more so than the catastrophic insurrection he'd lived through in support of the delayed *Granma* landing exactly eight months ago. In two days it would be August and perhaps all the bad luck would change.

He'd been arrested in March, but his defense attorney proved up to the task. When the pistol País was supposed to have been carrying couldn't be located, he'd been found innocent and released. He'd then attempted to open a Second Front in the Sierra Cristal, but the *Guardias Rurales* had been on to the plan and foiled the attempt. This failure to open a second front had been followed by the heartbreaking attempt on June 30th to disrupt Rolando Masferrer's pro-government rally in Santiago. 3,000 soldiers had filled the main square to hear Masferrer speak. His passion would have made Mussolini proud. Tanks lined the mustered ranks of the army while surrounding Masferrer were two hundred of his paramilitaries. They'd been sent to Santiago to root out the underground operations and flush Fidel and the guerrillas from the hills.

País had interrupted the radio broadcast, taking over the airwaves with the aid of sympathetic employees of the station, but then the action soon deteriorated. Several bombs and grenades meant to actuate disruption and sow panic had failed to explode, part of a batch from the Dominican that'd been buried in damp ground for too long. His younger brother Josué had been spotted by *Los Tigres* and his car sprayed with gunfire. The young País had jumped from the vehicle to return fire along with his two companions, only to be riddled with bullets.

Deep in hiding, Frank País hadn't even been able to attend the funeral on the following day. For the past three weeks he'd no contact with his fiancée, America, or his mother, Rosario. Before moving to this house, he at least had been able to watch America through an ancient spyglass. He'd sent her messages to stand on the street at certain times just so that he could get a glimpse of his tall, blonde, and beautiful girlfriend. *It all seemed to be slipping away,* he thought.

Raúl Pujol came into the house, slamming the door. "Frank!"

"What is it?" País had flirted with death so many times that there wasn't much that scared him anymore, or was it that he didn't care anymore?

"The police...we have to leave." Pujol's face was white, for he knew that if he were caught harboring País, there was little chance that he'd survive the interrogation by Colonel Cañizares.

"Do you have the taxi?"

"It's out there, but it's parked right next to the police. I think we should walk down the street and hail another ride."

País nodded, standing and grabbing the bag at his feet. The two men left the building by the only door, directly onto the street. There were four officers almost at the entrance with more behind them in the street when they exited, quickly turning to the right and moving away as if hurrying to an appointment. País heard a voice say, "That's him." The sound of scurrying feet from behind suggested approaching mayhem, but he knew there was no chance for flight or fight, so he merely kept walking. A blinding light flashed through his head as a rifle butt crashed into the base of his skull. The cobblestones came rushing up to meet him and he fell, hard.

País felt himself being lifted on either side, burly arms raising his slight frame from the street and dragging him to the police car. He heard screaming, and recognized the voice as Pujol's wife, Nena, who had just returned home from picking their son up from school. Next to him in the backseat was Raúl Pujol with blood streaming down his face.

They'd gone no more than two blocks when Pujol smashed the window and climbed through, but not before the car slammed to a stop. The driver stepped out of the car and shot Pujol in front of his wife and son as they came running down the block. The door was jerked violently open and a police officer grabbed País and dragged him from the car. A crowd began to appear from nowhere, apparitions from the ancient city of Santiago. He stumbled, and then fell on his knees, the lapel of his shirt clamped in the vise-like grip of a powerful policeman.

The day was hot, even for Cuba, the sky filled with whiteness like the center of a flame. A tocororo flew overhead, the deep blue crown with a white upper chest and a red bottom vibrant in the pale sky. Its wings flapped lazily, conserving strength, escaping captivity within which it could not live. This was the last sight País would see, for a blackness descended upon him, followed by a sharp report, just a glimmer of pain, and then nothing.

* * *

Fidel,

The situation here in Santiago is ripe to explode. Bosses, workers, students, everybody you can imagine, just decided to shut down the city. By dusk on the day Frank was assassinated the streets were empty. The police withdrew into their barracks and the soldiers cowered in Moncada. Not a single merchant was open. I told Rosario that she had to go claim the body of her son. And she did, bless her heart. With the help of Frank's fiancée, America, and her brother, Taras, they brought Frank's body to their house. They wanted to dress him in a suit and tie, but I insisted that he be buried in uniform, the same he had worn during the uprising to coincide with your arrival in Cuba. We put a beret on his chest with a white rose, and a red and black armband with the white M-26-7 emblem.

The next morning, the women of the city protested when the new US Ambassador, Earl Smith, gave a speech in Céspedes Park. The police attempted to disperse them with fire hoses, but they knelt and refused to leave, forcing the assassins to drag them away to be arrested, but then those women were replaced by more, until fifty respectable women of Santiago resided in jail. The only remorse I heard after was that they were saddened to miss the funeral that afternoon.

The procession included tens of thousands of people, all walking to the Santa Ifigenia cemetery where Frank was buried in the family plot, along with his brother. Six women schoolteachers, who had worked with Frank before the Batista coup, led the mourners carrying garlands of flowers, each connected to the next by a wide silk ribbon. The cobblestones rang with the National Anthem, sung loudly by everyone—the young and old, man and woman, whites, negroes, yellows, mestizos—all united in their love of this valiant young hero of the revolution and in their hatred of the oppressive regime.

Hugs,
Vilma

Sophia Franco stood silently in front of Fidel as he read Vilma's letter relating the events following the assassination of Frank País. While she waited for him to finish reading, Sophia's mind drifted back, like fingers rubbing a newly healed scar, to the immediate aftermath of her rape. After Rolando Masferrer had extracted the information he wanted, he'd no choice but to have her killed and make her disappear forever. And so the silent untying of her hands, one goon leering as he threw her the ripped dress she donned as best she could, then the march across the sugar warehouse and into the back of a car.

As they left the city, Sophia was under no illusion that the drive into the countryside had any other purpose than her death and disposal of her body. But she also realized that they'd have one final side desire before murdering her, and it was to this end that she mentally prepared herself. She was subtly provocative, as much so as her tortured and abused body allowed, while docile at the same time. She didn't put up any resistance when the thug grabbed her by the hair and dragged her into the bushes. As his hands busied themselves with her breasts, her own sought out and found the pistol in his shoulder holster, tipping it back and pulling the trigger so that a bullet traveled upward through the bottom of his jaw to lodge in his skull. Her shredded dress drenched with his blood, she stepped from the brush and drew a bead on the larger man. He dropped the shovel he'd been using to dig her grave and frantically reached for his gun. Her first two shots were clean misses, and he got off a single shot as her third attempt drove his nose back into his head before he fell lifeless.

Four months later, Sophia now stood in front of Fidel with two pistols tucked into the waistband of the pants she'd stolen from a clothesline along with the tee shirt she wore. Her gaunt form had lost all its former proportions of shapely womanhood, her cheeks hollow and pinched, her feet bare, having blistered and then calloused like leather, far from the soft tender skin of a few months prior.

"And you are who?" Fidel looked up at her, his eyes rising above the black frames of his glasses.

"My name is Sophia Franco."

"That tells me little, Señorita Franco. Other than it would appear from your speech that you're *americana*?" He stood, towering over her slight frame, taking a cigar and lighting it. "What brings you to my humble abode in the Sierra with this communication?"

"I was a messenger for the DR in Havana. When the Palace attack failed, Rolando Masferrer and *Los Tigres* swept me up in the repression that followed. They tortured me and then brought me to the countryside to die, but I managed to escape. I came to Manzanillo searching for Celia Sánchez, whose name José Echeverría gave me before he was killed." Sophia refrained from telling Fidel that Vicente had given her the address of a house to which she could send letters, and that is where she'd initially gone upon arrival. "A man named Hector brought me to a farm where I hid with a group that was waiting to be guided in to join the revolution. After a few days, Celia came, and we had a chance to talk a bit, and she entrusted me with this correspondence, complaining that she fears many of her messages don't make it to you with the usual people."

Fidel squinted at her, his cigar in the corner of his mouth. He trusted the judgment of Celia impeccably, and in this well-spoken, obviously educated woman—but with a tempered edge of steel and flatness to her eyes—he sensed a kindred spirit that could be trusted. That day he was wearing a beret that was a gift from Che, a departure from his normal green field cap. "And you wish to stay?" He liked her straightforward manner and was not disappointed with her answer.

Sophia pulled the two pistols out of her belt, holding them pointed up. "From what I hear, with these I meet the pre-requisites to join your band."

Fidel laughed, a low chuckle, quiet, as sound carried on the Sierra breeze, and they never knew who might be listening and prepared to pounce. "Bringing your own weapons is certainly rule number one."

"And a hatred of Batista." There was no masking the raw hostility as she almost hissed the name of this man who just a year earlier she'd regarded as quite dapper and likeable.

"Do you want to be a courier?"

"Do couriers get to carry weapons and kill *Los Tigres y Guardias Rurales?*"

"No." Fidel liked the fire in this woman, and she'd soon be a valuable addition to his plans. He'd been tossing around in his mind the idea of developing a platoon of all women, but he knew that it wasn't time, not yet.

"Is a man named Vicente Bolívar with you?"

The question had come out in such a low whisper that Fidel was forced to lean in to hear what she said. "Ah, so you're *that* Sophia."

Sophia nodded almost imperceptibly.

"He's been assigned to the 4th Column under Ernesto Guevara." Fidel paused, the germ of an idea developing. "I was about to send a message to Che that I hesitate to trust with just a local guide. Vicente has spoken highly of you, and my instinct is that you're trustworthy. What is more, Che is setting up schooling for the local children in his region. I'd guess that you are educated and might be useful to him as a teacher?"

Sophia stared impassively for a few long seconds before nodding her head. "For now, yes. For the time being, I can teach—but also learn how to be a guerrilla, so that I may one day fight." This was a good solution. It would allow her to visit with Vicente, keep her with the rebels in the mountains, and eventually give her the chance to kill soldiers. Her fury at Masferrer had kept her alive in the warehouse, but the long journey here had only thrown oil on the fire she wanted to wield to destroy everything related to Batista. Masferrer was just a tool, a pawn to the dictator, but one so vile it must be smashed along the way. She'd spent many a day mulling over her own brutality in extinguishing a pair of souls, yet she could find no regret within herself, only a hunger for more vengeance boiling just below her skin.

Sophia brought the dispatch from Fidel to Che in El Hombrito, a village in the foothills of the Sierra Maestra where the 4th Column had encamped. It took her several days to realize there was no second or third column of the guerrilla army, but merely that Fidel wanted to perpetuate that idea to give the impression that their numbers were far larger than in reality. The 4th Column had about seventy-five men, expanding the "free territory" to an area just northeast of Pico Turquino, while the 1st Column continued to operate mostly southwest of that peak. This area was about thirty miles long and twenty miles wide, a swath of territory the army would only venture into in great numbers and with armored protection.

Sophia was waiting in the camp when Vicente returned from a patrol with Camilo Cienfuegos. Vicente didn't recognize her at first, dressed as a *campesino*, and a half-starved one at that. It wasn't unusual for new faces to come and go, as there was a steady influx of people wanting to join the revolution. The romantic notions of the bearded guerrilla fighting for social justice that Herbert Matthews had depicted in his *New York Times* article had attracted many adventure seekers. And just as often, the grueling marches, incessant insects, lack of food, and inadequate medicine drove more than half of them away again. He glanced again with only casual interest, wondering if this man was a guide, courier, or fresh recruit—and stopped dead in his tracks. "Sophia?"

She smiled, or rather tried to smile, happy to see him—but fearful of her reception. "I've missed you, Vicente," Sophia said, but at the same time wondering if he could tell that another man had violated her.

Vicente lurched awkwardly forward and pulled her into a tight embrace. "I've been worried because I haven't heard from you, but mail is spotty in Cuba, and horrendous in the Sierra." He held her back at arms length, inspecting her from head to foot. "What happened to you?"

"It's a long story," Sophia replied simply.

"Let's take a walk, and we'll pretend we're sitting on the Malecón with *café con leche y cake de ron*." He said warmly, referring to the rum-soaked pastries they had shared so many times during so many happier conversations. He tucked her arm snugly under his own and began to show her around the base camp they were setting up in El Hombrito. "That building is used for a shoe factory, and over here is a leather workshop, and just down the hill there's a blacksmith forge."

"It's very different than Fidel's camp."

"You saw Fidel?"

"Celia sent a message for him with me. A local woman guided me to him, which I understand is difficult, because he moves every single day to a new location."

Vicente silently processed the news that she'd already met Celia and Fidel, as well as had been entrusted with a correspondence.

"What brought you to the revolution?"

"After the DR's failed assassination attempt I was picked up for questioning." Sophia stumbled over the words, unable to continue.

"Was it the SIM?" Vicente suggested gently. They'd now gone past the last building, an armory with an electric lathe to construct the casings for bombs.

Sophia stopped and sat down on a rock. "No, it was *Los Tigres.* Masferrer himself took me from my hotel." Vicente mulled over the implications of this stark statement, knowing the man's brutality. He gave her time to continue, and after a minute she did. "He took me to a warehouse by the port and asked me questions. At first I didn't answer, but eventually, I told him the little I knew."

Vicente sat down next to her tenderly, and with equal care put his arm around her shoulders. She flinched at first, but then seemed to relax, allowing the physical contact. "I will kill that bastard," he murmured.

"I killed two men," Sophia blurted out. "They took me to the country and one dragged me off to…" She turned away at the unexpressed words. "The other was off digging my grave. I took his gun and shot him here," she said, jamming her forefinger hard under her own jaw. She was crying now, wracking sobs that tore at his heart. He held her more closely, still gently, hushing her until the words came again, more calmly, precisely, as if she were packing things away carefully in a box. "The second man must have thought I was dead. He was shocked when I came out. I pulled the trigger twice and nothing happened except he dropped his shovel. And then he fired once. And I aimed at his head and shot him in the face. I shot them both. And then I started walking."

"You walked the entire way?" Vicente asked in amazement,

suddenly compelled to look at her feet. She'd always been so proud of her perfectly formed feet with their carefully clipped and painted toenails. What he saw now were the feet of a peasant, nails cracked, coarse, dirty, and callouses visible at the heels. His mind flew over the road to the Sierra Maestra from Havana, long stretches with no towns, no farms, and little sign of life. For a woman alone, hiding out from the authorities, weak from torture, to make such a trip was unfathomable. "How did you even consider such a thing?"

"From you," Sophia interrupted him. "You told me of your ancestors Maria and Mateo who were caught up in a slave rebellion, planned by that man, Aponte, I think you said his name was. And when the plantation owners foiled their plans, they escaped by walking all the way across the country to take refuge here, in these mountains. I knew it'd be difficult, but in truth, I had no idea how difficult." Taking no chances of being recaptured and knowing she was hunted, she'd stayed off the road to avoid *Los Tigres*. The heavy revolvers were a comfort, even if a grim one, for she would rather put a bullet in her head than be taken again. "Each night I woke at sundown and walked alongside the road. When it grew light, I slept. If I found food, I ate it. I stole from farmers, from poor villagers. I had no shame."

Vicente knew that was enough for now. "I wish I could've been there for you."

"How long have you been here?" Sophia asked, waving her arm to encompass the bivouac that was progressing towards a more permanent state.

"We've been here since the beginning of July with the purpose of expanding the resistance in this area, but I suspect that it also had to do with the fact that Che was having a difficult time keeping up with the daily marches. He struggles with asthma, and in this high altitude," Vicente shrugged his shoulders. "I hope no one betrays our position, because the bombers would make light work of us if they knew we were here."

"Tell me about Fidel. The newspapers paint him as a desperado, an outlaw, but then I read the *Times* article and he seems like a real Robin Hood, taking from the rich and giving to the poor."

"Fidel is everything," Vicente replied. "It's his indomitable will that has kept us together when things have been the bleakest. There's not a man or woman here who wouldn't charge an enemy patrol single-handedly if he asked them to."

"It seems that he's a man with a great vision and one who means to make it real."

"That he is."

Sophia nodded in understanding. "And what happens if you win this revolution?"

"I hadn't thought that possible until recently," Vicente admitted. "Arrest Batista and try the bastard for his crimes, along with his cronies? Throw out United Fruit and the *Yanqui* gangsters." Vicente mentally kicked himself for adding the part about the American gangsters, remembering too late that Sophia's uncle was one of them, but she appeared unaffected by his gaffe. "After that, we'd set up a democracy with an elected president and senators based on the Constitution of 1940."

"And you think Fidel will allow this?"

"What do you mean?" They stopped on the edge of the camp, turning to survey the odd assortment of buildings barely visible, hidden as they were underneath the trees' dense canopy and surrounded by high brush.

Sophia swept her arm out in a movement meant to encompass all of the Sierra Maestra. "He is the ultimate ruler of this kingdom, however small. One day he'll control the entire country, every city, the banks, railroads, and radio stations. What makes you think he'll give up that authority once he is victorious?"

Vicente shrugged uncomfortably, acknowledging his unease at the question, before catching her arm and walking back into the camp.

The next few weeks they got to know each other again. In Havana, Vicente was a poor mulatto struggling to survive, and Sophia was a rich socialite come to enjoy the exotic island of Cuba. In the Sierra Maestra, they were revolutionaries, nothing more, nothing less. They built a bed of palm fronds for Sophia next to Vicente's hammock, both with poles from which hung the mosquito nets.

Vicente was busy on daily patrols most days, but returned at night, while Sophia began to organize a school for the children of El Hombrito, teaching these peasant youngsters to read, write, and do math at a rudimentary level. Sophia had now been in Cuba for over four years, and had become quite proficient in Spanish, even if she struggled initially with the local dialect.

Now, for the first time in her life, she began to build self-esteem through personal accomplishment. She'd long fought against the stereotype of being the delicate flower raised for the sole purpose of pleasing a man, but had never truly found a path to a sense of self-worth. Now, to see the smiling faces, however smudged in dirt, looking up at her with respect, the cries of—M*aestra Sophia! Maestra Sophia!*—following her wherever she went planted a seed of dignity within Sophia that grew with every day.

This blissful period was shattered by the arrival of a terrified peasant one night with news that the soldiers were on the march, and were in fact, camped just a few kilometers from the Sierra Maestra at the Zapatero farmstead. The guerrillas put on their boots, quickly gathered the few things they needed, and were gone, leaving behind a few peasants, a doctor and two patients in the hut that passed as the sick bay, and Sophia.

By dawn, Vicente was in a coffee grove watching the house and barn below come to life as soldiers emerged. Soon, a force of several hundred *casquitos* began marching up the hill to where the guerrillas lay in wait. They were spread out with little discipline, shouting bawdy jokes back and forth, and totally unprepared for what was about to happen.

A burst from Che's Browning machine gun from a raised hillock overlooking the ambush site signaled the beginning of the attack. Vicente pulled the trigger on his M-1, sending five shots at a man already diving away from him into the bushes on the side of the road. Of the entire company, not a single man remained to fight. Vicente scuttled across the road and fired down the ravine at the retreating soldiers, but chose not to pursue them.

Che marched them further out of the mountains to plant another ambush near a sawmill for the reinforcements that would certainly come. It took the army seven days to show up, but eventually they appeared. Five troop transport trucks and two Jeeps came trundling up the steep slope into the impending trap, their wheels spinning in the slick mud from the recent cloudburst that had left the rebels soaked to the bone. The lead truck downshifted, the gears grinding harshly as the wheels fought for traction on the slippery slope. Vicente could see the driver cursing the conditions while the man next to him appeared to be dozing.

Che had chosen Vicente to start the attack on this day, a great honor of which he meant to prove himself worthy. As the M35 cargo truck loaded with *casquitos* came abreast of him, Vicente took a careful breath and squeezed off five shots, taking out the front wheel, which caused it to lurch off the road, before aiming for the windshield, his bullets smashing it as the driver and navigator dove out the side doors. Soldiers spilled from the rear of the truck and scrambled behind a jumble of huge boulders strewn alongside the road.

The last two trucks had managed to turn around and were hurtling down the mountain, but the soldiers from the first three trucks put up a fierce resistance, filling the air with lead. Vicente advanced upon the trucks with his rifle sweeping in front of him, the poet Crucito at his side, searching for a target. Too late he saw the *casquito* peering around the tire from underneath the truck, a Garand aimed at them. In slow motion, Vicente tried to bring his own M-1 to bear, but a bullet struck him in the shoulder, slamming him off his feet.

From the ground he witnessed Crucito jerk several times, the close-in shots opening him up like a sieve. Vicente brought his rifle to bear on the soldier by the tire, sending several cartridges clanging off the bumper of the truck, and then he rolled to avoid being hit again, coming to rest on his stomach, staring across a space about thirty feet into the eyes of a terrified man, both of them pulling their triggers. The soldier's face disappeared in a shower of blood, his burst of fire going wide of its mark.

Che insisted on personally bandaging Vicente on a table in the sawmill while the others ate. The euphoria of surviving the battle was passing, and Vicente's shoulder was on fire, his skin clammy, his stomach churning unpleasantly. It was a through-and-through, Guevara told him, and barring infection should heal cleanly. He poured sulfa powder over the open wound, both sides, and gave him an injection of penicillin, but Vicente refused morphine, knowing its scarcity and value, and that it should be saved for pain much worse than this. They buried Crucito, sorry to see him gone, and not only as a brother revolutionary, but also as a poet—"the nightingale of the Maestra" the men called him. He'd brought much entertainment to nights by the fire and days on the march, putting their lives to verse.

Sophia was just letting a class of twelve youngsters out of the schoolroom when the Jeep pulled up in front of the rough-hewn field hospital. She saw Vicente rise stiffly from the vehicle, his arm in a sling. Her hand shot to her mouth as she realized he was wounded. It was as if the day froze, even the mosquitos congealed in the sudden chill that raced through the Sierra Maestra on the wings of Josef Mengele.

Vicente broke the spell by stumbling and Sophia ran across the open space to him. "Are you okay? What happened? Were you shot?"

Vicente chuckled, his face slightly paler than usual, but otherwise having recovered his equanimity. "I was. A bullet clean through the meat of my shoulder that didn't hit any bones or arteries."

She took his M-1 from his good hand. "Come. Let me nurse you at our home."

He stopped dead when he saw the green-leaf walls and roof that framed his living area. "Did you build this?" While he'd been gone she'd woven the palm fronds into a small *bohio*, aided by one of the peasant women whose child she taught. It'd rained just the night before, and the interior had remained completely dry, leaving Sophia with a pride she was not familiar with, having used her hands to successfully create something as important and necessary as a shelter.

"I did," Sophia replied with a rare smile. As they entered the hut, he brushed his arm on the door and grunted in pain. "Are you okay?" she asked.

"I am better than Crucito, who was next to me and then gone in the time it would take to say goodbye."

Sophia remembered the man well, his spontaneous poetry. She shook her head at his loss, here yesterday and today no more. Her own mortality had become abundantly clear when Rolando Masferrer had whisked her from the hotel and in a matter of hours changed her life irrevocably. Somehow, she hadn't quite understood this delicate balance of life in relation to others. "I could've lost you," she said simply. "I could still lose you."

Vicente looked at her with the perception of one who realizes a new door has just been opened, a door that let flood in the consciousness of pent up emotion, passion. "You will never lose me." He touched her cheek with his hand, his thumb brushing her skin lightly.

She grasped his hand and held it firm to her cheek. "You look terrible. You need to sleep and regain your strength."

"Che doesn't plan on returning for over a week." Vicente sat down heavily on the hammock. "So I have a bit of time to recover."

"It's not Che you have to recover for." Sophia dropped to her knees to pull his boots off. "And you don't have nearly that long."

Vicente struggled to process this as he reclined into the hammock, the blackness enveloping him in a warm embrace, and he was asleep. He woke to a stifling heat, the sun up and baking the *bohío* that Sophia had built, yet he didn't rise, his mind analyzing the last spoken words of the previous night, "*It's not Che you have to recover for.*" It could mean just about anything, but the mischievous way in which she said the words had certainly implied something…naughty, or had he just been imagining that?

At that moment Sophia swung the palm frond door inward and swept into the room, a tin cup of water and a hard-boiled egg in hand. "You're awake." He thirstily drank the water, but had to be prodded to eat the egg. "You're going to need your strength," Sophia said, running her hand up the inside of his leg.

Vicente choked on the egg, hurriedly drinking the last bit of water to wash it down. "For what?" he spluttered, embarrassed by his growing erection.

"When the doctor gives the okay for your sling to come off, we're going to make love like it's our last day on earth," she replied with a quiet candor that brooked no denial.

The physician in camp, a local doctor who'd joined the *Movimiento 26th de Julio*, couldn't be persuaded that day to allow Vicente to remove his sling, but the following day, perhaps cowed by the black look in

Vicente's eyes, he gave his consent. It was just before dusk, and Vicente found himself almost running to the hut he shared with Sophia. She was just about to exit the door when he met her, bending to kiss her ripe mouth savagely. Stepping inside, they explored with their lips and tongues, their hands grasping and pulling, their bodies hungry, but Vicente's sling created a buffer between them. "*El Doctor* says it's okay to take it off if I need to," he gasped, stepping back slightly.

"And do you need to?" she asked with a wicked smile, reaching up and sliding the rough sling over his head, freeing his arm so she could press into his body. Vicente could feel the dull ache in his shoulder but paid it no mind. His skin felt like it was on fire where she touched him, and her voice echoed in his head as if from afar, every sense other than touch dulled by this storm of emotion and feeling. Sophia turned her face up and their mouths again met ravenously, as if to devour the other. With a moan, low and deep, Vicente awkwardly attempted to lift her new olive green shirt over her head with one hand. She giggled at his clumsy efforts, and then stepped back to aid him, slipping the shirt up and off, exposing soft white breasts, such a contrast to her tanned face and arms. Sophia ripped the buttons of his uniform off in stripping him of his shirt, jamming her body into his, the skin of their naked chests cleaved into one.

Her hands found his belt, loosening his pants, and Vicente pushed them down and stepped out of them while she took care of her own trousers. For Vicente everything disappeared as soon as he entered into her, a blackness rising from his toes to his heart to his head, one thrust, two, and then a grunt and he exploded, feeling as if all of the molecules of his body were shooting off in different directions. It wasn't until just before dawn, the third time they made love, that either one could begin to experience a gentler, more comprehensible level of rapture.

The next few weeks were the most marvelous days of Vicente's life, a period when he discovered love and the delectation of carnal knowledge. For Sophia, it brought zest back to a soul that'd bordered on extinction after the brutal torture at the hands of Rolando Masferrer and *Los Tigres*. She spent her mornings educating peasant children for a suddenly brighter future, her afternoons helping build the new rebel base camp as her part in fighting Batista's corruption, and her nights delighting in the touch and words and love of a man through which the blood and life of Cuba flowed. By the time Che came riding back into camp ten days later astride a recently liberated mule, Vicente had mostly physically healed, and Sophia's spirit had reawakened, bringing vitality back to her being.

Che talked nightly to the men of the books he'd read, written by or about Marx, Lenin, FDR, and others, in which at the forefront was the concept of certain inalienable rights for all. Everybody should have access to health care and education, not just those born wealthy. He reproached the excessive wealth and greed of a tiny segment of the Cuban population, and the exploitation by foreigners, particularly the *Yanquis* to the north, who owned large tracts of Cuban farmland and industry such as sugar and mining, as well as valuable city real estate and beach property. These businessmen siphoned the profits from sugar, fruit, and mineral wealth, not to mention the gambling and tourism industries so dominated by foreigners, money that was moved out of Cuba and into the pockets of a few demigods who then used it to support a policy of repression and perpetual poverty for the masses, instead of sharing it with all of the people of Cuba.

"Fundamentally the hearts of the American people are good," Sophia murmured to Vicente as they lay in their hammock after one such fiery talk from Che. "They're not the enemy."

"It's not the people we fear," he replied. "It's the filthy rich tycoons who control the government."

"Americans won't back policies unjust to Cuba if they know the truth. We just need to get the word to the people of the social justice that the *Movimiento 26th de Julio* offers in opposition to the corruption and violence of Batista."

"Fidel is doing all that he can to stop the U.S. from supplying arms to Batista. Very important ambassadors like Haydée Santamaría and others are there as we speak, lobbying for an end to weapon shipments."

"But Cuba needs more than that if the revolution is to be

successful." Sophia flicked a lock of hair from her cheek. "Who's going to buy the sugar, coffee, and tobacco? Where will Cuba get appliances, automobiles, and other American products that aren't made here? Cuba needs the United States of America."

"We're not opposed to a cordial relationship with your country." Vicente adjusted his arm around Sophia's sinewy shoulders. "But we won't be bullied."

"How is it that America bullies Cuba?" Sophia rolled on her side to look him in the eye. "By building railroads? By supplying electricity?"

Vicente reflected upon this, the silence of the night interrupted by the snuffling of a solenodon hunting for his dinner. It was true that *norteamericanos* brought much to the island, but at what cost? "It is not so different than you and your uncle. He gives you a great many things, yet he doesn't allow you to be you. We just want to be Cuba."

PART FOUR

The Road Comes to an Intersection

Earl Smith
American Ambassador to Cuba
Habana, Cuba

May 1, 1958

John Foster Dulles
Secretary of State
United States of America

Dear Mr. Secretary,

Last week, President Batista was forced to once
again suspend all Constitutional guarantees due to
violence in the streets. While this reflects poorly
on his administration, there is no alternative. The
revolutionary elements are disorganized, splintered,
and lack a program with public appeal. If Batista
were assassinated, there is no responsible group to
take over the government. Vandalism, chaos, and
bloodshed would surely ensue.

This said, the capital continues to flourish. The
Habana Hilton opened at the end of March to great
acclaim. It is the largest hotel in Latin America at
25 stories and 500 rooms. Under the patronage of
President Batista, American businesses own 90%
of Cuba's mines, 80% of its public utilities, 50%
of its railways, and 40% of its sugar production.
It is doubtful that any other regime would be so
amenable to our interests.

I propose that for these reasons we continue to
supply military aid in dollars and training. The
Cuban army has planned a large-scale summer
offensive to flush out and exterminate the rebels
in the Sierra Maestra. President Batista is putting
12,000 soldiers into the field, supported by tanks

and airplanes. There is little chance that the mentally unbalanced Castro brothers will survive more than a few weeks.

I can assure you that Habana is thriving. As the Hilton proves, it is still a primary tourist destination, and its government is closely allied with ours. The recent failure of the planned April strike is just further proof that the opposition is disorganized and weak, and that we should maintain the status quo.

Sincerely,
Earl Smith

.

Eastern Cuba: The Oriente Province

10

May 3rd, 1958, in the heart of the Sierra Maestra

Fidel puffed on his cigar, shielding the orange glow of its tip by cupping his palm. The lights of the Toyota Land Cruiser Jeep had been purposely smeared with mud to help them avoid detection in the moonless night, for they were on their way to a very important meeting, indeed. The leaders of the disparate parts of the *Movimiento 26ᵗʰ de Julio* were all coming together to discuss the direction of the revolution.

The Jeep—far fancier than the U.S. Army surplus Willies—had been acquired a month earlier when an enemy patrol had fled an ambush, leaving it behind along with two dead soldiers. Fidel had claimed it for himself so that he could better move around the "Free Territory" that'd been carved out of the Sierra Maestra, several hundred square miles in total. He'd summoned Vicente from the 4ᵗʰ Column to be his driver, and Sophia had accompanied him and become his personal bodyguard. The fourth person in the Jeep was Celia Sánchez, who had become his top advisor, and also his lover.

Celia had bewitched him ever since he'd first heard about her exploits while imprisoned on the Isle of Pines. Her plans to meet and guide his invasion force aboard the *Granma* had been impeccable. And when their landing had been delayed, she'd picked up the pieces. Now, they spent their nights planning assaults and hatching visions of a new Cuba once they came to power—all intermixed with lengthy sexual encounters that left them wanting more, needing physical contact almost as much as oxygen.

Fidel had finally allowed the 1st Column, led by José Martí, to settle down in La Plata. The 4th Column under the command of Che Guevara was still located in El Hombrito. Recently, Raúl had persuaded Fidel to expand into the Sierra Cristal northeast of Santiago, and the newly created 6th Column had moved its operation there. Juan Almeida had been assigned the 3rd Column, roving a swath of the Sierra Maestra between La Plata and Santiago, giving the rebels a total of four base camps spread throughout the mountains of Oriente Province.

Fidel was well aware that when the long-awaited summer offensive began, they would be forced back from the perimeters of the territory they controlled, but he was confident that they could hold out in the area near the spine of the Sierra Maestra, on terrain that was twisting, rugged, confusing and difficult to maneuver within. No tank or any other vehicle could handle the bruising mountain tracks along routes that provided rich opportunities for ambush, harassment, and buried explosives.

In La Plata, several guerrillas had built a cabin used as a command center during the day, a necessity to meet the demands of the growing rebel army, but with a walled-off bedroom where Fidel and Celia slept at night. Around this original building had sprung up a hospital, a civil administration building, a guard shack, and various other cabins for lodging. Celia had put in place a series of dedicated mule teams to deliver supplies from the cities and surrounding farms, while actual metal hospital beds had arrived complete with white linens, a single luxury of the civilization they'd left behind.

Fidel's thoughts turned to the driver of the Jeep, Vicente Bolivar, and he was struck once again by his own ignorance of the lives of those around him, supporting him, believing in him so strongly as to risk their lives every day. Even as a young man, he chafed at the poor living conditions of the peasant laborers on his father's sugar plantation. What did he really know about the people who lived like slaves, no matter their race? Sometimes, to him, they all seemed like one mass that had risen up from the earth itself to inherit their world. But there was one thing he was equally certain of, which was that he'd fight to the death for their right to live.

The *Movimiento 26th de Julio* was growing financially stronger, and as a result, new supplies had started flowing in, particularly weaponry. Fidel had a runway cleared for airplanes, a few miles from the base camp, and a regular flow of munitions and supplies was arriving from Miami, Tampa, and Venezuela, and more recently, Costa Rica. Everything was accomplished with such subterfuge that the government planes couldn't locate this budding enclave in the mountains.

The most recent addition to their base camp had been a shack called the Mountain House to host the radio station. An electric generator was used to power the short-wave transmission from the highest peak, and radio stations as far away as Havana had picked up their broadcast and now shared the weekly Sunday updates, which criticized the slanted and often fictional government reports about what was occurring in the Sierra Maestra. It had become a far too regular occurrence for *Los Tigres* or the *Guardias Rurales* to kill everybody in a remote location after raping the women, and then blame these actions on the guerrillas.

Che was publishing a newspaper, *El Cubano Libre*, the name a nod to the men of the woods—the *mambises*—who had come before and paved the way. Soon enough, Fidel reflected, he'd follow in the footsteps of Antonio Maceo and bring the war to the west, right to the gates of Havana. He would not be ignored any longer by those privileged few in their private enclaves, insulated from the reality of Cuba, happy in the illusion that they'd created in the capital, a fantasy world in which no excess was too much, and where the only things that mattered were money and power, even when others lacked food, water, medical care, a roof.

Up to this point, Fidel and the *Movimiento 26th de Julio* had been one of many opposition groups to Batista, but these rivals had withered away over the past year. The DR's attempted assassination and uprising in Havana had met with harsh reprisals, and the death of the charismatic José Echeverría had substantially diminished the organization. In September, a group of navy officers had risen up with support from the *Llano* section of the *Movimiento 26th de Julio* headed by Faustino Perez. The plot had gathered many adherents within the navy and appeared to have a real chance at success—until Fidel sabotaged it. This brutal intentional internal betrayal with so many casualties haunted Fidel and Faustino both, but was necessary to bring about a revolutionary government capable of making real change. The treachery of the naval uprising was unavoidable, as Fidel's greatest fear was irrelevance.

The recent general strike of April 9th had been a dismal failure, and as a result, Fidel had called for a meeting of the leaders of the *Movimiento 26th de Julio* to discuss what had happened, and how they should move forward. It had been planned and implemented by the *Directorate Nacional*, the ruling group of the *Movimiento 26th de Julio*, and its failure was another opportunity for Fidel to cement his position as the sole commander of the revolution. Fidel had known that the urban underground was severely under armed, and so he welcomed this attempt by them to seize control of Havana, for their downfall would be his victory.

And then just days before the strike, a C-47 transport plane had landed at the secret landing strip near La Plata, sent by President José Figueres of Costa Rica, a great supporter of their revolution. The plane had brought the largest shipment of arms ever to be delivered to the mountain guerrillas. There were 250 Beretta machine guns, one million rounds of ammunition, mortars, bazookas, tripod machine guns, dynamite, and hand grenades. Fidel now possessed the firepower to arm the underground and bring the capital to a standstill. But as with the navy uprising, he knew that he couldn't allow the revolution to succeed before he'd secured complete control. He couldn't take the chance of being left out of the triumph, way up in the mountains.

"We're here," Vicente announced as the Jeep pulled up under the cover of a grove of orange trees. They'd chosen the El Naranjo Farm in Los Altos de Mompié in the heartland of the Sierra as their meeting place to discuss the aftershocks of the failed strike.

Later that morning the meeting commenced. Faustino Pérez was now overall director of the *Llano*; Haydée Santamaría spoke for Santiago as Armando Hart had been captured and imprisoned; Vilma Espín had come from the Sierra Cristal; Che Guevara from El Hombrito; and René Ramos Latour, who had led the Action Teams in the streets of Havana. Also present were David Salvador, Bruno Infant, Marcello Fernández, Luis Bosch, and Ñico Torres representing various pieces of the national program. They were in the modest home of the Mompié family, who'd made arrangements to absent themselves to allow this momentous occasion to proceed.

Fidel wasted little time with pleasantries but dove right into the matter at hand. "What's the damage, Faustino?"

"It's hard to tell for sure at this point as many men and women have simply disappeared. Whether or not they were arrested, assassinated, or are in hiding cannot be certain, but at least half of our active members were killed."

Fidel turned to David Salvador who was head of the National Workers Front. "I've heard that several organizations chose to not follow our lead in the strike and went about business as usual."

"The CTC and the Communists backed out when the government got wind of the plans and Batista decreed the use of any force necessary to disrupt the strike."

"That was your job, to ensure that all the groups worked together, was it not?" Fidel was pacing the cramped dining room that barely fit the twelve of them, but stopped to stare down at Salvador.

"The CTC ordered their workers to ignore the strike on March 31st," Salvador replied defiantly. "Perhaps you should've called it off as support was slipping away."

"I should have called off the strike?" Fidel managed to spit out, his face apoplectic. "What control do I have over the *Llano*? I'm here in the mountains doing my part, but you insist that the Sierra and *Llano* be run equally and separately."

"Why didn't you come out of the mountains and attack the cities in the Oriente as promised?" Bruno Infant retorted, defending his comrade.

"As promised? The plan was for the militia to take control of the streets, and thus force the workers to stay home, shutting down the city. That was supposed to allow us, then, and *only* then, to come out of the mountains to engage the superior military forces there, knowing some of them would've been called to the cities to help restore order. It's like a row of dominoes: the first one has to fall for the second to fall, and so on. The Sierra was the third domino, but the first was to take the streets, an effort which met with disaster." Fidel tugged at a beard that had indeed finally grown quite full. "The first domino was René and the action squads. Not only did that domino never fall, it barely swayed. Perhaps 'teetered weakly before stopping' is the phrase that best describes the pathetic showing of the *escuadrones de acción*?"

All eyes turned to René Ramos Latour who'd taken charge of the militia groups for the planned uprising to precede the strike. "We'd no weapons but Molotov cocktails and a few light caliber rifles. Batista had the streets filled with patrols of four men to a car, all armed with machine guns. *Los Tigres*, the SIM, and the police were out in full force as if they knew the date and time of the strike better than we ourselves did."

"You lost the confidence of the locale cadres who commanded the individual cells, and that is why you failed," Fidel thundered at him.

"If I lost their confidence it was because you didn't forward the munitions shipment from Costa Rica on to us," René retorted heatedly.

"You claim the urban underground is ready. You assure me they are the equal of the mountain guerrillas and that they will bring the government to its knees, yet you stand there and say the calamity was due to the fact that you didn't receive weapons that you didn't know existed until but a few days before the action?" Fidel's exasperation filled the small room, answered in intensity only by René's refusal to back down.

"The strike was supposed to be announced at noon, when the workers had arrived home for siesta," René responded, his voice rising to meet Fidel's explosive rumble. "Yet the call went out at 11 a.m., a full hour early when there were only housewives at home to hear the radio. The cadres hustled their cells into the streets, but it was disorganized chaos. Also, instead of being trapped at home, the workers were stuck at their jobs!"

"This is true," Faustino interjected. "The groups at the radio stations either panicked and jumped the gun or misunderstood very clear orders. I've not yet been able to discover which it was, since everybody has gone into hiding, and I myself fled out of necessity."

"A serious mistake." Fidel nodded, his brow furrowed. "But only one in a long line of blunders. What other excuses would you care to make?" He redirected his attention to René.

"A key part of the plan failed when the person tasked with blowing up the electric plant was picked up by the police," René stammered, not yet ready to accept blame.

"So you had an informant." Fidel let the words settle in, a thought that'd been in the back of the minds of many around the table. "And that alleviates you of blame how?" René bowed his head and did not reply, so Fidel continued, "Your militia was unprepared for battle, both psychologically and physically. Your strategy was unsound. But what I'm hearing is that throughout all of this, you somehow looked to me to fix these issues. While you claim the urban resistance to be the equivalent of the guerrilla mountain fighter, and our *Directorate Nacional* is dominated by members of the *Llano*, you continue to look to me in the Sierra to resolve your mess, clean up after you, ensure your success. What do I need of you, then?"

After a long silence, Fidel asked, "How do we move forward after this? This fiasco has put the revolution in the gravest possible danger, as time after time, we continue to disappoint our nation. I'm the face and supposed leader of the *Movimiento 26th de Julio,* and in the eyes of history, will take the brunt of the criticism for this debacle. I'm *una mierda* for allowing this to happen, nothing more than a giant shit. There is no schism in our ranks but no unity either. How can I be blocked from the decision-making process, and yet still be held accountable? If others command the movement in the cities, how is it somehow my fault that the uprising was such a cluster fuck?" Here he stared icily at Salvador. "It's my fault that I didn't forward weapons when I didn't realize they were needed and for that I apologize." The words belied his action as he slammed his fist on the table in front of

René. "How do we create unity when there is this separation in the leadership?"

"We need to reorganize the *Directorate Nacional*," Faustino spoke up in a hushed tone, his manner deferential. "I motion that we place all matters of army governance, including that of the militias, under the command of Fidel. That only works if we make him Secretary-General of the entire organization."

"I second the motion," Celia Sanchez said, "that Fidel Castro is named Commander-in-Chief of the military and Secretary-General of the entire organization."

The revolutionaries at the table mulled over these words, but there was really little choice. The authority of Salvador and René had been demolished and the prestige of Faustino severely tarnished. The vote was unanimous, handing Fidel Castro complete power of the *Movimiento 26ᵗʰ de Julio* for the first time.

"For the first order of business, I will make changes in command due to the recent circumstances." Fidel glanced around the table, his rage having subsided now that he'd gotten what he wanted. More business carried them through the night into the early morning hours. When the meeting finally concluded, Fidel asked Faustino to walk with him. "Thank you for your support, my friend," Fidel said once they were away from prying ears.

"It was difficult to watch so many good men die." Faustino looked away, a catch in his voice.

"It was for the good of the revolution."

* * *

Raúl Castro looked at his watch and realized the approaching headlights must be the bus filled with United States marines and sailors. They were returning from leave, a day and night filled with rum and prostitutes. It was a wonder they'd traveled the twenty miles to Guantanamo City just to get drunk and laid when Caimanera, just outside of their base on the bay, was filled with bars and bordellos. The bus was trundling along through the stubs of a sugar cane field that'd been recently harvested, *for the last time*, Raúl thought to himself, *for we will make sure to come this far south to burn it to the ground before profits can be reaped from it.* In a few minutes the bus would round a corner and enter rougher terrain where the rebels now waited. A pale-orange, almost translucent, scorpion scurried across his boot, causing him to look around cautiously before lowering himself to the ground to await the bus.

Three months earlier, Raúl had led the 6th Column to the Sierra Cristal, opening up the Second Front. Back in early March, they'd loaded seventy men into three Jeeps, three cars, and three trucks for the harrowing trip northeast across the *Llano*. After the comfort of the forests and mountain hideouts in the Sierra Maestra, crossing the plains was like walking naked down a busy street. For this reason they'd traveled fast, reaching the foothills of the Sierra Cristal in Gimbambay just east of Mangos de Baraguá in ten hours.

In the Sierra Cristal, Raúl had begun constructing the organization he'd spent countless hours imagining over the past year. He created the first revolutionary peasant committees of the *Movimiento 26th de Julio* consisting of three men each. The job of these groups would be to supply the guerrillas, provide them with communication and early warning of attack, and to establish patrols to keep order in the area. These councils were based upon communist ideology, but marked by the experience of what he'd learned to be successful in the Sierra Maestra. As they traveled through the mountains, his 6th Column would stop in every region, establishing these supporting networks, further interconnecting the guerrilla with the peasant.

Raúl glanced to his right and smiled at Vilma Espín, who lay with a Thompson machine gun nestled into her shoulder. She was not only his most trusted confidant but had become his lover as well. Vilma had been a student at the Massachusetts Institute of Technology just a few years earlier. She'd left her studies to join the revolutionary activity in Santiago under the leadership of Frank País, and had become a courier between País and Fidel, who was in exile in Mexico at the time. It was in Mexico that Raúl had first fallen in love with her. There was something about her thick black hair, aristocratic nose, shapely cheeks, and zest for life that he couldn't get out of his mind. When she left Santiago to join him in the Sierra Cristal, a spark had ignited dormant passions in Raúl that he hadn't known existed.

Raúl had just turned twenty-seven earlier that month, but his baby face made him appear ten years younger, and this coupled with the renown of being Fidel's little brother—a mark that was more stigma than boost—meant that he constantly had to prove himself. This was probably why he took it upon himself to administer the coup de grâce during executions of deserters, traitors, spies, murderers, and rapists. By his count, he had killed twenty-three men this way since coming to the Sierra Cristal. In this way, his 6th Column had organized the peasants, cleaned out the bandits, and secured the territory of the Sierra Cristal for the *Movimiento 26th de Julio*.

The army soldiers proved reluctant to enter Raul's kingdom, but recently the bombings had intensified, and Raúl had guessed that General Chaviano was about to launch an invasion. Short of munitions, he was at a complete loss on how they could possibly maintain their position in the face of such superior numbers with empty rifles. He had half-heartedly considered resorting to the machete charge of Antonio Maceo and the *mambises*.

And then proof surfaced that the *Yanquís* were still supplying the Batista forces with deadly rockets, even after a supposed embargo had been put in place on all arms shipments. The substantiation of this illegal arms trade came in the form of a requisition order smuggled out of the Cuban Embassy in Washington D.C. A spy for the *Movimiento 26th de Julio* had photographed the paperwork for 300 rocket heads and fuses to be transferred from the United States to the Cuban Army at the base in Guantanamo Bay.

Raúl had the inspiration he needed, and on June 22nd he published an executive order calling for the arrest of all *Yanquís* in the area under his control. Yesterday, rebels had taken control of the American-owned Moa Bay Mining Company on the northern coast of the Oriente Province, taking twelve hostages, two of who were Canadian and so released soon thereafter. They also requisitioned trucks, Jeeps, and other supplies. But the most delicate maneuver was this capture of American marines and sailors returning from a night of debauchery in Guantanamo City. He knew that the death of any one of these men would lead to immediate retaliation and set the colossus to the north firmly against them.

"Pull the bus over!" Lieutenant Jose Q. Sandino of the rebel army demanded, stepping into the road and firing his gun into the air.

The bus driver kept inching the flat-nosed, muddy-green bus forward and began yelling out the window. "*Estoy llevando a militares de Estados Unidos*. I'll not pull over for bandits to kill all of us." In the moonlit night, the anxious faces of the United States marines and sailors could be seen pressed to the bus windows.

Raúl stepped into the Jeep and gestured for Vilma and two others to join him. From the brush on the roadside rose fifty men led by Juan Almeida, surrounding the bus as Raúl raced down the gentle incline to the front of the bus. "I'm Raúl Castro," he shouted, standing up and leaning over the windshield of the buggy. "And I'll guarantee your safety if you stop."

Though he'd never been very athletic, the past year-and-a-half had made him sinewy, a coiled spring waiting to snap. He'd taken to shaving when he established his headquarters in Mayarí Arriba, but at the same time grew his hair down to his shoulders. His features were fine and delicate, even though he preferred to call them "chiseled." The brainstorm was that by capturing and holding *Yanquí* prisoners, he'd force the air force to cease bombing and the army to hold off its own attacks for fear of injuring or killing these hostages. This would gain the guerrillas valuable time to resupply.

Raúl jumped out of the Jeep and boarded the bus. "We mean you no harm. You'll be treated good and taken care of. We need to show you the harm that your government is causing our people and our land." Raúl said, using schoolbook English, removing the ten-gallon Stetson from his head. "I'm not here to hurt anybody." Che claimed the younger Castro looked like an Argentinian gaucho, more fit for riding the range and herding cattle than sneaking through the forest carrying out guerrilla warfare. Raúl agreed that the hat didn't really blend well into rebel life, but he didn't care, for he prized the image he must've made approaching the bus in his huge hat, rifle tipped casually in his arm, and leather boots up to his knees. "What's your name, soldier?" Raúl asked the marine sitting in front of him.

"Joseph Anderson, sah. My friends call me JJ."

"How about you ride with me, JJ, and we can talk. The rest of you sit tight. Some of my men are going to join you for a short ride to where we have some trucks waiting." Raúl hopped lightly down from the bus, waiting for Anderson to join him. Lester Rodriguez pulled up in the Jeep with MOA BAY MINING COMPANY in bright red block letters on the side, Vilma riding shotgun, and the two of them climbed in back. Lester instantly threw the vehicle into gear and tore back towards Mount Rus.

"This is nothing personal, JJ," Raúl yelled as the wind caught soft-spoken words and whipped them back towards Santiago. "But we're in the middle of a civil war in our country, and your government has sided with a dictator against the will of the Cuban people."

"I down't know much about whaht my govehnment tinks, sah, but mowst of the men I know are on youh side in this cohnflict." JJ bellowed back with a New York City accent, having spent most of his life in Queens before joining the military.

"You can forget that 'sir' shit, JJ, and just call me Raúl." He held out his hand and the other man hesitated only briefly before shaking it, then seemed to relax a bit, accepting a cigarette from Raúl, who then had trouble lighting it because of the breeze. "I've guessed that the people of America favor our just cause. But your capitalist officials are intent on protecting the big money interests here in Cuba that Batista kowtows to." The Jeep left the road then, heading up a jagged runoff into the hills.

"Didn't we just recently place an ahms embawrgo," JJ ventured, "cutting off the supply of weapohns? I believe our leaders might be changing their pehspective."

"I've proof that the Cuban air force planes are using your military base in Guantanamo Bay to refuel their planes and that a shipment of 300 rocket heads and fuses was recently delivered in direct violation of that arms embargo."

JJ bowed his head aware of the truth of the words. "I cahn attest dat dose sure are a pair of fahcts."

"And then the dictator's planes drops these incendiary bombs, delivered by your military on orders of the Secretary of State, on the people of Cuba. The bombers don't know where we are, so they drop them in villages to send fear into the local population, killing innocent men, women, and children. All this suffering is caused by your government."

JJ opened his mouth to respond then thought better of it with so many loaded weapons on hand. He spent the night in the mansion of a coffee plantation, and the next day was bundled into a caravan of Jeeps with ragged guerrillas and several other prisoners. A two-hour drive delivered them to the remains of a small village. Shacks that'd once been home to peasants were now jagged timber, scattered thatch, and ashes. Raúl led the hostages around the carnage as if a tour guide, sharing information about the peasants killed here. "We pulled eleven adults and seven children out of that fiery inferno, their bodies so severely disfigured that close relatives were unable to identify them."

JJ found himself walking next to a distinguished man in civilian clothes, a striped shirt with a tie loosely affixed. "JJ Anderson," he introduced himself.

"Howard Roach." The man held his hand sideways to shake. "They grabbed a bunch of us from the Moa Bay Mining Company a few days ago. I'm an engineer and work for Stebbins. We were brought in to design the new nickel and cobalt mines."

"I heahd dey got a big expahnsion prohject going on up there in the nohth." JJ was careful to remain formal, for this man was more like an officer than an enlisted man, even if he wasn't a marine.

"They did." Howard snorted. "Freeport Sulphur, the parent company, was putting $76 million into building new mines. I'm not sure they'll continue after what's happened."

Raúl toured them through several sites of devastation. He had pieces of the bombs that'd been dropped; including one with a serial number that he claimed matched those on a delivery sheet from the United States to Cuba. They then moved on to an enclave of buildings filled with rebels. Once the prisoners were settled in their rooms, Raúl drafted a letter to the United States ambassador.

Dear Mr. Earl T. Smith, June 30

I am currently hosting forty-eight guests from your country in the free territory of the Sierra Cristal and Guantanamo Mountains. I assure you that they are being well treated and will be released as long as certain conditions are met. The first is that the United States stop supplying the Batista Government with weapons, especially rockets. The second is that the American Military Base at Caimanera must cease allowing the Cuban Air Force to refuel their planes there.

Yours in good faith,
Raúl Castro
Major of the 6ᵗʰ Column and
Frank País Second Front

A few days later Raúl, Vilma, and Marro came hurtling into Calabazas, a substantial town of about 400 in rebel-held territory. Companies of guerrillas ringed the town in case Batista's army had set a trap. The meeting spot was a four-room frame house just across from the unused airstrip. A reporter and photographer from *Life* Magazine accompanied them in a separate Jeep, driven by Taras Domitro. These two journalists had braved their way past government blockades to interview the kidnappers. What they'd discovered so far was that the rebels were astonishingly well organized, that the hostages were being well treated, and, strangely enough, handled more like guests than prisoners. An easy, curious camaraderie had developed between the American marines, sailors, engineers, and the guerrillas.

The American Consul Park Wollam and his Vice Consul Robert Wiecha were already there, and in fact, were staying in the house courtesy of the family that owned it. As Raúl and his contingent swept into the dining room, three young children had to be shooed from under the table so that the negotiation might begin.

"We must first have proof that the Americans you took hostage are unharmed," Park Wollam said immediately after introductions had been made. To say he was in over his head was an understatement. He'd been appointed to this position just five days earlier, two days after his forty-first birthday, and the only thing he'd ever negotiated for in his life was a used car. This was certainly a different world than the town of Spiceland, Indiana, where he'd been born and raised.

Raúl hooked his thumb at the *Life* Magazine team. "Lee and George can speak to their well-being."

Lee Hall nodded his head. "We were able to see the civilians and military men. They are all healthy and in good spirits. As a matter of fact, one of them was even wearing a gun slung down low on his waist. Cowboy, they called him, but I believe his name was Thomas Mosness." Raúl had taken a liking to Mosness, initially due to the fact that he wore a Stetson hat identical to his own, but the man's easy-going nature and southern drawl had cemented the deal. When he beat Raúl to a challenged duel, with empty pistols, he'd been allowed to keep the gun, unloaded, at his waist.

"I've a letter here from Ambassador Smith." Park Wollam laid the envelope on the table in front of Raúl. "It's a guarantee that the arms embargo is in place and that the military base is not refueling government planes, so I don't know what this is all about."

Raúl tossed a Polaroid toward Park. "This was taken at your airstrip at Guantanamo Bay two weeks ago." It was a Cuban bomber being fueled, the air tower with the United States flag at Guantanamo Bay clearly in the background. "This was secretly photographed at the Cuban Embassy in Washington D.C." He leaned forward and placed another picture on the table. "It's dated May 28th and is a requisition form for 300 rockets. This is fully two months after the embargo went into effect."

Wollam read the photocopy, a hint of red creeping up his face, before handing it to his Vice Consul, Robert Wiecha. "Those were replacements for defective supplies." He swatted at a fly as multitudes buzzed around the room.

"I believe the intent of your embargo was to deny the dictator Batista weapons that would be used against the proletariat, yet you continue to supply his bourgeois regime with the means to commit genocide. Make no mistake, it's not guerrillas they're bombing, but innocent men, women, and children." Raúl had begun the meeting with a jovial air, but now his voice turned steely. "George has pictures of what your rockets are being used for, and Lee has spoken with the survivors of these raids to verify their accounts."

"You can't just kidnap Americans," Wollam interrupted, "and think that there'll be no retaliation. Secretary of State Dulles has taken your actions as an invitation to intervention, and Admiral Ellis has asked permission to come free the Americans by force."

"Maybe I'm talking to the wrong person? Perhaps I should be speaking with Ellis, or Dulles, or maybe even Ike himself?" Raúl retorted. "Because I have proof that you are directly supporting Batista in his fight against us, which means that you have chosen a side, which in turn means that we've taken prisoners of war."

The drone of a plane could be heard approaching and Vilma went to the window. She didn't think that Batista would be asinine enough to bomb them when conducting business with American diplomats, but she worried that perhaps the United States had deployed a rescue mission. "It looks like a Grumman Albatross," she said, identifying it as a plane the guerrillas knew the Americans had favored since their war in Korea. It was more of a spotter plane than a bomber or fighter, with the ability to land on water as well as land.

"It's set to fly overhead three times a day, at ten, two, and four, until all the hostages have been released."

Raúl slammed his hand on the table. "Prisoners of war."

Wollam continued on, oblivious to the interruption. "We have a simple signal system in place that will communicate whether or not to send in a helicopter to pick up… It was our only choice when you demanded no radio communication."

"Tomorrow you may signal them to bring the helicopter. After I receive an apology for your aid to the illegal government of Havana and a strict promise to cease your military support." Raúl stood and strode from the room, kicking a hen out of the way, as Vilma and Lester followed behind. A light afternoon rain had begun, but rather than cooling, the precipitation created a steam bath as it hit the scorched ground.

11

July 17th, 1958, La Comandancia, La Plata in the Sierra Maestra

You are listening to Radio *Rebelde, the voice of the Sierra Maestra, transmitting to all of Cuba on the 20-meter band at 5 and 9 pm daily. I am station director Captain Luis Orlando Rodríguez. The illegitimate dictator Batista has amassed an army of 12,000 men supported by tanks, armored vehicles, and mortars for its campaign against us. The Rebel Army has stymied them at every turn, led by the brilliant tactics of Fidel Castro and the able defense of his comrade Che Guevara. General Cantillo and the assassin, General Chaviano, lead the armies' offensive. On June 28th, two army battalions marched out of the Estrada Sugar Mill area. Commander Ernesto "Che" Guevara allowed them to move cautiously into the foothills of the Sierra Maestra, just prior to reaching Las Vegas de Jibacoa, before ambushing the advancing infantry. When the armored vehicles came up in support, the guerrillas led them into fields of land mines planted at every entrance into the mountains. Several vehicles were damaged so severely* *that nothing but mangled metal was left. As the battalions panicked, they began to run, dropping their weapons as a contribution to the revolution. The expert riflemen of the rebels picked off many soldiers as they ran away. Three brave comrades were killed in this battle, but the army suffered the loss of eighty-six soldiers. A word of warning to the soldiers of Batista from our supreme commander, Fidel Castro: "Every entrance to the Sierra Maestra is like the pass at Thermopylae. Enter at your own risk."*

Vicente balanced his M-1 on a rock in front of him and waited for the soldiers to come around the bend of the narrow mountain trail. Up until now, Che and the 4th Column had carried out the brunt of the fighting, setting a series of ambushes, and then retreats, only to set more surprise attacks. The total guerilla force in the Sierra was comprised of just 300 men, and they couldn't risk any direct confrontation that would lead to significant casualties, not when they faced 12,000 soldiers.

Frustrated with his inability to penetrate the mountains from the north or east, General Cantillo decided upon an amphibious assault from the south. For three straight days the air force had heavily bombed the area between the ocean and the mountains. The rebels had permitted the troop transport ship to land the 18th Battalion at the mouth of the La Plata River without intervention, and held their fire as the soldiers moved up the waterway as far as the River *El Jigüe* before ambushing them in a barrage of bullets. The panicked soldiers had fired back at unseen targets, while the rebels melted back into the jungle.

The officers of the 18th Battalion ordered the men to dig trenches in preparation for an attack. They'd already lost seven soldiers and three others were mortally wounded, two of them screaming in pain. The rebels had no inclination to assault a numerically superior force, and merely hunkered down in their hiding places to wait them out. For the past two days there'd been no contact, but now, with food and water running low, the army was beginning to probe for weaknesses.

The first soldier came around the corner, yet Vicente, who'd learned to be patient in such situations, still waited. The air was like a damp, hot sponge, the humidity formidable, but it certainly must feel better resting here in the shade of the rocks, he thought, than trudging up the mountain trail below. A second and third man appeared through the sultriness. Vicente wiped his brow with his sleeve and softly admonished himself to wait a few moments longer. Out of nowhere a huge white bird with distinctively hued feet soared on an updraft, startling the soldiers. Vicente knew it was a red-footed booby, because Sophia and he had seen them down by the sea, fishing. This one, his pink and blue beak somehow brighter in the thickness of the day, must've strayed from his coastal hunting pattern.

When the fifth man appeared, Vicente took a small breath, aiming for the lower half of the body. Knowing that when shooting downhill people tend to aim high, he adjusted even lower and squeezed the trigger, letting five bullets escape the chamber, *whap, whap, whap, whap, whap*. The recoil against his shoulder was comforting, as was the vision of his target crumpling to the ground, screaming in surprise and anguish. The other four had scrambled for cover, leaving one dying man and three rifles lying in the trail.

Fidel had just hung up the telephone with Che when he heard the spurt of gunfire coming from the hill. He heard no return fire. He waited a few seconds to make sure it wasn't the beginning of something larger, and then turned to Celia. "The 17th Battalion has made contact with Che outside of Las Vegas de Jibacoa."

"That's one of their veteran battalions is it not?" Celia took a tiny sip of coffee from a gourd, the bitter taste pleasing.

"Yes. Let's hope Che can prevent them from attacking us from the north. If he can hold them off we might just force the 18th to surrender." They'd surrounded the government troops on three sides and controlled their only escape route, which now presented a clear— and deadly—field of fire.

"If Che holds, Cantillo will have to try to send reinforcements via the sea." Celia stood and moved from her small desk to Fidel's side, striking a match as she approached to light his cigar, which had gone out while he spoke on the phone.

Fidel nodded absentmindedly, the cigar bobbing up and down preventing the match from finding its intended target. Celia patiently lit another match and was more successful as he stopped to think for a moment. "Send Sophia to Camilo and make sure that he has set up the .50 caliber guns on the cliffs overlooking the ocean. It's crucial that we dissuade them from any sort of landing attempt."

Celia stepped to the entranceway that was propped open with two six-foot sticks, one on either corner, for the door to their cabin was more like a wall that opened outward and upward, the length and height of their kitchen space. She motioned to Sophia, who lounged outside in the shade of a tree, today acting as one of two bodyguards who were constantly on watch. Over the past year the government had dispatched several assassins who'd infiltrated the guerrillas posing as rebels to get close enough to slit Fidel's throat and slide away into the jungle. Two weeks earlier just such a traitor had been exposed, tried in the courthouse, and shot. Celia passed on Fidel's orders to Sophia, and told her to hurry back.

Before returning to the intensity of Fidel's energy, Celia took a moment to listen to the gurgling brook down below. Their home was built into the craggy side of a ridge, its footings sunk into the inclined hill, which fell steeply down a hundred yards to the streambed below that'd been recently filled by daily thunderstorms. There was a trapdoor in the bottom of their back veranda with a ladder they'd used several times when the bombers had come too close. She stepped back in and took a pitcher of water from the refrigerator she'd brought in with mules, a backbreaking chore, a single luxury that always made her think of her father's house with a smile. The adjacent room was the bedroom they shared and had a similar door, allowing what little breeze there was to flow through. The mattress, a gift from the Medina family, the peasant musicians who lived less than a mile down the mountain, dominated their chamber.

"It's a nice life we have here," Celia said to Fidel, drinking the cold water and looking through the covering canopy of trees to the

valley in the distance. "I'm going to miss this when the war is over."
Fidel paused in his writing, leveling a glance at Celia's back.
"When this is over, we'll be rewriting the history books."

"Yes," Celia replied. "But these moments in the Sierra Maestra
will always be the closest to my heart."

"Don't get too romantic or I'll remind you about the insects, the
heat, and those bombers overhead."

Celia sighed. "You should talk to the soldiers, make them think
about what they're dying for. Just hearing your voice will shock them,
perhaps weaken their will to fight." She sat down at her desk. There
was no sidestepping the fact that this first fighting phase of the
revolution was coming to a climax.

"How do you propose I do that?" Fidel asked. He didn't doubt
that there was a reasonable solution already formed in the mind of
his main advisor.

Sophia found Camilo Cienfuegos on a cliff overlooking the beach
at the mouth of the La Plata River, his normal broad smile widening
even further when he saw her approaching. He was a very handsome
man, athletic and happy-go-lucky. He had the largest beard of any of
the men, wild, tangled, and which overwhelmed his angular features.
"Sophia." He rolled her name off of his tongue with pleasure. "What
can I do for you?"

She smiled in return. "Fidel sent me to ensure the .50 calibers
were prepared to repel any reinforcements." She looked at the large
machine gun lying on its side, nestled into the rocks and the scrub
trees dotting the terrain.

"That man is just not very trusting, is he?" Camilo joked, gesturing
to the parapet and the three men who would aid him in working the
large gun. "The other one is about five miles down the coast, but I
believe this is where the landing will come." He pointed out to sea
where a naval frigate was creeping its way in. "But you should stay a
bit and talk."

"I need to get back."

Camilo took her arm. "Give it a few minutes, or at least until the bombers are gone."

Sophia became aware of the growling of airplanes approaching, a sound that she'd ignored as if to wish the planes away. She allowed him to pull her into a small crevice in the rocks and smiled, but didn't complain, when he wrapped his arms protectively around her. He was popular with the women, but she knew that he respected her relationship with Vicente.

The bombers came from the United States base at Guantanamo, where the planes, *Yanquí* leftovers from World War II, were refueled by Cuban crews and flown by Cuban pilots trained in America. They came sweeping up the coast from the east, the first bombs landing a few miles away and approaching like the footsteps of some colossus, the very earth shifting below them from the blasts, the rocks groaning in protests, and the trees splintering. As quickly as it began, it was over, and Sophia extricated herself from Camilo's arms and crawled out. The other men were already propping up the machine gun on its tripod and preparing it for the landing. The naval frigate had anchored a few hundred yards out to sea, and eight long boats filled with soldiers were lowered to the water.

"Yes, that's it," Camilo murmured as he wrapped his fingers around the trigger, caressing the butt with his cheek. "Come to Poppa." He allowed the boats to get halfway to shore before squeezing the trigger, the heavy casings kicking into the air and scattering into the rocks, their clacking drowned out by the earsplitting din of the big gun. The first round passed harmlessly over the boats, and Camilo cursed, lowering the muzzle slightly. The men in the boats stared into the cliffs trying to locate the source of the gunfire. Some of them caught the flash of the sun on the barrel, others saw the spark from the muzzle, and the ones who weren't hit may have seen the smoke drift away before they hastened to crowd themselves into bottom of the landing boats, fighting each other for position.

Many of the men—peasants conscripted from rural areas—were unable to swim, never having seen the ocean before, and the wide expanse of water was even more terrifying than the invisible death speeding their way from the cliffs above. Water began to seep in from the holes punctured in the bottom of the boats by the large caliber projectiles, the salt water mixing in with the piss of frightened men. The gun laid waste to the exposed men, blowing them into the sea, tearing off limbs, severing one man's trunk so that he fell face forward into the sea leaving his legs in the boat. The only thing that surprised Sophia, who'd witnessed her share of combat violence by then, was that the boats didn't turn back, but plodded forward, several off course and obviously with no one at the tiller.

"Die you bastards, you rat fuckers." While he raked the boat, Camilo kept up a string of curses that would've made Sophia blush a year earlier. Now she didn't even notice. "That's right, turn around you pigs." Finally, the boats began to turn back towards the frigate, whose deck gun had begun to hurl shells in the general direction of the cliffs but with no discernable effect. With a flourish he stepped back from the tripod, clapping his hands together like a blackjack dealer leaving the table, and looked around with a hyperexcited expression verging on mania. "You can tell Fidel that there'll be no support coming from the sea."

Vicente had shifted his position knowing that his vantage point had been compromised and that a bomber would soon try to flush him out with explosives. He was fairly certain, however, that the army wouldn't be attempting to infiltrate men using that narrow trail again any time soon. He was now propped between a fallen tree and a rock guarding access up the hill. His perch overlooked an open, eroded area where rivulets of rainwater had cut the trail, creating an opening through which any and all would have to pass to start their climb. He took a can of sardines from the small bag on his belt, opening it with his knife.

Vicente understood the concept of skirmishing only when the advantage was hugely in their favor, but that didn't make the waiting any easier. He'd always been one to tackle issues head on, and here lay the problem, right at the base of the cliffs. Yet, they merely waited. The small patrol he'd shot at earlier hadn't been their first foray, but was one of a series of constant probes. Earlier he'd taken cover as the bombers had made their run, hearing shortly after the heavy-duty machine gun rattling away at some distance, the sound drifting up to his perch on the sea breeze. That'd been a few hours ago, now, nothing. Into that serenity suddenly thundered the voice of Fidel Castro, so loud that Vicente wondered idly if the man had finally made the transformation from mere mortal to god. Then he realized Fidel was talking into a megaphone hooked up to amplifiers from the radio station.

> *You have no chance of survival, and this is not your fight to begin with. The illegitimate dictator, Batista, has conscripted you and now uses you to silence me, Fidel Castro, for he fears my ideas and the men of the* Movimiento 26th de Julio. *What are my ideas, you ask? I believe in a duly elected government. I believe in giving every man and woman a piece of land and in the sharing of wealth. I believe that a man who works hard should be rewarded with the fruits of his labor instead of his effort just filling the pockets of the rich. Today you receive a paycheck. Tomorrow you will again be cast out. Your leaders refuse to surrender because they don't care if you live or die. We, this revolution, are the only ones who give a damn about any of you and we are offering a hand, a gesture of life. We do not torture and kill prisoners like your army, an army commanded, by the way, by a dictator and his chief-of-staff who are safely tucked away in Havana while you bleed and die for them. Surrender, and we will feed you. Surrender, and we will give you water. Surrender, and we will release you to the Red Cross and in a few days you will be home in the arms of your loved ones.*

Vicente grinned as he listened. He knew the persuasive power of Fidel Castro and was certain that the man could convince you it was night when you were basking in the sun and day when the darkness enveloped you. Fidel blared at Batista's army for hours, and when duty called him away, he played the national anthem and various patriotic songs, the notes tumbling and echoing through the canyons and crevices of the spine of the Sierra Maestra.

Major José Quevedo Pérez sat with his back against a tree, reading the note brought to him by Eulogio Rodriguez, the cook from the 103rd Company of his battalion. Eulogio had been captured several days earlier, but had shown up this afternoon, an emissary, with a request to surrender from Fidel Castro. *How is it possible,* Quevedo wondered, *that in the midst of such a delicate situation, this man Fidel could express himself in such a respectful manner to someone who has been fighting against him and was still doing so?* It was in complete contrast to the bumbling, corrupt chain of command in the Cuban Army he served, an army in whose honor he'd lost faith ever since Batista's 1952 coup. Quevedo had grown up in a military family, his father a colonel at *Fortaleza de San Carlos de la Cabaña,* the fortress protecting Havana harbor, while he'd joined the cadets program at *El Morro* in 1943, also located across the narrows from Havana.

It's not possible that a bunch of rag-tag civilians hiding in the mountains could possibly overthrow the government, Quevedo thought, *but here I am surrounded with every avenue of escape eliminated.*

They'd landed on the beach five miles southeast of the Turquino Peak at the mouth of the La Plata River nine days earlier and rapidly moved up the waterway to reach the forest. When they reached the point where the La Plata River met the El Jigüe stream, the rebels opened fire. Quevedo was certain that this opening salvo would be followed by a horde of rebels charging down the mountain, and he'd ordered the men to dig trenches and wait for an attack that never came. Patrols sent for supplies had been decimated, reinforcements had been rebuffed, and when they tried to move forward, the resistance had been extreme. Then the messages over the loudspeaker had begun, requesting their surrender.

What am I holding out for, Quevedo asked himself. *If anything, I side with these rebels over Batista. Thus far, I've done my duty as an officer of the army, but for what? To protect that which I oppose?*

The next day, a pale Major Quevedo and his aide approached the rebel lines waving a white flag, clambering up the rocky trail, several guns trained upon them as they were brought to meet with Fidel. As they approached *La Comandancia,* the unmistakable hum of aircraft could be heard coming in low over the mountains. Fidel Castro stood on the far side of a small clearing with a woman at his side who Quevedo knew must be Celia Sánchez. As bombs began exploding nearby, Major Quevedo couldn't help flinching. He noticed that neither Fidel nor Celia seemed to pay the slightest bit of attention to the detonations around them. "There's a cave just over this way that might be safer for our talk, Major."

"It would indeed be a shame to survive you and be killed by my own air force," Major Quevedo confessed.

Once safely in a cavern with an oil lamp throwing odd shadows upon the walls, Fidel broached the subject of surrender. "You've done all you could, Major." He spoke deferentially, now that he suspected he'd won. "Turn over your men and I'll allow officers to keep their side arms. As well, I'll immediately begin making arrangements with the Red Cross to release your soldiers if they agree to no longer participate in the fighting."

Major Quevedo bowed his head in acceptance, for there was little choice. "I'll give the orders for my men to lay down their weapons immediately," he said with finality. The truth was, Fidel had offered more than Quevedo was going to ask for, and had done so in the friendly, respectful manner of one commanding officer dealing honorably with an equal.

"We were at the University together, you and me." Fidel veered off into a tangent, lessening the sting of defeat. "You were in officer training and law, and I was the teaching assistant designated to cram information into you. You had a knack for the law, much more so than many of the other officers I worked with."

Major Quevedo stared at the most feared man in all of Cuba, a small green kepi pushed down on his head as if to contain his hair, intense eyes magnified by black glasses perched upon his prominent nose, that heavy beard—and felt himself in the presence of history. Standing casually in a cave in the mountains as bombers dumped their payloads all around, chatting about their university years as if they'd met at the grocery store and were catching up on old times. "I can't say that I remember you," he finally admitted, his voice tentative, the deprivation and worries of the past ten days having worn him down. "Of course, after Moncada, I remembered the name. I just can't remember working with you."

"It appears that the bombings have stopped," Fidel commented, "and so perhaps we should proceed with the surrender."

Quevedo pursed his lips, breathed out, nodded his head, and then cocked his ear to listen to the silence signifying the end of the raid. Fidel stepped out of the cave first, signaling the end of the meeting to those who awaited them. They started back to the camp, but along the way, came to a fork in the trail. Fidel pointed off to the left with a casual wave of his hand. "We've a host of prisoners that we've taken from your battalion just down that trail. Would you like to visit with them?"

Major Quevedo nodded. "That would be much appreciated if I could just have a few minutes."

"Go. When you're finished, have one of the guards show you up to my command center, and we'll draw up terms."

Major Quevedo was surprised to be allowed to pay a visit, unguarded and still wearing his pistol, to his imprisoned men. He silently compared this to the treatment prisoners received from his own superior officers, especially the barbarous General Chaviano who was as savage and uncouth as they came. If the roles had been reversed, Quevedo realized that Castro and all of his men would've been executed on the spot, likely after having been tortured for sport first.

Three days later a deal was brokered with the army. With the Red Cross as an intermediary, 250 soldiers were released from captivity in exchange for medical supplies. Major Quevedo would remain in La Plata with several other officers as prisoners of war, but the enlisted soldiers would all be released. As he watched his troops fly away in several helicopters, he noticed a man sitting on a mule watching, a man he recognized as Che Guevara.

"That bastard Mosquera and his battalion have finally ventured into the hills. I believe we can isolate him and finally achieve justice for his atrocities," Che said as he speared peaches out of the can with his knife and shoved them in his mouth. This was a rare delicacy that he cherished, and so Celia tried to put them by for him whenever she was able.

"If he's exposed himself, you can believe it's for a reason," Camilo Cienfuegos replied from where he squatted in the corner.

"Whether he's using himself as bait to lure us in or not is of no matter," René Latour said. "If we've the opportunity to get that cocksucker, we have to try." René had transformed from urban underground leader into a very capable field commander. He was now in charge of the 10th Column, a small group of about forty men, and had proven himself more than up to the task.

Fidel chewed the end of his cigar, listening to the back and forth of his top leaders as he surveyed a large map of the area spread out on the table in the center of the room. He knew that Mosquera's presence was most likely a trap of some sort, but he was also aware that if the opportunity to kill Colonel Sánchez Mosquera slipped through their grasp, the morale of the men would suffer. Even before the revolution, the area they were now in had been the personal fiefdom of Mosquera and his *Guardias Rurales*. Since the arrival of the guerrillas, the repression had become much worse. Innocent *campesinos* were lynched to send a message, homes and occasionally entire villages were torched, and mass murders became commonplace. If a woman lived alone, it was assumed that her husband had joined the rebels and she was summarily raped and killed.

"Gather round," Fidel said decisively. "René and Ramón," he continued, his fingers coming down on the map, "will take their columns in advance to make sure that Mosquera and his 11th Battalion aren't able to unite with the 17th Battalion. I'll follow with the 1st

Column and encircle them. Che, you'll hold your defensive position at Las Vegas de Jibacoa so that Cantillo can't sneak past and attack La Plata while we're away. Camilo, you'll loop around Pico Turquino to the east and share the plans with Crescencio, and then come to support us from that direction. Juan, you will flank my column to the right and slightly behind. Ramiro, you'll stay here with your men. Make sure you remain in communication via the telephone with Che in Las Vegas de Jibacoa, as I will be sending couriers with updates to him there."

Major's René and Ramón gathered their men and started off immediately. Fidel had ordered Vicente to join René's 10th Column for this engagement, perhaps to have a true *Fidelista* with them. René still harbored some resentment at being blamed for the failed Havana uprising and general strike, and often expressed disagreement with orders, but there was no arguing the fact that he was a markedly capable leader.

Three days later, the various columns were in place. Vicente chewed on a malanga root as he squatted on his heels next to René in the sparse shade provided by several scraggly pine trees. Over the past few days he'd gotten to know and like this man quite a bit, finding him to truly care for what was best for Cuba. "All I'm saying," Vicente commented, "is that once we defeat Batista, many radical adjustments will need to be made if this revolution is to be about more than just a change of power."

"I've no problem with land redistribution." René took a swig from his canteen, letting the tepid water trickle down his throat. He wiped his mustache, newly grown since arriving in the Sierra Maestra. "I don't much care for how the rich treat everybody else, but I do have concerns about nationalizing property and businesses that belong to the United States."

"You don't actually believe they deserve to keep what they've stolen from us over the years, do you?" Vicente asked incredulously.

René took off his beret and poured a bit of water into it, and then placed it back on his head in a futile attempt to cool down. "I just don't think they'll allow it, is all."

"If I've learned anything from following Fidel, it's that you can't be fearful that you're not ready, or not strong enough. He shared a speech by Patrick Henry to me one night, and one part really stuck with me, so I asked Fidel to write it down so I could memorize it." He cleared his throat, suddenly a bit embarrassed, and then began to declaim. "*They tell us, sir, that we are weak; unable to cope with so formidable an adversary. But when shall we be stronger? Will it be the next week, or the next year? Will it be when we are totally disarmed, and when a British guard shall be stationed in every house? Shall we gather strength by irresolution and inaction? Shall we acquire the means of effectual resistance, by lying supinely on our backs, and hugging the delusive phantom of hope, until our enemies shall have bound us hand and foot?*" He paused. "I don't know if you know Patrick Henry or not, but he was from the United States and ends the speech with the famous line, *I know not what course others may take; but as for me, give me liberty or give me death!* It seems that his words have some relevance to our situation, wouldn't you say?"

"What year did you say you dropped out of school?" René laughed and shook his head. "And here you are reciting speeches from the founding fathers of the *Yanquís*. Okay, so we kick the foreigners out. How about the Marxist?"

Vicente knew that was how René referred to Che due to his political philosophies. "Is it his nationality or his politics that you disagree with?"

"Both," René replied. "I don't understand how a state-controlled system would be better than a democracy, and I certainly don't need some doctor from Argentina forcing that down my throat."

Before Vicente could reply, the sound of gunfire erupted from the direction of Santo Domingo where Major Ramón was busy keeping the 11th Battalion bottled up on top of a hill. Thus far, Mosquera had shown little interest in coming down from his lofty perch, and the guerrillas had followed their main tenet of engaging in open conflict only when the terrain and situation favored them greatly. There was no need to give an order. The men rose to their feet and filtered into the trees towards the distant firing.

Vicente flitted from tree to tree, the noise of battle growing in intensity. Soon, he saw guerrillas falling back as the numerically superior army soldiers pressed forward. Vicente realized that the troops were about to flank the rebels on both sides and encircle them, trapping them in an enfilade of fire to be cut to pieces. The forty men of Rene's 10th Column closed to point-blank range. Disciplined, they took up position and waited for the Major to commence the ambush.

There were two soldiers stumbling through the underbrush not ten feet from Vicente when the signal gunshot rang out, and he immediately emptied a thirty round clip into first those two, and then the main body of soldiers, the hunters suddenly becoming the hunted. For the first time since this insurrection had begun, the men had weapons and ammunition in abundance. Some 31,000 rounds of ammunition had been acquired when the 18th Battalion had surrendered a few days earlier, along with all of their mortars, bazookas, grenades, machine guns, and hundreds of rifles.

Vicente slid another clip into his M-1 and rose to his feet, scuttling forward, sweeping the rifle back and forth as he moved, weary of a downed soldier playing possum. The soldiers who'd survived the initial onslaught had fled back into the center, but Colonel Mosquera managed to stem the stampede, turning the men around and forcing them into defensive positions. The guerrillas knew their roles well and sank to the ground, choosing not to charge into a dug-in adversary with superior numbers.

René crawled over to Vicente. "What do you think?"

"They're going to pull back up the hill, and we should let them go."

"We gave them a pretty good shot in the kisser, though." René chuckled.

"We take any casualties?" Vicente asked, looking around the small wooded area, able to discern a few rebels using the natural cover.

"Pascal had a bullet graze his side. Nothing serious. Why don't you slide over and check on Ramón and see how he and his men fared."

Vicente circled back around, taking almost an hour to reach the position occupied by Ramón Paz and the sixty men under his command. "Where's the Major?" he whispered to the first man he came upon, the man merely jerking his head back over his right shoulder without replying. Vicente came to a group of four men huddled over the dead body of Major Ramón Paz.

"He died instantly," a guerrilla said flatly. Vicente didn't recognize him. He was most likely a recent product of the recruitment school in Minas del Frio. "Two others are dead and several injured."

"Major René Latour is just over that way." Vicente waved back in the direction from which he'd come. "I suggest you pull back closer to him until a new commander is appointed."

Two days later they were given orders to cut off the escape route of the 11th Battalion. In the process they captured a soldier who claimed he was deserting. If Colonel Mosquera could leave, why couldn't he? "Sure enough," the man claimed, "a *helicóptero* came in yesterday and the Colonel got on board with his staff and left. Nobody even knows who's in charge and a whole passel of us decided it would be best just to leave."

"Let's hit them now, while they're in disarray," René suggested, though part of his mind wondered if it wouldn't be best to just let them go. *What was the point in engaging, defeating, and capturing them if they were just going to release them in a few days?* But orders were orders, and he knew better than to disobey Fidel. "I'll take my company and get around behind them to the west and ambush them at El Jobal near the Yara River. If they're truly leaderless, this will cause them to turn to the east and head towards the safety of the Estrada Palma Sugar Mill. Vicente, you'll command Major Paz's company setting up an ambush in that direction, and we'll crush them between us."

It was late afternoon before Vicente heard the shots ring out, suggesting that Major René Latour had confronted the enemy. But that was followed by mortar fire, and the rebels hadn't brought any with them. And then there was the unmistakable boom of a tank and Vicente knew that something had gone horribly wrong.

"Pascal, come with me. The rest of you give us a few hundred yards and then follow behind heading for El Jobal." He and Pascal began to carefully slide their way forward through the trees towards the heavy fire. Figures appeared ahead coming at them, and Vicente raised his hand cautioning Pascal not to shoot. As they drew closer he saw that they wore the olive green of the guerrilla. "It's Vicente Bolivar with Major Paz's Company coming up behind," he called from the protection of a tree. "What is the situation?" he asked, stepping out.

"Where's René?"

"He's been wounded," a man named Marcos gasped. "We set the ambush like planned, then a new battalion hit us from behind. The *hijos de putas* had mortars and a tank. We had no idea they were there."

"Where is René?" Vicente demanded again.

"He should be coming right along." Marcos paused to collect himself. "Juan and his brother are carrying him in a hammock. He took mortar fragments in his lower belly. It don't look very good."

"Pascal, take Marcos and the rest of the men back to our company and set up an ambush. Surprise them, and then withdraw. Do not get pinned down. We have no idea what we're dealing with here."

With that, Vicente followed the gunfire in search of René. He found the Alfonso brothers struggling along with the man moaning softly in pain at every step they took. "This way," he directed them, circling away from the planned ambush to a small hamlet that'd been deserted some time ago. They set him down on the ground inside one of the palm frond shacks. "Juan, go see if you can find Che. He should be back between here and Santo Domingo."

René mumbled something unintelligible and Vicente tipped a sip of water to the man's lips, a froth of blood bubbling from his mouth. He coughed, and then spoke in a barely audible whisper. "I don't want that communist poking around inside of me."

Vicente chuckled grimly, understanding that while the men disagreed about politics, there was mutual respect between them. "He should be just a few miles back, and I don't think his politics will affect his medical skills."

René's lower belly was torn apart. His intestines hung out from his stomach with jagged pieces of metal jutting forth. The frothy blood on his lips meant a puncture of the lungs, and each breath was labored and painful. Vicente doubted that the man would last until Che's arrival. He died half-an-hour later right after exacting a promise from Vicente to tell his wife and children that he loved them.

* * *

General Eulogio Cantillo stood over a sizeable map of the area surrounding Las Mercedes, Cuba. "You've done your job well, luring the rebels after you," he said to Colonel Mosquera. Cantillo didn't much care for Mosquera, but the fact was that he was a very effective soldier, and capable officers were hard to find these days.

"Now we have to finish the job." Mosquera had a weak chin that quivered when he spoke, but his heavy-handed, often violent tactics were legendary in Oriente Province.

"Castro took the bait and fell right into our trap. He's surrounded between our forces in this triangle." Cantillo used a pointer to touch the three small towns of Arryones, Sao Grande, and Las Mercedes. "He came to support his 10th Column, believing there to be only two of our battalions in the field. He was quite shocked when we came at him with seven tanks, a bazooka squad, and 1,500 men."

"I did appreciate the airlift from the hill," Mosquera said drily. Things had been tight for a few days as he'd been cornered with the rebel forces closing in on him, but then a helicopter had flown him and his general staff to safety, leaving his 11th Battalion stranded on a hilltop. This had been enough to bring Castro running with his 1st Column, the greedy rebel pig.

Cantillo set his hat down on the table, revealing a receding hairline. That, coupled with a paunchy build, caused many men to underestimate him. "We have eight battalions bearing down on him and he has, what, a couple hundred men? It shouldn't be long now."

12

July 3,1958, Sierra Cristal

rue to his word, the next day, Raúl brought five of the
prisoners back with him, along with an armed escort of twenty
men, arriving in three Jeeps and a transport truck. The guerrillas
pulled up to the house where the Americans were staying, but were
told that Wollam and Wiecha were on the airstrip speaking with the
pilots of the three transport helicopters that'd arrived a few minutes
earlier. The convoy cut across the small ditch and through the scrub
brush that'd grown up in the years the field had been unused. A group
of children had gathered around the choppers, the youngest crowding
forward, while those older hung back and tried to look disinterested.

Raúl approached the Americans gathered at the helicopter doors.
"Here are the prisoners as promised," he said. He'd chosen the
older, more fragile, less healthy of the lot to return, understanding
fully that he'd be blamed by the Americans for any sickness or,
God forbid, a death that would undoubtedly lead to harsh and
immediate retaliation. It was a dangerous game he was playing, but
it had bought the guerrillas a reprieve of a week so far. One supply
plane had already arrived, and several more were expected over the
next two weeks, and then the rebels would be well prepared for any
assault that might come.

"These are the prisoners?" Wollam uttered, trying to keep his temper in check. "You have forty-three more hostages by my count. Where are they? We have three helicopters on the airstrip ready to transport fifty men, and you bring only five?"

"Prisoners," Raúl corrected him softly. "They're being held further away. It'll take some time yet to get them here."

"So, we should bring these helicopters back tomorrow?"

Raúl laughed. "Tomorrow? Of course not. Tomorrow we celebrate American independence. We'll have a barbecue for our guests. Maybe the next day."

Howard Roach had walked over and heard these last words even as the helicopters turned their engines on and the whirling blades began their deafening beat. "What's this I hear about a barbecue? Can I change my mind and stay another few days?"

Raúl smiled broadly. "No, Howie, you must leave today and get your high blood pressure pills, or Dulles is going to get permission from Ike to send the marines of Ellis into the mountains to eradicate the evil Raúl Castro and his cronies." He hugged the man and prodded him towards the eggbeaters.

Howard grinned back, lingered on a hug with Vilma, who was looking particularly appealing in a plaid shirt instead of the normal olive green, with blue jersey pedal pushers, and a red kerchief holding her hair in place. He then walked down an honor guard of twenty guerrillas. Several of the men had been at the coffee plantation with him, and he shook their hands heartily, liking these young rebels.

Raúl played the game for two more weeks, releasing a few guests every other day. This slow repatriation appeased the Yanquís enough that they didn't feel the need to send in troops, and all the while gained time for the rebels to build their strength. On the night of July 17th, Juan Almeida arrived at the headquarters Raúl had established at an old plantation on the outskirts of Mayari Arriba. He delivered the orders from Fidel to release the last of the prisoners.

"Not a problem. We've had several arms shipments and restocked our ammo and are ready to fight again." Raúl grinned. "So, we no longer have need of our anti-aircraft batteries." This is what they'd come to call the captured Americans who'd been more useful than actual weapons in preventing air raids. "I'll liberate the last of them tomorrow. Is there anything else?"

"Santiago tells us the CIA is sending a spy to find out if you're a damn commie. He's a former Marine who goes by the name Captain Rex. Fidel wants you to keep him close, perhaps use him to train new recruits in technique, and impress upon him your democratic leanings."

Raúl smiled sarcastically, and then bid his friend *adiós*, as Juan had to get back to his own column.

"He's not here to kill you, is he?" Vilma asked, once Juan was gone.

"No, not as long as we can pull the wool over his eyes," Raúl replied.

Vilma stepped closer, running her hand down his smooth chest inside the unbuttoned uniform. "I don't think I could live without you."

"You won't have to," Raúl reassured her, one arm wrapping around the small of her back and the other hand cupping her neck.

"We could just kill him and be sure."

"No. We'll use him for our purposes. We've hundreds of new recruits pouring in. Men willing to fight who we can now arm, yet they're no good to us without training. We'll have this Captain Rex establish a school and educate them in the art of war."

Vilma ground her hips into his midsection. "You'd have the CIA help you with your Marxist Revolution?" she asked in a husky tone.

Raúl nuzzled his lips into her shoulder, his teeth sending shivers down her body. "Marx had many good ideas, but so did Thomas Jefferson, Abraham Lincoln, and Franklin Delano Roosevelt. Once we've finished with Batista, we'll create something totally new here in Cuba."

"A new government based upon equality." She bit the lobe of his ear roughly.

"A place where neither color, gender, wealth, nor birth will dictate social status." He began to unbutton her plaid shirt, his hands crawling inside, still intrigued by the bullet bra she wore, but impatient to unhook the pointed undergarment.

Vilma undid his belt, letting his pistol and cartridges drop to the ground. "Mm. You talk too much."

Raúl groaned in reply, his hands pushing her jersey pedal pushers down around her ankles and lifting her onto the table.

* * *

"We're trapped," Crescencio Pérez said quietly. "They've surrounded us with at least seven battalions—at least 1,500 men, including tanks and mortars." He tapped the map showing the placement of the enemy units around their position just outside the town of Las Mercedes.

"Can we break through back towards Minas del Frio?" Fidel pointed in the direction of the heights of the Sierra Maestra they'd so foolishly abandoned. It was only a few miles, and not much further was *La Comandancia* at La Plata, but they both might as well have been on the other side of Cuba.

"Not without a huge loss of men. Every battalion has mortars, bazookas, and at least one tank. If they don't know exactly where we are, they will by morning, and the air force will be bombing the hell out of us." Crescencio spat into the dirt. "I can get you out of here, along with maybe five or six others. We could slip through at night."

"I won't leave my men behind," Fidel declared.

"If you don't, the revolution is over."

"Che and Camilo are outside the military cordon," Fidel spoke slowly. "But if the military captures two-thirds of our already small force, we may as well concede defeat. There has to be another way."

"You are an able strategist," Celia spoke up. "And you have terrific skills planning and fighting battles, but it isn't what you do best."

"And what is it I do best?" Fidel growled.

"Talk." Celia was careful to not smile, for this was a delicate matter.

"Talk?" Fidel glowered at her. The others studiously looked at the ground, their faces burning as they pretended to search the map for a way out of the steel cordon surrounding them.

"Call for a truce to negotiate the terms of surrender," Celia urged.

Fidel swore, deep in his throat, his face growing purple. "I'll die before I'll ever surrender."

"I didn't say that we *would* surrender," Celia replied calmly. "Send a messenger to General Cantillo that you wish to negotiate terms. And then you'll fill his ears with as much rhetoric and mumbo jumbo as he can take. I know you. You can talk for days. In the meantime, we'll start slipping men through their lines in small groups of three or four until everybody is safely away."

On the verge of exploding in rage, Fidel abruptly froze, for once in his life at a loss for words. "That might just work," he finally said.

"You should stress that you wish to put an end to the bloodshed," Celia added.

The very next day, General Cantillo, Fidel's surrender proposal in hand, found himself on a small plane on his way to Varadero Beach where Fulgencio Batista was vacationing. Cantillo flew into a small airport in Matanzas then hopped into a waiting car for the short ride to Batista's beach home ten miles out o a very narrow peninsula, a route that was heavily guarded. Cantillo sneered to himself, knowing that while he was putting his life on the line, this man was living in opulent splendor protected by more men than comprised an entire battalion.

For the first time, Cantillo began to wonder what he was doing. Why should he endanger his life so that others could wield all the power and realize the benefits? Perhaps he could play Castro against Batista, letting them kill each other, and then he could swoop in and take control of the government. He already had the support of most of the army. Would they side with that fat bastard Tabernilla or the sadistic bully Chaviano? Neither was likely. Cantillo was the only general actually in the field. If he could just eliminate Batista and Castro both, there was a chance that this could all be his.

Once he passed through all the guards and arrived at the villa, Batista had him wait by the pool as if he were some common delivery boy. After an hour he appeared in a bathing suit, dark glasses, and gold chains around his thick neck. A servant held a robe for him, which he slipped on, slapped the ass of the beautiful young woman with him, and ambled over to Cantillo like he'd just spotted him at a resort. "What is so important that you have to interrupt my vacation, General?"

"We've received a correspondence from Castro suggesting he's ready to end the bloodshed." Cantillo didn't believe this himself, but he decided on the spot to make Batista believe it.

Batista sat down at a small wicker table and indicated Cantillo should follow suit. "Do you really believe that Castro wants a truce?"

"We have him surrounded. He has little choice."

"And he has no chance of escape?"

Cantillo was sitting with the sun directly in his face, a position he was certain Batista had intended. "He could probably slip away," he conceded. "But the bulk of his force would be captured. It'd be a devastating blow."

Batista knew that Cantillo wasn't telling the whole truth. He hadn't risen to become the most powerful man in Cuba without a great deal of political savvy, and he certainly knew when he heard a mistruth, even one of omission rather than commission. What he was not sure of was when he had stopped caring about the people of Cuba. It was he who'd brought schools to the rural population in 1936, taxing the sugar companies to pay for them, and sending army sergeants to be teachers. His triennial plan in 1937 had called for distribution of state land to the poor, health insurance for working mothers, and a housing program for the elderly, as well as many more reform-minded government goals.

Where had he gone wrong? Was it the affair that he'd started with the seventeen-year-old beauty, Marta Fernández Miranda? He had, to be fair, divorced his wife and married this younger woman. Not that he was faithful to her either, as could be seen by the young actress he'd brought with him on vacation. He'd always had a weakness for women, ever since the aging prostitute had taken him in when he was homeless in Santa Clara, before he joined the military.

"Sir?" Cantillo interrupted Batista's reverie. "Do I have your permission to meet with Castro to negotiate peace?"

Batista was brought back from his youthful idealism to his less idealistic present. "I've asked my prosecutor general, Lieutenant Colonel Fernando Neugarti, to come out from Havana. He should be here shortly. You'll bring him back to Bayamo with you, and send him to hear what Castro is offering." *That should wipe the sneer off your smug face*, Batista thought. Whatever Cantillo thought he was gaining by brokering a peace with Castro had effectively been removed by sending his own man to reflect the credit back on himself.

Cantillo and Neugarti arrived back in Bayamo that very night, and the next morning Neugarti flew into Las Mercedes in a helicopter, bringing with him the medical supplies that'd been one request, the other being that a ceasefire be adhered to during the negotiation. Neugarti was a slender man with a keen legal mind. He was eager to make a name for himself, and he saw no better way to do so than to broker a peace between the army and the rebels. Fidel personally greeted Neugarti and ushered him into an old brick building belonging to the coffee plantation in the town. The brick outer wall had but one entrance, a high arch that Fidel brought Neugarti through as they went to the main room.

For the next three days Fidel harangued the government, advocated for the people, showed contempt for the corruption prevalent in Cuba, and reviewed the entire history of insurrection, going back as far as the time of Hatüey. The only other person who spoke ever was Neugarti, who made fragile efforts to steer the talks to some sort of negotiation of the truce. Each evening he'd return to Bayamo to fill in General Cantillo, and all the while guerrillas were being slipped out of the town in small groups.

The third day, in desperation, Neugarti presented his own plan to Fidel, involving a call for general elections among other things. To his surprise, Fidel immediately agreed that the plan had merit. It was decided that Neugarti would return to Havana to get approval from Batista, and then the treaty could be drawn up formally, before they all gathered in Bayamo to make it official.

An ecstatic Neugarti barely stopped long enough to tell Cantillo the good news before proceeding to the airport. As the plane carrying Neugarti lifted off the runway in Bayamo, Fidel was in his Jeep with Celia and Sophia in the back as Vicente drove, following Crescencio on horseback, the last of the guerrillas to slip through the cracks and back to their mountain stronghold.

The very next evening, Fidel went on the radio to announce the government's pathetic failure.

Now for Radio Rebelde, the voice of the Sierra Maestra, transmitting for all Cuba on the 20 meter band at 5 and 9 pm daily. This is Fidel Castro bringing you the truth from the battlefront. The summer offensive has ended with a decisive victory for the Movimiento 26th de Julio.

The rebels suffered twenty-five killed, men who will go down as martyrs of Cuban independence. The army suffered 231 deaths, with more than 400 prisoners taken, allowing the rebels to capture over 500 rifles, eleven .50 caliber machine guns, two tanks, one cannon, one anti-aircraft gun, countless mortars and bazookas, and another 100 submachine guns. We would like to thank the dictator, Fulgencio Batista, for providing these weapons.

Our revolution is not against the soldiers who should be standing shoulder to shoulder with us as we fight against the graft and corruption of the officers, those men who gained their position not through merit but as favors from the dictator Batista, and now use their status to line their pockets at the expense of the people of Cuba. Soon, the men and women of the Movimiento 26th de Julio *will leave the Sierra Maestra and bring the battle to the doorstep of those most guilty. I urge the soldiers to lay down their arms, or better yet, join us in our campaign to free Cuba.*

For those of you who wish this Civil War to end, these are my conditions. First, the illegitimate dictator, Fulgencio Batista, must be arrested and delivered to the tribunals of justice. Second, all political leaders involved in the illegal seizure of power, or who have enriched themselves at the expense of the Republic's resources, must be arrested to face justice. Finally, all army officers who have committed crimes in the cities or countryside and enriched themselves through illicit means including smuggling, extortion, or gambling must be turned over to the rebel army for trial.

*We await the answer of the present regime on the march,
for we are coming for you.*

* * *

Fulgencio Batista entered the room at one in the afternoon, looking dapper as always in a gray suit and dark tie, a crisp white shirt, and brightly polished shoes. He'd just come off the elevator from his residence on the third floor of the Presidential Palace to the administrative offices on the second floor. The previous night he'd stayed up late again, until the early morning hours, watching movies, finishing with one of his all-time favorites, *Casablanca*.

His mind was still puzzling out Rick's decision to send the love of his life away and remain in Morocco even though it probably meant arrest and possibly death. *Would it not be better to take the money and the girl and go someplace safe?* He flashed a smile and greeting to his secretary, a beautiful dark-haired white woman in a low-cut black dress. Maybe today he'd send his wife to their Kuquine estate in the country so that he could invite his secretary to share a movie with him upstairs. It'd been over a week since he'd enjoyed the pleasure of her company.

The others were waiting for him in the conference room. Batista took the time to walk around the table and greet each of them personally. General Cantillo had flown in with Colonel Mosquera to update them on the situation in the Sierra Maestra. General Chaviano was there bringing news from the Sierra Cristal, and Rolando Masferrer had come from Santiago. Of course, his close friend, and chairman of the Joint Chiefs of Staff, General Francisco Tabernilla, was there. Batista made a point of asking after wives and children, pausing at each man's side to carefully listen to their reply.

As soon as he sat down, however, it was all business. "General Cantillo, let's start with the Sierra Maestra. It's my understanding that the peace negotiations of ten days ago were just a ruse to gain an advantage. I believe that when you came to consult with me, I voiced this concern, but you were adamant that we hear Fidel out." Batista's voice was steely, a reminder that he'd once been a formidable foe, though it had been some time since he had been near a battlefield. "What's the prognosis?"

General Cantillo was impassive on the exterior, but inwardly he smiled to himself. Of course he'd known that Castro's request had been but a scheme to buy more time. The truth was, it couldn't have worked out better. Fidel hadn't been destroyed, and he now trusted Cantillo. When the time came to broker a peace between the two forces, it would be him, Eulogio Cantillo, who would be calling the shots. "It's not good, sir. We were forced to withdraw from Las Mercedes under intense pressure from the guerrillas. The morale of the men is so low that I doubt we can get them to leave the safety of their garrisons any time soon."

"You have twelve thousand soldiers in the field, yet you've been beaten into submission." Batista threw up his hands in exasperation. "I hear different reports on how many guerrillas there are. What's your estimate?" Batista had removed his Rolex from his wrist and was absently tapping it on the solid oak table.

"If I had to venture a guess, sir, I'd go with two thousand in the Sierra Maestra, and an equal number in the Sierra Cristal. That doesn't include the thousands more they have in the urban areas." Cantillo knew the number was actually much lower, but was hesitant to admit to taking a drubbing by so few.

"You outnumber them five to one," Batista let the numbers sink in, then added, "and yet are defeated at every turn."

"The rebels have the better ground to defend, sir. They're also more committed than the peasants that make up my army."

"What's this I hear of an invasion of the west?" Batista was only half-listening, thinking again of *Casablanca*, of Rick Blaine choosing to stay.

"Fidel has ordered three of his columns to move west under the command of Che Guevara, Camilo Cienfuegos, and Jaime Vega."

"Can we stop them?" Batista slid his watch back onto his wrist and leaned forward over the table.

"We've annihilated the column led by Vega," Cantillo said proudly.

"And the other two?"

General Tabernilla interrupted, his long mortician's face appropriately grave. "We've mobilized all of the military units between Santa Clara and Oriente Province. My intelligence tells me they are less than 500 men, traveling hundreds of miles, with no transportation or supplies. We'll stop them. And then we'll kill them."

General Cantillo bowed his head to this assessment from his superior officer. "I hope that General Tabernilla is correct."

Batista turned to his brother-in-law, Colonel Albert del Río Chaviano, a man who he didn't much care for, but tolerated because he was family. "What is to report from the Sierra Cristal?"

Colonel Chaviano had a well-groomed mustache that did nothing to soften the meanness of his eyes. "The guerrillas under Raúl Castro have cemented their defense in the mountains. While we're unable to penetrate their lair, they don't leave the safety of their haven to confront us either."

"And they can't be bombed out?"

"We've tried, but they've built bunkers into the ground, and at the sound of approaching planes, they disappear from sight. Tanks and armored vehicles can't penetrate the rugged terrain, and the soldiers are on the verge of desertion if forced to march into the hills."

"We'll have to be satisfied with keeping them isolated on the eastern tip of the country," Batista said half-heartedly, realizing that his empire was crumbling and that the people were turning against him. "How's Santiago holding up?"

Rolando Masferrer had recently returned from Santiago where he'd been rooting out insurgents. "Between the army, the police, and *Los Tigres*, we have firm control of Santiago, but there is a fresh bombing incident nightly. A guerrilla group under the leadership of Juan Almeida has taken control of the heights to the west of the city. As long as the rebels don't cut us off from Santa Clara and Havana, Santiago should hold fine." He knew this was what Batista wanted to hear, but the truth was, Masferrer had no plans to go back to that city. He'd never wanted to be a martyr. No, he was a survivor, and he'd already begun to plan his escape.

* * *

Vicente had been assigned to the 8th Column under the command of Camilo Cienfuegos for the invasion of the west, part of two groups that had left the safety of Orient Province at the end of August. A third had been ambushed and wiped out before barely getting started. As the Batista offensive faltered, Fidel had decided to go on the attack, sending his best commanders to drive the war to the doorstep of the capital. Che Guevara had led the 2nd Column to attack Santa Clara, less than two hundred miles from Havana. Camilo had been tasked with capturing Yaguajay, just southeast of Santa Clara, and then to aid Che in capturing that city.

The trip across Camagüey had proven so difficult it could've been the thirteenth labor of Hercules. Hidden in bunkers buried into the ground, the army had set up a cordon of soldiers to ambush them and halt their progress. These companies of soldiers infested the Baraguá District, forcing the guerrillas to the southern coast where rains had saturated the area, creating endless waist-deep bogs of mud that meant hours of slogging, the rebels' rifles and cartridges held high overhead to keep them dry. They'd traveled fifteen straight days with mud clutching at their elbows without respite from the torrential downpours. When the clouds finally cleared and the sun came out, the rebels had collapsed in a small clearing in the center of a copse, stripping their clothes to be dried, and fumbling for the last of their food and water.

Vicente took two volunteers and went to hunt for more substantial food. After about an hour of futile searching, he spotted a deer, but before he could fire, a shot rang out, and the animal toppled to the ground. He raised his hand, cautioning the two rebels with him to stay still. Three government soldiers approached the fallen deer, and if it wasn't for the hunger for real meat, Vicente might've let them go. Oh, what a morale boost that fresh venison would provide for the 8th Column! Two of the soldiers propped the deer on its back while the third drew a tapered knife and sliced the belly open from genitals to sternum. It was at this moment that Vicente stepped from behind the tree and leveled his M-1.

"We're soldiers." The man with the knife had the insignia of a corporal on his sleeve and was the first to speak.

"And you are now prisoners of the 8th Column of Fidel Castro under the command of Camilo Cienfuegos." Vicente managed a smile through the dirt caked on his face. "Drop your weapons and pick up that deer."

They waited until dark to build a small fire under a cluster of pine trees, hoping the needles would dissipate the smoke and the darkness would conceal what little light trickled into the night sky. This was the first meat they'd eaten since the horse, a pack animal they'd slaughtered six days earlier, slicing raw pieces of flesh from its body in their desperation. If any of the men had suffered stomach pains from that incident, they'd kept it to themselves.

"There are two full battalions spread out ready to ambush you." The corporal looked around at the bedraggled group of just over one hundred men. "You've no chance to make it through."

"But you know where all of these men lie in wait?" Camilo asked gently.

"That I do." The corporal could not contain a bit of bragging. "I personally gave the orders for their deployment."

"So, you could guide us through safely?" Vicente took another small bite from his ration of the deer.

"Why would I do that?"

The next night they silently made their way single file through the ambush sites, the corporal leading the way. Quite simply, the rebels had promised that if they were fired upon, he'd be the first to die. Once they'd moved safely through the maze of ambush sites, the corporal and two soldiers were set loose, left to ponder the choice of returning to their homes or going back to the army to admit what they'd done. After thirty-one days of marching through the muck and around the soldiers, the guerrillas reached the Jatibonico River and crossed over the swollen waterway into Las Villas Province.

In the ensuing six weeks, the 8th Column tightened the cordon around the Yaguajay military barracks by capturing one by one the lesser garrisons in the surrounding small towns. They then created civilian networks to support their efforts much like Raúl Castro was doing in the Sierra Cristal. As for the beleaguered Yaguajay barracks, reinforcements had arrived three days earlier in the form of Captain Abón Ly and the 11th Battalion. Ly had replaced Colonel Mosquera who had suffered a debilitating back injury, and now commanded 300 well-trained career soldiers who were posted around the city in the tallest buildings to protect the water and electricity supplies, bolstering the city's already formidable defenses.

Camilo established the guerrilla headquarters in a brothel whose Madame was a firm supporter of the movement. She told the girls that there'd be no charge for the rebels, and the men eagerly accepted this opportunity to tryst before what they all knew was the coming battle. Vicente abstained, missing Sophia's company even more in such surroundings. He told himself that the quicker they were able to subdue the city, the faster he'd be reunited with the woman who stirred his passion even from afar. Yesterday the townspeople had invited them to honor *Nochebuena*, but Camilo had stipulated they could only celebrate the night before Christmas if they drove the soldiers from the city and back to their military barracks on the edge of town. This was plenty of motivation for the rebels to prepare an assault on the entrenched soldiers.

When the sun fully emerged above the horizon at their backs, the opening shot rang out, building to a crescendo of rifle fire mixed with the heavy booms of the bazookas. Vicente had targeted a soldier on the roof of a two-story building who seemed to be serenely watching the dawning of the new day, unaware of the impending doom below him. Several bullets from Vicente's rifle almost severed his head from his body, flopping backwards as if hinged, before he slowly collapsed to the rooftop.

Vicente was up and running before the man hit the ground, sprinting to the protection of a corner market, where he stood with his back to the wall, gathering his breath, before peering around the side. Bullets crashed into the stone sending jagged slivers tearing at his face. He jerked back, cursing, his hand feeling the blood on his cheek. He slid down the wall to a sitting position, and then taking a deep breath, rolled around the corner cradling the M-1. A machine gun nest on a building across the way opened up, but the bullets hit high, several feet above his head. Vicente gently squeezed the trigger, sending a burst aimed at the two soldiers on the rooftop, and they dove for cover.

Commander Camilo Cienfuegos came around the corner, his rifle blazing away as he stepped over the prone figure of Vicente. He wore a light jacket in the early morning hour, flapped open in the breeze, his cowboy hat perched jauntily upon his head and a cigar hanging out of the corner of his mouth. "Quit lying around Bolívar. We've a town to clear." Camilo had built his reputation as a point man, utterly fearless as he led companies through the mountains on patrols and ambushes. On one such surprise attack, he allowed the lead soldier to get close enough before opening fire that after he killed him, Camilo had caught the man's rifle before it hit the ground.

Vicente scrambled to his feet, sweeping his rifle in front of him as he moved to the left of his commander. Several soldiers were visibly retreating towards their barracks, dropping their weapons in flight, and Camilo aimed carefully and brought one such man down, twisting and convulsing on the ground. He waved at the building from which they'd been taking fire, indicating that Vicente should make sure it had been cleared of soldiers. Vicente ran across the central plaza and through the front door of the town hall building. He paused at the bottom of the stairs, counted to three, and then began to clamber up the steps.

As he reached the second floor, a soldier appeared, swinging his rifle in a wide arc that connected with Vicente's upraised arm, his fingers grasping the weapon and hanging on. The man snarled, released the rifle, and produced a bone knife from the sheath on his belt. He slashed at Vicente, drawing blood from his torso, a shallow cut through the heavy cloth of his uniform. Vicente jammed the man's own rifle into his face, the impact leaving the man teetering on the edge of the staircase. The soldier threw a punch, and all Vicente could do was grab his arm and hang on as they both tumbled down the stairs. When they finally came to rest on the first landing, Vicente noted the awkward angle of the soldier's neck and realized the man was dead. He pocketed the knife. The rifle could be retrieved later. He performed a cursory sweep of the building to ensure it was now empty before returning to the street.

As Vicente returned to the street, Camilo pulled next to him in a Jeep, honking the horn, "Bolívar, get in, you look a mess."

Vicente climbed into the vehicle. He realized how comfortable it was to sit down, aware of the rock splinters in his cheek and the scratch across his chest. "Where are we going, sir?"

"Sir?" Camilo snorted. "Do I look like some fat son-of-a-bitch like Tabernilla? Don't insult me." They drove through the streets, finding their forces firmly in control of Yaguajay. The next step would be to capture the barracks. As they passed by the Narcisa Sugar Refinery, Camilo suddenly slammed on the brakes and leapt out. Vicente followed slowly as Camilo approached an old derelict bulldozer sitting behind one of the outlying buildings.

"What is it?"

"It's how we'll drive the army from their barracks," Camilo said excitedly, cavorting around the long-neglected piece of farm equipment. "Do you know the tale of Don Quixote?"

"I can't say that I do, Camilo."

"You need to read it, Bolívar. It's only the single most important piece of literature ever produced by a Spaniard. Don Quixote is an errant knight living in a fantasy world in which he imagines windmills to be giants. In this contraption I see a fire-breathing dragon that will chase the soldiers from the safety of their garrison. See if it will start up. Never mind, I'll check it myself."

Camilo jumped into the seat of the bulldozer and began fiddling with the controls. "Did you know that I started off my adult life as a student at the art school in San Alejandro?" He opened a panel in the front and realized there was no battery. It'd need to be started with the crank handle, which he promptly turned over. The tractor wheezed, coughed, and then indeed came to life. "I wasn't there long due to some money troubles, meaning I didn't have any, and the school expected payment. Anyway, in my short time there, I studied the sculptures and works of Leonardo da Vinci. Did you know he was an accomplished inventor as well?"

"Leonardo who?" Most of the schooling Vicente had been

exposed to, including his recent political education, had been of more practical matters than literature and art.

"Never mind who he is, only know that he had a penchant for devices, an interest that I myself have shared. Imagine this machine with a flame thrower, belching fire, rumbling into Captain Ly and his men, torching their buildings and walls, so that they have to emerge from their fortifications to be confronted on equal ground."

What Vicente was actually thinking was that this slow-moving bulldozer might prove to be a deathtrap for those occupying it and not opposing it, but he knew enough to nod wisely and keep his counsel. Camilo took the machine back to the empty lot next to the brothel and immediately started working on it. He raised the Caterpillar bucket and welded metal plates around the radiator, including the cab. He then tested it by firing into the casing, adding sandbags for extra protection. Next, he moved onto the armaments. He took a field sprayer and attached it to a compressor with a tiny motor that would ignite and shoot gasoline in a fiery streak over ten yards, which meant it would have to be within close range to be effective. He mounted a .50 caliber machine gun in the cab with the barrel poking out a slit in the armor two feet long to compensate for the jury-rigged, fire-spouting tank's single greatest flaw—the spped of its one functioning gear was a torturous crawl.

Over the next few days he launched three assaults in the dark period before sunrise, a time where the dragon would be most effective in creating terror and confusion. To little avail, however, as each time it struggled to get within flame-throwing range of the barracks before well-aimed bazookas dismantled the machine. Finally, Camilo gave it up.

None of the men were all that interested in a direct assault on a well-entrenched enemy, and besides, the women of the brothel were providing them free services as heroes of the revolution. Meanwhile, Fidel was impatient that Camilo secure this city. Once Yaguajay succumbed, then Camilo and Che's combined forces would make short work of Santa Clara. This, Fidel reasoned, would have the domino effect of allowing Raúl Castro and Juan Almeida to take Santiago, thus isolating Havana from the rest of the country. And so the commander continued to brainstorm ideas of how to unseat the army from their fortifications.

On December 28th, after nine days of siege, Captain Abon Ly came out of the garrison under a white flag to negotiate surrender. "We'll give up the barracks if you let us withdraw with our weapons."

Camilo was uncharacteristically grave in his reply. "My men are used to sleeping on the ground. We've no need of your barracks. It's you and your weapons that we desire. And that's what we shall have."

"No. No surrender." Ly shook his head. "I have direct orders from General Tabernilla that nothing is to fall into your hands. I'm sorry that we do not see eye to eye on this matter."

"We've captured the reinforcements sent by sea," Camilo replied, puffing on his cigar. "We have also cut you off in every direction from which relief could come. I know that you must be short on food and water. The stench of your dead is unbearable all the way over here, so I can only imagine what it is like in the barracks. You can't have much ammunition left." He smiled broadly. "A wise officer would see to the wellbeing of his men and surrender without further pointless death."

"I'll speak with my officers." Captain Ly rose stiffly from the small table they sat around. "If we do not get the necessary reinforcements…" He left unsaid the possibility of surrender.

"Once you are back, the ceasefire is null and void."

"See me safely to the barracks and the battle may resume."

Camilo's next strategy for unseating the army was to fill a train with explosives and run it into the garrison. The tracks led to within fifty yards of the fortress. He ventured that with enough speed; the locomotive would reach the outer wall and explode on impact. This ploy failed when the locomotive didn't reach the buildings, and also didn't actually explode. "We need a mortar if we're going to dislodge them," Camilo mused, his field glasses trained on the enemy barracks. "Vicente, take a Jeep and another man over to Santa Clara. I believe Che may have a mortar in his possession, as long as he didn't lose it in his travels. Once we get some serious firepower, they'll surrender in no time at all."

And so Vicente immediately set off on the fifty-mile journey to Santa Clara to see if they could borrow a mortar.

PART FIVE

The Road to Victory

Earl Smith
American Ambassador to Cuba
Habana, Cuba

August 20, 1958

John Foster Dulles
Secretary of State
United States of America

Dear Mr. Secretary,

It pains me to inform you that operation *Verano*, the summer offensive by the Batista forces against the guerrilla communists of Fidel Castro, has failed. The *Movimiento 26 de Julio* has now begun an invasion of the west, sending two columns of troops to that purpose.

The only possibility for President Batista to stay in power is for the United States to renew military support with money and weapons. I am aware that there are some serious shortcomings in the current regime, but I can assure you that it is far better than any alternative. My understanding is that the 4th Floor diplomats who work for you are making many policy decisions in regards to Cuba. It is for this reason I am writing directly to you so that you are truly aware of the crisis here in Cuba.

The CIA, under the tutelage of your brother, Allen, appears to be seriously underestimating Fidel Castro as a communist threat. Castro has been clear that he plans to nationalize businesses and spread the wealth of the country throughout the population. The U.S. will never be able to do business with him as he won't honor international obligations or maintain law and order.

President Batista is not the perfect ruler of Cuba, but he is far better than any of the alternatives. He has proven himself a valuable economic ally, and I recommend we avert our eyes to his shortcomings, at least until we have a replacement ready. Perhaps a military junta of army officers would be acceptable?

I would be happy to fly to Washington to discuss this with you directly.

Sincerely,
E.T. Smith

13

September 4th, 1958, La Comandancia at La Plata in the Sierra Maestra

After Camilo and Che's columns—named in honor of heroes Antonio Maceo and Ciro Redondo—had begun the western invasion, Fidel began to shore up his own column. He'd sent his best leaders and men away, and now needed to shape true guerrillas from the recent recruits of the training school at Minas del Frio. These fresh volunteers had been trained in combat, but had seen little actual action, something he intended to change. In his home in La Plata he'd gathered an important group to begin implementing an integral piece of his plan.

"Comrades," Fidel greeted the assembled women once they were all present. He usually held council in a small area just outside with a table and stools, but desired more privacy for this particular gathering. It was good they'd crowded into his and Celia's home, as a cool rain came whipping across the ridge on strong gusts of winds, and they dropped the large swinging door into place, sheltering them securely against the elements. Celia offered each in turn cheese, bread, and wine, delicacies she secreted away for just such special occasions.

"I've brought you together today to tell you that I'm finally ready to capitulate to your collective demands. I want you to fight."

Sophia looked around the room, seeing the mirror image of her own grim satisfaction emanating from the faces of the others. Teté Puebla, only seventeen years old, had arrived at La Plata the same time as Sophia. She'd grown up the oldest of eight on a small farm in Yara, more interested in playing baseball with the boys than with dolls or clothes. Soon after Fidel had arrived in the Sierra Maestra, so had members of *Los Tigres*. One of these paramilitary ruffians, Juventino Sutil, had killed a friend of Teté's when she was fourteen by tying the victim up, stuffing him in a bag, pouring gasoline over him, and setting him on fire. Two weeks later, her cousin was gang-raped by fifty soldiers from Manzanillo. Soon after that, Teté starting carrying munitions to the guerrillas in the girdle underneath her wide skirt. A year later, when the authorities became suspicious of her, she'd fled to *La Comandancia* along with Ileana Rodés, who now sat next to her. Sophia, Celia, Teté, and Ileana were joined by Isabel Rielo to make a total of five women meeting around Fidel.

"Good. Can we first hunt down that bastard Masferrer and cut his dick off?" Sophia asked, ebullient to finally get an opportunity for retribution.

Fidel smiled. "Such words from a *gringa senorita*! You'll become guerrillas fighting for freedom, not assassins bent upon revenge."

"So our first order will be to attack Sánchez Mosquera?" Teté knew that it was common practice for Mosquera's soldiers to enter a village and tie the men to poles, rape the women, and then kill everyone, burning the evidence to hide their perversions. They'd report back that they'd killed a platoon of guerrillas in a firefight. It was his battalion that'd raped her cousin, leaving the young woman for dead.

"I'm establishing a brand new platoon, made up of thirteen women. It will be called *Mariana Grajales*, after the mother of Antonio Maceo." Fidel said. Grajales had sent eight family members into the battle for independence, sacrificing many of the people she loved for her country. "There'll be opposition to this plan, though, and I need to make sure we're all agreed and speak the same message after it's announced."

"Many of the men won't like it," Isabel agreed. She was tall and thin with black hair that stretched flat down her back. Born to a peasant family outside of Santiago, she'd shown remarkable promise in her schooling. Isabel's parents had managed to send her to the University in Havana, where she'd first become involved in revolutionary activity. After the failed strike in April of the past year, she and her sister, Lidia, were forced to flee into the Sierra Maestra and join the *Fidelistas*.

"I'll first enlist you as my private security detail to demonstrate publicly the faith that I have in you. As the men become accustomed to the idea of women fighting, I'll split your platoon, sending some of you into battle while retaining the rest as my bodyguards."

"No offense, Commandant, but guarding you tucked safely away in the Sierra Maestra is not the same as fighting," Sophia retorted. She was certain that she'd be kept in the detail protecting Fidel, and wanted no part of that, if the other option was killing soldiers.

"I don't plan to stay 'tucked safely away' for much longer," Fidel replied heatedly. "Soon we'll all leave the mountains and begin tightening the noose on Santiago."

Later that day they met with the leaders of the 1ˢᵗ Column to break the news that the new platoon was being established. Many of the officers were newly appointed, as Che and Camilo had taken the most experienced men with them on their invasion of the west. Eddy Suñol, a recent graduate of Minas del Frio, was the first and last to argue. "How can you give these women weapons when there aren't enough rifles for all of the men?"

A veteran guerrilla would have known better than to openly confront Fidel. "Because they are better soldiers than you. They are more disciplined," he replied with a bluntness that brooked no argument.

Over the next few months Fidel was busy communicating with and orchestrating Che, Camilo, Raúl, and Juan in directing actions in their respective fronts, as well as the urban underground leaders in Havana, Santiago, and other smaller cities. Since the guerrillas had bested Batista's summer offensive, Fidel and the *Movimiento 26ᵗʰ de Julio* were being treated with a new deference by some of the lesser opposition groups, and *La Comandancia* at La Plata had seen a steady flow of visitors. Men and women streamed in wanting to join the guerrillas and were cycled into the military school at Minas del Frio.

In times past, they would've been turned away because of lack of arms, but suddenly cash and weapons had become plentiful. Wealthy landowners, mine owners, industrialists, both Cuban and American, realized that they'd better hedge their bets and back this *Fidelista* movement. Powerful and rich exiles and foreign governments started sending supplies, weapons, and cash. Politicians and journalists trekked into the mountains to meet with the *Barbudos*, thus nicknamed the 'bearded ones' by the country that had begun to idolize them, especially the cigar smoking, passionate, yet always-eloquent Fidel Castro.

One night after a particularly hectic day in which Celia had ushered in supplicator after supplicator to meet with Fidel, he broached the subject they'd both been avoiding. "It's all coming to an end."

"Yes, it is," Celia, replied sadly.

Fidel didn't notice the regret tingeing her words. "I believe the broadcast on Radio Rebelde regarding agrarian reform has resonated with the peasants."

"I doubt there is a soul in Cuba who isn't listening to Radio Rebelde," Celia responded. "And the thought of owning their own land? Of seeing the results of their own blood and sweat realized? It was a master stroke." She leaned over and pulled a Lucky Strike from the pack and lit it with Fidel's cigar.

Fidel admired her bare back, the lithe muscles rippling over her tiny frame. "Every day," he observed, "more and more soldiers and officers cross over to join our cause."

"Tabernilla kicked himself in the ass when he ordered that deserters were to be executed immediately. It opened the door for you to invite them to join the cause free of repercussions." She blew a puff of smoke to the ceiling of the hut.

Fidel swung his feet to the ground and walked naked to the window. "Camilo is prepared to attack Yaguajay. Che is tightening his grip on Santa Clara. Raúl and Juan will crank up the pressure on the garrisons outside of Santiago, and we'll prevent any reinforcement from Camagüey. In little more than a month we'll command all of Cuba outside of Havana, and Batista will have no choice but to surrender."

"The only real concern is what the United States will do." Celia slid from bed, setting her cigarette aside, and padded across the floor, wrapping her arms around the muscular body of her lover. As he'd said, it wouldn't be long before the war ended, and everything would change.

"They made their intentions clear when they devised a plan to get that rat Carlos Márquez Sterling elected. Ambassadors Gardner and Smith are in cahoots with Batista. They should've known better than to trust him."

"You can't allow the United States to interfere with the true revolution and all that we've planned for after the triumph."

"We must neutralize the army. Then it's imperative we delegitimize any opposition so that there's nobody for the United States to replace us with who the people will accept. Then, and only then, when our position is solidified, can we begin nationalizing the interests of Americans and wealthy Cubans."

"Many of those wealthy Cubans endorse your efforts now." Celia began brushing her hair. "How do you plan to tame them after you take their factories and their plantations?"

Fidel turned and faced Celia, wrapping his arms around her. She looked up into his face, the eyes unfocused, and his mind miles away from passion though he held her close and naked. She knew he'd never once thought about what victory would do to their relationship. He saw every political and military move three steps ahead of most people, but his mind was not programmed to process emotion equally well.

"My first step," he was saying, "will be to nationalize my father's plantation. After that, I'll have the support of the people. They'll understand that I have their best interests at heart."

* * *

Sophia squirmed her way forward, placing the stacks of dynamite at the footings of the arching structure, one of the last railroad bridges in the entire province. She ran the electric wire back from the gunpowder, attaching it to the leads on the magneto in the plunger box, and then she waited for the train. They'd come a long way since the days of planting unexploded bombs salvaged from air force bomb runs and then shooting at them so they went off. Sophia gazed at the Cauto River below, fifty miles northwest of Bayamo, the longest river in all of Cuba, its lazy water inching by with the pace of the hutia, the slow moving rat-like rodent she'd been forced to eat on more than one occasion.

Up above, Teté waved her hat, the signal for the train's arrival. Built by Fiat, this kind of four-car train was commonplace in Cuba. Running on diesel, it linked the sugar cane plantations to the major hubs and was now used by the military to bring in reinforcements and supplies to the beleaguered Oriente Province. When Sophia thought the time had come, she made herself count to ten before depressing the plunger.

The magneto sent a spark down the coils and into the clustered explosives, which ignited spectacularly, crumpling the wooden bridge supports and sending it, along with the train, plummeting into the serene Cauto River. She disengaged the wire from the box and took the contraption with her as she climbed up the ravine behind her. *May Rolando Masferrer have been on that train,* she silently wished.

Sophia crested the ridge, moving towards the rendezvous spot, when the earth exploded in front of her, hurtling her back down the steep incline in a shower of dirt and debris. She clambered to her feet, ears ringing, a bit of blood dripping from her right nostril. She wasn't sure what'd happened, but knew she had to move. Her rifle secured on her back, she left the battery and plunger behind, moving up the slope at an angle from where she'd just tumbled. Muffled shouts pierced her dampened hearing, and then she saw the first *casquito* peer over the edge. The Infantryman hollered, pointing towards her scrambling figure as she clawed her way to the top some fifty yards from him.

A burst of bullets broke through the sound of her hoarse breathing, and Sophia tried to use what scrub vegetation there was as cover. She rolled over the brink, pulling her M-1 from her back and prepared to return fire, and became shockingly aware of what the initial explosion had been. A tank was bearing down upon her with a company of about twenty soldiers creeping along behind. With a curse, she crab-walked back over the edge at the spot where she'd been mushroomed into the air in a mass of rock, soil, and sticks. Using the contour of the rim for protection she squirmed her way forward, scuttling on all fours. Several soldiers jumped over the edge and rained bullets around her, and then gave pursuit when she slipped past a ledge that cut her off from view.

Sophia wasn't sure if she heard the whistle first or saw Teté's figure in the distance, but either way, when Sophia looked in that direction, Teté waved her into the ravine back towards the river. Throwing herself downward, her feet giving out, Sophia flipped head over heels, ending in a pile quite abruptly against another rock outcropping. She looked back up to see the tank cresting the ridge, positioning to get an angle while the soldiers rushed forward to kill her.

This is how it ends, she thought. And immediately there was an explosion underneath the tank. The earth opening up an immense cavern down which the vehicle spilled sideways, tumbling end over end. Picking up speed it rolled past her almost all the way to the river. Several of the soldiers had been blown to bits by the detonation, while others whizzed down the hill in shock. Those remaining at the top suddenly found themselves facing the business end of the rifles carried by the *Marianas* and quickly retreated.

"When we saw them chasing you, we planted the rest of the dynamite just under the edge and hoped you'd continue leading them this way," Isabel said grimly, once they'd pulled Sophia up and patched her scratches.

"I was bait?"

Teté laughed. "It didn't start out that way. *Las putas sin madres,*" she spat to emphasize her insult about whores without mothers, "came out of nowhere, from our blind spot. It was the best we could do, facing a tank and a company of soldiers."

"And you shot the dynamite, causing it to explode, and sent the tank tumbling down to the river." Sophia nodded her head, seeing it now. "*Madre di Dios* that was lucky. But how did you know that it wasn't going to roll right over on top of me?" It did not appear that the Mother of God had an answer for that.

* * *

Fidel set the meeting in a coconut grove, the only cover before venturing into the killing fields. From where they were, the Guisa/ Bayamo road stretched north up a small incline. It was this vantage point that allowed the guerrillas to see reinforcements approaching for the garrison. On November 20th, the rebels had encircled Guisa with its fort, the town perched within striking distance of the Sierra Maestra, but firmly within the *Llano*. They'd intercepted and destroyed the daily patrol traveling the twelve miles to Bayamo, signaling the beginning of the siege.

Fidel ordered his men to apply pressure to the garrison, and then promptly set up ambush sites, the majority of the rebels gathering along this road to Bayamo where over 5,000 soldiers with tanks, mortars, and armored cars resided. Fidel's 1st Column had had only 180 men when the battle began, but they'd brought along 500 porters to carry munitions and supplies. These porters were, in reality, to become warriors when new weapons were captured. In the five days of the siege thus far, seventy of these men had gone from porter to rebel, and the ranks now swelled to 250 men.

Fidel, Celia, Universo Sanchez, and Sophia were gathered around Braulio "Cordolun" Coroneaux. "They're not screwing around this time," Cordolun stated emphatically. "They're bringing two Sherman tanks and fourteen trucks filled with soldiers."

"How long until they get here?" Fidel's gaze fell upon a coconut tree, the lopsided bumps circling the tree another form of time, each scar indicating where the great fronds had grown and fallen each year, the tree growing larger with a smooth expanse of bark, before repeating the process.

"They'll be here within the hour."

"Can we stop them?" Fidel asked.

Cordolun drew a rough map in the dirt at their feet, no more than a straight line indicating the road, a slight rise and fall to show the hill he was positioned on. "They're coming this way from Bayamo.

When they reach the bottom of the rise, we'll detonate a mine that is buried in the road." He jabbed the ground with a stick to show where the mine had been placed. "With any luck we'll blow the shit out of the lead tank," he said, spitting to the side. "On the hill, I've twenty-two men and seven *Marianas* who'll stop them from moving forward. Hidden in the Guinea grass are another eighty men, who will concentrate fire and pin the *hijos de putas* down."

Sophia had drawn the short straw and was tasked with detonating the mine. She now sat with her back against an abandoned car, some casualty from before this battle, an old Buick pulled to the side of the road and gutted over time. She was using a car battery for the electric current that would run down the wire, blowing the mercury fulminate detonator, causing the TNT to explode. These detonators had been stolen from the manganese mines of Charco Redondo, a few miles to the east. Blowing the charge wasn't the hard part. It was close to a suicide mission and escape wouldn't be easy. She had to wait until the lead tank was no more than fifty feet from her, and then escape up the hill with no cover other than thick grass to reach the first trench four hundred yards away.

Sophia could hear the rumble of the tanks clanking along the pebble road, and the quieter noise of the trucks trundling along behind. There was also the whine of two spotter planes, probably the PA-22's, like the one they'd managed to shoot down on the first day of the battle. These planes had belt-fed machine guns mounted on the front and would make short work of her if she was seen. When the aircraft had passed overhead, two yellow birds in the sky, Sophia peeked around the corner, anxious to time this explosion exactly.

Their cache of dynamite having run out, the charge was improvised, TNT from unexploded mines packed into a fifteen-gallon milk churn and buried just below the surface of the road. There was no counting to ten this time, merely waiting for the lead tank to reach the spot marked by a solitary stocky fan palm, the type that grew best on unfertile ground. Sophia held her breath, and touched the two wires together, the current zipping down the line, creating a minor explosion, a pause, and then the car she was hidden behind lurched into her back and knocked her sprawling.

Without looking back, she scrambled to her feet and began running, her ears ringing with the noise of the charge soon followed by Cordolun's heavy-duty machine gun and the *rat-tat-tat* of over a hundred rebels opening fire simultaneously. Bullets streamed around her like minnows in a lake, spitting up small puffs of dirt around her feet as she ran. When she was halfway there, the road under her feet heaved, the heavy boom of the 75mm tank echoing in her ears. The grass was burning around her as she began crawling forward, a stinging sensation in her back. After what seemed eons, she tumbled into the trench. Teté was there, providing covering fire, her long curly black hair matching the soot on her round face.

"Did I get it?" Sophia asked, spitting dirt from her mouth.

"Blew the piece of *mierda* right upside down." Teté took a break from shooting, and tucked her head back into the trench for cover.

Sophia risked a glance over the edge, only to realize the burning grass had created a smoke too thick to see through. "Is my back bleeding?"

Teté nodded her head yes. "It looks like you've half the road stuck to it. You better work your way to the rear and get a medic to look at you."

Sophia was lying naked on her stomach with a towel covering her bottom while a doctor plucked pebbles and other debris from her posterior when Fidel and Celia swept into the cave they were using for headquarters and the field hospital. These caverns were the most extensive in all of Cuba and provided a terrific command center for the rebels.

"Brilliant work, Sophia." Fidel was ebullient. "When you blew up that Sherman, it threw the entire convoy into disarray. The soldiers have circled the trucks as a barricade and are now hiding behind them with the remaining tank tucked safely back in the middle. We've dug trenches to prevent their escape towards Bayamo and are closing the net upon them as we speak."

"Glad to hear it," Sophia gave a muffled reply, gritting her teeth against the pain.

Two days later, Sophia was happy to rejoin her friend, Teté, in a trench, squeezing in between her and another *Mariana*. No sooner was she settled than spotter planes came low over the hill, strafing the ground with machine gun fire as the guerrillas tried to grind themselves lower into the ground, the planks and earth overhead slim protection from the powerful projectiles. On the heels of the plane came the tanks, bent upon a rescue mission for the soldiers trapped in the road, spread four abreast, the large cannon turrets belching forth the 75mm explosives ravaging the incline and the fields the others had burrowed into.

When they were within range, Cordolun started returning fire with his machine gun, while some of the others tried to drop bullets down into the soldiers following behind the tanks. Picking up the sparks from the machine gun post, two of the tanks began sending their projectiles at Cordolun. One shell landed directly on the machine gun, tearing Cordolun to shreds and killing the three men helping him with the large gun. Sophia watched in horror, bowing her head to take a moment to honor the man she'd just recently met, but had come to like and respect.

Two days later the government troops attacked in force from three directions, coming again along the road from Bayamo to Guisa, but also from Santa Rita and Corojo. This thinned the already-sparse rebel forces, spreading them over wider terrain. In each location they held firm, never realizing the attacks were a feint meant to distract them, allowing the soldiers in the garrison to escape. With their backs to the fort, the rebels were not ready for the exodus that occurred, as the 200 men pinned down inside fled in a collection of transport trucks and Jeeps, driving fast and hard down the highway towards Bayamo. The rebels managed to inflict a number of casualties, but the soldiers were able to make their withdrawal mostly intact.

Fidel and his 1st Column entered Guisa on November 30th; disappointed the soldiers had escaped, but jubilant at their triumph. Over the next three weeks they marched towards Santiago, capturing several small garrisons and the weapons stored in each and thus arming more and more men. On December 20th, they secured the large fort at Palma Soriano, effectively cutting off any reinforcements for Santiago.

Juan Almeida continued to tighten his grip on the west of Santiago from the Sierra Maestra, while Raúl wiped up everything north and east of the city, in rapid succession capturing Mayarí, Holguin, Sagua de Tanamo, and Baracoa. Raúl also controlled Santiago Harbor, having placed eight heavy machine guns on the heights around the bay, trapping two frigates whose guns were useless at a range of 300 yards.

On Christmas Eve morning Fidel called Sophia to his headquarters in the Central America sugar cane mill in Palma Soriano. He was planning on visiting his mother and brother, Ramón, at his childhood home in Birán, and wanted her to come as a bodyguard. They left in the faded sky-blue Land Rover that had become Fidel's vehicle of choice. Sophia rode in the single backseat, directly behind the passenger seat in which Celia rode, while Fidel drove. Sophia had driven this vehicle before, but she found her short stature made it hard to see over the spare tire mounted on the front hood, which wasn't an issue for Fidel. It was only a thirty-mile drive from the headquarters at Palma Soriano, through territory completely under the control of the guerrillas. Their only fear was aircraft passing overhead.

As they came down the dirt road to the home where Fidel had been born in the town that owed its livelihood to his father Ángel, Teté Puebla stepped out with her rifle pointing upward. She was part of the advance detail that had come to secure the plantation for the visit. Fidel slowed and nodded, and then continued on to the house.

Fidel rarely spent time thinking about his father, but the town and home brought back a flood of memories. Ángel Castro had treated his wife and children like he treated his workers, which is to say, poorly. He thrived on conflict and getting his way, taking pleasure in making others knuckle under to his aggressive nature. It was this drive to conquer everybody and everything in his path that'd led him to wealth and influence.

Fidel had spent the first three years of his life in the peasant quarters before his father even recognized his legitimacy. By fleeing Birán to go to Havana for university, Fidel had accepted defeat at the hands of his father, an irksome detail that rankled his subconscious and created overt angry behaviors whenever he was told "no." He'd fought every authoritarian figure who had ever confronted him, starting with teachers, and then running the gamut of gangsters, police, soldiers, and politicians. He dreamed of the day he'd return and stand up to his father, and then the man had died of a stroke while Fidel was exiled in Mexico. Here, on the edge of triumph, with the government teetering on the brink of defeat, with his forces poised to conquer Cuba, Fidel began to realize that in some ways, he was not so different from his father.

They passed several buildings where clusters of peasants congregated; they were mostly Haitians who worked the sugar cane for the Castro family. The cock-fighting pit was empty, perhaps in honor of Christmas Eve, or maybe on Ramón's orders. The house was a large structure, built on stilts so that animals could take shelter underneath it. A few cattle were all that was left of a large herd after years of supplying the rebels. They went upstairs to a wide veranda where Ramón, Fidel's older brother, met them at the top with an effusive hug. Ramón had steered clear of the politics of revolution. He'd never wanted anything more than to become a farmer and marry his local sweetheart, but he'd been instrumental in getting supplies to his brothers in the mountains over the past, desperate year.

"Fidel." His mother, Lina Ruz, came out of the house onto the veranda. "I prayed that I'd see you again, and the gods have been good to me." She pulled him into a tight embrace. At fifty-five she was still quite strong. She pushed her black-rimmed glasses back up on her nose and held him at arm's length. "Come inside and say hello to Grandmother Ruz."

"It's good to see you again, Mother." Fidel followed the spry lady into the house he'd grown up in.

Grandmother Ruz was nestled into a rocking chair, a wool blanket wrapped around her even in the warmth of the day. Fidel knelt and kissed her cheek, marveling at this woman. After generations of living in Pinar del Río, she and her husband had packed an ox-cart with all of their belongings and walked the almost 700 miles to Birán. Grandfather Ruz and his sons had worked in the cane fields for Ángel Castro and his daughter, Lina, had become the Castro housekeeper. Soon after being pulled into the main house, Lina gave birth to Angela, Fidel's older sister, then Ramón, Fidel, Raúl, Juanita,

Emma, and Agustina. Somewhere during that time period, Ángel's first wife had disappeared, never to be seen again. Fidel often thought that he might try to find her one day. He felt sorry for this woman who'd been so betrayed by his domineering father.

"I've saved a turkey for just this occasion," Ramón announced as he came in, accompanied by Raúl and Vilma. For a brief few hours on this Christmas Eve, the commanders of the First and Second Fronts were away from their posts, but there was little fear of attack, as the army was cowering behind the walls of Santiago hoping for reinforcements from Havana that would never come. "Mama and my wife have spent the day cooking, and I may've even helped more than I got in the way." Ramón was excited to see his two younger brothers, living as he did with all women, his wife, mother, and grandmother.

Fidel and Raúl introduced Celia and Vilma to their mother. This was the first time she'd met either of these women so important in her son's lives. "*Tal vez te gustaría afeitarte antes de comer?*" Lina asked Fidel if he wished to shave before eating with the familiar edge to her tone he remembered so well.

"No, thank you, Mother. Our beards have become a symbol of our movement, and thus I must keep it," Fidel replied carefully.

Luckily, her attention was distracted by a chuckle from Raúl. "And what are you laughing at?" Lina grasped a lock of Raúl's long hair and gave it a firm jerk. "Perhaps you'd like a haircut?" Several chickens fluttered past, distracting those gathered from the confrontation between mother and sons. Celia mentally made a note to bring one of the birds with her for a meal the following day.

The turkey, along with roast pork, rice, beans, and several other spicy dishes, was soon served. *Yuca con mojo* had always been a favorite of Fidel's; perhaps it was the sharp garlic flavoring the root vegetable that he enjoyed. Celia had two glasses of the *Sidra*, sparkling hard apple cider, giving her a case of the giggles. They talked of their childhood; the three boys were just seven years apart in age and so had had many adventures together. They laughed at Ramón who'd never wanted to leave *Finca Manacas*, as the farm was called, and at Fidel for his hot-headedness and stubbornness.

"Remember when you threatened to burn down the house if mama and papa didn't let you go back to school?" Ramón asked Fidel. "I pleaded with them to do so, because the look in your eye told me you were as serious as a cow giving birth. I would've been afraid to sleep here if they hadn't."

They moved to the veranda and sat staring off at the mountains. The sun had now set, and the shadowy outlines hinted more at their power than beauty, the craggy ridges and towering pinnacles the creation of two super colossal forces colliding. With no give on either side, a new, original landform had risen up into the sky, dwarfing the terrain surrounding it. *Not a bad metaphor for the Cuban Revolution,* Fidel thought as Ramón offered cigars from a box. "Dunhill?" Fidel asked with pleasure, carefully pulling out a torpedo, one of the largest.

"The Upmanns, to be specific. I bought these in Santiago last month."

"It's been a while since I've been to Santiago," Raúl commented as he chose a smaller cigar. "But I expect to be in the city any day now."

"The revolution has been going well as of late," Ramón said quietly.

"Was it really necessary to burn our cane fields?" Lina interjected, an edge to her voice.

"Mother, we're not going to talk of such things," Ramón spoke firmly. "Fidel and Raúl are doing what they must to end the tyranny our country faces."

"And they're going to do that by taking our *finca* away from us? Don't think I don't listen to the radio. I heard the speech about giving the large estates to the peasants who work them."

"I've also saved some fine brandy," Ramón interrupted, retreating into the house to fetch the liquor that would complement the cigars.

"We're attempting to rectify the entire corrupt bourgeois system, and removing Batista is only the first step, Mama." Fidel restrained his normal booming voice to almost an entreaty. "We only want to provide all Cubans with food, education, and medical care."

With the arrival of the brandy, the conversation shifted back onto more cordial themes. Raúl told the story of taking the Americans hostages. Everybody laughed uproariously when he mimicked the face of Park Wollam, the American Consul, when he'd realized that Raúl was turning over five men, and not all fifty. That prompted Celia to share the details of the three days in which Fidel had spoken with General Cantillo as he bought time for his guerrillas to slip away.

Fidel had fallen into a rambling speech on agrarian reform around midnight when Celia stood up abruptly and suggested it was time to go. "We meet with General Cantillo in a couple of days as he negotiates for peace," she said. "Let's hope we don't have to listen to him speak for three days about nothing like Fidel. Those were possibly the most boring days of my life." With lingering embraces and hearty waves, they parted ways, the rebels to their camp and the revolution.

While Fidel was celebrating Christmas with his family, General Eulogio Cantillo was meeting with a group of generals plotting the overthrow of President Batista. General Cantillo left the meeting hiding his anger at the fat general and his family that ruled the Cuban military. Francisco "Silito" Tabernilla had attached himself to Batista back in the 1930's with the Sergeant's Revolt and clung to his coattails ever since. He, too, probably had a nest egg in West Palm Beach, just waiting for him if, and when, he decided to leave Cuba. Cantillo was forced to sit there and listen to this ass-kisser dictate policy as his sons all nodded their heads in agreement. They had the gall to order him to meet with Castro and bring their terms for peace to the man, not realizing that he, Cantillo, had already put out feelers to that end. *It was time to grab some of the glory instead of straggling along picking up the crumbs left by other, inferior men,* he thought.

The meeting was set for December 28th, and Cantillo made sure that all flights over the area were cancelled. He wouldn't put it past the fat bastard, Tabernilla, to try and take Castro out using Cantillo as bait. He took his most trusted man, Orlando Izquierdo, to fly the helicopter into the sugar plantation known as "Central America." When he saw the gathered rebel leaders, he did think it would, perhaps, have been worth the double-cross, for not only was Fidel present, but so was Celia Sánchez, Raúl Castro, Vilma Espín, the traitor Major Quevedo, as well as Raúl Chibás, the civilian leader who was brother to the late Eddie Chibás.

"Good to see you, Commander." Cantillo forced a smile, his thoughts still stinging from that meeting in Havana.

"You know everybody?" Fidel asked, turning to encompass the rebel leadership.

Cantillo assented that he did. "I have an offer of peace from Chief-of-Staff Tabernilla."

"Have you been on a sugar cane plantation, General?" Fidel queried.

Cantillo raised his eyebrows. "Several, Commander. As a matter of fact my headquarters for a time last summer was the Estrada Palma Sugar Mill."

"Yes, of course, of course. And so, you realize, that sugar is the very lifeblood of Cuba?"

"I do, and that's why your policy of burning that very lifeblood has at times left me confused as to your true purpose."

Fidel laughed. "Walk with me, General." He flipped open his Zippo lighter and lit a cigar, and then snapped it shut. "Cigar?" When Cantillo declined, he continued, "The system is flawed and only favors a few. Sometimes drastic measures have to be taken to make change. It seems to me that there is plenty of wealth so that nobody should go hungry."

Cantillo knew better than to enter a philosophical discussion, and thus got right to the business at hand. "General Tabernilla wishes to know if you'd be open to a military junta. Fulgencio Batista, his cabinet, and the worst of his officers will leave the country. The military will take control of Havana, opening the door for reconciliation with you and your forces. We'd be happy to place loyal officers such as Colonel Ramón Barquín in positions of power."

"You say 'we,' General, so I'm to assume that you'd also be part of the junta?" Fidel asked.

"It's been suggested that I'd be a strong liaison between the army and your guerrillas, and if I can be of service to Cuba, then I'm happy to participate. I want this strife to end, this senseless loss of life."

"On March 10th of 1952, Fulgencio Batista stripped away the liberty of Cuba with one snap of his fingers. He's since imposed censorship, sold our souls to foreigners, filled his own pockets, allowed the rape of thousands of women, and killed our children." Fidel puffed urgently on his cigar. "Batista enjoyed the sheer power of complete control—and complete corruption—and then he began to make mistakes.

He never took the *Movimiento 26ᵗʰ de Julio* or me seriously. When he finally realized the threat we posed, he threw the weight of his army at us, and we defeated him soundly. Why? Because of that very corruption. He tethered good officers like you to the imbecile Chaviano, not because he thought it best, but because he owed them for familial obligations, or in return for bribes that lined his pockets. And where does that leave us?"

"So you will not accept the terms proposed?" Cantillo asked finally. He had never thought that Fidel would, but that is how a negotiation began, was it not?

"Those were not terms. That was a fantasy proposed by a desperate madman with no understanding of the predicament that he's in. I'll tell you the terms that are acceptable. The first and most important is that Batista shall not leave Cuba. He'll remain here to face charges for his crimes against his country. This is true for all of these war criminals, whether a member of his government, the army, the police force, or any other military organization such as that of Rolando Masferrer and his perverted *Tigres*. Point two is that there will be no military uprising in Havana. I will personally lead the march on Havana once Santa Clara and Santiago have fallen. I'll enter the city as a conquering hero, not as a puppet to the existing military. The third mandate is that you'll have no contact with the United States Embassy. We will not repeat the Revolution of 1895 when the Americans swooped in and took over. There'll be no deals, no aid, and no collusion. If you can abide by those three conditions, then I'll agree that you will lead a military uprising in Santiago, which will open the gates of the city to my Second Front."

Cantillo struggled to formulate a response to conditions to which he knew he couldn't agree. They'd stopped in the middle of the sugar cane field; the burnt stalks still smoldering, thin tendrils of smoke creeping into the sky. The main building had survived the fire, but the sugar mill and several of the smaller structures had gone up in the recent blaze. "There are interesting points to your plan, but I see no way to prevent Batista from leaving the country. He still controls the army, the air force, and the navy. If he decides to fly out of the country, there's nothing I, nor you, can do about it." Cantillo was not sure whose demands were more outlandish, those of Tabernilla, or Castro. "But I can bring your proposal back to General Tabernilla for consideration."

"No need. Send a message. I need an answer within two days, for every moment wasted brings United States intervention closer." Fidel had finished negotiating. "And this is a deal with you, and not Tabernilla, who'll soon be facing a court for his crimes."

Cantillo managed to keep his calm demeanor, but what he'd only suspected he now knew was true: Fidel trusted him. "Give me three days and I'll have your answer."

Fidel relented slightly. "On December 31st at 3 p.m. exactly, we'll attack Santiago. You have until then to join the winning side. After that, you'll be considered an *enemigo de la revolución*."

14

December 28th, 1958, Havana

Vicente pulled around the circular drive at Las Villas University in Santa Clara. The building was new, built of concrete and brick, and was currently the headquarters of Che and the staff of the 2nd Column. "Luis, keep an eye on the Jeep while I find the Comandante. We don't need any of our boys liberating the vehicle for their own uses." He strode up the steps into the administrative building, finding Che and his commanders grouped around a table, a short wave radio cackling in the background.

"Bolívar! *Che*, hopefully you're here to tell me that Camilo is close behind with the 8th Column?" Che asked, rising to kiss his cheek and shake his hand.

"No such thing." Vicente hugged the Argentinian back, careful of the sling supporting the other man's broken arm. "I hear you survived the journey here only to fall off a wall and break your arm? Had you been drinking?"

Che gave a small, savage smile. "It was not one of my more agile moments, but I'm certain the fall saved my life. Those soldiers had a bead on me, *che*."

"Well, I'm glad of your clumsiness, then."

At Che's side was a young lady, less emaciated than most of the guerrillas. Her light brown hair was streaked with blond highlights and she had dark eyes. He now pulled her forward by the elbow. "Aleida has been taking care of me."

The young woman stepped forward boldly and stuck out her hand. "Aleida March."

"Vicente Bolivar." He clasped her hand firmly. "I've heard of the schoolteacher-turned-guerrilla."

"Aleida knows her way around Las Villas, especially Santa Clara, so she has become my walking map," Che explained.

"And a very pretty map indeed," Vicente added, well aware of Che's lingering looks at the attractive Aleida. "Is that your red Toyota Jeep outside?" Che nodded his assent. "Kind of grabs your attention. I imagine it helps the bombers zero in on you quite well."

Che snorted in disdain. "*Che*, I am busy finishing my invasion of central Cuba, so enough of this idle chat. Come with me and tell me what you need." He took Vicente's arm and steered him outside to the red Toyota. Vicente had barely settled into his seat when Che floored the gas and sent the vehicle hurtling into the street.

Once he gathered himself, Vicente nodded. "I do need something."

"As you can see, we've little to offer. Rolando Cubela and the DR are bogged down attacking Barracks 31, there are reinforcements attempting to come from the west, and Colonel Casillas has sent out an armored train with 400 soldiers to impede our attack on the city. They're sitting right up there on Capiro Hill as we speak."

"You have no need of your mortar then?" Vicente asked.

"*Che*, I told that damn tailor to bring more heavy weapons, but he didn't want to be slowed down on his trip across the provinces. Where has that left you?" Even though he smiled when he said this, there was an undercurrent of painful truth. The 2nd Column had struggled more than the 8th Column in the trip across Camaguey Province. Things had started poorly when the plane bringing them ammunition and gasoline had been destroyed, which meant they'd had to leave on foot without trucks. As a result of their slog across the flooded plains, many of the men had developed the ghastly foot disease the region's peasants called *mazamorra*, a painful affliction that made walking torturous. "If I give him my mortar, what do I get in return?" Che asked.

"Captain Ly has hunkered down in the garrison in Yaguajay," Vicente explained, "and can't be tempted out. He's low on ammunition, water, and food, but still resists. He claims it is a matter of honor, and his orders are to hold the fort." Vicente glanced out the window at the war-torn streets of Santa Clara. Burning cars blocked streets that were devoid of people. "He'll succumb eventually, but," here Vicente shrugged his shoulders, "a mortar would certainly hasten the outcome, allowing Camilo to bring our column down here with many fresh weapons to arm those wanting to join us."

Che had driven just a short distance from his headquarters, tires screeching as he slammed on the brakes. "Come with me. I need to make an announcement to the people of Santa Clara." They went into the radio station, a squat building with a metal antennae reaching into the sky. Several rebels stood at the entrance, rifles at the ready. They broke into smiles at the sight of their fiery commander, but shyly nodded in recognition, afraid to address him.

"How do we get on the air?" he demanded of the man inside.

The man half-saluted, picked up the microphone and handed it to Che, and finally managed to speak, "Flip that switch and speak into this."

Che hit the switch and immediately began passionately spouting into the microphone. "This is Che Guevara of the *Movimiento 26th de Julio*. Our army is here in Santa Clara and victory is imminent. We're sweeping the corrupt and immoral *policía* and soldiers here in front of us like the trash they are and will soon liberate the city. You can aid in this movement by blockading the streets to prevent their tanks from traveling through the city and terrorizing you in your homes. If you work in the water or electric facilities, I need you to cut the supply so that we can force the army to surrender. Without electricity and water, they won't last long. Let the ruling classes tremble at revolution. You have nothing to lose but your chains and a world to win. The moment is at hand and the time is now. Act to liberate Cuba from tyranny." He dropped the microphone on the table, nodded to the guerrilla still sitting there, and strode back out the door.

"That was certainly to the point," Vicente said drily once they were back in the jeep.

"I'll give him my mortar." Che ignored the comment, pausing to look Vicente in the eye before driving off. "But I want you in return." Vicente had never considered himself an item of barter before and didn't know how to reply. Che continued, "If we're to take the city of Santa Clara, we'll need to drive the soldiers from Capiro Hill to gain entrance into the city limits. To do this, I'll send in Vaquerito's suicide squad. They're a group of youngsters, barely old enough to wipe their own asses—but courageous beyond belief. It'd be very beneficial to Vaquerito to have another veteran present in this attack, *che*."

As they pulled back into the University, Vicente nodded. "I'll stay if you send one of your men back with Luis and the mortar." Vicente didn't relish joining the suicide squad, but orders were orders. The group was fearless, always the first into the breach. Led by the legendary Vaquerito, they gained glory by walking the line between life and death, with more martyrs among their ranks than he cared to think about.

"Done. I'll include a message to Camilo letting him know I requisitioned you." Che clapped his hands, but paused in the doorway and grasped Vicente's arm. "I'm going to marry her, you know."

"Who?" Vicente had met Che's wife what seemed a decade ago in Mexico and knew the couple had a daughter together.

"Aleida March," Che said in a dreamy voice that was completely out of place with the whine of fighter planes and the heavier roar of bombers that could suddenly be heard approaching from the west. "Quickly, come in here." Che led Vicente into the center of the building, and they crouched on the floor under the table until they heard the thick booms of the bombs exploding several miles away.

"I think that many of the pilots refuse to bomb the city," Che said with a smile. "There are rumors they're dropping their explosives at sea rather than destroying Santa Clara and her people." He spread out a map of the city on the floor and showed Vicente the key points: the *estación de policía*, jail, hotel, courthouse, palace, Barracks

31, the Leoncio Vidal Garrison, and Capiro Hill behind which he'd sketched a crude train. "Capturing this train is the key to our success."

At dawn Vaquerito and Vicente led half of the suicide squad in an attack on the railroad station, ensuring there'd only be one direction for the train to flee, towards the fort and tracks that had been vandalized the night before in preparation for this assault. There were only four soldiers guarding the depot, men who, when surrounded by a company of young but intent rebels carrying hand grenades and rifles, couldn't surrender quickly enough.

As they led the prisoners out the door, the phone rang and a young guerrilla, First Lieutenant Hugo del Río, picked it up. A military chief on the other end demanded to know what was going on. Hugo replied, "The guerrillas are all over the street."

To which the chief said, "Don't worry, the *policía* will soon restore order."

Hugo laughed brazenly into the phone and stated, "That is not likely."

"Are you with the guards or the *policía?*" the chief demanded, outraged at the impertinence.

The young first lieutenant retorted, "Neither. I'm a *Barbudos*, and we now control this part of the city."

A few hours later Vicente found himself charging uphill with ninety rebels too young to even attend the University in whose buildings they'd just spent the night. They carried hand grenades and machine guns, their faces tense with purpose, creeping silently forward until they were a few hundred yards from the top, and then sprinting on Vicente's signal. A blaze of gunfire dropped a boy to Vicente's right, and he threw a grenade that exploded just short of the soldiers. True to Che's prediction, the few sentries on Capiro Hill quickly fled back to the train with the suicide squad in fast pursuit.

Vicente dashed forward to keep ahead of the others, his stamina greater than these fresh recruits, but his speed no match for many of these youngsters. He stuck the grenade in a pocket and pulled the M-1 from his back, spraying lead at the fleeing soldiers. One of them hitched up and toppled to the ground, trying to drag himself forward with his hands.

Captain Gabriel Gil, just a lad of seventeen years, was leading the suicide squad in hot pursuit, an honor bestowed on him by Vaquerito, when the boy abruptly toppled forward, dead before he hit the ground. As the fleeing soldiers neared the train, bullets spewed from the armored train cars. The guerrillas pulled up and took cover, most gasping for breath and bent over, as the two locomotive engines began to push the carriages back towards the safety of the Vidal Garrison.

"Follow me," Vicente ordered, jogging after the train. Most of the rebels didn't know that just a half-mile further the tracks had been ripped up. Within moments, brakes screeched, and then they heard the thunderous sound of rending metal. They rounded a bend and witnessed three of the carriages overbalancing after smashing into a corrugated tin garage that had ripped open like a sardine can, while the engines and the other nineteen cars came to a shuddering stop.

Men spilled out of the fallen armored transports as the suicide squad fired fiercely in their direction, sending a withering hail of lead at the disoriented soldiers. Lieutenant Roberto Espinosa of the guerrillas was the first to reach them, demanding their surrender. He captured forty-one soldiers while Vaquerito and Vicente laid down a covering fire on the remaining carriages.

"Get the .30 caliber machine gun set up on that roof there," Vicente shouted, pointing to a building about fifty yards from the stationary train.

From buildings, streets, and alleyways, men and women began to appear, carrying Molotov cocktails. A swarthy man about forty years old puffed on his cigar, and then held the lit end to the rag stuffed into the contoured Coca-Cola bottle. As the material lit, he held it casually for about ten seconds, before sending it hurtling through the air to crash upon the metal roof of one of the train cars, smashing and spreading burning gasoline across the roof.

A young woman whose face told a tale of hardship pulled up to them in a truck filled with empty Hatuey beer bottles. Several men appeared with cans of gasoline and began to fill the bottles as explosions flooded the air. The urban underground of Santa Clara was awakening after years of living in secret, and now in exultation, began to openly strike back at the tyranny that had destroyed their community, rising up as Fidel had known they would all along. In less than an hour, a white flag attached to the end of a rifle waved from the doorway of a carriage car.

Vicente wasn't quite sure how it happened, but a half hour later he found himself sharing a cigarette with one of the soldiers while several of the officers negotiated terms of surrender with Che. There was no question of their submission as the last of the soldiers emerged from the oven-like heat of the burning train carriages. "Where are you from?"

The soldier spit a fleck of tobacco out before replying. "Matanzas."

"I grew up there, until just before the revolution. Vicente Bolívar."

"Alvaro Torres," he replied. "Where did you live?"

"Just off 49th street on the northwest side of the harbor." Vicente tried to envision his home, but all that came to mind was his grandmother in her rocking chair, the house a blur behind her. "How 'bout you?"

"I live with my parents right in the old city at *Plaza de La Vigia*. My backyard is the San Juan River." Torres wished he were casting a line into that river right about now. "I knew some Bolívars. One I knew had a fishing boat."

"That'd be my uncle. I haven't seen him in eight years, nor been back to Matanzas."

Torres didn't ask about the absence from his family. These were difficult times. "What's this all about?"

Vicente thought out his answer carefully before replying. It was a topic that had consumed him for a few weeks now, as the tides of war had shifted in their favor, and it appeared that victory was actually possible. "It's about what's right." He lit another cigarette. With wandering eyes, he took in the smoldering ruins of Santa Clara, the upended, smoking train cars, the automobiles and barriers in the streets, and above all else, the man in front of him. "You and I aren't so different. We're just pawns in the game of power and money, and we've always lived on the wrong side of the tracks." He paused, before continuing, "I'm trying to figure out what is right, finally."

"Can't say I ever cared for Batista, but I got a family to feed and a man's got to work. Hell, I'm not even supposed to be a soldier. I joined the army as an engineer." He looked over his shoulder at the other troops from the train. "They sent us out here to fix bridges, but now they have us defending the actual soldiers who spend their time hiding in the barracks."

"We all have to make our choices in life." Vicente crushed his cigarette with the heel of his boot and walked away, feeling that something had changed, something important, something he was a part of for better or worse.

The surrender details were worked out, the prisoners stripped of their weapons and sent to Caibarién, where they would be put on a navy frigate and taken to Havana. It was a demoralizing blow for 400 soldiers to return to the capital not just defeated but humiliated at having been outsmarted by a small group of young "inexperienced" fighters.

For the rebels, it was like Christmas, for the armored train was a virtual traveling arsenal, a treasure trove of bazookas, machine guns, a 20mm cannon, 600 rifles, and almost one million rounds of ammunition. More importantly, there were many fresh recruits waiting for any available weapon to join the ranks of the insurgent guerrillas, and as a result, their numbers swelled.

That very afternoon, Che ordered an attack on the police headquarters where hundreds of law enforcement officers were holed up. The building was in the center of the city across the street from the del Carmen Park, within protective range of sniper fire from Masferrer's *Los Tigres* dug in on the tenth floor of the Grand Hotel, and just 500 yards from the army barracks of Leoncio Vidal and the 1,300 soldiers stationed there. The streets surrounding the station had been filled with automobiles, many now burning as a result of the 77mm high velocity shells from the two British-made Comet tanks positioned in front of the headquarters.

Vicente had gone to recon the police station with a baby-faced guerrilla named Emérido, and in the process had been almost blown to smithereens by one of the tanks and a wall of *policía*. They reported back to the new command post where they found Che,

Aleida, Vaquerito, and Hugo del Río discussing strategy in the living room of a deserted apartment.

"*Che*, you two look terrible," Che commented, taking in their blackened faces with streaks of red, and the debris that adorned their tattered uniforms.

"We can't get close enough with any sort of manpower to force them into surrendering," Emérido complained. His hat was riddled with bullet holes from peering around corners.

"Now that the water and electricity are turned off it'll be just a matter of days before they're forced to raise their arms," Vicente declared.

"We don't have days," Che stated in a low voice. "Fidel has been clear that we have to get this done before Batista and his cronies can escape the country."

"Colonel Rojas will never let them surrender. He knows that would be signing his death warrant," Hugo added bleakly. For Rojas, capitulation meant only one thing, and that was execution. His barbarous reputation was well known throughout Santa Clara, and retribution would be swift and anything but merciful.

"I have an idea." Vaquerito smiled broadly, a grin as wide as his cowboy hat. He walked over to the wall and banged his fist lightly against it. "What do you suppose is on the other side of this wall?"

"An alleyway?" Emérido asked, puzzled.

"No." Vaquerito shook his head. "Another wall."

"I assume you're going somewhere with this?" Che interjected with exasperation.

"And on the other side of that wall is a room leading to another wall beyond which is another room and so on and so on right to the corner across from the police headquarters." Vaquerito laughed. "I suggest that we break through the walls and prepare an assault from those advanced points. The others will support us from the roofs."

An hour later, Vicente was crawling across the skyline of Santa Clara searching for a clear view of the police headquarters. A building on Garofalo Street, which was just about fifty yards from the station, provided them with ample protection and a clear line of fire. The Comet tank was parked intimidatingly in front of the *estación de policía*, facing a park with Saint Carmen's Church situated in the middle. In the corner of the plaza closest to them, seven granite pillars surrounded a large Tamarind tree, each representing one of the original families of Santa Clara.

Two seasoned fighters, Beltrán and Tamayo, were with Vicente and Vaquerito. "You need to keep your head down or some sniper is going to put one right in your noggin," Vicente cautioned, judging Vaquerito too cavalier with his safety.

Vaquerito chuckled. "You never hear the bullet that's going to get you," he replied. "It can happen leading a charge or cowering behind the skirt that is fear. I'd prefer that when my time comes, death finds in my breast a courageous heart. I'm no gutless *cobarde*." If anything, Vaquerito was the exact opposite of a coward.

Without warning, six soldiers loped into view in the park. Vaquerito stood to see them better as he sent a burst of fire in their direction. Tamayo yelled at him, "Kid, hit the deck or they'll kill you for sure."

Vicente had risen to one knee and saw the tank by the station swiveling the machine gun turret, the deadly .30 caliber weapon zeroing in on their position. "Get down!" he yelled, dropping to his face behind the short wall as the heavy-duty gun spewed death towards their position. When the *rat-a-tat-tat* concluded some twenty seconds later, he risked a glance over the edge and saw a park devoid of soldiers and the tank lumbering on down the street. "Everybody okay?"

"There's a soldier in the window at nine o'clock," Tamayo warned in a whisper. "You should have a clean line of fire from your position, Vaquerito. A dollar says you miss." Vaquerito remained huddled behind the lip of the wall without moving. Tamayo crawled towards him. He grasped his shoulder and gave a tug. "Hey, what's up, why aren't you firing?" Vaquerito's head yawed sideways, covered in blood.

They carried the dead captain back across the rooftops and down to the streets of Santa Clara. As they toted the young hero past other guerrillas, each man removed his hat and marked the passing. Vaquerito had been vastly popular, a charismatic fun-loving kid with the courage of the *Mambí* and the kindness of a grandmother.

Che was returning from his meeting with Rolando Cubela and saw them on the street. He swerved to the side and jumped from the Jeep. "It's as if they've killed a hundred of my men." He touched Vaquerito's cheek, and pulled his hand back to inspect the blood upon his fingers. Che shook his head and climbed back into the Jeep, leaning his head out as if to say something, and then abruptly driving off.

All that night and the next morning the guerrillas tunneled their way through the buildings of Santa Clara until they were able to fire upon the *estación de policía* from cover. The finest position was the Saint Carmen Church just across from the headquarters, and this is where Vicente and Tamayo found themselves in the afternoon of the last day of 1958. Directing a steady fire into the windows of the building, they wore down the *policía*, wounding and killing several, but more importantly, depleting their ammunition and giving them no rest. The two tanks had taken it upon themselves to retreat to the garrison.

Around four o'clock a white flag waved out a window, and a request was made for a cease-fire to allow for the injured be released and treated, as well as for the removal of the numerous corpses. Some hadn't died at the hand of the guerrillas, for Colonel Rojas had personally shot several men who'd spoken of surrender. Che had promoted Tamayo to the head of the attack, and he met with Colonel Rojas in the middle of the street to discuss the wounded and dead. Still livid with anger over the death of his friend the previous day, Tamayo nevertheless agreed to halt the attack for two hours for humanitarian purposes.

"What if I just go inside the station and announce that any man who hasn't committed a crime against the nation may lay down their arms and simply walk out the door?" Tamayo directed the question at Vicente as they smoked cigarettes and pondered their next move.

"There are almost 400 men in there, hungry, tired, and terrified," Vicente mused.

"Many of them have families they'd like to see again," Tamayo replied.

"They must know that there is little chance of reinforcements arriving and saving them at this point."

"The *policía* know that we treat prisoners humanely," Tamayo reasoned.

"This may be their best opportunity to exit the fighting without dying first and with some honor intact at having held out so long," Vicente concluded. "I think if we bypass the officers and present peace to the men, they'll grasp at it like shipwrecked sailors to a life raft in the middle of the ocean."

As the two-hour cease-fire wound to a close, Tamayo and Vicente once again met in the street between the church and the *estación de policía* with Colonel Rojas. "I ask you again to surrender," Tamayo demanded of the corpulent man.

"We will not do so unless you guarantee the safety of every man in the barracks." Rojas whined, wondering how his comfortable life could've taken this drastic turn to chaos and defeat.

"Any man accused of crimes against the population will face a trial and consequences for their actions." Vicente interrupted the man's thoughts. "Everyone else will be returned to Havana."

Rojas sighed. "I cannot agree to that."

Tamayo brushed past the man and pushed his way through several *policía* on his way into the station. Vicente followed him to the door, pausing to look at Rojas still standing in the exact same position, facing the Saint Carmen Church, his figure forlorn in the empty street.

"Our men control the city of Yaguajay and Cienfuegos. There'll be no reinforcements by land or sea." Tamayo began preaching to the exhausted men. "You have two choices. You can follow the orders of your officers and fight to the death, or you can lay down your weapons and walk out of here right now. If you surrender, you'll be given food and water and returned to Havana within the day."

There was a long pause when Tamayo finished, a moment in which their lives hung in the balance, and then the first *policía* put down his rifle and walked out the door. Once the barrier was broken, a rush of men lay down their guns and filed out the door quickly, as if afraid that Tamayo might change his mind.

As Tamayo and Vicente emerged from the *estación de policía*, an ebullient Che met them. "Congratulations. Fidel will be very happy." He waved his pipe in a circle leaving rings that drifted up into the sky. "There's more good news. The garrison at Yaguajay has finally surrendered. Camilo should be here tomorrow with the 8th Column to help us strangle Leoncio Vidal, and then onward to Havana."

* * *

Fulgencio Batista was enjoying a last moment in the office of his summer estate, *Finca Kuquine*. He picked up the solid gold telephone, a gift from the American Telephone and Telegraph Company, and wondered if he should take it with him. People didn't think he should've accepted it in the first place. But isn't that how you got things done? *Quid pro quo*, you rub my back, and I rub yours. Hell, President Prío had a solid gold flush handle on his toilet.

It was New Year's Eve, and yet he felt little reason for celebration. At 9 p.m. he'd met with his chief of staff who told him that they couldn't hold Las Villas Province. That damn Marxist agitator, Che Guevara, now controlled the city of Santa Clara and was cutting off reinforcements to the Leoncio Vidal Garrison. Batista had then taken a phone call from Colonel Lumpuy in Santa Clara, who told him that, absent those reinforcements, he'd soon have to surrender the garrison. Batista courteously hinted to the man that there would be no aid, and it might be time to get out.

More bad news had followed, as General Cantillo, back from the east, informed him that the last bastion in Oriente Province, Santiago, was about to fall to the guerrillas. He was well aware that Cantillo was jockeying for power, hoping to step in and pick up the scraps, maybe even become the military dictator of Cuba. *Well, he could have it, the whole mess, and see where that gets him*, Batista thought. The *Barbudos* had been drastically underestimated; their persistence was undeniable, especially that *bastardo*, Fidel Castro. He tossed back the last bit of Scotch in his glass and rose from his desk. It was time to go.

He found his wife, Marta, waiting in the kitchen with their oldest son, Jorge, and the two youngest children as well. The middle two boys had been sent to the United States to visit their grandfather a few days prior, a precautionary move, although not even his family knew that all of them would soon follow suit. His wife, like most of the elites in Havana, had little idea how bad things had grown in the country. They were driven the short distance to their Camp Columbia home in Havana, the very place from where he'd orchestrated his coup almost seven years earlier.

As tradition dictated, his top military commanders, government officials, and closest family were gathered for New Year's Eve at his home, awaiting his lavish gifts. Their expectations grew greedily every year. Tonight he entered the upstairs living room at exactly midnight, just in time to celebrate the New Year, making sure to spend a few minutes chatting with each of his wife's closest friends, knowing that any perceived snub would cost him the ire of his beautiful but moody spouse. Raising a glass, he made a toast to everybody's health, gave out presents, and quietly told his top commanders to meet him in his office at 2 a.m.

The week before, Ambassador Smith had summoned Batista to his office in the American Embassy, where a special envoy from President Eisenhower tried to convince him to leave Cuba. Batista considered Smith an arrogant prick who was probably miffed because his golf game had been interrupted. He acted as if he were the ruler of Cuba rather than Batista, which in retrospect, may have been true. The United States owned the majority of sugar and tobacco fields and almost all of the mineral and oil reserves as well as the public utilities.

Well, he'd have the last laugh, for by selling out to American companies and gangsters, he'd amassed a fortune of $400 million secreted away in foreign banks. If the Americans wanted to play kingmaker and back General Cantillo in a new government, so be it. This Cuban peasant, the poor boy of mixed race who'd once worked for Ángel Castro in Birán, was going to retire and disappear into the lap of luxury. In the background, his military leaders droned on about how hopeless the situation was, but at the same time refused to face the reality staring each of them in the face.

When he had heard enough, Batista stood up, slamming his chair down in the process. "There are three airplanes waiting on the tarmac outside. There's room for each of you and your wives on those planes. I'd suggest that you don't waste any time, as they'll be leaving in less than one hour with or without you. General Tabernilla has the list of who is to go on what plane. If the name is not on the list, the person will not board. Thank you and good luck."

Batista strode out of the room and found his wife with their three children as he'd directed, still unsure what was going on. "We're leaving the country," he told them abruptly. They exited the house, as men scrambled madly to find their wives, and call home to have servants bring their children. There was no time to gather their hidden caches of money if they wanted to escape Cuba alive.

The airstrip was just a short distance away, and Batista herded his family onto the first airplane, one of three Aerovías Q civilian aircraft, along with forty of his closest friends and advisors. Batista had requested exile in his Palm Beach home, but Smith had told him in no uncertain words that the situation was too fragile, and therefore, the United States could not accept him at this time. Thus, their destination was Santo Domingo. The other two airplanes, both with about forty passengers, would be allowed to fly to the States. As his plane taxied down the runway, Batista stared at the lights of Havana and mumbled to himself, "Cuba, I think this is the end of a beautiful friendship."

Even at 2:30 a.m. the ring of the phone didn't surprise Rolando Masferrer. He'd gone to the Cabaret earlier in the evening for a show and then brought one of the showgirls back with him. It was a trivial matter to him whether the woman desired him or was scared of him. He had just kicked her out and lit a cigarette when the call came through. The conversation was short as the party on the other side was rushing to catch a plane, but the message was clear. Batista was leaving Cuba, and it was time for Rolando Masferrer to do the same. His bag had been packed for some weeks now, so he had merely to dress, pull on his white cowboy hat, and grab his luggage for the short trip to the marina where his yacht was tied up. West Palm Beach wasn't far, and he'd had the foresight to buy a house there and open a bank account. He had not survived the Spanish Civil War, the gangster years of the 1940s, and the Batista coup for a lack of preparation and intelligence.

Meyer Lansky, the head of organized crime in Havana, was sitting in the Hotel Plaza in the early morning hours of the New Year with his beautiful mistress when Charles White came through the door, scanned the room, and approached his booth. The man leaned down and whispered into Lansky's ear, "Batista has fled the island."

As if he expected this to happen, Lansky rose and motioned for his chauffeur. "Take the women home and meet me back here with the car." He paused. "The *Barbudos* have won the war."

Lansky told the casino manager to separate all of the American money from Cuban money, secure it in lockboxes, and deliver it to a safe house. He knew there was a good chance that riots would ensue, and that the casinos would very likely be targets of the hordes. Just as he feared, when the morning came, the mob vandalized several casinos, including the Plaza, the Deauville, and the Biltmore. Worst of all, at Lansky's pride and joy, the Riviera, a truckload of pigs was released and tracked mud and shit throughout the lobby and gaming room.

James Noel, the CIA station chief in Havana, was standing on the balcony of his apartment in Havana at just after three in the morning when he saw the lights of a plane leaving the airstrip at Columbia, followed shortly by a second, and then a third plane. He knew there were no scheduled flights at this hour. He surmised that what he'd just witnessed was President Fulgencio Batista and his cronies fleeing Cuba.

Noel had been considering sleep, but instead he flicked his cigar over the railing, put on his sports jacket, and went out the door. It would be a busy day at the office, and he might as well get started. No matter what, it was imperative to prevent Fidel Castro from taking power. Yes, the man had Marxist leanings, but more importantly, his ideas about land distribution and the nationalization of important industries would negatively affect American interests. Even more worrisome, his oversized ego made the man believe he was more than just a revolutionary, but rather, the second coming of Christ himself.

15

January 1, 1959

The radio crackled to life, and the voice of Rolando Cubela suddenly filled the room of the building downtown where Che had moved his command post in Santa Clara. "Is Commander Che there?"

It wasn't yet light out on the first day of 1959, but already Che was busy planning the final stage of victory in Santa Clara. He sat with Aleida, Vicente, Tamayo, and Hugo. None of them had slept that night. He reached for the handset and replied, "This is Che."

"Captain Millán has just surrendered Barracks 31." Cubela's excited voice flooded the dark room lit only by a flickering gas lamp. "But that's not all. The word is that Batista has left the country."

Che cursed and kicked the table. "It'd be a shame if that pig escapes the justice he deserves."

"It would appear that the state is not abolished, but merely flies away." Vicente deadpanned, but was met merely by a glare from Che.

He had no sooner hung up than a call came through from Leoncio Vidal. "I'd like to begin negotiations for an indefinite peace," Colonel Hernández' exhausted voice wheezed over the patrol car headset. He'd assumed command this morning when it was discovered that Colonel Lumpuy had gone missing after a phone call from Batista.

"There can be no peace without unconditional surrender," Che replied in a steely voice.

"We have just received word from General Cantillo that Batista has fled the country. A provisional government has been put in place with the support of Castro."

"None of that matters," Che bellowed over the radio waves. "My orders from Fidel are quite clear. Unconditional surrender. I also know that Fidel wouldn't have agreed to any plan that involved a military coup in Havana. Nor would he have allowed Batista and his cronies to flee."

"Perhaps we could talk face to face," Colonel Hernández wheedled, increasingly desperate. When things were going well he had no authority, and now, on the verge of defeat, the decision to continue fighting or lay down arms rested squarely on his shoulders.

"I'll come to you," Che said. "I'll be there in ten minutes, *che*." He knew that time was of the essence. Not only were war criminals escaping the country, but also opposition parties were jockeying for power. Meanwhile, this colonel was stalling for time. "Vicente, get my Toyota."

Eight minutes and a precipitous car ride later, they were walking through the front gate of the barracks. Che spent no time beating around the bush. "I hope you've decided to turn over your barracks to my command."

"I have been ordered by my superior officer *not* to do that." The day was not hot, yet sweat dripped down the cheeks of the olive-skinned army officer. "Perhaps we can call a temporary truce while we work out the details. It's possible we're on the same side now."

"Look, commander, I've already discussed this with Fidel. It's unconditional surrender or fire, real fire, and with no quarter. The city is already in our hands. At 12:30, I will give the order to resume the attack using all of our forces. We'll take the barracks at all costs, and you'll be responsible for the bloodshed." Che had raised his voice so that the other officers and soldiers could hear his words. "Furthermore, you must be aware of the possibility that the U.S. government will intervene militarily in Cuba. If that happens, it will be even more of a crime to Fidel as you will be supporting a foreign invader. In that event, our only option will be to execute you as guilty of treason against Cuba."

The beaten colonel hung his head. "I must speak with my fellow officers."

Che nodded and strode out. They went back to the public works building, where he ordered Vicente to prepare for the final assault. With just ten minutes left before the resumption of firing, Colonel Hernández emerged with a white flag, and Che met with him. It was just after noon on New Year's Day. "Have you come to your decision, Colonel?"

Colonel Hernández looked around at the faces of the rebels. Any other New Year's Day, these youngsters would still be sleeping off the night's excesses. He recognized the pride in their bearing. Unlike the men in the barracks, these guerrillas believed in what they were fighting for. He turned to Che and nodded.

Che gave him a short nod back, commending him for his wise decision, and then stepped past him to yell to the soldiers in the barracks. "Lay down your weapons and come out with your hands up and you will be returned to Havana unharmed. That, of course, excludes any of your number who have committed crimes against the population of Santa Clara."

Even before he had finished talking, soldiers were laying down their arms, and walking out into the rebel lines where they shared cigarettes. The majority of them were peasants from the countryside, fighting for a paycheck and not out of patriotism. The news that their commander-in-chief Batista had fled, coupled with the disappearance of their immediate superior Lumpuy, decimated what little illusion that they had left about the legitimacy of this war.

A few hours later Camilo and the 8th Column rolled into town in a parade of trucks, Jeeps, and automobiles. Hungry from their recent victory in Yaguajay and subsequent rush to aid in the final assault of Santa Clara, they immediately prepared and devoured hundreds of sandwiches, washing them down with twenty-four cases of Hatuey beer. Most of the men then fell into the deep slumber of the completely exhausted, as they would move on Havana first thing in the morning.

Fidel had ordered that Camilo Cienfuegos should be the first into Havana with his column and occupy Camp Columbia. As the supreme commander of the invasion, the honor should've belonged to Che, but Fidel was worried how the people of Havana would accept a foreigner, and what the United States would make of the presence of a known Marxist in the role of conquering hero. Camilo was jovial, likeable, and most importantly, a citizen of Havana. He was a man who the people would stand and cheer for, whose tall frame and bearded face represented the face they knew as the revolution.

"We rushed here as quickly as possible," Camilo said as he lounged on the floor with his back reclined against a sack of grain in the public works building. Slouched around him were Vicente, Che, and several others. "I mean to say, right after I shared the victory with a pretty little *señorita* who I'd had my eye on for a couple of days." He lazily smoked a cigar, blowing fat rings into the air. He described the sexual escapades that'd taken place in the failed flame-throwing bulldozer, finishing the tale with, "She was quite impressed with the firepower."

The others laughed tiredly. "Throw me an apple, Vicente." Che requested, puffing upon his pipe. He took several bites. "Camilo, you will leave in the morning, and I'll follow in the afternoon." He stood up, thinking that it might be time to turn in and curl up with Aleida for another type of celebration. "Vicente, I have a message for you to deliver to Fidel, so I'd ask that you leave immediately. There is a Buick outside with a full tank of gas."

Camilo and the 8th Column continued on in their journey to Havana just as the sun started to rise. They arrived in the capital at just after five in the afternoon and were greeted warmly by Colonel Ramón Barquín. In April of 1956, Barquín had led an attempted coup against Batista that was called "the conspiracy of the pure," due to the spotless record of the army officers involved. When the uprising failed, Barquín was arrested and sentenced to six years imprisonment on the Isle of Pines. General Cantillo had had him released to appease the approaching guerrilla forces the previous night, but the plan had backfired.

Cantillo was trying to create a place for himself in the new regime and thought that putting Barquín in charge of the army at Camp

Columbia would seem a welcome peace offering to Fidel and the rebels. Instead, the Colonel, wisely counseled by Armando Hart, had arrested Cantillo while the general slept, a present for Camilo when he arrived. Hart also greeted Camilo, and the two men hugged fiercely, jubilant to have survived battles and years of prison to meet again. Armando and Camilo had both become involved in the movement before the attack on the Moncada Barracks. The previous year, Armando had been arrested in Santiago and imprisoned on the Isle of Pines for his participation in "revolutionary activities." He'd been released the night before along with Colonel Barquín.

When the 8th Column wound its way into the city, hundreds of thousands of cheering Cubans greeted them, each fighting for a better view of the arriving *Barbudos*, who had taken on the status of folk heroes and patriotic liberators in Havana. The sight of these "bearded ones" from the mountains was no less exciting than if Jesus or Changó had entered the city riding on a tank.

* * *

Fidel and Celia spent New Year's Eve at the home of Rammón Ruiz, who was the chief engineer of the Central America sugar mill that had become their base over the past few days. They made love in the early morning before drifting into sleep for a few hours, though slumber was more elusive for Celia as she realized her idyllic time was coming to an end. She was sipping coffee in the kitchen when Fidel emerged. "Today is a new year," he said, stretching. "I sense that today will be the day it all comes crashing down."

Celia handed him a cup of coffee. "Change is in the air," she agreed.

"We will be the face of the people as we reclaim liberties for everybody." Fidel sipped the black coffee.

"*You* will be the face of the people." Celia stated impassively. Before Fidel could respond, Rammón and his wife entered the room and set about making a simple breakfast of eggs and bread for them to eat. A few other rebel leaders entered from outside. They'd spent the night in the mill's mostly empty employee housing.

They had just taken their first bites when the door burst open, and a young man of no more than fifteen charged into the room. "The American radio station has said that Batista has fled Cuba."

"What?" Fidel was immediately on his feet and in a towering rage. "I knew that Cantillo couldn't be trusted. When he didn't get in contact yesterday about the deadline for the uprising in Santiago, I should've realized that the yellow coward was working both ends against the middle. I'll have his heart skewered on a pole for letting this happen."

Celia fiddled with the radio during this rant, and suddenly the voice of the CMQ announcer in Havana filled the room. "This morning before dawn, President Fulgencio Batista and his top advisors, generals, officials, and closest friends flew the coop. Carlos Manuel Piedra of the Supreme Court has filled the void as the president while General Cantillo has been put in charge of the army." He went on to describe the dazed crowds spilling onto the Havana streets.

"We must go to the Radio Rebelde transmitter." Fidel paused momentarily. "Have the men prepare to invade Santiago. There's not a moment to be wasted."

As Celia drove the Jeep to the transmitter, Fidel frantically wrote on tiny scraps of paper and cursed Cantillo as a traitor. She followed behind as he stormed into the shack where the radio and antennae had been set up, surprising two rebels playing canasta. Castro took the microphone, flipped the switch to transmit, and immediately began speaking. "This is Fidel Castro talking to you from the outskirts of Santiago as Cuban liberty—*your* liberty—is once again being usurped by a dictator. The news of Cantillo's power grab this morning is chilling. The general had reached out a conciliatory hand to the *Movimiento 26th de Julio* a few days ago only to stab us in the back today. He has allowed the dictator, Fulgencio Batista, to flee the island and escape revolutionary justice. He has formed a military junta in Havana putting himself at its head and refuses to surrender the Leoncio Vidal Garrison in Santa Clara. Our forces must continue to attack on every front against the illegal regime. Revolution? Yes! Coup d'état? No! Revolution? Yes! Coup d'état? No! This triumph over tyranny will not be snatched from the people at our moment of certain victory. We must not let it happen. Never shall we experience another March 10th. The victory of the people, the will of the people, the success of the people must be absolute. It cannot be halfway, or close, or good enough. Workers of Cuba must be prepared for a revolutionary strike that will be announced soon, stopping the machinery of tyranny that attempts to grip our island. The columns of Camilo Cienfuegos and Che Guevara must secure Santa Clara and march upon Havana. Here is what you can expect, people of Cuba. The forces under my command will march upon Santiago at once. Hubert Matos and Juan Almeida will sweep in from the southwest, and Raúl Castro and his columns will attack from the southeast. Revolution? Yes! Coup d'état? No!"

Fidel handed the microphone back to the rebel named Carlos and demanded, "Can you get Colonel Rego Rubido on the radio for me?"

Several hours later, Sophia drove Fidel and Celia to Escande on the outskirts of Santiago to meet with Colonel Rubido, the ranking officer of the Moncada Barracks. With Batista gone, and his men already under siege from an increasingly violent urban population, Rubido and his top officers agreed to surrender the city to Fidel. At 9 p.m. on January 2nd of 1959, Fidel Castro rode into Santiago with Celia Sánchez at the head of his liberating army.

The first stop was the ceremonial surrender of the Moncada Barracks by Colonel Rego Rubido. The symbolism was lost on no one, least of all Celia, who remembered reading her father's leftover newspaper one day in late July of 1953 in her small village of Pilón. This is where she first heard of the courageous group of men and women that had struck a blow against the dictator Batista and his army by attacking these very barracks, an assault that had failed miserably. Along with everyone else in Cuba, she'd followed the rumors, transmitted on the radio, and printed in the newspaper, as the rebels were slowly hunted down and killed or captured. News of the trial and imprisonment were kept relatively muted, although a few stories leaked out. But the following summer when she read Fidel Castro's momentous speech, "History Will Absolve Me," she knew there was no option but to join the revolution. Celia had never imagined that she would fall in love with this brash lawyer, or that she'd become his most trusted advisor. At the same time, she realized that the reality of Havana was not the same as the insular, sometimes desperate, always intimate world of the Sierra Maestra.

They moved to the town hall building where they met with the Lions and the Rotarians, powerful organizations in Cuba that had backed Fidel from the early days. Their officers now sat in wicker chairs reaping the benefits of that decision. Just after midnight, Fidel stepped onto the balcony overlooking Céspedes Square in Santiago to speak to the cheering throngs that had gathered to celebrate the victory of the guerrillas. As he stood at the railing in front of the adoring crowd, Fidel took a long moment to relish the achievement. In less than six years, he had gone from being dragged through these very same streets as a prisoner portrayed as a threat to Cuban society and its social order to a conquering hero of the people, beloved by so many, a figure whose victory was already reverberating around the world.

Behind him sat Dr. Manuel Urrutia, the man whom Fidel had slated for the interim president of the new government, and the Archbishop of Santiago, Enrique Pérez Serantes, who had baptized him in his childhood and saved his life after Moncada. To his left was the *Hotel Casa Granda,* and across the square was the *Catedral de Nuestra de Senora de la Asuncion.* To his right lay shops and the neighborhoods of Santiago. In front of him were his people.

Vicente had arrived in Santiago just before Fidel appeared on the balcony, and followed the noise to Céspedes Square. Tens of thousands of people filled the streets blowing horns and drinking rum. Strings of bare bulbs were hung around the square, dancing in the wind and throwing eerie shadows across the buildings. He fought his way through the crowd towards the town hall building where he figured Fidel was, but he was still a good hundred yards away when a hush descended upon the crowd. Looking up, Vicente saw Fidel Castro standing at the railing with an expression of triumph upon his bearded face, his eyes looking down on them, black glasses roosting upon his nose. A pair of klieg lights illuminated him and the balcony as if day had come hours early.

"What greater glory than the love of the people? What greater reward than these thousands of waving arms, so full of hope, faith, and affection? No satisfaction and no prize are greater than that of fulfilling our duty, as we have been doing up to now, and as we shall always do. Frank País is not here with us today, nor many others, but they are here spiritually—and only the satisfaction that their death was not in vain can compensate for the immense emptiness they left behind."

Vicente looked over his shoulder, as if he might glimpse these spirits among them celebrating the culmination of their efforts. He thought of those brave friends who had perished at Moncada and in the horrific retaliation afterwards. His ruminations drifted to the lionhearted men aboard the *Granma*, who were annihilated by the army on their arrival back in Cuba with so few survivors. Even as their numbers had swelled in the mountains, numerous men and women had given their lives fighting, up to the last bloody invasion of Las Villas Province on the plains that had become a common grave to so many. And then there were the countless souls in the urban underground slain serving the cause, many tortured, some raped, all of them made to pay in blood for their beliefs.

Castro's booming voice brought Vicente's attention back to the balcony. "In Havana, a group of military officers conspire to take power in the vacuum left by the flight of the coward Batista. General Cantillo met with me in good faith and then broke his vow, greedy to achieve his own personal ambitions over the common good. They are attempting to steal the revolution from the very people who have fought for it. Most of the men in the armed forces are honorable men, merely fulfilling their duty in fighting against our revolution through misguided notions. But a small minority of officers is guilty of crimes so heinous that I cannot speak of them now in our moment of celebration. You, the people, know of these men and their depraved transgressions." He paused and surveyed the crowd. "Who wants General Cantillo to be the President of Cuba?" he bellowed to the masses below.

There was the slightest pause as the throngs processed his words, and then like ten thousand trumpets they roared their response in the negative. "*Nunca! Nunca! Nunca!*"

"Who wants General Tabernilla to become President?" Fidel went through lists of the most vile of Cubans before he finally turned to Dr. Manuel Urrutia. "I do not call for power for myself, as I am only an instrument of the people. So I propose that until free and fair elections are held, that a man of our own interests, a man of honor, a man of Santiago fill the role of president of Cuba. Who here wants Dr. Manuel Urrutia to be president of Cuba?"

Vicente found himself screaming his assent along with the rest, caught up in the moment and swept away on a sea of patriotism. The people and Fidel were uniting under a single banner that opened the door to a golden future for Cuba.

"When I landed with eighty-two men on the beaches of Cuba, people asked us why we thought we could win the war. 'Because we have the people behind us!' we told them. And when we were defeated for the first time, and only a handful of us were left and yet we persisted in the struggle, we knew that this would be the outcome, because we had faith in the people. When they dispersed us five times in forty-five days, and we met together again and renewed the struggle, it was because we had faith in the people. Today is the proof that our faith was justified."

The first glimmer of dawn began to streak the sky to the east as Fidel continued. "A few days ago I stopped during the night at the monument to the protest of Baraguá near Birán. At Baraguá, Maceo, defeated and powerless, nevertheless refused to accept the terms imposed by the victorious Spanish general because the terms did not include independence and the abolition of slavery. At that late hour, we were the only people present in that place. We thought of the daring feats of our wars of independence, and how those men fought for thirty years and in the end did not see their dream realized. We can tell them that their dreams are soon to be fulfilled, and that the time has finally come when you, our people, our noble people, our people who are so enthusiastic and have so much faith, our people who demand nothing in return for their affection, who demand nothing in return for their trust, the time has come, I say, when you will have everything you need. I will always speak to the people with loyalty and frankness. Hatred, that shadow of ambition and tyranny, is now expelled from the republic."

The crowds surged forward and backward like a living thing, and Vicente felt like a small part of a greater organism, the thoughts of those around him were his own, the movement an extension of his own mind, his responses mimicked by thousands of lips.

"There is no longer black and white in Cuba. I have also come to the realization that there should be no separation between the sexes in terms of social, economic, or career aspirations in Cuba. Since the beginning of our revolution a core group of women have ensured the success of the *Movimiento 26th de Julio.* These women have been couriers, nurses, cooks, members of the urban underground, and finally soldiers in our columns. Many have died horrific deaths at the hands of the enemy, but never once did they shirk from their duty. Full of daring, cunning, and courage, they impressed me so much I formed a platoon made up solely of the daughters of Cuba christened as the *Mariana Grajales* in honor of the mother of Antonio Maceo, who gave her entire family as martyrs to independence. No longer shall they be relegated to the role of homemaker and nurse. They will now take their positions side by side with the sons of Cuba in forging a new world in which people are judged by their merits and not their wealth, color, or sex."

The vision of Sophia Franco casually carrying her rifle like an extension of her arm flashed into Vicente's mind and he had a deep and abrupt urge to be in her presence. He began fighting his way forward, intent on delivering Che's message to Fidel so that he could find his love and the two might revel together in this glorious achievement.

* * *

January 9th, 1959, Matanzas, east of Havana...

It was just after 2 a.m. when Ed Sullivan entered the room for the arranged television interview with Fidel Castro in the town of Matanzas some sixty miles east of Havana. Fidel had led the 1st Column out of Santiago on January 3rd in a thick fog at the front of a motorcade of cars, troop transport trucks, and Jeeps. For 500 miles, in every town, city, and village that they passed, people had lined the streets throwing flowers and cheering for all they were worth. Once in the town center, Fidel would stand up in the back of the Jeep and give a short victory speech about the success of the revolution and what to expect next. He praised the people for their support and promised to bring them jobs, education, and health care. When he was done, those with automobiles pulled in behind the procession and followed along beeping their horns.

"Are you ready to begin?" Sullivan asked, picking up the microphone from the table in front of him.

"Yes," Fidel replied simply.

Ed Sullivan switched the microphone on and began speaking into it. "You know that the Batista propagandists to our country and other countries around the world don't represent you as young revolutionaries. Rather, they call you communists." Sullivan's delivery was deadpan, his expression aloof and unreadable. "But I look around, and I see many of the youngsters with you are wearing medals, rosaries, scapulars, and carrying bibles. I know that Cuba is mostly Catholic. How about you? Are you Catholic?" The room was filled with bearded guerrillas and smooth-shaven urban resistance fighters, many carrying tommy guns and wearing sunglasses even at this dark hour. Smoke from various cigars, pipes, and cigarettes wafted through the air creating a swirling miasma, as each rebel tried to position his or her body within the camera's view.

"I was brought up Catholic and went to Catholic schools," Fidel said softly. He was exhausted and stumbled slightly over the English words.

"In school you were a fine student and athlete." Ed Sullivan sat next to Fidel trying to ignore the weapons held casually by almost everyone in the room, one rifle almost pressed against his forehead. "You were a pitcher, weren't you?"

"Yes. I played all sports. I did basketball, track, and swimming— every sport. This helped prepare my stamina for the endless treks in the mountains over the past few years."

They talked in generalities for a minute or two and then Sullivan paused, his visage if anything even more serious. "I have to ask you a few questions about the situation here in Cuba. How many Cuban people do you think were tortured and killed by Batista?"

Fidel remained stoic outwardly, but did pause before answering. "It's hard to say. Thousands? Tens of thousands? Tortured? I'd say that maybe as many as twenty thousand Cubans have suffered inhumane physical abuse at Batista's hands. And many thousands killed as well." Vicente found himself craning forward to hear Fidel, who was speaking in a hushed tone that was unusual for him.

"It is ten minutes past two in the morning and you have to be up in a couple of hours." Ed Sullivan stood to emphasize his next question, jabbing his finger inches from the notebook in Fidel's left front pocket of his shirt. "In Latin American countries, dictators come in and steal and torture and kill all the time. How do you propose ending that cycle in Cuba?"

"You can be assured that Batista will be the last dictator because we're going to improve our…" Fidel searched for the correct words as he also stood, towering over Sullivan. "We're going to improve our democratic institutions so that force can no longer rule."

"The people of the United States have great admiration for you and your men because you are made in the real American tradition of a George Washington or any man who takes on another powerful nation and wins. How do you feel about the United States?" Ed Sullivan asked.

"The people of the United States are very focused and work extremely hard. I think this is because they've come from all over the world, places where they were mistreated and persecuted, and then came together in the United States to form a great nation." Fidel was careful to praise the people, while at the same time, ignoring the government of the United States.

Ed Sullivan smiled. "We want you to like us and we like you and Cuba. It has been an honor to meet you and your men."

"I'm honored by your interview," Fidel stated. "And I apologize for my tiredness." The two men shook hands, one to return to the United States and the other to get two hours of sleep before finishing off the final steps on the long road to the capital of Cuba.

The cavalcade continued the next morning before sunrise, stopping on the outskirts of Havana to pick up nine-year-old Fidelito, who'd flown in from the United States with his mother to join his father in the triumph. His ex-wife was not happy about this, but she knew better than to deny him the presence of his son. The parade of cars, Jeeps, military trucks, tanks, and people on foot wound its way through the old industrial city of Guanabacoa and along the harbor road past the freight yards, factories, and refineries. In the port, Fidel spotted the hulk of the *Granma* rocking gently against the quay. A Cuban flag flew from her bow, and he asked the driver to stop for a moment, leaping from the back of the Jeep to run over to visit the boat that'd brought him back to Cuba from Mexico just over two years earlier.

As they passed the Shrine of the Virgin of the Road, Fidel again leapt from the Jeep, pulling Fidelito along with him, and climbed up on a tank, joining Camilo Cienfuegos and Che Guevara. The noise became deafening as they trundled their way through the crowds swarming the streets of Havana. More than one million people cheered one word in unison as they viewed the conquering hero atop the tank. "Fidel—Fidel—FIDEL—FIDEL!" Church bells rang, factory whistles blew, ship sirens pealed, and naval gun salutes boomed out over the intoxicated masses.

They went first to the Palace and held a press conference in the Hall of Mirrors, site of the failed assassination attempt by the DR. The reconstituted DR, now under the leadership of Faure Chomón as Secretary General and Rolando Cubela as the military commander, had entered Havana immediately after Batista had fled, and the men quickly laid claim to the Palace. They were trying to assert their right to at least a part of the victory and the power up for grabs, as they had been rebelling against the Batista regime for as long as the *Movimiento 26th de Julio*. It took a threat of violence from Camilo and Che to coerce them to vacate the premises so that Fidel's chosen president, Manuel Urrutia, could move in. On January 7th, the United States of America extended diplomatic relations to the new government. By the time Fidel arrived in Havana, control had been solidified, except for the still-fuming DR, who had moved their base up to University Hill, taking with them a stockpile of weapons from the arsenal at the air force base.

Celia knew that her life would never be the same. Fidel Castro had emerged from their mountain hideout as an idol to the people. The men wanted to be him, and the women wanted to be with him. At each town along the way from Santiago, she'd watched as the people thronged their vehicles, desperate to see Fidel, frantic to hear his voice, and praying to have him look upon them. Women threw him flowers and begged him to father their children. Celia understood that she couldn't compete with the multitude of gorgeous and vibrant women who flung themselves on the ground in front of Fidel, as she well knew his voracious sexual appetite. The socialite beauty, Naty Revuelta, was somewhere in the wings waiting to sink her talons into Fidel once again, as she'd done before and after his imprisonment at the Isle of Pines. Revuelta hadn't been willing to leave the comforts of her wealthy life in Havana to go into the mountains and lead an austere and dangerous life as a guerrilla. But now that Fidel was back in the capital, Celia had no doubt that she'd soon be offering herself once again to the savior of Cuba.

Nonetheless, Celia knew that she had become invaluable to Fidel as an advisor, and that she could hold a prominent position in his life as well as the government just as long as she didn't allow her jealousies to interfere. He'd still look to her for advice on important issues, and, she imagined, that bond would lead to mutual physical comfort based upon need and nostalgia. Celia looked proudly out at the throngs of millions and felt warmth fill her body, an almost maternal instinct for the people and the future of Cuba surging through her veins. She understood that the honeymoon period had ended. It was time to leave the sensual explorations of youth behind and take her place fulfilling the role of mother to Cuba. Her children needed her.

The entourage made its way as planned to Camp Columbia where Fidel was slated to greet the people. He started out riding in the back of a limousine with bulletproof glass that had been liberated from the departed dictator. But as they started up La Rampa, the street that climbs from the sea to the Vedado neighborhood, Fidel couldn't remain isolated from his admirers any longer and moved into a Jeep along with Juan Almeida. From the windows and balconies of the tall buildings, flowers and confetti rained down upon the procession, and people emerged from the underground nightclubs with drinks raised in celebration.

A well-dressed, middle-aged man held a parking meter over his head jubilantly, one of the few casualties after Batista's flight. The meters had once filled the pockets of government officials with a steady supply of cash; they would no longer. They pulled into the wrong road to enter Camp Columbia and couldn't turn around, such was the traffic backed up behind them. But it didn't matter. Fidel led the way, goodheartedly climbing the short fence and trekking across a field towards the newly-made stage looming above the hordes of people.

Fidel climbed the structure and materialized above the crowd with his arm raised high over his head. Cuba erupted in joyous screams of ecstasy. Across the training fields, airfields, and open spaces of Camp Columbia swarmed over a million people, come to see their messiah, the man from the mountains who'd promised to halt the corruption and evict the loathsome leaders of the debauched Batista government. With only twelve survivors after the failed *Granma* landing, the story went, these apostles had taken refuge in the Sierra. They'd grown in number and strength before emerging from their sanctuary to sweep away the rotting dogs of evil before them to present Cuba with true freedom for the first time in her existence.

Vicente stood with Sophia to the side of the stage, overflowing with patriotism for his country, yet heavy-hearted at the end of a chapter. He had some idea of the changes that had to follow. He watched as Fidel finally raised his arms to quiet the crowd, and a million voices dwindled down to one.

"We led a quieter life in the hills than we are going to have from now on. Now, we are going to purify our country. The first thing we who have made this Revolution must ask ourselves is, why did we make it? Speaking here tonight, I am presented with one of the most difficult obligations in this long struggle, which began in Santiago on November 30, 1956. The people are listening, the revolutionaries are listening, and the soldiers whose destinies are in other hands are listening also. This is a decisive moment in our history: the tyranny has been overthrown, but there is still much to be done. Let us not fool ourselves into believing that the future will be easy. To tell the truth is the first duty of all revolutionaries; to fool the people always brings the worst consequences. The rebel army won the war by telling the truth. The tyranny lost the war by fooling the public and the soldiers. When we were defeated, we announced it over Radio Rebelde. That was not the way of the army units, many of which repeatedly committed errors because the officers were never told the truth. That is why I want to continue this simple concept of always telling the people the truth."

Three doves roosting atop a nearby house, awakened by the clamor and the applause of the people, flew aloft and then, attracted by the spotlights that shone brilliantly on Fidel, they began to flutter around him. One of them landed on his left shoulder while the other two walked along the edge of the podium. Some people placed their hands over their hearts, while others fell to their knees in awe at this symbol of peace delivered by some higher power.

Fidel reveled in the moment before continuing, "Nevertheless, we should not be complacent. A battling army no longer leads the revolution. The worst enemies the Cuban revolution can face are the revolutionaries themselves. That is why we have always dealt with the wrongs of our own fighters so severely. The first thing that we must ask ourselves is: why did we do it? Did any of us have any special ambition, any ignoble objective?" He paused for a long moment, his gaze sweeping the crowd, letting the question sink in.

"As soon as possible, I will take the rifles off the streets. There are no more enemies, there is no longer anything to fight against, and if some day, any foreigner or any movement comes up against the revolution, all the people will fight. The weapons belong in the barracks. No one has the right to have private armies here. I want to warn the people and tell the Cuban mothers that I will try to solve every problem without shedding blood. I want to tell the Cuban mothers that no more shots will be fired. And I want to ask the people to help us solve this problem. For now, the festivities are over. It is time for us to go to work. Tomorrow we will need many things, money to pay for food, electricity, and to rebuild. These are the same problems faced by the revolutionary government. All of us have to work harder on behalf of the nation. Anyone who returns here after two years will not recognize the republic. I see an extraordinary spirit of cooperation everywhere. I see that the press and the journalists are all willing to help. All of Cuba has learned much during these recent years. Now we have a big job to do." Here, Fidel paused, and turned to Camilo Cienfuegos who stood slightly behind him. "Am I doing alright, Camilo?"

Camilo, smiled widely and replied, "You are doing well, my friend."

Sophia took Vicente's hand and led him away from the thundering voice of Fidel Castro and the equally vigorous cheers of his throngs of admirers. They climbed back over the fence and walked to the small building where they had parked. "What is it?" he asked her, but he already knew the answer.

"I have to go," Sophia said simply.

"Go where?" Vicente tried to ward off the truth he already knew.

"Back to the United States." She pressed her hands into his chest, her chin uplifted to see his face. "Home."

"How will you get there?"

"My Uncle Sam has a plane on a private airfield on the outskirts of the city. He had a message delivered to me last night in Matanzas that there was a spot for me."

Vicente stared down into those beautiful eyes as he rubbed his left eye with his fist. "You won't be coming back?"

"There's no place in Cuba for me any longer," Sophia said simply. "You could come with me?"

Vicente shook his head. "I am Cuba."

Epilogue

November 30, 1975, Havana

Vicente didn't open his mail until he returned to his apartment in the Vedado District of Havana, for even after all this time, he recognized the handwriting on the envelope. The past sixteen years had held as many trials and tribulations as the years in rebellion, if not more. After taking power, the *Movimiento 26th de Julio* had proceeded to solidify their position by eliminating every enemy through executions. There had been so many deaths and so much blood as the corruption and vice was cleaned from the city.

Once the rotten had been extirpated, the revolutionary government had enacted the land reform that Fidel had always planned. The new policies redistributing the wealth of the island went hand in hand with nationalizing all American interests in Cuba, leading the United States to impose an embargo on the country. When this boycott didn't resolve the main problem in the U.S.'s eyes—that commie rat Fidel Castro sitting in the seat of power—President Kennedy had then backed an invasion led by Cubans exiles that failed miserably, an offensive now known as the Bay of Pigs, and a misadventure that further cemented the position of Fidel as ruler of Cuba.

Fidel had not become president, but had appointed those who took the title, but everybody knew whom the real power broker in Cuba was. Due to the boycott, the Cubans had no choice but to ally with the Soviet Union. Vicente reflected upon the hard times he and all the people of Cuba had faced over the past years, but there had been many victories as well. Education had improved dramatically, medical care was now available to the whole country, not just the cities, and everybody had a job.

Vicente pulled his knife from the sheath at his belt, the same blade he had acquired in Yaguajay from the dead soldier, now hidden by a suit jacket instead of the olive green camouflage of a guerrilla. He had been rewarded with a high-ranking job in the Ministry of Agriculture even though he had initially known little about farming. Over time, he had proven his worth. With shaking hands, he slit the envelope open and two pieces of paper dropped onto the table. He picked up the newspaper article first.

The New York Times
November 1, 1975

Batista Ex-Aide Killed by Bomb

Miami, Oct. 31—Rolando Masferrer Rojas, the feared head of the secret police in pre-Castro Cuba, was killed today when a dynamite bomb exploded as he started his 1968 Ford Torino automobile at 10:58 a.m. The 56-year-old associate of the former Cuban dictator Fulgencio Batista was killed in the driveway of his home in the southwest section of the city. The high yield bomb, apparently planted last night, blew the roof from the car.

The bombing was the latest and most dramatic in a series of terrorist blasts in the Cuban community here in recent weeks. It is the first such blast to result in death. There was fear in the Cuban community that Mr. Masferrer's death would trigger reprisals.

Vicente put the article away before reading to the end, instead turning his attention to the brief note folded into the story.

Dearest Vicente,

As you can see, my demons have finally been laid to rest. It has been a difficult trail since the pig allied himself with powerful mobsters like Santo Trafficante, but it makes the revenge only that much sweeter. I think of you and our time together every single day, and look forward to a time when the relations between our countries might improve so that I might visit you.

I will always love you.
Sophia

He shook his head and smiled, thinking of the Italian girl from America who had lost her innocence in Cuba. Sometimes violence was the only answer, and revenge was gratifying. Vicente had a wife and three children now, but he too looked forward to an era in which Cuba and the United States could put aside their differences. He felt certain that Sophia would one day fill a niche in his new life, but as a friend rather than a lover. Vicente carefully folded the papers and placed them back in the envelope. *Some day.*

About the Author

Matthew Langdon Cost has wanted to be a writer since age eight. This is his first traditionally published novel, but he has written two other works of historical fiction, as well as a mystery trilogy. Over the years, Cost has owned a video store, a mystery bookstore, and a gym. He has also taught history and coached just about every sport imaginable. He now lives in Brunswick, Maine, with his wife, Harper. There are four grown children: Brittany, Pearson, Miranda, and Ryan. A Chocolate Lab and a Bassett Hound round out the mix. He now spends his days at the computer, writing.

Made in the USA
San Bernardino, CA
20 June 2020

73619456R00185